The
HUSTLE
A Means to an End

D1521890

A Novel By

DONISHA DERICE
JAI DARLENE

HOPE
STREET
publishing

ISBN: 978-0-9853515-5-7

Cover photo and design: RJ Jacques
Cover models: Terralyn Marie, Carlos Williams, and Farra of Team Nocturnal Models
Makeup artists: Rosemary Ashley (Red Lip Savage) and Aleascha Carper (Dollface Makeup Artistry)

Hope Street Publishing
P.O. Box 2705
Philadelphia, PA 19120
www.HopeStreetPublishing.com

Prologue

Bella

"You want to fuck me?" I ask the pasty-skinned white boy who is trying to sweet talk me out of my panties. He nods his head yes. "Well, at least go get me a drink first. Damn." The boy runs off to get us drinks. I can tell from his eagerness that he is a freshman, just starting his college year here at Notre Dame. Eager to party, eager to get white boy wasted, and eager to fuck some hos. I glance at my sister and roll my eyes. Beau is with a tall white boy. To be so short she is steady attracting tall guys. I whisper to Beau, "Man, this is so fucked up. Daddy only left us 50 G's." I grit my teeth.

"Damn, Daddy didn't get murdered on purpose. Shit, it's not like he intentionally left us only with $50,000. The feds took everything when they killed him," Beau whispers back. Beau is delusional. Daddy was the top drug lord in Indiana. Usually people in that occupation don't have a long life span. Daddy should have known better and stashed away more money for us to survive on in case he was ever killed or jailed. Instead, he left two high school teenagers to fend for themselves. I don't think I can forgive him for that.

Yeah, $50,000 sounds like a lot of money, but it really ain't shit. After paying for rent, private school tuition, and other living expenses, that $50,000 is dwindling quickly. I'm not trying to be homeless and hungry. So here we are, hustling just to get by; letting strangers be all up in our faces and touch us. It creeps me out. I will never forgive our father for leaving us like this.

"How much money do we have left?" I ask Beau as I watch the pasty white boy making his way through the crowd of partygoers with two red plastic cups filled with spiked punch.

"Not much. Did you have to buy that hooker outfit?" Beau asks, gesturing to the Prada dress I'd bought earlier that day.

I shrug my shoulders. "What? It was on sale." The pasty white boy finally makes his way to us. "Kenny likes my dress," I say loud enough for him to hear me over the music. The dress was an investment to catch the attention of rich white boys and it is paying off. I rub his chest to prove my point as I grab one of the red cups from his hand.

1

"My name is Kevin. And, oh yeah, I love it."

I take the other cup from his hand and give it to Beau. "Kenny. Kevin. Whatever. In an hour or so your name will be *Oh, God! Oh, God!*" I laugh and the tall white boy Beau is with looks at her with excitement. I can see from the imprint in his pants he is ready to leave this kegger and get the real party started.

Beau

I watch Bella get into the driver's seat of Kevin's Jeep. "Greta!" I yell at Bella before she pulls off. She winks. I want to make sure she has her gun with her just in case shit goes bad. I got a little .22 strapped to my left thigh. I feel the cold metal and it makes me feel secure, even though I hate carrying guns. I know I have it if I need it. Shit, I should have reminded Bella's trigger-happy ass to keep her hands off Greta unless absolutely necessary.

"Man, I've never done anything like this before," Phil says as his long, skinny fingers grip my ass tight.

"Mmmm, me either," I moan, rolling my eyes. This shit is crazy. What have I gotten myself into?

"What you say?" Phil yells into my ear. He is so gone. I am sure he won't remember shit in the morning. "Umm, I got like $300 on me right now. That's enough, right?" He starts digging in his pockets. Shit, if that is all the money we can expect to get each time, Bella and I are going to have to do this a whole damn lot or think of something else.

"What the fuck? Do I look like some low class bitch to you?" I stop on the sidewalk in front of his hunter green BMW. "My fucking shoes cost more than that." I look down at my Valentino heels.

"Yeah, they do look expensive. They are nice," Phil smiles at my shoes. Hell yeah. He's in a Beemer, rocking a Rolex, and he can spot some expensive heels. He got money. "I got a lot more money at home, though," Phil slurs.

That's what I'm talking about. Show me the money. "Good, I'll drive." Phil walks closely behind me and I can feel that his dick is hard and ready as he presses it against my ass. I snatch the keys out of his hand. "Lets go," I say, hopping into the driver's seat.

I feel butterflies in my stomach as I drive. I can't believe I'm doing this. This is not how I imagined life at 16. I am sure this isn't how my parents imagined my life, either. Hell, I never thought I would be orphaned due to both of my parents being murdered by the time I was 16. Man, Bella and I have had some fucked up lives. Her mother overdosed when she was two years old. My mother was murdered when we were 10. And our dad was killed earlier this year. Fuck it. Here goes nothing.

I feel Phil's hand on my thigh as we pull up to his apartment. I got undergrad and law school to think about and the scholarship I received isn't going to cover all my expenses. Not to mention both my sisters and my grandma have to be good, too. Hustle it is, then. Bella and I got to do what we got to do to make this money.

DONISHA DERICE & JAI DARLENE

1
Hustle Down

Beau

5 years later…

"No, no, no, and no," I roll my eyes and sip my Grey Goose and cranberry. It is obvious that Bella hasn't learned anything from last night or any of the other losers she has picked up before. Nice clothes and shoes don't equate money. Every one of the guys she pointed out appears to have money, but I can tell they don't. The first sign of a dude with no real money is the fact that he is standing around drinking what's on tap just like all the other regulars. If you're not in VIP popping bottles, you ain't got enough money to get me or my sister.

While Bella tends to focus on the physical, I look deeper and analyze each potential mark.

"What, Beau? Damn. I fucked up last night but don't start acting funny and shit. Most of the time I'm on point. Anyway, it's still my turn to choose," Bella snaps back at me. It's true, she doesn't mess up often, but the mistake she made last night was epic. She chose these two cats based solely on their appearances. Yeah, they were spending. Yeah, they were dressed well. Yeah, they were even in VIP, but when we were done with them we only got a thousand dollars and that was between the both of their broke asses. A stack is the lowest amount we have ever gotten, so we decided to hit up another city before the end of the weekend. Twice in one weekend is a first. We usually only hustle once per weekend. But here we are in Houston at Black Diamond Nightclub about to get it in again. We've flown from Indianapolis to Seattle to Houston in less than 24 hours, and I plan on making it worth our while.

Bella loves money just as much as I do, but I sometimes tease her, saying she can't be Daddy's daughter because she lacks his hustling gene. But shit, he couldn't deny either one of us. At a first glance, Bella and I look as different as night and day—ebony and ivory. Bella is tall, towering at 5'10". Her Italian mother's DNA mixed with our African-American father's to give her a light caramel skin tone, green cat-like eyes, jet black curly tresses that cascade down her back, and a big booty that frames her slender, modelesque physique. I, on the other hand, am

5'2", dark brown-skinned, thick, and, as my grandma always says, bow-legged from the split down. Don't get me wrong, though, we have more similarities than differences. We both have the same full lips, big booty, and dimple in our left cheeks. And to look into our almond-shaped eyes, if you knew our father you'd know they were his. You'd know we are both the daughters of Beaunifide Upendo Jones and hustling runs through our veins just a strong as blood does.

"Here you go, ladies," the bartender says, sitting two glasses in front of us.

Bella rolls her eyes at him. "We didn't order this."

"I know. It's from the owners of the club." The bartender points to the VIP section upstairs, where two men standing on the balcony raise their glasses at us. They are both tall and dark-skinned. One is nicely built—probably 200 pounds or so. The other dude is bigger—shit, maybe pushing 300 pounds. Bella and I raise our glasses to them and then place them back on the bar without taking a sip.

"What is this?" Bella questions the bartender.

"Louis XIII Black Pearl. By far our most expensive cognac at $350 a shot."

"Nice choice," I say to Bella. "Now that's how men with money act. Looks like you won't have to choose tonight. We've already been chosen." I nudge Bella as we walk away from the bar and the hustle begins.

"Whatever, Beau. I'm not taking the big one with his Rick Ross-looking ass. I always get the big ones," Bella pouts.

"Why do you care what he looks like? You need to be concerned with how his pockets look," I laugh as we head to the dance floor. We know they are still watching us, especially since we left the drinks they bought, so we start dancing. Some song about big booty girls is playing. We make sure to put on a show, popping our asses and rolling our hips. This is usually how the hustle begins. Within the next five minutes or so, one of them dudes will be down here to get us. Our hustle thus far has been foolproof. Aside from those broke dudes from last night and the occasional minor bullshit, we have it down to a science. It is thrilling and exciting to hustle, but money is always the motivation and we are definitely in it to get paid.

"That's rude," a deep voice whispers in my ear from behind as a strong hand grabs my waist. He came quicker than I thought he would. The song about big booty girls is still playing. I turn around to face him.

It is the smaller of the two guys. Bella is right; she usually attracts the big dudes. He is about 6'3" and dark chocolate with a low caesar haircut. He has a serious look on his handsome face.

"Excuse me," I smirk. "You can't just start feeling up on women like that. It's rude." I remove his hand from my waist and continue to dance. He pulls me in close.

"Nah, it's rude of you to leave the drink I bought you," he smiles. His confidence reminds me of my father. I can tell he is used to getting what he wants. He takes my hand.

"I don't take drinks from strangers," I inform him, snatching my hand away. He pulls me in close to him again. He is wearing Acqua Di Gio cologne. Damn, he smells good and damn, it actually feels good to be in his arms. My stomach momentarily flutters as we lock eyes.

"Well, let's fix that," he whispers in my ear. "I'm Israel. You can call me Real, though. Come to VIP with me." He leads the way toward the stairs and I grab Bella's hand and follow him.

The big dude is waiting at the top of the stairs. I laugh to myself. His ass does look a lot like Rick Ross. He is tall and dark-skinned with a bald head and full beard.

"Damn, you gorgeous," he says, taking Bella's hand. "I've been watching you since you came in here." She looks back at me. You know the saying, *if looks could kill*...Well, the look Bella gives me has me feeling like I was shot five times like 2Pac. We all walk over to a private area that is secluded and roped off from the rest of VIP. There is a sectional couch and a table full of bottles and glasses. Bella and I sit next to each other.

"Bella, play nice," I whisper.

"Yeah, yeah, yeah. But see, I told you I always get the big ones. It looks like he needs a double dose," Bella whines. I just mug her.

"No whispering. We're supposed to get to know each other so you'll accept a drink from me. What's your name?" Real smiles. We never make up fake names. Too easy to forget and get caught up. Plus, they won't remember our names by the morning, anyway.

"Beau," I smile.

"Bo?" Real stares at me. "You don't look like a Bo." He looks me up and down as if I just gave him a fake name.

"And what exactly does a person named Beau look like?" I ask, frowning.

"Shit, I don't know. Like some cat from the 'hood with a grill

DONISHA DERICE & JAI DARLENE

full of gold, a herringbone chain, and some cornrows," he laughs.

I roll my eyes and try to stifle my laugh. I have to admit, he is funny. I glance over at Bella and her Rick Ross look-alike. She is playing her role, smiling and flirting with him. I look Real over. He is wearing a diamond-encrusted rope chain and his watch is a Bulgari that's worth about $10,000.

"I'll have that drink now, even though you just told me my name sounds like it belongs to a thug." I pick up a glass, gesturing for him to fill it.

"My apologies, beautiful. You make the name look damn good, and to be honest, it does fit you."

"Yeah?"

"Yeah, girl, you bow-legged like a mug." Again this man has me laughing.

As we sip our drinks, Real and I sit and talk for what seems like hours. We chat about music, entertainment, and even politics. We have so much in common, especially music. We both love Pac and agree that a lot of the new music out right now lacks meaning and depth. I like his vibe—really like it.

Several drink later, Real's conversation starts to get personal.

"So where's your man at?"

"I'm single." It's the truth. It's not like this hustle business leaves a lot of room for dating.

"I mean, you are smart and beautiful. You can't be single."

"Where's your girl?" I ask, ignoring his compliment.

"She's sitting right in front of me. We just haven't made it official yet." He gives me a slick smile.

"Whatever." I roll my eyes in disbelief. There's no way his fine ass is single.

"For real. I'm not down with cheating. If I'm fucking with some other broad what am I supposed to believe my girl is doing? You get what you giving, right?"

I nod my head, agreeing with him. Whether he's bullshitting or not, I like his answer. Our conversation gets deeper as we discuss life and relationships. It seems like he has all the right answers. If I had a checklist for the perfect man, Real would be hitting all the marks. I am feeling everything about him. I notice myself laughing and flirting with him, which is so not me, but there's something about him. I know I am not supposed to like him, but I can't help it. The more I sit here

8

conversing with Real, the more I want to get to know him. He couldn't be more different then the ignorant, nothing ass dudes I usually meet in these clubs. Real is smart, cute, and intelligent. I watch his sexy lips as he speaks and when I look into his eyes, they are deep and focused only on me. It's weird, but this connection I am feeling with him…damn…it's indescribable.

Bella taps my leg, signaling that it's almost time to make our move. I snap myself out of Real's trance and try to get back into hustle mode. He is just another victim of the hustle and nothing can come of this. After tonight I will never see him again. An up-tempo song starts to play and Bella and I simultaneously stand and begin dancing. While our marks are focusing on our asses, we slip Special K into their drinks. Ketamine hydrochloride, AKA Special K, is a liquid anesthetic that will slowly numb your body and knock you the hell out.

"Let's dance," Bella says, grabbing her guy's hand to pull him up. "But first…" She grabs her drink and raises it to toast. "To fine ass women, long nights, and good sex!" Bella laughs. She is doing a good job of selling the dream, because I can see in big boy's eyes that he is buying that shit up. He's probably imagining fucking her right now.

We put it on them on the dance floor, making sure to put all those moves we learned in our Latin and hip-hop dance classes to good use. I feel Real's hands on my thighs and his dick poking my ass.

"I like you," he slurs into my ear. I turn around to look him in his eyes.

"I can tell." I look down at his pants, smiling.

"Nah, fuck that. I really like you. I can tell you aren't the average money-hungry chick. Believe me, it ain't just about fucking." He looks me deep in my eyes and I know he is serious. He is telling the truth and it hurts a little. I have done hundreds of hustles and I have never felt like this about any mark. I like him, too.

Real is right, though; I am nothing like the average money-hungry chick. I don't fuck for money and I don't beg for it. I am a taker. I take what I want and usually, I want money. But tonight, I want him. Damn, I want him—like *really* want him. I lay my head on Real's chest as we slow dance to Beyoncé, and I do something I never do; I allow myself to let go and enjoy him. I smell his cologne. I hold onto his neck, softly and slowly stroking it. I revel in the feeling of his hands caressing my body. I dance with him as if he is mine, and when he leans in to kiss me, I kiss him back. I don't turn my cheek like I normally would. I tongue him down like he is my man. I kiss him like I have known and loved and cherished him forever. Even though I know the drinks and the drugs are taking over his mind, his kiss feels real.

"Excuse us." It doesn't take Bella long to break up whatever it is I call myself doing with Real. She grabs my hand and pulls me toward the restroom. She makes sure it is empty and locks the door behind us before she starts going in on me.

"What the fuck are you doing?" Her disgusted glare almost burns a hole through my face.

"He is wearing a Bulgari watch. He tipped the waitress $100 from a bankroll he pulled from his pocket. I figure he has at least $5,000 cash on him." I recite Real's stats to Bella in an attempt to change the subject. She eyes me suspiciously for a few moments before walking to the mirror to check her makeup. Talking money worked. Bella seems to have forgotten about scolding me for kissing Real.

"The big dude just went to pull the money from the door and the bar." Bella's green eyes gleam. I laugh. She must have forgotten his name already. "Let's see, admission is $30 per person and the maximum capacity for the club is around 800. If at least 650 people paid to get in, that's what?" She pauses to tally the numbers in her head. "$19,500? And then there's the bar money and whatever he has in his pockets. Let's get this money." Bella finishes up in the mirror and applies some lip-gloss. I do the same before we exit the bathroom.

Back at the table, two thirsty ass waitresses are all up on our marks. Another common happening when we hustle is hos trying to intercept. I remember once we lost some dudes when we had gone to the restroom to discuss business. We came out and saw them heading out the door with some other chicks. Bella isn't about to let that shit happen tonight and I am not about to let Bella start a fight—yup, that has happened in the past, too.

"Hey, did y'all tip them? Let's go." Bella moves past the waitresses and stands in between them and the guys. One of the waitresses starts running off at the mouth. I can't tell what she is saying as her lips are flapping a mile a minute, but I can tell from her body language she isn't happy.

"I hope it isn't common practice here to allow the help to disrespect your guests," Bella says in her most calm yet snooty demeanor.

The big guy hands the mouthy waitress his empty glass and shoos her off as he grabs Bella around her waist. Saved by the Bella. We sashay out the club with our moneyed marks draped over us like pricey mink scarves.

By now the boys are really feeling good. They stagger to a tricked out Mercedes-Benz sitting on 22s. Bella snatches the keys and hops into the driver's seat. She pulls out of the packed parking lot, headed for the motel, then cracks the windows and turns on the radio to try to keep the boys awake. Real lays his head on my shoulder and I can see Bella mean mugging me through the rearview mirror. I can't lie; I am thinking about Real and not his money. *Focus, Beau, focus.* I close my eyes and take a deep breath.

Bella pulls up to Nites Tale Motel. We have already gotten three rooms but I go through the motions like we hadn't. Room 211 is mine and Bella is right next door in 213. Room 215 is the extra room where we keep our stuff until we leave. Walking to the room, Bella's guy is stumbling hard but still trying to focus on sliding his hand up her dress. They disappear into their room.

Real is smiling at me as we walk into our room. He sits on the edge of the bed, still smiling. I stand in front of the other bed, staring at him while mentally counting down the time it will take him to pass out. I need to keep my distance. I feel like if he touches me just the right way, it could be a wrap. And the one thing I cannot do is fuck him.

This is crazy. I have never had feelings this quick for a man. I bet the sex would be good, though. It's been a while for me. *Focus, Beau, focus.* I try to clear my head. I start to walk towards the bathroom where I will wait for him to pass out. I hit the light switch as I pass by it hoping the darkness will make him sleepy.

"Hey, come over here." Real grabs my hand and pulls me down on top of him before I can make it to the bathroom.

"No, wait. I need to…" He kisses me before I can finish my sentence. I know I should get up, but I don't want to. Those lips. Those damn lips. How could I not kiss them back? As our mouths melt together, he slowly unzips my dress. I try to pull away, but not very hard, though. I don't want to fight it and he's not going to let me. He knows I am feeling him. He's turns me over and lays me on the bed. Real's soft lips caress my breasts as he unhooks my bra. Gently moving his tongue down my stomach, he makes his way to my treasure. Yeah, I call my pussy a treasure because that's exactly what it is, and it is priceless. He pulls off my panties and starts French kissing my other lips, pausing briefly to tell me he usually doesn't do this. I giggle at the irony.

"Neither do I," I whisper, barely audibly, as he dives back down below. He kisses, licks, and sucks my treasure until it pulsates and the bed is soaking wet beneath me. It is the absolute best ever. It's so good I can barely handle it. I try to crawl away—not because I want him to stop, but because it is so good I am about to climb these damn motel room walls. I grip the bed sheets and bite my lip, afraid if I open my mouth the moans and screams of pleasure will echo throughout the whole building. Before I even notice, Real stops kissing me down there and enters me. It happens so fast that I know he didn't put on a condom. I open my mouth to say something, but no words come out—just love sounds.

Real starts off slow with me. I feel every stroke gently entering and slightly exiting. He fits like a glove. His moans start at a whisper and slowly get louder. I cover his mouth with my hand and shush him. Then I pull him down onto the bed and climb on top of him. I ride him slowly at first, feeling every inch of him sliding in and out. I catch a glimpse of the time on his watch. It is 4:08. Shit, I have to be ready to go within the next 40 minutes. I speed things up and begin riding as fast as I can. Real is unable to hold back his moans of pleasure. I can tell he is loving it, and I am, too. He feels so good I really don't want to stop. Real's hands grip the small of my back as he screams out, and we both climax together. My body shudders as I roll onto the bed and close my eyes. Now the pleasure and ecstasy are gone. All that's left is the unmistakable feeling of regret. What the fuck did I just do? I did that. I had sex with Real. I had sex with a mark.

Focus, Beau, focus. Too late. Damn, it was so good. I take a deep breath and sit up. Real has been still for the past few minutes. I lean over him and realize he's knocked out. I think under normal circumstances I would be pissed if a guy went to sleep on me right after we had sex but, shit, I'm glad. It's 4:25. I run into the bathroom to take a quick shower. I wish we could leave the money. I wish I could go back and lie beside him. I wish I could wake up to his smile, and enjoy breakfast with him. But Bella ain't letting that money go, so I can forget about any of that happening. I hear my phone vibrating in my bag. It's too early for it to be my alarm. It must be Bella. I wonder if she heard Real's moans. If she did, she will never let me live this down.

I put on my clothes and then I reach for Real's pants. He's got a nice little knot in his pocket. I don't know how much it is. I don't even count it. I decide I can't take it. I am not going to hustle him, like he was just some mark, because he wasn't. Okay, he was *supposed* to be, but he was more than that. More importantly, taking his money would make me look like a real whore and prove that I am, in fact, just another money-hungry chick. I know I shouldn't care what he thinks of me. After all, I am never going to see him again. But I *do*. I can't deny the fact that I do care what he thinks. Regardless of whether or not I'll ever see him again, I don't want him to think badly of me. That's it; I am not taking the money. My phone vibrates again. It's Bella calling me. As I walk back into the bathroom so I can answer, I turn and take one last look back at Real, who is sound asleep.

DONISHA DERICE & JAI DARLENE

2
When the Joke's on You

Bella

"So how old are you?"

"I'm 21."

"For real? How old is your sister?"

"She's 21."

"What?! Y'all ain't sisters and the same age...unless y'all some 'hood twins." The jolly Rick Ross-looking ass fool jiggles in the front passenger seat as he laughs. We're headed to the motel, and if I wasn't driving I would slap him, even though what he's saying is true. I was born on November 21st. Beau was born a couple weeks before me on November 12th. Our daddy was a ho. He has three kids that we know of by three different women. All his baby mommas are of different ethnicities: black, Italian, and Colombian. It's like his dick was the rainbow coalition, uniting all the races of the world.

"I'm not gonna lie; y'all don't look nothing alike, but yo' daddy must've been a pimp 'cause y'all both fine as hell." I look in the rearview mirror to see if Beau can hear this motherfucka' clowning us, but she's too busy being cuddled up in the back making kissy faces with Real. They look like a damn couple. I am appalled. What part the hustle is this? I can't believe she really likes one of our marks.

I take a deep breath to calm myself down. I decide right then to just let it go. She can fall in love if she wants to, as long as she gets that money and cuts me my half. I have bigger problems, like being broke as fuck. I haven't been this desperate for cash since I was 16. Five years in the game and I don't have shit to show for it, all because I was dumb enough to let myself get hustled. I take comfort in knowing that I have at least another three months to hustle before Beau quits to start law school. I won't even be close to where I used to be financially, but at least I won't have to donate blood for money to pay my mortgage.

I can't help but to think about what my dad taught me. According to him, in life you have two options; either you hustle or you get hustled. If someone was able to take what is rightfully yours, you've been hustled. If you are spending half of your waking hours earning pennies to make a corporation millions, you are getting hustled. If you are spending everything to fulfill an addiction, you are being hustled. In my Daddy's words, "Put a hustler in any environment and they are bound to come out on top." If Dad was alive he would be so disappointed. Damn, I fucked up.

Ever since I got hustled I've been debating whether or not to tell Beau my dilemma. I don't want to have to come to her for help. I put myself in this situation so I will get myself out of it. But I never keep secrets from my best friend and I withheld this one long enough. I decide I'll tell her when we get back to Indianapolis tomorrow. Shoot, maybe telling her will be like therapy. Holding all this inside has been wrecking me. I don't know when was the last time I had a good night's rest or a decent appetite. Hell, I even messed up the last hustle because I'm so stressed about money.

I overhear Real saying, "I don't want this night to ever end. What y'all doing tomorrow?" I interject before Beau can start making future plans with this mark. "Tomorrow is Make Money Monday. We got work to do." Everyone laughs. I want to know what the hell is so funny. I know why Beau's laughing. The thought of me working a regular nine to five amuses her. These other two don't know what the fuck I do, though—but they 'bout to learn tonight. I wonder how funny it will be when they wake up in the morning to find their pockets turned inside out. I laugh to myself imagining the looks on their faces.

"Make Money Monday, huh? I know that's right. How do you make yo' money?" Real asks. Beau leans in and kisses him on the cheek. I am hoping that kiss is to distract him from asking too many personal questions, but I know it's not. I can tell she is enjoying him.

The big motherfucka' chimes in. "She works at Superhead Taught Me, Incorporated. Girl, you know you ain't never worked a day in yo' life." They all laugh at his joke, comparing me to the infamous whore known for giving head to celebrities.

"Yo, bro, chill out," Real says, patting his shoulder.

"I'm just saying, with a face like *wow* and body like *damn* she ain't working no regular nine to five, bruh. Let's be real. I know she a video vixen or some rich dude's baby momma or somethin'."

Beau steps in. "You right. She ain't no hustla'. Not a drop of it in her blood. Just know we some daddy's girls." I see her smiling at me. She got jokes. She knows how I feel when she says I ain't no real hustla'.

"Let's go." I turn off the engine and am the first one out of the car. I mean mug Beau as she fronts like she is getting the keys for the motel. She doesn't think I'm a hustler, huh? If she would say that to some strangers then she must really believe it. I decided there's no way I can tell Beau I got hustled. I'll never hear the end of it. I already take too much shit from her just because I didn't go to college like her and I invested a lot of money into my condo. She'll say it's just jokes, but I take that shit to heart. Words hurt.

Beau notices I'm giving her the death stare as she hands me the room keys. She is about to say something but Real stumbles over, attempting to grab her by the waist. She had to catch him before he fell to the ground. I go back to the car and almost pull my back out helping that big ass dude to the room. Thank goodness our rooms are on the first floor.

Once we're alone, he immediately tries to unzip my dress. I kick off my heels and run to the other side of the room to get away from him. For a big guy, he is pretty quick; his ass is stumbling right behind me so closely he almost falls on top of me.

"Oh yeah, I like to chase the cat. Ain't nothing but the dog in me. Woof!" he sings. This dude is still full of energy. The Special K is barely having an effect on him. I have to give him another dose to knock him out. He grabs me by the waist and turns me around so that I'm facing him. He sticks his face in my cleavage and licks in between my breasts.

"Whoa, whoa, Rick. Let's have a toast!" I exclaim. I push him back and rush into the bathroom to grab a bottle of vodka and two cups from my overnight bag. I'm glad I didn't leave my bag in the third room like I normally do.

"My name is not Rick. It's Cliff. Clifford James. And there's nothing else to toast to. We've been toasting all night," he complains.

"But toasting makes my panties wet," I moan seductively.

"One more toast won't hurt," he quickly agrees.

I already have one of the cups laced with Special K so I don't have to worry about trying to sneak it in his cup without him seeing it. We toast and I watch him drink it all down in several chugs. I tell him I need to go to the bathroom to freshen up and that I'll be right out. I hide in the bathroom from his ol' extra energetic horny ass and wait for the drug to kick in.

After about 15 minutes, I peep out the door to see if he has passed out yet. To my relief he is sprawled out across the floor. I tiptoe over to him and wave my hand over his face. Nothing. Yup, he is knocked dead out. He has money in his pants pockets and in his wallet—

all big bills. He also has a nice little ostrich skin backpack that he is carrying. "I'm keeping this," I smile to myself. I check inside it. Bingo! All the money he made from the club that night is in the bag. I can hear the cha-chings ringing in my head as I put the money that I took from his pockets into the backpack and go back into the bathroom to count it. Then I realize I left his Rolex on his wrist. I'm taking that, too.

As I tiptoe back towards him, I trip over my heels I left on the floor and fall on top of him. I freeze in position. "No, no, no, don't wake up!" I stare into his face, expecting to see his eyes twitch or flutter, but to my surprise he is still knocked out. I've never accidentally fallen on top of a drugged mark before, but I don't think he should still be knocked out like this. He didn't budge at all. I check his breath. He isn't breathing. I panic. "Oh no, oh no, he's dead. I killed him!" I climb off of Cliff's massive body and sit on the bed, shaking and crying as I try to calm myself enough to figure out what I'm going to do.

I run to my phone and try to call Beau. She doesn't pick up. I look back at the body. I'm a murderer. I didn't mean to kill him, but there he is, lying on the floor dead. Bile begins to creep up my throat. I run to the toilet and throw up. I try to call Beau again. No answer. I call her again. No answer. I hear a farting noise. I saw once on the Discovery Channel that dead bodies can still make noises as they release bodily gasses and fluids. I throw up again at the thought of a dead body farting less than ten feet from me. I call Beau again. No answer.

I am still trembling with fear as I think about the possible consequences. The first thing that comes to mind is jail. That thought alone causes me to almost lose control of my bladder. There's no way I can go to prison. I have to cover this up. I try to remember what they do on those real life detective shows. You know, the ones based on true stories where the criminal almost gets away. Well, I need to do the opposite of what they do, because I don't want to *almost* get away. I need to make sure there's nothing leading this back to me so I don't get caught. I take a washcloth from the bathroom and wipe down everything I touched. On my hands and knees, I search the floor for any hairs I might have shed. Then I go to the car and wipe down everything in it. Hopefully I covered all my bases and got rid of any fingerprints and DNA. I guess I'll find out soon enough.

Standing next to the car, I see lightening crack across the black sky and hear the roar of thunder. Rain begins to pours down on me, merging with the tears already running down my face. I am trying my hardest not to throw up again. I want to have a heads-up if my efforts aren't enough, so I put a Google alert on the name Clifford James from my phone. I want to be notified of all news concerning him. I call Beau again and finally she answers. I can smell the sex through the phone. She has the unmistakable *I just got laid* voice. I'm over here having a life and death emergency and she's too busy getting her rocks off to pick up the phone.

I lie and tell Beau that Cliff is breathing funny and that his breaths are shallow. Beau says she is going to call for an ambulance over at the gas station and tells me to call a cab and meet her there. I don't tell her the truth because I want to protect her. I know she couldn't handle it if she knew he was already dead, so I leave her a little bit of hope. I don't want her to feel what I'm feeling right now, even if I am mad at her for fucking Real. I hang up with Beau and wipe the last of the tears from my face. "No more crying," I coach myself. There is no point in shedding tears over what's already done. I didn't mean to overdose Clifford, but there is risk involved with the hustle. I tell myself to toughen up. I still have to take care of my family and myself. Tears can't pay my mortgage or keep me out of jail. I force myself to chuckle out loud. Ain't a damn thing funny. But I laugh so I won't cry.

DONISHA DERICE & JAI DARLENE

3
Change

Beau

There are three major rules to the hustle that up until tonight Bella and I had never broken. But within this one night we have broken all three. We rank the rules by severity of the punishment. Rule number one: Never, by any means, go over the dosage amount. Possible consequences of this, which we may learn tonight firsthand, are death and first-degree murder charges. Rule number two: Never fuck a mark. This could also be a death sentence. HIV, a litany of other STDs, or even a child could come from fucking a mark. Not to mention drugging someone and then having sex with them is rape. Damn, am I a rapist? Rule number three: Never, ever leave the money. Hell, if there is going to be the risk of prison or other harm we might as well achieve the goal we set out for. Money has always been our motivation.

I want to tell Bella that I had broken the rules too—that I fucked Real and that is why I didn't take his money. It didn't have anything to with her overdosing Real's brother. But I am too worried and upset to bring it up. Other than Bella whispering apologies, it is silent between us for the three-hour plane ride back home to Nap. I am in shock and I do something I don't think I've ever done before, at least not seriously. I pray. I pray for what seems like the whole three hours. *God, please let him be okay*, I repeat over and over again in my head.

I never thought our hustle would kill someone. We are always prepared and careful. We have plans and instructions in place in case we ever feel endangered. We both keep tasers under our pillows at the motels. We wouldn't use them on anyone unless it was absolutely necessary, but if it was, we would use them to get out of the room and hide in the third rented room we always keep. We also take proper precautions when measuring the Special K. We researched it and we know exactly how much to use. So I cannot understand why Bella would give dude so much. He isn't even the biggest man we have dealt with and the regular dose has always worked. My mind wanders to what Real might be thinking now and how he feels. I know that was some crazy shit for him to wake up to; his brother being carried off in an ambulance and the women they hooked up with gone. How the fuck did we let this happen?

Once at my house with the door closed, Bella and I speak simultaneously as we often do, but the words that come out of our mouths could not be more different.

"We are done," I calmly say as Bella informs me that she has gotten $70,000 from Cliff.

Our next words are also spoken simultaneously, but this time we say the same thing: "What?" We both look confused.

"A man may be dead and you still talking money!" I yell. At that moment I feel like my sister, my best friend, my only confidant, has lost her soul in the hustle. "Who gives a fuck how much money you got? It's blood money if he dies!"

"We are hustlas, Beau. This is the life we have chosen and in this game there can be casualties," Bella argues. She sounds like our father, who never hid the fact that people die in the hustle game, both the wrong and the innocent.

"We are not pushing drugs. We are not drug lords. You mean to tell me that because he thought he might get to fuck some woman he just met, he should accept the fact that he might die?" I try to reason with her. I can't believe she is comparing what we do to what our father did.

"Regardless of what form it takes, hustling is hustling. You think we are the first women to rob men for their money? Hell nah. We just chose to be as logical and precise about it as possible. And please believe people have died getting robbed," Bella continues to argue. She has valid points, but she just seems so heartless about the situation. "I didn't want him to get hurt, and I definitely don't want him to die. But fuck, Beau, what would you have me do now? Take the money back? Turn myself in?" Bella asks emotionlessly, knowing I don't expect her to do either one of those things.

"I would think you would show some real emotion—some actual regret about what you did." To be honest with myself, I don't think she can. Bella and I embody the two conflicting sides of our father. Yes, Beaunifide Upendo Jones was a hustla'. The drugs he distributed took many lives, not to mention the lives he took with his own hands and reckoned as casualties of the hustle. But he still had a heart and a conscious. He did feel bad for some of the wrong he did and the anguish it caused.

Bella and I stand silent for a while. When I finally speak, I just repeat what I had said earlier. "We are done." I can tell Bella is pissed.

"This is some bullshit. You can't just quit on me—not now. I can't hustle by myself. He's probably alright, anyway," Bella tries to persuade me. "You don't know that he's dead. You're just assuming."

"I don't care," I snap. "The mere possibility that we may have killed someone should be enough to stop." I walk out of the living room as Bella continues yelling whatever. A few seconds later the door slams. We have just had our first real argument. We've disagreed before, but never like this.

Between what may have happened to Cliff, thinking about Real, and the argument with Bella, I can't eat or sleep. I sit around thinking about what's next. I wiped down the truck. I am sure Bella took care of her room. I even removed the sheets—I knew my DNA was all over them. I remember Real's still body as I moved him around the bed to get the sheets. I leaned in close to his face and felt his warm breath on my ear. I felt like the most gutter person on earth but I knew it was necessary. I grabbed the towels I showered with and wiped down his dick, too, balls and all. I tossed the sheets and towels in a dumpster near the gas station before calling the ambulance. I think Bella and I did a good job of covering our tracks, but I can't shake the feeling that we might get caught up. I lay in bed tossing and turning, waiting for the FBI to kick in my door. Two o'clock, three o'clock, and four o'clock roll by. By 5 PM I finally close my eyes with the sun still beaming down on me through the window.

* * * * *

I roll over in bed and my head is banging. It's Tuesday morning and I have slept for over 15 hours but still feel like shit. As I lay, the same thoughts continue to cross my mind. Shit, I thought these Tempur-Pedic mattresses were supposed to make you feel like you are in heaven but I feel the exact opposite. I slept in my clothes. I didn't wrap my hair either. So not only do I feel like hell; I look like it, too.

My phone starts singing 2pac's *Only God Can Judge Me*. I laugh at the irony. Although I don't talk to God that often, I still believe that truth—only God can judge me. I wonder what he is thinking of me right now. I let the call go to voicemail. I'm not really in the mood to talk. I roll out of bed and cook a good ol' omelet with bacon, sausage, ham, green peppers, onions, jalapeno peppers, and a lot of cheese. I make hash browns and biscuits, and then I pour some OJ.

Hustlin' wasn't the only thing my father taught my sister and me. After my mother passed away, he was always a single man, at least as far as we knew. So he showed us how to be ladies. What better way to learn how a woman should act than from a man with high standards? We had chefs and maids, but he still took the time to teach us how to cook, clean, speak different languages, and, most importantly, how to hustle. He showed us the ropes. Yeah, Daddy did it all. He kept the house immaculate and expected us to do the same. As far as cooking, shit, I'd rather eat some home-cooked meatloaf, mashed potatoes, cabbage, and cornbread than go to a restaurant. My dad said he learned all he knew about cooking and cleaning from his mother, our gorgeous grandma, GG.

When it came to fashion, Daddy had his attorney, Jacqueline Price show us the ropes. Ms. Jacqueline grew up in the 'hood with my parents. She was my mom's best friend. According to my dad, she is a hustla', too. He told us that attorneys are the best legal hustlas ever. Guess that is why I decided I would go to law school. I know I will be a great attorney—that is if I'm not in the pen doing 20 to life for murder.

Shit, I almost forgot. I sit my plate down and run to my phone. Thinking about Ms. Jacqueline reminds me that today is orientation for law school. I have two missed calls and a voicemail message from her.

"I don't even want to know what excuse you have for missing orientation," her message begins. "Lucky for you, I signed you up for the afternoon one. It's the last one, so I expect you to be in attendance, and I want to see you in my office by noon."

It's 10:45. I jump in the shower, lotion up, and throw my hair in a ponytail. I put on a black A-line pencil skirt, a white blouse, and black Christian Louboutin pumps and hop in the Maserati Daddy had bought me when I turned 16. Bella and I kept our cars, because they were some of the few things we had left from him that didn't get seized by the government.

I reach the law school in 30 minutes. I am nervous as hell, heading to Ms. Jacqueline's office. She don't hold no punches or put up with any bullshit. She took me under her wing after I told her how much I wanted to be an attorney. To be late for whatever reason is not acceptable. I close the door as soon as I enter her office.

"I don't even want to know why you weren't here this morning," she begins. "You are your father's daughter and that is all I need to know." I can't focus on what she is saying as my mind begins to wander back to the other night. I can't stop thinking about the dude Bella overdosed. I want to know if he is okay, but I have no idea what his or Israel's full names are. I don't think I can live with myself if he dies. God, let him be okay.

"Beaunifide, what the hell? Are you listening?" Ms. Jacqueline yells.

"Look, Ms. Jacqueline, I overslept. It won't happen again." I stand up and give her a hug. I can see she is worried about me, but something she taught me is plausible deniability which means the less you know the easier it is to deny it. I cannot and will never tell her—or anybody else—what happened. Bella and I will take this shit to our graves.

I leave Ms. Jacqueline's office and head to orientation. I must have missed the "dress casual" memo. I am looking like I'm ready for court while everyone else has on jeans, T-shirts, sneakers, and flip-flops. It doesn't take long to notice that I am the only black person who is a recipient of the Ethan Rose and Company Scholarship for Future Attorneys. I walk to the registration table and grab my nametag and orientation packet. All first year law students are placed into groups and those in your group will basically have the same class schedule with you throughout law school. I am hoping to get some cool people in my group. I have a strong intolerance for stupidity, ignorance, and arrogance. Unfortunately, it seems like I got a little bit of it all in my group. Since I am in a summer program for the Ethan Rose scholarship recipients, my group is small and full of ignorant elitist assholes.

Orientation is a momentary distraction from the shit that just went down less than 48 hours ago, but the reality that a man might be dead because of our hustling ways soon creeps back into my mind. And so does Real. Head still spinning from everything, I go to my car, longing for the comforts of my home.

The first thing I notice when I walk in the house is a stack of money on the end table by the door. Bella must have put it there before she left. I don't want anything to do with that money. Checking the time I notice I have an hour before the bank closes at six. I grab the money and head right back out the door.

Showing up to the bank with $35,000 in cash to deposit might seem suspicious, but Daddy taught us how to make hustling look legit. Bella and I own a farm that is managed and maintained by our father's close business associates, "Uncle Frank," so any large sums of cash can be attributed to farm profits or the sale of farming equipment.

Our personal banker, Samantha Stone is one of several bank managers our father would use to move money around. Once Bella and I started needing someone to help us with our hustle money, we contacted her. For $20,000 a year Samantha can wash and clean anything we bring to her. I go directly to her office when I arrive at the bank.

"I'd like this placed into Bella's checking account," I tell her, laying the money on her desk, Samantha doesn't ask any questions. In less than ten minutes I am done and on my way back home.

As soon as I walk back into the house, my phone starts singing Scarface's *Mary Jane*. It's my GG. Damn, we missed Sunday dinner. GG is about to go in on me.

"Hey GG," I answer the phone. She skips the formalities. No *hi*. No *how you doing, baby*. She gets right down to business.

"What happened to y'all Sunday, Beaunifide? I cooked all this food and you and Bella didn't come over, didn't call, or anything. Is everything alright? You know I'm constantly praying for y'all girls to get your lives together," GG chides me.

"I'm sorry, GG. I didn't mean to miss dinner. I promise I will be on time this Sunday. I'll even bake you an apple pie."

"And what about church? Will you be attending Sunday?"

GG is a hustla' too—for real. She's been hustling up souls and getting them saved in the name of the Lord for over 50 years.

One thing I don't do is lie to my GG. I keep it real with her always. "I can't make any promises, GG. I went to orientation for law school today, though," I quickly change the subject.

"Good, baby, that's real good. I am proud of you, Beaunifide. Now you and Bella can stop that foolishness y'all into," GG fusses.

"What foolishness, GG?" I laugh. GG ain't no fool. She doesn't know how Bella and I are making money, but she knows we are hustling somehow.

"Beaunifide Love Jones, don't try to play with me, girl. I raised your daddy, your momma, your sisters, and you. I know you out there some kind of way and it is God's grace and mercy protecting you," GG preaches. She preaches the same thing to me every time I speak to her but it's hitting home today, especially with what went down. I remember praying for Real's brother.

"GG, this guy I know might be in trouble. Can you say a special prayer for him?" I ask.

"Of course, baby. He will be alright. I pray God's mercy over him and that anything ailing and hurting him will be fixed."

After hanging up with GG I read the first hundred pages of my Tort Law book and work on outlining my notes before getting ready for bed. When I finally lay my head on my pillow I can't fall asleep. I feel tortured by the thoughts of what may have happened to ol' dude. I think about Israel. I close my eyes and think about his smile. I wonder what he thinks of me now. Before having sex with Israel I hadn't had sex in almost two years. I had been in one relationship but never in love. I do want love, though. Although my life has always been about hustling and money, deep down I want normalcy. I want the same thing my father wanted for my sister and me. He showed us how he hustled and the life he lived so we wouldn't want to live it. He told us how our mothers died because of his hustle so we would be scared of it. He wanted us to be able to lead normal lives without crime.

Daddy also told us life is a hustle and we had to choose our hustles wisely—and we thought we did. Robbing dudes wasn't going to be a lifelong thing for Bella or me. Actually, it would have never been our hustle if our father hadn't been murdered. Before he died, Daddy sat us down and asked us what our legal hustles would be. He talked to us about all sorts of legal hustles. He even told us GG's pastor was a hustla'. We laughed, but he was serious. He said, "You see how people listen to him? How people's faith in God is built up because of his sermons? Yeah, he is hustling for the Lord." He told us he would do the best he could to help us master whatever hustle we chose. I told Daddy I wanted to be an attorney like Ms. Jacqueline. He said I would be even better than her and that him putting me in private school and having me learn five foreign languages would help. He also signed me up for the Ethan Rose and Company Scholarship for Future Attorneys when I was in my junior year of high school. Although the scholarship is usually only offered to seniors, my father showed the school that I had already received a full scholarship to Notre Dame, and that I was number one in my class and the class president. Once they received my essay, I was awarded the scholarship.

Bella's dream hustle was to marry rich. Daddy laughed but entertained her hustle idea anyway. "Hell, I already did all the work to get you into your hustle," he said. He explained how Bella was beautiful because he had mixed his DNA with a model's. He'd sent Bella to the most prestigious private school in the city, giving her first pick of the elite future moneymakers. And he kept her dressing fresh so she would catch the eye of any man she wanted.

Our dad did a lot for us before he died, but he could have never imagined he would leave us so soon. So when we thought of our own illegal hustle we tried to make it as fool-proof as possible to make sure we stayed out of harm's way just like Daddy wanted. As I've learned, though, nothing is fool-proof and mistakes can and will take their toll on a hustla'.

Still up at 1:30 in the morning, I decide to Google the name of the club. As soon as I type 'Black Diamond Club Houston', tons of articles pop up. I click on the first one and my heart skips a beat as I read the title of the Houston Herald article: **PRO BASKETBALL PLAYER ISRAEL JAMES' TWIN BROTHER HOSPITALIZED AFTER WILD NIGHT OF PARTYING**. I breathe a sigh of relief. It said hospitalized, not dead. He's alive. I read the article which states the brothers stayed at a motel near their club after partying until the wee hours of the morning. It says that when Israel went to get his brother, Clifford James, so they could go home, Israel immediately noticed Clifford's shallow and labored breathing and called for help. At the hospital, tests were run and Clifford was diagnosed with sleep apnea. The article goes on to describe symptoms and causes of sleep apnea, one of which is being overweight. There is no mention of any drugs being in his system. I exhale deeply and mouth a silent "Thank you, Jesus." We didn't kill anyone. In fact, the Special K probably had nothing to do with what was going on with him. I am beyond relieved.

My mind wanders to Israel. He probably hates me but I can't stop thinking of him. Like my daddy always said, the hustle has its sacrifices and I truly feel like Israel is a sacrifice. I can only imagine what could have been between us, other than good ass sex, of course. I stare at his picture in the news article. We had spent hours together and he never mentioned he was a basketball player. He wasn't flashing money or being arrogant. He was real. For a moment I mull over the possibility of fixing this situation. Maybe I could contact him. If he doesn't know about the drugs it will be easy to come up with a story. And as for Clifford's money, I can pay him back. "Yeah fucking right!" I laugh out loud. That is never going to happen. Israel probably thinks I am some ratchet ass whore and I sure as hell ain't got time to fight with Clifford's big ass, because I know he is beyond pissed. Bella hustled the shit out of him.

I sit at my desk debating whether or not to tell Bella tonight. Maybe I should make her sweat. Honestly, it doesn't seem like she cares. Bella has pretty much chalked Clifford up as a casualty of the hustle. But I am so damn happy I can't wait to tell her. It has to be in person; I want to see her face when I tell her the good news. I throw on a T-shirt, Bebe jogging pants, and Jordans, and head over to Bella's condo.

Driving to Bella's, I think about how lucrative the hustle has been. I mean, who knew robbing men was such good money? For five years Bella and I hustled almost every weekend. We took the occasional break for holidays, but other than that we were constantly on it. We averaged $10,000 each time, about 40 times a year. Not to mention all the expensive jewelry we were able to get money for. Five years in the game and we have made over $3.5 million.

With that money Bella and I did a lot of shit. But the most important thing we did was make sure we would always have a home. Being ripped from the Geist neighborhood we grew up in and then losing the home our dad worked so hard to provide for us, Bella and I decided that it would be better to own instead of rent. I opted to pay $450,000 cash for a 4,500-square-foot, 5-bedroom, 5½-bath house sitting on an acre of land out in Zionsville. Bella, on the other hand, chose to get a mortgage on one the most expensive condos in downtown Indianapolis. Her 1,500-square-foot, 2-bedroom, 2½-bath condo cost $1.2 million. It is ultra modern, super sleek, and totally her style. The apartment has every possible amenity one could ever want, including a concierge, maid, and dry cleaning service.

I park in Bella's second spot and use the spare key card she had given me to access the elevator in the garage. On the way up, I smile at my reflection in the fancy glass and mirror-lined elevator. I exit the elevator at the penthouse floor and ring the doorbell instead of using my key. All I can hear on the other side of the door are a bunch of expletives and something about shooting the stupid motherfucka' dumb enough to try her.

"It's me, Bella," I quickly announce myself so as not to get shot. "Damn, stand down, soldier."

"Shit, Beau," is her response when she finally answers the door with her purple .22 at her side. I guess at 2:30 AM it is a little late for someone to be popping up. But despite the time, somehow Bella manages to answer the door looking like a million bucks. She is wearing a short, black silk nightie with six-inch Jimmy Choos. Her hair is flowing perfectly down her back with not a single strand out of place.

"You look good," I laugh. "Why the hell are you looking so good at two in the morning?"

"Well, I was thinking that whatever bold ass stalker got past the doorman and decided to knock at my door at this time of the night had to be crazy as hell. I figured I was most definitely gonna have to shoot his weirdo ass. If I shot his ass the police would get called and then Fox, Wish TV 8, and all of them other news channels would be here," she explains. We sit on her couch, a handcrafted sofa flown in from Spain, laughing as she pours us some wine. It is as if we had never gotten into the fight. It feels like it always does. "And you know me, Beau," she continues. "I'd be damned if they were gone plaster my face all over the news with me looking anything less than flawless." I can't help but laugh at her rationale. I still don't know how she managed to get herself together so quickly. We sit back laughing and joking about how the news reports would sound as we sip our wine.

Bella and I are having such a good time that I had momentarily forgotten why I stopped by in the first place. I pull the printed news article out of my pocket and hand it to her. Bella seems to just skim over the article without really reading it and hands it back to me. She already knows. I can tell by how nonchalantly she looks at the paper.

"So how long have you known?" I ask as I place the paper back in my pocket.

"I knew there was something familiar about that dude you fucked." Bella's response catches me off guard. "Yeah, I know that, too," she smiles. "I don't know what you thought you were doing. We ain't living an Usher song. Ain't no love in the club. Money is the motivation. And since dude is okay and it probably didn't have shit to do with the drugs, we can forget this shit and get back to hustling." Bella's gleaming eyes peer at me as she awaits a response.

I am silent for a minute as I choose my words carefully. Bella is right about the drugs not hurting Clifford, but I am not about to let her post up on her high horse like she didn't do shit wrong. And having sex with Real isn't the reason why I am done hustling.

"What the fuck ever, Bella. I don't understand how the possibility of hurting or killing someone wouldn't make you want to quit. Hustla' or not, I ain't for that shit. Besides, you knew this wasn't going to be a forever thing. I start school in less than a week and in one night I almost saw all my hard work ruined." I shake my head.

Before we started hustling, we decided that it would end by the time we began our legal hustles. I didn't think I'd be in law school until this fall, but my scholarship requires that I attend the summer session.

"You aren't a lawyer yet, Beau. And I damn sure don't see a ring on my finger or a man in my bed, so we should still be on our hustle shit. You weren't supposed to start school this early, anyway. You changed the plans!" Bella yells.

"Fuck all that. I am done and that's the end of it. My focus from here on out is law school and making good on the legal hustle I told Daddy I wanted—the legal hustle I've been preparing for and looking forward to. You done had a basketball player, a doctor, a Fortune 500 CEO, and an astronaut propose to you. A real life walk-on-the-moon astronaut! Shit, I am starting to think you don't want to go legal." I feel like Bella has fallen in love with the hustle and hasn't really been looking for a husband or to settle down like she said she would someday do. She has set her standards so high that no man can seem to reach them. I guess she sees our hustle as the best way to keep making steady money. But Bella is being selfish. I bet she never even considered the time and work I am going to have to put in to succeed in law school. She probably figures shit will be just like when I was in undergrad, which was easy. During the week, I went to my classes and studied; on weekends we hustled. But I know law school, with its law clinics, internships, and the ridiculous amount of reading and studying, will require more of my time and attention. It will not be a cakewalk like undergrad was.

It is now Bella's turn to sit and deliberate on her next words. She knows that once my mind is made up there really isn't anything that can change it. "You know what Beau? You always tease me and say that I ain't no real hustla', but look at yo' ass. In less than three hours a dude hustled you out of your panties and your pussy. Now you wanna quit, 'cause some mark done laid the pipe good. You are so fucking weak!" Bella yells.

Before I can fully digest what she said I hurl my glass at her. Although I missed on purpose, she got the message.

"You should know bout being hustled! Look at you being hustled by Louie, Prada, and Gucci. Look at this ridiculously expensive apartment. You being hustled by a lifestyle you're dying to keep up with and going broke in the process!" I snatch my keys off the marble table and head toward the door.

"You wear the same brands I do!" Bella screams. "Get the fuck out my house, you hypocritical bitch!"

"Fuck you!" I yell back. "This ain't even yo' shit. This the bank's shit!" As I storm out the door, a glass Bella has thrown smashes into the doorframe just inches from my head. By the time I reach the garage, security is there waiting for me and demanding that I return my keys and elevator access card. My initial thought is to cuss the Rent-A-Cop out and demand he makes Bella be a woman and come get them herself, but I am done with her and have no desire to see her simple ass anymore tonight.

4
When You Ain't Ready

Bella

The water is pouring down on my head, drenching me and making my straight dark hair turn curly. Whenever I wear my hair in its natural curly state people mistake me for being Hispanic. They ask me if I speak Spanish or try to guess which South American country I'm from. When it's straight they just ask what I am. It's frustrating that people feel the need to classify me. They want to know *what* I am as opposed to *who* I am, as if I'm nothing more than my race and what they see on the outside.

Even my own right hand, my sister, doesn't know me. At least Beau doesn't know me as well as she thinks she does. It's apparent from the hateful words she spit at me that she thinks I'm just a dumb broad trying to keep up with the Joneses. My daddy was Beaunifide Jones. I AM the Joneses, damn it! I don't need to keep up with shit. Yes, I dress fly and spend thousands on my clothes, but I consider my wardrobe an investment. In a society where people focus so much on outward appearances, it's important to make the best first impression, especially when I'm hustling. Ain't no man with any real money trying to holla at a broke down looking chick wearing a dress from Rave. If you want to attract money, you better look like money. Besides, Louboutins make me happy.

Shit, my condo is currently worth $2.4 million. I was able to mortgage both the condos on the top floor of my building for $1.2 million and I'm currently renovating them so that it will be one big player ass penthouse. Once the renovations are done the condo will be worth $4.6 million, netting me at $3.4 million dollars. Beau must not know how much I have in assets. Who gives a fuck that I pay a mortgage? Technically, my net worth is almost $5 million. She doesn't look beneath the surface. All she sees is a two-bedroom apartment and a bunch of clothes. She obviously has no clue as to how investments work. Disrespectful bitch.

I hold my face close to the showerhead, letting the water be my tears. I am more angry than sad, but the sadness is there too. I can't

33

believe what just went down only minutes ago in my condo. I feel like I just lost my best friend. I wasn't expecting to lose my temper, but she hit below the belt. She verbally attacked me and she tore up my shit. That was an $800 crystal wine glass she threw. If she was mad, she should've gone home and tore up her own damn house.

She pissed me off so much that when I threw my wine glass at her, I wasn't trying to miss. In that moment I was so angry I aimed that glass right at her little short, square, block head. But in hindsight, I'm glad I did miss. If I seriously injured her I would hate myself.

Interrupting my self-venting I hear the lyrics of *Hey Big Spender*, a classic song by Shirley Bassey. It's my cell phone ringing. From the ringtone I know it is one of the dudes I keep in rotation. I don't feel like being bothered. Besides, it's 3:30 in the morning. Whoever it is knows better than to call me in the middle of the night like I'm some booty call, and if they don't know, they will soon find out because I am not answering. I let the phone go to voicemail without bothering to hit the ignore button. I am not about to leave the comfort of my hot shower. I sit on my built-in shower bench and let the steam engulf me like a warm embrace. I really need a fucking hug and this shower is as close as I am going to get to one tonight.

Beau is right about one thing and she doesn't even know it: I am broke. Well, that is, unless I liquidate my assets, and that shit is not about to happen. Besides, if I start selling all my shit for cash, Beau will know something is up and I'm not giving that self-righteous know-it-all the satisfaction. I have to figure out how to rebuild my empire on my own and I know one thing for sure, I'm never going back to Haughville again. I don't care how broke I am.

My dad and mom—well, Beau's mother that I considered my mom, too—were born and hustled together in Haughville. It's the typical 'hood you see across America; violent crime, drugs, teen pregnancies, and gang activity that has triggered, what those in the upper echelon call, urban decay. We lived in the 'hood, but we were rich and everybody knew it. That made our home a target. It was my mom's death that led to my dad moving us out of Haughville to Geist, one of the most affluent neighborhoods of Indianapolis. Otherwise he would have never left the place where he grew up. It was also my mom's death that made my dad a legend.

My mother's death was gruesome. It's the type of murder that would have been on that show *Unsolved Mysteries*. She was in our home in Haughville when some close associates of my dad's broke in while he was away on business. They ransacked our house, looking for Daddy's safe. My mom was so loyal to him that she refused to tell them anything. When she wouldn't aid them in their endeavors, they cut off her fingers for motivation. When they deemed her useless, they shot her in the vagina and splattered her brains all over our living room floor. Days later, her body was found in the White River. But before my mother's body was found, heads had already rolled. Daddy personally hacked off the heads of every person involved in my mother's murder, and a few people who weren't, just for good measure. His rampage solidified his spot as the king pin in Indiana. There was nothing on this Earth that my dad wouldn't do four us, but he could never bring my mom back. Every time I go visit GG, who still lives in the old neighborhood, my mother crosses my mind and I am reminded why I'll never live in the 'hood again.

Hey big spender, my phone rings again. Irritated, I swing the ceiling-to-floor glass shower door open and snatch my cell phone off the sink. I don't even care enough to look on the caller ID to see who it is. It doesn't matter. Whoever it is wants to get cussed clean out for calling this late.

"What?!" I bark into the phone. "What, man, what?! What is so damn important that you're repeatedly calling me at almost four in the fucking morning?!"

"Oh, did-did I wa-wa-wake you?" the voice on the other line stutters. I immediately know it is Reggie's whack ass. Picturing this annoyingly clingy fool makes me even more pissed.

"What the fuck are you thinking, you stuttering motherfucka'? What the hell could you possibly want this late at night?" Without pausing to give Reggie an opportunity to reply, I continue to lay his ass out. Somebody is going to feel my wrath. If it can't be Beau, and Reggie's dumb ass wants to call me at this hour like he has no sense, then he deserves to be on the receiving end of my tirade. Besides, I already have a bone to pick with him. "I got an email from the bank about my mortgage being due next week. Why haven't you paid it? The bank shouldn't be emailing me about shit because you should've already taken care of it!" Shit, he has been paying my mortgage for the last three months. Might as well make it four. I have to set my expectations high. He shouldn't be calling me unless he is taking care of my bills. Otherwise, he can hit the bricks.

Reggie changes the subject. "Wha-what do you mean k-k-keep

calling you? Is someone bothering my cinnamon gelato? I want to see you. I'm on my way." The thought of this dork in my home and his hands on me makes me nauseous. I made that mistake once with him and I'm not going to let it happen again. We were getting ready to go out on a date and when he came to pick me up I wasn't ready. I buzzed him up so he could wait in my living room while I finished getting ready. This dude did his best not to leave my place. He was trying to take a "tour" of my house that he was hoping would lead to my bedroom. Never has he and never will he ever, ever, ever touch me ever. Ewww. If he wants to wine and dine me, great, but he's not getting any of my peaches in exchange. It's so much easier to just drug and rob these dudes. They always expect something from you when you try to do things the right way.

"Yeah, come over here and I'm going to greet you at the door with Greta," I threaten.

"Who's Greta? I thought you didn't get down like that, baby. I'm excited."

With irritation seeping through my voice, I say, "Greta is my pretty purple pistol, fool. And I will fire her on sight. Don't call me again until you've paid my mortgage." I hang up on him and place my phone on vibrate, half wishing it was a landline so I could slam the receiver down in his ear. I grab a towel and dry off. I rub some Aveda moisturizer all over my skin and hit the sack.

'*And going broke in the process.*' As I lie in bed Beau's words are replaying in my mind like a bad song that I can't get out of my head. I still can't believe her. She's trying to leave me like everybody else. Tears run down my face until I fall asleep.

I wake up to my phone vibrating. It's 1:26 PM. I have nine text messages. One of the messages is from Angel, our younger sister. She wants to know if she and her friends can still crash at my condo this weekend after a party they're attending. The other eight texts are from Reggie. Ugh, we have a level-ten clinger here. I read the first message: ***Baby, I took care of the mortgage this morning. I want to see you, my sweet cannoli. How about dinner at Bone Fish?***

That's one burden off my shoulders. I don't want to be rude to Reggie now, so I hit him with a quick reply: ***Thanks, baby. I knew you would come through. I'm busy tonight. Maybe next weekend. I'll be thinking of you, xoxoxo.***

I delete his other seven messages without reading them. They are irrelevant. He paid my mortgage and that's all I need to know. To be smart enough to have become a software engineer, Reggie is dumb as hell. The way I cussed him out last night and then hung up on him, I didn't think he would pay my mortgage at all. But it seems the meaner I am to him the more he wants me. I may have to bench him, though, before he gets too crazy on me.

I climb the stairs to the roof and lay out next to the pool with my laptop in one hand and a mimosa in the other. I log onto my online bank account and see an extra $35,000 in my account. Beau's ass is still on her high horse and put her half of the money in my account. I'm not going for that shit. As much as I need the money, I have a point to prove. We always split the money 50/50, and this time will be no different. She's taking this money whether she wants it or not. Beau needs to learn that putting it in my account will not make that night disappear. I do an online transfer and put the money into her personal checking account. My instant messenger pops up. It's Reggie, again. *Amore mio. My little scoop of Neapolitan ice cream. I miss you. You need to start making time for me.*

I sigh and block him. I wish I would've never confided in him about my ethnicity. Look how he is using it to manipulate me; calling me Italian desserts and shit. If you can't trust a dude with simple information like that, then you can't trust them at all. Maybe if I continue to ignore him he will go away.

I log into my email account, and my eyes light up when I see a new email from a prestigious Chicago modeling agency I submitted my portfolio to a couple of weeks ago. I badly need some cash flow. I don't want to have to hustle by myself. Hustling is like a formed habit. Habits kick in once a cue tells your brain to automatically follow a set pattern, but take that cue away and things fall apart. Beau is my cue. If she's out, I'm not sure I can do it on my own, especially after having her as my partner for the past five years. I'm not ready to give up the hustle, but I can't do it on my own, either.

As I click on the email, I cross my fingers in hopes of a good response. If Sophia, my deadbeat crack head egg donor, could be a model, so can I. I almost leap out of my lounge chair with joy when I read that they want to see me in person this Friday morning in Chicago. Finally, some good news! I run and grab my phone so I can call Beau with the good news. But I immediately put it back down when I remember I'm not speaking to her punk ass.

Beau's officially on my list of people who have deserted me. The first is Sophia, who didn't love me enough to want to get off drugs to care for me. I refuse to refer to her as my mother, because no real mother would dump her only child on another woman to raise just so she could snort cocaine. She gave me up to my dad and Beau's mom, Tanya, shortly after I was born. Tanya was a complete stranger to Sophia; she didn't know how she would treat me. Considering Sophia was my dad's side piece, Tanya could've been jealous and abused me. Luckily for me, she raised me like her own. I consider her my real momma, but Tanya left me, too. She chose the hustle and our father over me and Beau. Even if it wasn't of her own free will, she still left me. Even Daddy ultimately left me. And now Beau. To hell with them all. I can only depend on myself. I can't even depend on God. How can I when He let all this happen to me?

The next day I somberly pack my bags and jump in my McLaren, a gift from my ex, to make the three-hour drive to Chicago. Typically I fly, but it's cheaper to drive, plus I need this road trip to clear my head. I've been rejected by modeling agencies before and I can't help but feel like this time will be no different.

Just after passing Lafayette, I notice a car behind me; the same damn car that was behind me when I was driving through downtown Indianapolis to get to I-65. I'm being followed. I can't tell who is in the car because of the tint on the windows. I reach in the glove compartment to grab Greta. I don't know who it is or why they are following me. But I got something for their ass if they think they're about to run up on me.

I slow down below the speed limit, hoping the car will pass me. I look in my rearview mirror and see it slowing down as well. Damn. I speed up my car to match the tempo of my heartbeat. I blaze down the highway at 85 miles per hour. I check my mirror again to see if the car is still behind me. A little Honda cuts me off and I swerve to avoid hitting the raggedy car. I accelerate to 90 miles per hour. I dip around an Escalade and then press the gas until I'm approaching 95 miles per hour. This asshole is still behind me. Shit, I wish I drove the Hummer so I could ram the car and run it off the road. I smash the gas to 100 miles per hour but still can't shake him. Where are the fucking police when you need them? This is the shit I be talking about. You can't rely on anybody. I'm being chased down the interstate at 100 miles per hour and there is no state trooper anywhere in sight. I grab my cell phone and dial 9-1-1 as I take the next exit. An operator answers and I use my best victimized valley girl voice to tell her I'm being followed, and I'm frightened, and

I'm pulling up into a gas station,.

I park in front of the gas station's convenience store, making sure my vehicle is visible to the surveillance cameras. I lock my doors, gripping my cell phone in my left hand and Greta in my right. The car pulls up right next to me. I stay facing forward, trying to avoid making eye contact to diffuse whatever situation is about to go down. This bold motherfucka' walks right up to my car and knocks on the window, forcing me to make eye contact with him.

"Reggie?!" I exclaim in disbelief. I crack the window half an inch—enough for him to be able to hear my voice, but not enough for him to be able to stick his hand through the window, if he feels inclined to try.

"Why are you following me?" I speak slowly and calmly, doing my best not to antagonize him with the slew of curse words that are going through my mind. His mental state has to be in bad place for him to go through the trouble of following me from Nap to Lafayette.

"My dainty tiramisu," he begins. I turn my head so he can't see me rolling my eyes. "Remember wh-wh-when you said that men kept calling you all through the night? I ju-ju-ju-just wanted to make sure you were alright. You weren't returning my calls." Let's be accurate. I am not returning your calls, text messages, emails, or instant messages.

Reggie just graduated from a bug-a-boo to a stalker in one night.

"Listen to me, Reggie. You need to back off. You just followed me for over an hour. That is not okay."

"I've been paying your mortgage. I have a right to make sure my little ricotta is okay. I'm invested in your well-being."

Oh hell no. I'm about to put an end to this right now. I reach into my purse, pull out my checkbook, and write a check for $28,000—the amount of my mortgage payments he made for the last four months.

"Here's everything you've given me," I say, throwing the check at him through the cracked window. "You're no longer invested in shit I do. I can't believe you chased me down the highway. Where they do that at?!" I scream. Ain't nothing normal about this dude and now it's costing me money that I do not have. My heart drops at the large sum of money I am giving back to him. Once the check clears I will only have $7,000 to my name. But it is worth it to get rid of his weirdo ass. I'm about to get this modeling job anyway, I tell myself. I can make it all back.

The police squad car pulls up just after I toss Reggie the check. I tell the officer about Reggie's stalking ways. I don't want him arrested, but I do want a restraining order. The officer gives Reggie a stern order for him to stay away, and advises me to get a protective order in my city. He assures me he will stay with Reggie for 30 minutes to give me a chance to leave without being followed. My wheels screech as I take off from the gas station, eager to quickly get away from Reggie's level-ten clinger ass.

5
Beef Amongst Sisters

Beau

By Friday I am just as pissed about what happened with Bella as I was Wednesday when it went down. And the call from Samantha Stone, our banker, doesn't make it any better. Bella transferred the $35,000 into my account and Samantha is making sure Bella and I know we can't play tag with that much money. I make my way to the bank to take care of it. I told Bella I don't want that blood money and I mean it.

"What is going on with you two?" Samantha starts in on me as soon as I walk into her office.

I don't waste any time getting to the point. "Put the money into a savings account so it can accrue the most interest possible," I request. I am good on money but I know Bella probably needs it, especially with the renovations she is making to her condos, although she is too damn prideful, stubborn, and bull-headed to admit it.

"Are you sure you all don't need it?" Samantha looks at her computer screen like she knows something I don't.

"I am sure you see that I am good with my financial situation and it is well under control. If Bella needs it, she should have kept it." I stand up to leave. I am not going to worry about what the hell Bella has going on. I have my own life to get together. I have always been the responsible one. Yeah, Bella is about her business, but when shit goes wrong like the last hustle did, Bella acts as if she really doesn't give one single fuck. I, on the other hand, still feel chills thinking about what could have happened to that man. For Bella, though, it is on to next one. I am done trying to be her conscious and voice of reason—done. As I'm leaving the bank, my cell phone begins ringing.

"Hey GG. How you doing?" I am used to talking to GG every day, but I must admit, I've been avoiding her a little lately. She somehow always knows when something is up with me. With the way I've been feeling for the past couple of days, she would have read through whatever front I tried to put on.

"Baby, are you busy?" GG doesn't sound like her usual cheery self.

"Never too busy for you. What's up?"

"Well, if you aren't busy can you stop by?" GG asks, knowing I would never say no, even if I was busy. I tell GG I will be there in about 20 minutes.

I already know there can only be one of two things bothering GG: Bella or Angel. I'm placing my bets on Angel. GG is too easy on our younger sister. I swear she would let the girl get away with murder. I don't play that with Angel, so I am usually left to be the strict one. I just want what's best for her. We all feel bad that she never got a chance to meet Daddy, so we spoil her. Bella and I bought her a new Maserati for her 16th birthday and we give her a $1,000 monthly allowance, which was what Daddy had done for Bella and I. I am so glad that she's living in Indy with us, even though I never thought that GG, along with help from Bella and I, would be raising a kid.

"Hey, baby," I hear GG call out to me from the dining room. As soon as I sit down at the table, GG hands me a letter from Angel's high school.

Dear Mrs. Jones,

This letter is to inform you that Angel Jimenez-Jones' academic performance for the last semester is not up to standard with our requirements. We pride ourselves in the academic success of our students. Angel received a grade of D in advanced chemistry, a grade of D in calculus, and a grade of C in Spanish. Although those grades are not failing, they have brought her GPA down to 2.2. Per our requirements, all students must maintain a 3.0 GPA, which is a B average. We cannot require that Angel attend summer school, but it is highly recommended. If Angel does not bring her GPA up by the end of the fall semester, we will unfortunately have no choice but to remove her from the school.
Respectfully,
Aaron Yatz
Dean of Academic Affairs

The next page is a copy of Angel's report card. I am so hot that I could have incinerated those papers with my bare hands. This sneaky little girl has been lying to us. When she brought home C's last semester, she promised to start staying after school for tutoring and, as far as we knew, that is what she's been doing. But it's obvious she hasn't.

"Why didn't you say something to me sooner, GG, like when she got her midterm grades?" I look over at GG who has her head in her hands.

"Sometimes you are too hard on her, Beaunifide. She doesn't want to disappoint you, but maybe, baby, she's just not as smart as you." GG rubs my cheek and stares at me with her big brown, hoping, loving, faithful, and honest eyes. I love GG so much, and I know she is trying to give her youngest granddaughter the benefit of the doubt, but she is getting played by Angel. I have done so many wrong things in my young life. But one thing I have tried to never do, and to date have not done, is lie to my GG. I expect the same of my sisters. I know Bella feels the way I do, but that damn Angel is another story.

"I will take care of it, GG." I smile at her as I get up to leave. As usual, before I can make it to the door GG offers me something to eat.

"I made salmon, potatoes, fried apples, and biscuits," she smiles at me. She knows food is the way to my heart and she has fixed one of my favorite meals. As I sit there with GG smashing every bite of her delicious food, I know what I am about to do will have Angel beefing with me, too. Must I always be the responsible one? Is being accountable worth fighting with my sisters? I don't know, but I am who I am and my core values will not allow me to compromise.

As I head to my car I can feel the stares of some of the young dudes on the block and hear them calling out to me; dudes posted up on the block doing nothing with themselves and their lives. Ugh, I hope this is not where my little sister is wasting her time. I sincerely hope that she's not hanging with these no-future-having little boys instead of studying. It is obvious they do not know whose daughter I am. Either my father's legend has died down in the streets, or they are just too damn ignorant to respect hustle royalty. I ignore them as they continue to call out.

"Shut up, y'all," I hear a familiar voice yell at the little dudes on the street as I pull off. I look over and see Jason standing in Keyona Mayfield's yard holding their son. He still looks fine as hell; a tall, light-skinned pretty boy but a thug and a hustler all the same. He was once my father's protégée and my boyfriend. I chose Jason back when I was 15 because he reminded me so much of my father. It turns out that Jason was too much like my father. He cheated on me just like my dad cheated on my mother. That is how Jason had little J. I have always sworn to myself that I would never be like my mother, so that was the end of us.

I don't care that Jason has gone legit and owns a successful auto body shop and some real estate. I don't care that he proposed to me, swore that it was just a one night stand while I was off at Notre Dame, or that he was drunk in the club. I saw my mother give her all to my father in spite of his cheating ways, and I was not down for that shit at all. I roll by smiling at Jason and Keyona. I want him to know I am good and not concerned with him in the least bit. I see him and Keyona staring as I drive down the street, thinking about Angel.

I know what I am about to do is harsh but, oh well. If I have to take time out of my damn day to deal with her mess there needs to be consequences for her actions. I know GG's pushover self and Bella's irresponsible ass won't discipline her so it's up to me. She may be able to get over on them but I'm sure as hell not about to play these games with Angel. She gone learn today, and I don't have any problem being the one to teach her.

I have a taxi pick me up at home and drop me off at her school. I walk into the office and I am pleasantly greeted by the secretaries. Some of the school administration still remember me from my days there. I don't mean to toot my own horn, but I was class valedictorian, class president, led the school to three state debate championships, and helped form the Student Conflict Mediation Council. Every time I come up here for Angel they tell me how they wish they had more students like me. Toot, toot!

Angel's school is full of rich spoiled kids who feel entitled to the best of everything in life and treat teachers and other staff like their servants. Yes, of course there are kids like me, who are focused on getting good grades, being awarded scholarships, and getting into the best colleges. I'd say about between 25 to 30 percent are like that. The rest, though, are like Angel. They only care about partying with their little friends and looking good in their designer clothes and luxury cars. After I sign Angel up for summer school I walk to her car. I pass row after row of hundred-thousand-dollar vehicles. Not a hooptie in sight. Approaching her Maserati, I consider that maybe we spoil Angel too much; the car, the clothes, the shoes, the money. Bella and I want to make sure she has everything Daddy had given us, so we do exactly what he had done for us. But the one thing that our father had given us that is impossible to replicate, no matter how hard we try, is his wisdom. As I sit in Angel's car, I realize that wisdom is the one thing she needs the most. Bella and I always share the stories and advice that Daddy had given us, but I know it's not the same coming from secondary sources.

I see Angel approaching from a distance. Her tanned caramel skin glistens in the sun. She is darker than Bella, but lighter than me. She has on her school uniform. At 5'5" her blue pleated skirt shows off her legs and her expensive ass Vince Camuto pumps. I check my watch. It's only 1:15. The little heifa' is leaving school early. I can't believe this girl. I start the car up and pull out of her parking spot. One of the girls Angel is walking with points to the car and appears to be asking Angel if it's hers.

"Hey! Hey!" Angel screams, moving toward the car as fast as her heels can carry her. Her two friends are scurrying along right behind her. They look like a gang of Barbie goons running up on me. If I were a real car thief, what were they going to do? Attack me with their MAC make-up and lipstick me to death?

Angel finally realizes it's me and tells her friends to wait for her across the street. I roll the window down as she walks up.

"What the hell, Beau?" Angel looks shocked but relieved to see me. "I thought somebody was stealing my car. Wait a minute. Oh my gosh! Y'all got me a new car?!" Angel's eyes light up. This girl has got to be delusional. I just caught her skipping out on school and I am sure she is aware of her horrible grades. Angel starts looking around the parking lot, trying to guess which car is hers. I can't help but to laugh. She is dead serious.

"Are you for real? You are not getting a new car. I am taking this car. You're on punishment." Her smile instantly fades when she realizes I am not smiling and not joking.

"No," she says, shaking her head as her eyes fill with tears. "You are not doing this to me, Beau. You can't!"

"I can and I am. Driving this car is a privilege—one that you've proven you don't deserve."

"You know what, Beau, just because you lost your mom when you were young doesn't mean I need you to be mine. I got a mom." Angel throws a low blow. She knows how I feel about losing my mom when I was little. It's cool, though. I know her feelings are hurt and she is probably feeling embarrassed. "What am I supposed to tell my friends?" Angel whines, gesturing to the two girls who are still waiting for her across the street.

45

"I don't give a damn what you tell them. You'll get the car back when you get serious about school and start doing what you're supposed to be doing.

"You call yourself taking my car because I am messing up in school, but how I am going to get to school now?"

"Don't act worried about school now. You're dipping out early and barely passing. How the hell you get a C in Spanish, Angel? You are Colombian! You lived in Colombia, where Spanish is the national language. Get yo' simple self in the car," I scoff. Angel doesn't answer my question. She just screams that she hates me and walks away from the car. I know I am doing what needs to be done, but I am now at odds with both my sisters. Sunday dinner is going to be a blast. I hope GG is serving chicken 'cause I done had more than enough beef this week.

6
When Plan B Fails

Bella

Friday I wake up at 6:30 AM in my room at the W Hotel. To save money I asked for a single room instead of a suite. See, I can be price conscious. It is still a little expensive at $250 a night, but I need the comfort after all the drama I just experienced with Reggie.

I shower and put on a white plain baby tee and a pair of crisp dark blue Armani jeans that hug my hips just right. I unwrap my hair and brush it so it is pulled away from my face and flowing down my back. I don't put on any makeup, because modeling agencies like to see a fresh, natural face. They want to see a canvas that they can paint on. I don't wear too much makeup on a regular basis, anyhow—usually only eyeliner and lipstick. Like Daddy would say, you don't need makeup when you have the genes of a Jones. Beauty and hustling come naturally.

I am too nervous to eat, so I skip breakfast, and I call the front desk to have valet bring my car around. I grab my taser from the nightstand next to the bed and grin at the smiley face stickers Angel put on its handle. I place it in my purse, just in case. Reggie could pop up again or, even worse, there is always a chance that someone I hustled might recognize me. You never know.

I am waiting in my room for valet to bring my car around when my cell phone begins to ring. I'm focused on getting signed with this modeling agency and I don't want any more distractions, but it is GG and I can't ignore her call. I've been avoiding her all week.

"Greetings and blessings to you, GG," I answer with slight sarcasm. I know she is calling to go off on me. I missed church last Sunday and GG is not having it.

"Chile, you can take that sarcasm out of your voice or I can slap it out of you." GG is gangsta'. She holds no punches. I check my attitude. I know she isn't playing about slapping me. "I'm disappointed you missed church and Sunday dinner, Bella. I'm even more disappointed that you haven't called. I shouldn't have to hunt you down. At least call to let me know you are alive."

"I'm sorry I missed church and Sunday dinner, GG. I will make it up to you."

I conveniently leave out that I missed church because I was too busy hustling like she is getting hustled by the church for what they call 'tithes and offering.' I'm real enough with myself to know that I may lie to GG by omission, but I won't outright tell her false words.

"You can make it up to me by making sure you don't miss church this Sunday," she says.

"I can't make any promises, because I'm in Chicago right now, GG. I have an interview with a modeling agency today. Not sure when I'll get back to Indianapolis."

"I am so proud of my babies. Finally, both of y'all can stop that mess y'all into and do something worthy of Jesus." Oh Lawd, here she goes. I try to figure out a reason to rush GG off the phone before she starts preaching. I am not trying to hear that mess. The hotel phone rings. Yes! Saved by the bell.

"GG, that's valet with my car. I gotta go. Wish me luck." GG wants to tell me something about Angel and say a prayer with me before I get off the phone, but I tell her I don't want to be late, which is the truth. GG will pray until her wig falls off and Jesus comes back. I don't have time for that.

I arrive at the modeling agency in a great mood. I'm feeling bubbly and am all smiles. Judi, a secretary for the agency, greets me as soon as I walk in the door. Her jaw drops as she looks me up and down. "Absolutely stunning. Those eyes! If you can't get signed I don't know who can." My confidence goes straight through the roof. I just walked in the door and I'm already turning heads. This has to be a sign.

Judi takes some pictures of me to see how photogenic I am. Then she ushers me into the room where I will do my interview with the modeling agents who will make the final decision. They ask me a slew of questions, then they request that I walk for them. I imagine that I am on a runway and give them the fiercest walk I can muster. When I reach the end of my imaginary catwalk I ignore the frown on the dark-skinned man wearing skinny jeans and stilettos, and focus on the other two smiling faces. At least I have someone's attention. They thank me and ask me to wait in the waiting area while they discuss whether or not they are going to sign me.

While waiting, I think over my financial predicament. Even if I sign with the agency I still won't be able to stop hustling. Who knows when I will get a pay check. I can't believe I'm checking for a paycheck.

This is a first. But my cash flow is running low, so I have to do something. Now let's see, I only have about $7,000 to work with. No, wait, $6,650 after paying for the hotel and other expenses for this trip. Shit, I don't even have enough money to cover my mortgage payment next month. "Broke. Broke. Broke," I accidently say out loud.

"Did you say something?" Judi's voice breaks in. Embarrassed, I tell her I am talking to myself.

I have $6,650 to my name. I doubt that little chunk of change will last me a week. My car insurance for all three of my cars is due in two weeks. I'm going to have to do at least one more hustle. If I play my cards right I can get at least $10,000. I search the Internet from my cell phone to see which clubs in the Chi are going to be jumping tonight or tomorrow night. Konflict East is in town for the weekend. I will have to stay one more night. Konflict is one of the most prolific rapper-producers in the game and he hails from Chicago. Staying one more night will leave me down to $6,400. Beau or no Beau I have to make this hustle work.

"Bella, you can come with me," Judi announces. I quickly stand up. I am so nervous I feel a little dizzy. I am led back to the same room I auditioned in. The panel of three has dwindled down to one. That must be a good sign. You only need one person to say congratulations. Multiple people are meant to be witnesses just in case things go left when an applicant is turned away. I put on a big smile and sit down.

"Bella, I just want to begin by telling you that you are very, very beautiful. Unfortunately, though, you don't have the look."

"The look?"

"Yes, Bella. Your walk is great, however, your look is too commercial. We are looking for something more...high fashion. Oh, and your derriere is too big for your body frame. You might want to consider seeing a plastic surgeon about liposuction."

I don't like the way this bitch says my name in such a mocking and condescending tone. And that remark about my ass was just uncalled for. I've been trying to break into the modeling business since I was teenager and I have been constantly told that my ass is too big. Fuck them and fuck her. She's just mad because she looks like someone splattered hot fried bologna grease in her face. I take a deep breath and focus on the task of restraining myself from snatching her cheap, synthetic extensions off her doughnut-shaped head and slapping her in the face with them. As the silence between us grows, she looks uncomfortable and squirms in her chair a little bit. If I know one thing it's how to keep my composure and show no emotion. So, I smile and thank her like my hopes aren't shattered. I sashay out of that office like I am on the runway rockin' Givenchy at Fashion Week. Damn right I'm gonna show these dream snatchers the profits they're going to lose by letting me walk out the door. Commercial my ass. I can wear a trashcan and make it look good.

I drive to an upscale vegetarian restaurant located in the Inner Loop. It's 11 o'clock and it's time for brunch. Once I get to the restaurant I circle around the block looking for parking. After finally spotting an open space four blocks from the restaurant, I parallel park into the tight spot. I turn the engine off and just sit there for a moment in thought. Looking at my reflection in the rearview mirror, I question why I am parking so far from the restaurant. I always valet my car, but now that my money flow is slowing up, I am going the cheaper route.

"Fuck this!" I crank the engine up and quickly pull out of the spot. If I start acting broke now, I am going to be broke. It's all a state of mind. Besides, it's backwards to spend money at an expensive restaurant while being too cheap to valet my car. I pull up in front of the restaurant, hop out, and toss the valet my keys. Then I strut my long, lean legs inside as if I am still on that runway. I don't need that agency. The whole world is a runway for Bella Amore Jones.

I ask the hostess to seat me in a quiet, secluded area. After being seated I order a carbonated water with lemon. I could really use a cocktail, but it is still too early in the day to drink, so sparkling water will have to do. The waiter comes back with a glass and a bottle of S. Pellegrino and asks for my order. I order eggplant parmesan. I'm a weekday vegetarian. I eat mostly fruits and vegetables, but hell, sometimes I want some bacon or a good steak. I'm not willing to give up meat entirely.

As I wait on my food, I sip on my S. Pellegrino imagining that it is a cosmo. A handsome white man appearing to be in his late twenties approaches my table and sits down uninvited. My eyes widen at his audacity. I take a good look at him. He is nicely built with dirty blonde hair, blue eyes, and perfect white teeth. I am not easily impressed, but his smile...it is like a glimpse of heaven. He is manly and pretty all at the same time. He looks like the type that has women falling all over themselves just to get his attention.

He looks somewhat familiar. And if he looks familiar to me, it must mean he has bank. For a moment I consider making him my next mark, but the thought leaves my mind just as quickly as it had entered. That would be too messy. To sit at my table without asking permission shows he has already been watching me. He probably spotted me as soon as I walked through the door. At this point it will be too easy for him to identify me to the police. I could just make him my man candy and get in his pockets that way, but after what happened with Reggie yesterday, I don't have the energy or the interest to engage him in any type of relationship just to take his money. Right now I'm 100 percent about my hustle. I have bills to pay, shopping to do, and charities to donate to. There is no way I can make money off of him. Simply put it, he's a waste of time, and he is in my space.

"I never knew someone could make carbonated water look so good," the man compliments. You should be a S. Pellegrino spokes model." The agent's words of rejection replay in my mind. *"You don't have the look. Your look is too commercial."* I suck my teeth, slowly becoming infuriated.

"Go away," I sternly reply. A look of shock crosses his face. He didn't expect me to be so standoffish.

He quickly gains his composure and tries again. "When I see a beautiful woman sitting by herself I tend to not want to leave her all alone. You never know who might be lurking around." He grins that heavenly smile of his. I try to keep myself from falling into his deep blue eyes. I look away to avoid being hypnotized by them.

"Go away," I repeat. I can tell he is getting frustrated because I'm not throwing myself at him like he is, most likely, accustomed to women doing.

"May I ask why you want me to leave?"

"Why? Because you sat down uninvited. That's rude."

He stands up next to my table and asks, "May I sit down?" He flashes that picture-perfect sparkling grin of his. But as much as I am lost in his divine smile, I am not amused.

"No. Go away," I snap. He sits down again anyway, just as the waiter arrives with my food. Before he can put the plate down on my table I ask him to box it. I don't know if I am dealing with another Reggie or what, but I am ready to go. Annoying stalkers that don't understand boundaries make me lose my appetite. "Give the bill to my friend here and mark it with 50 percent gratuity. He's very, very generous. No is NOT in his vocabulary." I shoot Mr. Colgate Smile a sharp look, then, not even bothering to wait for my food, I sashay out the restaurant as if I am still on my runway. When I go to pay for the valet, the attendant tells me it has already been paid on my behalf. Shocked, I jump in my car and speed off.

Back at the hotel I change into some workout gear and go for a jog down Lake Shore Drive. There is nothing like summertime Chi. It is a beautiful sunny day. It seems that everybody is out on the shore enjoying the lake. The run does me some good and momentarily allows me to forget my worries.

After my run I go back to the hotel and hit the sauna. There is only one other person there; a brown-skinned man of average height whose left cheek appears swollen. I almost failed to recognize him without the diamond jewelry and flashy clothes, but then it dawns on me who he is.

"You're Konflict East, right? I love your album *School Truancy*. Real Talk."

"Yeah, that's me. And you are? You some type of model or somethin'?"

"I'm Bella Amore, and nah, I don't model. I just hustle. You know, investments and whatnot. That's why I love your album so much. What's the point of going to college when I can stack millions without it?"

"Yeah, yeah. Exactly. Bella Love, the self-proclaimed female hustla'. I like that. You're a diva. I'm doing a party appearance at Vision tonight. Come through. I'll put you on the list."

"Okay, I'll check it out. I was looking for something to get into tonight, anyway."

"Cool, see you tonight."

Konflict leaves me alone in the sauna. I'm hype. Things are looking up. Running into a celebrity must be a sign. I will definitely find my mark tonight at Club Vision. I can't leave Chicago without making some money. After all, this was supposed to be a business trip. Leaving with no modeling contract and no money would make it a complete waste of time.

Back in my room, I shower and lay down for a nap. I only get about an hour of sleep before I am awakened by my phone ringing. As soon as I answer, I hear Angel's frantic voice on the other end.

"She took it, Bella, she took it! Tell her to give it back! You paid half for it, too."

"Huh? Who took what?"

"Beau took my car while I was at school! It was so embarrassing. I thought someone stole it."

"Wait, what? I'm confused. Calm down and speak slowly."

"While I was in class Beau took my Maserati. When I got out of school the car was missing. I always park it in the same spot so I thought someone stole it. Then Beau rolled up in my car and was all like, 'You lookin' for this? Yeah, I took it. Get yo' grades up and you might get it back.' She did this in front of everyone, Bella. I can't stand her!"

"So how did you get home? Your school is all the way on the North side and you live in Haughville."

"Exactly. Beau tried to make me get in the car with her so she could take me home. But I refuse to sit shotgun in my own shit. I had one of my school friends drive me to your place. I don't want anyone at school knowing I live in the 'hood with GG. I would just die. I could never show my face at school again, ever. Next week is the last week of school and I don't know how I'm going to get there. And then we have that party downtown this weekend. I can't be without wheels like some broke busta'. How am I supposed to save face?"

"See, this is the shit I be talking about. How is she going to take your car without discussing it with me first? She always thinks her way is the best way. I'm tired of her shit. Fuck her."

"Yeah! You went half on that car. Tell her to give it back, Bella."

"Don't even it worry about it. I got you. You can drive the Hummer. The spare keys are in the kitchen drawer...the one right next to the refrigerator."

"The Hummer? It's too big, Bella. Let me get the McLaren."

"Girl, bye. Drive the Hummer or walk. And we are going to talk about your grades when I get back. You know you have to keep a certain GPA to stay in that school or they will kick you out." I'm not as hard on her as Beau, but I do gently keep her in line.

"I'm doing my best, Bella. I need a tutor or something. I'm not as smart as you and Beau."

"Yes you are. Ain't no idiots in our bloodline. You speak three languages. So I know what you are capable of when you get focused. But we'll talk about what you need to do to get your grades up later. I have to go. Love you."

"Love you, too."

"Hey, make sure GG knows where you are. I don't want her to worry."

"Okay, bye Bella."

It's almost 5 PM when I hang up the phone and I can hear my stomach growling. I don't know when I last ate and I am starving. I don't want to go to a restaurant. Apparently I have a knack for picking up strays at restaurants. I just want to be left alone, so I order room service. They take forever bringing my food. I'm damn near not hungry by the time my food comes. I take a few bites before pushing it aside. I don't have time to gorge myself on food. I have to get out and find a dress before the stores close. I packed a few outfits, but I need something new and sexy to strike the attention of a potential mark tonight.

I drive down high-end-store-lined Michigan Avenue. I could've walked from my hotel, but why walk when I can floss in my whip? As I cruise down the Magnificent Mile, I keep my eyes peeled for a boutique. I pass Chanel. Too classic for club gear. I pass Louis Vuitton. I want my purse to be a Louis, not my dress. When I come to Niemen Marcus, I park, go inside and browse through the dresses. I see a couple of cute dresses, but nothing really wows me until I come across an emerald lace Valentino dress with a nude liner. It's worth at least trying on. The dress is the last one on the rack and it's a size two—my size. Inside the fitting room, I slip the dress on and take a look at myself in the floor length mirror. The dress is form fitting, designed to hug every curve on my body. It is mid-thigh length and the nude lining magically matches my skin tone perfectly. In the front, the nude lining has a heart shaped neckline, showing the cleavage of my ample B-cups. I turn around and see that the dress is completely backless. If it were cut any lower I'd be flaunting major ass cleavage.

I snap a picture of myself in the dress to send to Beau to get her opinion. I know I look good; I just want to show the dress off. Then I remember I'm not talking to her. I'm even more upset with her after that scandalous shit she pulled on Angel. So I send the pic to Angel instead. Angel, of course, loves the dress and wants me to get her one, too. If I had the extra cash, I would. Well, not this exact one—we can't be running around looking like the damn Bobbsey Twins. Instead of telling her I'm broke I just send her a smiley face and ignore her request altogether. I peel the dress off my body and go to the cash register. The cashier rings up my dress at $2,200. I hand her my credit card without flinching. I knew a Valentino dress wouldn't be cheap. This is an investment. I'll spend $2,200 on this dress and make at least $22,000 tonight.

Back at the hotel, I shower and pull my hair into a simple, classic topknot. I spritz myself with Chanel No. 5 perfume and slide into my dress. Nude open-toe stilettos, a matching leather clutch, and dangling gold earrings complete my ensemble. Turning in each direction, I look myself over in the mirror one last time before leaving, and when I see my lean, toned back I am damn glad I work out. I call valet to get me a cab and then I head downstairs.

It's almost show time. Lights. Camera. Action.

7
Something in the Air

Beau

No lie, I am a stress eater. Thank God for a high metabolism. After getting home I smash some cookies and cream flavored ice cream with whipped cream and chocolate syrup. I turn my phone on silent. I am sure somebody will have something to say about what happened with Angel today and I don't want to hear it. I sit on the couch and try to focus on my reading assignments, but can't.

Looking around at my place, it seems like I really have my shit together to be only 21. I own a nice ass house with a custom walk-in closet that even the trendiest fashionista would drool over. I have money in the bank. I am beautiful, in shape, and three years away from being an attorney and partner at my own law firm. (Ms. Jacqueline has already agreed to go into private practice with me if I graduate in the top ten percent of my class.) But despite all that I have and all that I have accomplished, I feel so alone and empty.

I feel like so much has changed in less than a week. Although I know Bella didn't mean half the foul shit she said about me hooking up with Real, it has hit a nerve. Being with Real for that brief moment made me realize how much I want love; some forever shit that my father spoke about having with my mother. He said when they met, he instantly knew she was the one. She was 14, he was 16, and still, he knew. Even though he fucked up and messed around, he always only loved her. He was in love with her, even if he didn't know how to show it.

The one thing Daddy never taught us was how to be in a relationship. I guess it was because he didn't know how himself. So I'm left to figure it out on my own. I have determined that love is just another hustle. Actually, being in love with someone is the worst hustle ever. People do the craziest shit for love; they'll fight and kill for love. Sacrifice everything for love. Even die for love. I'm not willing to be crazy for love, so for the most part, I've never been in love.

The craziest thing is, even though all I have ever seen is the bad in love, I still want it. I still want marriage and maybe someday kids. I have strategically planned out my life; what universities I will attend,

57

what career I will have, and even who I will love and be with. For a long time I thought it would be Jason Campbell.

Jason was as close as I have ever been to being in love. I could have fallen in love with him. I had already deeply cared about him, but he ruined it. Jason and I started dating when I was 15 and he was 18. He was my dad's shadow. Other than the obvious physical differences, Jason and my father were very similar. Jason has striking hazel eyes, light skin, curly hair, and is 5'9". His personality and values are very similar to my dad's. That is why I chose him; I felt like he was a logical choice. He's a hard worker, smart, physically attractive, and, most importantly, my father trusted him. That was a huge thing for me, considering the love and respect I had for my dad. Regardless, Daddy didn't approve of me dating Jason for one big reason: he saw himself in Jason just like I did. Ain't that some shit?

Jason and I only dated for about nine months before he got arrested and my dad was killed. Jason got locked up for disorderly conduct the same day my father was killed. The charges weren't filed, though. He would have been released if he hadn't snapped when he saw the news of my father's death. He took it hard. He got into a fight with a deputy in jail and ended up serving 1 ½ years for battery on an officer.

Having been bred and raised to be a real down ass chick, I did what any other woman riding for her man would do. I waited for him. I wrote, visited, and kept money on his books. But when he got out I could tell things wouldn't be the same. He still felt some kind of way for not being there when my dad died and not being there to take care of me. At the advice of my father, Jason had stopped hustling months before my dad died. In retrospect, the way my father was conducting business, it kind of seems like he knew his demise was upon him. My father was almost out of the dope game and had begun investing his money into legit businesses, some of which were managed by Jason. So when my father's empire fell, not only were Bella and I forced to start from scratch; Jason was too.

Jason went back to hustling when he got out, and I sort of understood why. When he told me it was only until he got his money up again and could start some legit business ventures, I believed him. That didn't change the fact that I had seen everything I loved lost to the drug hustle and I despised the fact that Jason was back in it. But by then Bella and I had started our own hustle and, even though we weren't pushing drugs, we were on some illegal shit, nonetheless. So it seemed hypocritical of me to ask him to stop hustling when I was doing the same.

With Jason hitting the streets again, me enrolled in college at Notre Dame, and Bella and I doing our own hustle on the weekends, Jason and I were seeing each other less and less. I remember him asking if I was cheating with some preppy college dude. I laughed it off. Those college boys weren't really my type, but I could tell Jason was insecure about it so I gave myself to him my freshman year. I allowed him to have my prized possession, my virginity, because I still didn't want to deviate from my perfect, strategically thought out plans. I thought sharing myself with him would make him more confident that I was his, but it did the exact opposite. Jason started randomly popping up on campus, especially on the weekends when Bella and I were out hustling. Seeing that I was not there furthered his suspicions about me being with other men, but there was no way I could tell him the truth about what I was really doing. And, in his mind, my failure to adequately explain my absence confirmed his suspicions. I saw why Daddy didn't know how to be in love—that shit is hard.

The most fucked up part is that Jason's ass was the one who wound up cheating. What made it even worse is who he cheated with: ghetto ass Keyona Mayfield. I had to find out about it through her when I came home to visit. She was at least five months pregnant and rubbing it in my face. I felt like she was just posted up waiting to catch me so she could gloat that she had been with my man. There I was outside GG's house all hugged up with Jason after Sunday dinner. As soon as she walked into the yard, he stood between us, and I instantly knew something was up.

"Beaunifide, I'm sure Jason already told you and please don't think I was setting out to get yo' man..." That was all she got out her mouth before I punched Jason in the side of his face. I didn't need or want to hear any more. I knew exactly what it was. I haven't spoken to Jason since that day. Almost two years later he still calls, leaves voicemails, send letters, and tries to leave messages with GG and Bella. I was done, though. When I was younger, I saw how my dad, mom, and Bella's mom went through that bullshit, and I swore to myself I would never be that chick. Now Jason is miserable with a little boy by a ratchet 'hood rat instead of living the beautiful life I'd planned for us.

As I walk through my empty house and climb into my big, lonely king-sized bed, I think about Jason and what could have been. I think about Real and how things might have turned out differently if we'd met under different circumstances. The one thing I want the most I can't seem to get. I feel like I am doomed to be alone. I curl up with my blanket, turn the lights off, and drift off to sleep with memories of past men haunting my mental.

The sun streaming through my cracked curtains wakes me up early Saturday morning. I tiptoe barefoot into my garden, which is full of vividly colored fruits, vegetables, and flowers in full bloom. It's a beautiful day. The morning breeze smells sweet like the strawberries growing ripe. Butterflies flutter by and I can hear bees buzzing. I decorated the garden to be peaceful and tranquil. There are two Italian marble benches at the entrance and a large bench swing. In the middle of the garden sits a stone fountain and a pond full of koi fish.

I often retreat to the garden when I need to relax and think. I climb onto the swing and take in the serenity around me. My phone vibrates in the pocket of my robe, disrupting my peaceful relaxation. It is GG. I assume she is calling about Angel. I'm sure Angel has told her some over-exaggerated version of what went down. But it turns out GG is actually calling to ask about my friend I asked her to pray for. I tell her that he is doing well and everything is okay. After a few *amens* and *thank you, Jesuses*, GG lets me know she wasn't worried and that she knew God would protect my friend.

"Beau, you and your friend are children of God and God protects his children," GG explains. "Now, is this young man your boyfriend?" she asks. She is definitely interested in my love life. She talks about me getting married all the time, to a good God-fearing, church-going man, of course. GG has gone as far as inviting some of the guys from church over for Sunday dinner trying to play matchmaker.

"No, GG," I laugh. "I promise, if I get a man, you will be the first to know. But right now my main focus is law school and being at the top of my class."

"That's real good, baby. GG is proud of you."

"Thanks GG."

"Jason stopped by yesterday after you left. You know he always asks about you. He's been coming to church, too. You would know that if you came yourself sometimes. Beaunifide, he has really changed his life around."

Every so often GG starts talking about Jason. She has a soft spot for him, but I don't. I don't care if he shows up at GG's with Jesus himself, a 20-carat diamond ring, and a choir of singing angels. I am done with him.

I don't respond. GG and I sit on the phone in silence for a minute before she starts up about God and God's love.

"You know the beauty of God," she preaches. "Jeremiah 29:11 says, 'For I know the plans I have for you,' declares the Lord, 'plans to prosper you and not to harm you, plans to give you hope and a future.'" I usually cut her off, but this morning I am receptive to her message. It seems like something I may benefit from; something I need to hear. "You keep that in mind, baby. God has a plan for you."

GG hangs up to do her morning prayer, leaving me to my thoughts in the garden. I wonder if God really answered my prayers and protected Cliff. I mean, he is okay, and from what I know about overdosing on Special K, he could have been seriously hurt or dead. If God saved Cliff, he saved Bella and me, too. Even though I didn't specifically pray for God to save my ass by saving Cliff, he did. If he had died I would've been dead too—maybe not physically, but my life as I know it would have been over. No law school, no law practice, no big ass house in the 'burbs, no beautiful garden to sit and meditate in, no bank accounts holding over half a million. If Cliff had died, I'd be facing 20 to life and would become part of the most horrific hustle ever, the prison system. Maybe GG is right; God's plans for me are good.

I whisper, "Thank you God" into the air and it feels good to say it and mean it. All my life I have lived by everything my father taught Bella and I. The things he didn't teach us, I figured weren't important enough for me to give a damn about. God was not one of the things my father taught us about. He made us go to church with GG every Sunday up until he died, but I never really paid attention. All the preaching went into one ear and out the other. I have actually read the Bible, though. It is a good read with stories of war, kings and queens, money, greed, and love. But, I never looked at the Bible as an instructional how-to-live guide like GG does. Not saying I didn't believe in God or the word of God. I just didn't see the importance of God in my life. Maybe that is changing.

Maybe I have never really thought about God because up until this point in my life I didn't think he thought much of me or my sisters. God has allowed my mother to die, Bella's mother to die, Angel's mother to abandon her, and he took our father. I figured a God who loves and cares for me wouldn't take away the people I love and need the most. Then again, he has spared my life, kept me from going to jail, and helped

61

me make it through college. Maybe it's time I give God a shot. After all, he just got me out of some deep shit. Before I have enough time to change my mind, I call GG back and tell her I will go to church with her.

"Hallelujah!" she shouts through the phone. I laugh at how excited she is, but am glad to have made her day. Man, I hope I don't regret this.

8
Hustle Them Before They Hustle You

Bella

When the elevator doors open, I see Konflict and his entourage occupying it. "Got damn!" one of them yells out as I step onto the elevator.

"Hey, Miss Me Amore. You headed to Club Vision?" Konflict asks.

"Yeah, actually I am."

"Where ya' girls at? How you getting there?" he probes.

"Damn, you nosey," I giggle. "I'm solo dolo. And I'm whipping that yellow cab." I'd never drive any of my flashy cars to a hustle. They'd make me more identifiable if my marks decided to go to the police. Ain't too many chicks out here whipping McLaren sports cars.

"Nah, I'm a gentleman. I can't let you go out like that. You rolling with me in the stretch Hummer. You're welcome." His smugness catches me off guard and I want to say something slick to him, but I tell myself to be nice. Technically, I did need to thank him. He is saving me money on a cab and he is unknowingly going to help me land my next mark. I smile and shrug my shoulders to indicate that I am cool with riding with him.

Konflict has me cracking up on the way to the club. He has jokes for days and helps cut the tension and nervousness I'm feeling. It's make or break time. Either I can hustle by myself or I can't. Konflict leans close to me.

"I like you, Bella Amore. You should be my in-town girl." This basically means he wants me to be his sidepiece whenever he comes to my city for events, concerts, promos, or whatever. It means that whenever he calls me I will have to come running, and when he's not in town he is free to do whatever he likes. The average chicken head would be flattered and jump at the opportunity, but I ain't that fucking chick. Nah, I'm good on that.

"Hmmm," I hum, pretending to contemplate his request. "Maybe, if you're a good boy." Konflict would be a good hustle in the long run, but I don't have time for that. I need cold hard cash now. I don't have the time, the patience, or the interest to spend weeks trying to get whatever gifts he decides to give me in exchange for being his arm candy. And I am definitely not looking for love. My heart still aches from the last time I was in so-called love. Never again. Like I said before, it's easier to just hustle. Besides, he doesn't even know where I'm from to be his in-town girl.

I need to find a way to use the fact that Konflict is interested in me without letting him cock-block my hustle. I can't hustle him. Not only does he know too much about me, but he has a whole team constantly surrounding him. I'm not trying to get caught up by being too ambitious.

We arrive at Vision and are quickly ushered inside and shown to the VIP booth sectioned off from the rest of the club. The waitresses bring out bottles of champagne and pop them. The DJ gives Konflict a shout out over the sound system and starts playing all his hits. I scan the packed club. Everyone is dressed to impress and seems to be having a blast.

Looking at me, you'd never be able to tell that I'm nervous as hell. This is my first hustle by myself and I'm not sure I can pull it off. Konflict calls me to sit down on the couch next to him. I pretend I don't hear him; I'm not trying to be cuddled up. I need to see and be seen. I'm searching for my mark and catching looks from men trying not to stare. Hell, even a few women are looking. I don't discriminate. If she has enough money, I'll hustle a woman just like I hustle these men. Money is money. It's not like I'm actually fucking these marks, unlike Beau, so what do I care if I lead a bitch on just so I can take her coins?

A medium-built, brown-skinned guy with a bald head walks across my line of view and catches my attention. Actually his Movado watch catches my attention. It isn't blinged out or anything flashy, but I can tell a Movado from 30 feet away. The cheapest Movado costs at least $1,500 and his is on the higher end. This dude has guap. When he sees me, he stops dead in his tracks and locks eyes with me for about 15 seconds. He motions for me to come to him. I shake my head. There is no way I'm going to him. I need to see if Mr. Movado has enough money to make his way up to VIP. I motion for him to come to me. He approaches the bouncers who are vigilantly guarding the entrance. With a celebrity in the building the security is tight. Mr. Movado pulls out a wad of cash, peels off a couple of bills, and hands it to one of the bouncers. Bingo. I found my mark.

64

Satisfied, I turn around and see a gaggle of groupies surrounding Konflict on the couch. I walk over and he immediately makes the two girls to his left get up so I can sit down. I ignore the groupies' angry glares. They don't want it. I am secure in the fact that I have my taser in my purse. Even though I'm outnumbered, if anything pops off I will tase the shit out of those bitches. I sit down and try to keep myself from breaking down from nervousness. Typically, during a hustle either Beau or I would distract the dudes while the other slipped the Special K in their drinks. I have no fucking clue how I am going to do it by myself.

I look over at the scowling groupies and I get an idea. If I'm going to make this hustle work I will just have to adapt to my environment and use what I have around me. I seductively motion for the light-skinned one to come sit on my lap. "Awww baby, don't be mad. Come over here and sit on momma's lap and tell me all about it." All the dudes go crazy with excitement and she doesn't hesitate to take my bait. As she is making herself comfortable on my lap, Mr. Movado comes over. "Can you hold her for a sec?" I ask Konflict, passing her on like the ho bag she most likely is. Her dress rides up as she sits on his lap.

"Whoa, pull ya' dress down, girl," says Konflict. "I don't want no skid marks on my jeans." Only the guy sitting to his right and I hear his joke. I want to laugh so hard, but instead I just crack a smile. Konflict is surrounded by a group of followers, so if I start laughing that will egg his right hand man on to continue the jokes. I can't have her running off in embarrassment. Even though Groupie Number One laughs I know she has to be embarrassed by that joke.

I stand up and give Mr. Movado a hug like he is a really good friend I haven't seen for a while. I don't know his name so I introduce him to Konflict as 'my buddy.' I sit back down next to Konflict and make room for Mr. Movado. The waitress comes back with more bottles and makes drinks for everyone in our section. Once everyone has drinks in their hands I call over Groupie Number Two. "We don't want to leave you out, sexy. Get over here." She looks ecstatic that I even acknowledge her, let alone call her sexy in front of everyone. She sits on my lap, even though I motioned for her to sit in between Konflict and me. She is a little bit thicker than Groupie Number One and she is heavy on my lap. I really want to push her big ass off of me.

"Ma, you got a phat ass!" I yell over the music. "Let me see you drop it to the flo'. How low can you go?" I smack her ass and thankfully, she gets up to dance. She puts on a show, bouncing her butt up and down, isolating her left butt cheek, then her right. While all the dudes are entranced with her ass, I lean over to Konflict and ask, "Don't you want to see them kiss?" Konflict nods his head and smiles. "Go tongue her down for Konflict," I whisper to Groupie Number One. "This might be your only chance to impress him."

Like clockwork, she grabs her friend and they start slobbing each other down. Konflict, his entourage, and even Mr. Movado start hooting and howling like they are in a strip club. Some of them even start throwing dollars at them. I quickly slip some Special K into Mr. Movado's drink while everyone is distracted. Then I announce a toast. "Cheers to great times, great people, and great sex!" I sigh in relief as Mr. Movado downs his laced drink. The hard part is over.

I rub Mr. Movado's knee. "Fuck these hos and fuck Konflict, too," he whispers in my ear. "I came over here for you." Exactly. I lead him out of VIP to the general area by the bar. It's quieter over there. Since I got it popping in VIP, it is the center of attention with everybody trying to get in. Maybe I should become a party promoter. I wonder how much it pays. Probably not enough. I need a million cash to put me back on track to where I was before I got hustled. I know I can make that much money hustling, but I don't know about party promoting.

I make general conversation with Mr. Movado and I make sure the bartender keeps the drinks coming. I can tell he isn't used to a boss chick taking care of the tab and he likes it. Truth be told, I'm not really paying for shit. The bartender knows I came in with Konflict and he is putting everything on his tab. But Mr. Movado doesn't need to know that.

I convince Mr. Movado to go back to my hotel so we can get to know each other better. It really doesn't take that much convincing. Before I know it, I'm driving his Lexus to the nearest motel. As usual, I already made reservations under an alias earlier. As I am driving, he places a gun in the glove box and locks it. At least I know he's not planning on killing me—well, not until after he figures out I hustled him. More importantly, I notice a stack of cash in his glove compartment. I make a mental note to take what's in the car after I take what's in his pockets.

We arrive at the motel and Mr. Movado strips butt naked before I can even close the door. The only thing he has on is his socks and Movado watch. "Slow down, cowboy. We have all night," I tell him as I check my watch. He should pass out any minute now.

"Well, you already look naked in that dress. Come here so I can see what's under that lace." I dodge him when he reaches for my arm and he falls face-flat onto the bed. The Special K finally kicked in. I'm relieved that I didn't botch this hustle and that it's going smoothly.

I take all the cash out of his pockets and wallet, as well as his Movado off his wrist. I grab his car keys and go into the bathroom to call a taxi. It will be 20 minutes before the cab gets here, so while I wait, I count, then recount the cash. He had nothing but hundred and $50 bills on him. I place hundred-dollar bills into piles until there are nine stacks sitting on the bathroom counter. The total comes out to be $9,250. "Yes!" I exclaim out loud and do a happy dance. I just paid my mortgage in one night. It's not as much as I was hoping for, but it'll do. When I get back to Indy, I will sell the Movado to my jewelry connect and he will sell it on the street for a profit. We never sell the jewelry ourselves. It's too messy. I check my watch and the cab should be here in five minutes. Boy, time flies when you are counting money. I still need to get the cash I saw in his Lexus. I pick up all the stacks of money and shove them in my purse before heading to Mr. Movado's car.

In the parking lot, I take the cash out of the glove compartment. I leave the keys in the cup holder and lock the car with the button on the door. I shut the passenger side door and turn around, slamming into someone. "What the fu—Reggie?! How did you find me?" I yelp. I don't know if I am more terrified or angry. This motherfucka' done stalked me all the way to Chicago even after I called the police on him!

"I thought you were my sweet innocent florentine, but you ain't nothin' but a stank ho," Reggie says with hurt in his voice and anger flaring in his eyes. He must have watched me go up to the motel room with Mr. Movado, and I guess he thinks I just finished screwing him. "You said you weren't giving it up to nobody, but I've seen you entering and leaving hotels with men all night. How many men have you fucked tonight?" Before I can even say anything he grabs my arm. "How many?" he growls. "You've been getting run through all night. I want my turn." He yanks my arm hard, making my whole body jerk. I am scared out of my mind. I've had clingers before, but I've never been attacked like this.

"Ho, get in the back of the car. I'm going to bang the shit out of you." In a panic, I muster all my strength and punch Reggie in his Adam's apple as hard as I can. Gasping for breath, he releases my arm. I quickly grab my taser and jolt Reggie over and over again. He falls to the ground shaking and squirming.

"How did you find me? Tell me now!" I demand over his

agonized screams.

"Your laptop," is all he can manage to say.

I stop tasing him so that he can speak.

"Fuck you mean my laptop?"

"There's a tracking device in it," he says breathlessly. "I put it in there that one time I came to your condo. It enables me to monitor what websites you visit and locate the laptop anywhere. I tracked you to the W and every time you left the hotel I followed you. I love you, my tender almond biscotti! I just wanted to see you and make sure you were okay. You broke my heart!"

Reggie is one fucked up individual, and this is definitely a fucked up situation. I am enraged. I scream out my utter frustration and hatred for this man as I continue to tase him. I pull Greta out and place the barrel at his temple.

I speak slowly to ensure he comprehends just how sincere I am. "If you ever come near me again, I won't hesitate to blow your fucking brains right out the back of your skull!" I consider shooting him in the foot to show him I'm serious, but instead I repeatedly pistol whip him in the head with the butt of my gun until I see blood flowing down his face. "I'm nobody's whore," I spit through clenched teeth. I kick him in the balls with my stilettos and silently vow to myself that nobody is ever going to take anything from me again. I've already been hustled out of my money; I'll be damned if I let someone hustle me out of my panties, as well.

Back at the hotel I pack up all my things. Before I leave, I lift my laptop over my head and slam it to the floor. I jump up and down on it on it, smashing it to pieces. Yeah, I could've taken it somewhere and had the tracking software removed, but I feel so violated that I don't even want the stupid thing anymore. As I take all my frustrations out on the computer, my emotions begin to well up until I can no longer suppress them. All at once, the pain resurfaces; pain that I keep buried deep down inside; pain over the situations with my daddy, my mom, Sophia, Beau, my ex-boyfriend, and Reggie. I want to cry, but the tears don't come. So I just continue releasing my rage on what's left of my laptop. I use every ounce of energy within me to relentlessly stomp it until I am sweaty and breathless. I leave it mangled in pieces on the floor and check out of the hotel to drive back to Indianapolis.

I arrive back home around 7:30 Saturday morning and the place looks like a pigsty. Angel hasn't even been at my condo for a full 24 hours, yet she managed to pile up the dishes in the sink, leave food containers out on the counter, and has the trash overflowing. I can't stand a dirty house. Steaming, I walk back to the guest bedroom. There are two big suitcases thrown on the floor and clothes are tossed all around the room. Angel is sprawled across the bed sleeping. She looks like she is wearing the clothes she had on the night before—a purple mini skirt and my white Donna Karan blouse. I nudge her.

"Bella!" Angel exclaims with saliva running from her mouth. She rubs the sleep from her eyes and gives me a hug.

"What's up with all this luggage?" I ask.

"I'm moving in."

"I don't think I heard you correctly," I say in a tone of voice that is full of attitude. "Did you just *tell* me what you are going to do?" I am beginning to get irritated with Angel. She has some nerve thinking she can just move right in without consulting me first. Of course I will let her move in, but she could have at least asked.

"No, Bella. I was waiting for you to get back so we could talk about it. I haven't brought all my stuff; just my clothes. We can get the rest of my stuff Sunday after dinner with GG." This girl has a quick wit. She knew I was getting angry and she covered her tracks before I completely shut down her plans without hearing her out. "Bella, can I pretty please move in? GG is too strict." I can believe that. That was one of the reasons why Beau and I moved out at Angel's age. "And Beau stole my car. I feel so violated." I can understand that, too. I guess we were both feeling violated this week from people trying to take what's ours. "And since I don't have a car," Angel further pleas her case, "my friends would have to come to the house to pick me up when we hang out this summer and GG lives in the 'hood. I don't want to be—"

I wave my hand cutting her off. There is no need for her to finish. I know she doesn't want to be embarrassed and judged by her snobby, rich private school friends. Neither did I when I went to that school. I'm fully sympathetic; I know how ruthless those private school kids can be if they perceive you as weak. And when you attend the top private school in the state, being thought of as poor can definitely make you a target. Everyone is expected to excel and everyone is assumed to come from money. However, I am not about to let her run over me just because I'm sympathetic to her situation.

"There will be rules if I let you stay here," I tell her in my sternest voice.

69

Angel bear hugs me. "Thank you, thank you, thank you!"

I gently nudge her off me and begin to lay down the law. "Rule number one: Clean up after yourself. I am not your maid and I refuse to live in filth. I want this place sparkling like it was before you got here. Rule number two: Stay out of my closet." I pop the collar of my blouse that she's wearing. "Rule number three..." I hesitate. I've never had to take care of anyone full time and lay down the law. I don't know what the third rule should be. "Rule number three: You are the one that is going to tell GG you're moving out." I don't know how GG is going to take the news. Better Angel take the heat from GG than me. I smile at my little sister. I see myself in her, and yelling and fussing at her will only shut her down. She admires me and is more likely to take my advice than listen to GG's demands.

After talking to Angel, I call Samantha to stop payment on the check I wrote Reggie. He's going to pay for trying to rape me. I beat his ass and I'm not paying him back. I go to bed and turn my cell phone on silent so my sleep won't be interrupted. My mattress feels like a bed of feathers so I never have trouble falling asleep. I turn over to get more comfortable and I see Lorenzo, my ex, lounging in my bed. My heart flutters, I have no clue how he got into my room. I haven't seen him since he skipped out on me and I had the locks changed. Lorenzo and I were together for almost eight months. He was the only guy I ever dated that I thought looked past my beauty and examined my heart. And at one point I was even willing to give him my heart. He was the only man that knew what truly motivated me, and despite what anyone thinks, it's not money. Money comes and I'm learning the hard way that money goes.

Lorenzo is grinning and looking me up and down, making me feel uncomfortable. I don't know what he can possibly want. He has already has taken so much from me.

"You spent so much time building these walls," he says, lifting his arms, gesturing to my condo. "How long has it been since you started construction? Uno anni? Dos?" I stare at him with dead eyes. I want to run but my feet feel like concrete. He snaps his fingers, my condo crumbles, and I begin to fall. Lorenzo casually levitates in the air above me. In a mocking tone he yells down to me, "It only took me seconds to get in and tear it down." He laughs as I continue falling. Just when I'm about to hit the ground face first, I wake up in a cold sweat panting heavily.

I sit up in bed, trying to interpret the meaning of my dream as I catch my breath. Shit, I guess it means I'm getting stalked even in my dreams.

I glance at my cell phone and see the LED light is blinking. It is 6 PM. I can't believe I just slept for almost 12 hours straight. I have a text message and a missed call from Caleb, the son of GG's pastor. Caleb has beautiful mahogany skin and wears the cutest little black nerdy glasses. He's had a crush on me ever since we were kids.

After Daddy was murdered, Beau stopped attending church but I continue to go every now and then, even though I don't believe in religious institutions or care for God. I mean, he doesn't care for me so why should I care for him? My sisters and I have been through so much and he never once intervened to help us. We had to help ourselves. I only go to church because it is something small that makes GG happy.

Anyways, Caleb never had enough confidence to ask me out. Like most guys, he only pays attention to my body and was intimidated. I would see him out of the corner of my eye staring at my ass as I walked up the center aisle to give my offering. He always complimented me and told me how nice I looked, but would never ask me out on a date—until I called him out on it.

One Sunday Caleb approached me to tell me I looked pretty in my dress. I asked him if he really thought I looked pretty why he hadn't asked me out yet. He looked stunned at my boldness. Here I was, the no-life-having daughter of a whore, at least that's how his mother referred to me. She hates to see me flirting with the most holy, ordained blessed-by-Jesus-himself son of a preacher man. Before he could even get his thoughts together to reply, I answered for him. "Because your mother controls you. She thinks I come to church dressed like a street walker and that I'm unworthy of you." Embarrassed, Caleb denied it. We exchanged numbers and he asked me out.

At first, a part of me only wanted to go out with Caleb to get under his mother's skin. Even though we kept our rendezvous to ourselves, every time I went on a date with him I felt like I was sticking it to his mother. Another part of me genuinely wanted to see what he was all about. And I found out he isn't about shit. I quickly dumped him in the category of ain't-shit men. He's constantly throwing money at me because that is what he thinks I want, and he's constantly trying to get in my panties. Come to find out he has a squad of chicks, but I guess I'm his ultimate prize. I may not be saved, but I'm pretty sure that's not the Christian way, especially for a preacher's son. His mother is so busy

71

worrying about my family background and referring to me as a jezebel, she is blind to the fact that her own son is the real whore. I know what some may think; if he ain't shit then why do I still allow him to text and call me? Why haven't I just ended things with him? Because I'm a motherfuckin' Jones, that's why. He wants to use me—hustle me out of my Victoria's Secrets, so I'm going to use him instead—hustle him out of his money, and make sure he never gets these panties.

Caleb's text says he wants to treat me to Mo's Steakhouse. It's my absolute favorite restaurant in the city, however, I am not trying to be seen in public right now. After being stalked and almost raped by Reggie, I want to lay low. I'd rather count the money that I made from the Chicago hustle than stuff myself with a steak. I politely decline Caleb's offer and tell him I might see him at church Sunday. I let him know I am tight on cash and I have to work this weekend. He is disappointed on the missed opportunity to try to get in my panties, but I'm sure he has some bird on deck that is ready to swoop in to replace me.

I reach for my purse and empty it onto my bed. Stacks of cash flow into a big pile between my legs. Forget a hard dick. I'd rather have cold hard cash any day. At least I know what it's good for. I count the money and it comes out to be a total of $32,650. Cool. Now let's see; I have $32,650 from the hustle, $28,000 from the stopped check I wrote Reggie, plus the $4,200 left over from what I spent in Chicago. Okay, I'm not balling out of control, but I'm good for a few months.

I still need to figure out how to keep the cash flow coming. I decide that, even though I don't want to, I have to keep the hustle going, at least until I can figure out a legal hustle or meet my wealthy prince charming. My last two hustles were botched. First I almost kill someone, then I almost get raped and killed. Cliff and Reggie got me shook. I can still do a hustle here and there, but not every weekend like I used to. No way in hell I will hustle that often by myself. I'm just going to have to cut back on my spending. Ha, good luck with that! At least I can slow down the construction I'm doing on my condo. That should save me some money. I definitely need to hurry and find my prince.

9
Takers

Beau

I thought about skipping out on church no sooner than I told GG I was going, but like I said, I don't lie to GG. Besides, she sounded so happy and excited when I told her I was coming. I can't let her down.

Sunday morning my alarm goes off at 9:30. I have enough time to cook and get ready before the 11 o'clock service. I asked GG about the 8 o'clock service so I could get in and out as soon as possible, but she already knew what I was thinking and said to be at the 11 o'clock service, which is the one she always attends.

I pull out the least tight black dress I own. It is fitted at the waist and flares out. It's sleeveless so I grab a black sweater to wear over it, along with some black Christian Louboutin pumps and a small black clutch. Aside from the red soles on my shoes, I'm wearing all black like I'm dressing for a funeral. While driving to the church, I kind of feel that dreadfulness like I really am on my way to a funeral. My heart is racing and I feel butterflies in my stomach. You'd have thought I was going to run into God himself at the church. Well, I guess that is sort of the point of going to church, huh?

GG's church is Greater Love, Faith, and Peace Apostolic Evangelical Pentecostal Baptist Catholic House of Prayer and Church of God in Christ. Whew, that's a mouthful. I laugh every time I think of that name. The church is non-denominational and I'm sure that's why the pastor named it that. It's only about ten minutes from my house.

The parking lot is packed. There are Benzes, Lexuses, and BMWs all throughout it. Man, God is big business. Looks like he is answering all kinds of prayers in this lot. Right up front with a sign stating 'Reserved for Pastor' sits a Buick. I like the fact that Pastor Lewis isn't all extra flashy. I always liked the pastor—whenever I have come to church, that is.

I can hear praise and worship going on as I enter the church. Beautiful angelic voices singing praises to God flow through me as I make my way up front, where I know GG will be. I feel like Pac with *all eyes on me* as I walk by and feel the stares making me a little self-conscious. I don't know if they are staring because I haven't been to church since my father died five years ago, or because this dress is tighter than I thought. The men are probably staring at my bum. The women are probably staring because they're mad their husbands are staring at my bum.

The church is packed, but GG has saved a few seats right next to her. She hugs me tightly, probably to make sure I'm not a figment of her imagination. She looks cute in her blood-of-Jesus-red suit and floppy church hat.

"Thank you, God!" GG screams out after she releases me from her hug. I just smile, partly out of embarrassment, but mostly because I don't know when I have ever seen GG's eyes shine so brightly. If making my GG happy is all that I accomplish by coming to church today, I am happy.

I can tell people in the church are really feeling the praise and worship, but I'm not expecting anything much out of service. After the praise team is done there is a scripture reading and a prayer. Immediately after prayer, Pastor Gideon Lewis comes to the pulpit. He is of average height and looks to be in his early fifties with snow-white hair cut into a low fade. He's wearing a nicely tailored black suit, white dress shirt, and navy blue tie with loafers.

"This morning I won't be preaching the sermon I had originally planned," Pastor begins in his warm and inviting voice. "God came to me and let me know he had something to say to somebody here this morning. Someone who hasn't been to church in a long while. Someone who he feels he may lose for an even longer time if he doesn't touch them today." It sure feels like he's speaking directly to me. But he can't be. I'm sure I am not the only person here this morning that hasn't been to church in a while.

"Today I am going to preach about takers," he continues, "People that go after what they want, when they want, with no regard for other people's feelings or the inevitable consequences that come from taking something that is not theirs." He *is* talking about me. I feel a queasiness in my stomach as I am instantly reminded of the hustle and the taking I have done. I feel like shrinking in the pew and disappearing right then and there.

Pastor Lewis goes on to discuss King David and Bathsheba. He tells the congregation how David saw Bathsheba from his balcony and wanted her. He didn't care that she was married. He took her.

"Now Uriah was the husband of Bathsheba. He was a soldier. David had taken Uriah's wife, laid with her, and got her pregnant. David and Bathsheba knew the baby couldn't be Uriah's, so he devised a plot to fix the problem. King David tried to get Uriah to go into his home and sleep with Bathsheba. But because many soldiers were still out there fighting away from their families, being the honorable man that he was, Uriah refused to do so. The Bible states that Uriah slept outside and did not lay with his wife. So King David sent Uriah back to war and sent a letter ordering that Uriah be put at the front of the battle where he would surely die. As planned, Uriah died, King David took Bathsheba as his wife, and it seemed that all was well. But as I said at the beginning of this sermon, there will always be consequences for taking what is not yours." As Pastor Lewis preaches, I sit entranced by the sermon. I feel like God has looked into my heart and whispered in Pastor Lewis's ear.

"King David had done everything right in the sight of God except in the matter of Uriah," the pastor enlightens the congregation. "David had to pay for his sin even though God had forgiven him. After their son was born, the baby became very ill and died. You see, even those chosen by God fail and do wrong and take. David was a taker, but he repented for his sin. And, as we all know, David was the greatest king of Israel and a man after God's own heart," Pastor finishes.

GG stands up, waving her hands. "Preach, Pastor, preach!" she shouts. Everyone in the sanctuary stands as the organist starts playing that melodic Holy Ghost beat—you know, that one every church has that gets the congregation all riled up. People are shouting in the aisle and dancing across the church. The spirit has taken over, but all I can do is stare into space, deep in thought. I am a taker. I have taken so much from so many men. And the one time I meet a man I really like, I take advantage of him, too. I can never have Real. I will never know what could have been. All I'm left with is the memory of our short time together—and regret. My heart is racing rapidly. God, what have I done with my life?

Once the church is settled down it is time for offering. I pull out my checkbook and my hand trembles the whole time I'm writing. I had initially planned on giving an offering of five hundred dollars, but as I write the check, I just keep adding zeroes. When I am finished I've written a check for $50,000 and don't think twice about it.

After service, I see the first lady smiling at me from a distance. "Hi, baby," she says, walking over to me with outstretched arms. She is always so nice to me when she sees me. I think it's because on the surface I look like I have my stuff together. She congratulates me on graduating Magna Cum Laude from Notre Dame and starting law school. No doubt she has heard all about my accomplishments from GG's testimonies. First Lady continues to toot my horn for me while also telling me about the things her son Caleb is doing. "He has a master's in chemical engineering and will be working on his doctorate starting this fall," she recites, beaming with pride.

She has big plans for her son, as any mother would, and sees me as an asset. I think I remind her of herself. Bella, on the other hand, she sees as a liability, and the irony of it all is that Bella is who Caleb wants. I chuckle at the thought of how First Lady despises my sister solely based on her outer appearance. She can't stand Bella. And please believe the feeling is mutual. Bella can't stand people who judge her based on her physical appearance—especially someone who should be living by the Bible. Judge not lest ye be judged.

First Lady grabs my hands and pats them with her soft, warm palms. She is beautiful; her skin is dark chocolate, soft, and smooth as cocoa butter. Her long silver hair gracefully frames her small face. Her frame is also petite. She's the same height as me but smaller in size. Her beauty is only overshadowed by her desire for perfection. She hopes that Caleb will someday take over the pulpit and image is very important to her.

Meredith Lewis was groomed to be a first lady. Her father was the minister of the church before her husband. She sang on the praise team and in the choir, taught Sunday school, and knows the word of God like her own heartbeat. She holds a political science degree from Indiana University and would have made a wonderful politician. She handles the church as if it is the white house and her family as if they are the first family. God and family come first, ergo Caleb is her 'golden child.'

First Lady is very calculated. I can tell every move she makes and every word she chooses is well planned and thought out...like when she waves Caleb over. She is trying to push something that is not there. I have absolutely no interest in Caleb. For one, he has a thing for Bella. Secondly, Caleb is a ho. As badly as he wants Bella, he can't help poking any and every open hole. What's so crazy about it is that First Lady thinks her son is an angel and that Bella is a loose, money-hungry harlot. To say she doesn't think Bella is first lady material is an understatement.

I smile at Caleb as he approaches. His long chocolate arms reach in to give me a hug. Don't get me wrong; from outward appearances, Caleb has his stuff together. He's handsome, dark chocolate, and tall with a set of pearly whites that could convince anyone that he is an angel. I guess that is how he has his momma fooled.

"Well, I will let you two catch up," First Lady smiles and walks away. I can't help but to shake my head and roll my eyes. Caleb isn't paying me any attention. He keeps surveying the church, hoping to see Bella pop out of thin air. I know he noticed she wasn't sitting next to GG this morning. He is full of some stuff I can't say in church. Caleb knows I know he is looking for Bella, so he doesn't waste any time getting to the point.

"So where's Bella?" He gives me that winning smile. I almost burst out laughing, but hold it in and minimize it to a little snicker. I start looking around and peek over Caleb's shoulder as if I am expecting Bella to walk up at any moment. Caleb's dumb self gets all giddy and turns around, expecting to see Bella.

"Did you see her sitting next to me during the service?" I ask Caleb. I roll my eyes. "Is she standing next to me right now?"

Finally catching on, Caleb chuckles. "Well, I know you will see her soon. Can you give her this, please?" He pulls a thick white envelope from his suit pocket. No doubt it is money. He is so infatuated with Bella that he doesn't even realize she is playing him like a fool.

"You know what? GG is going to see her this evening and I am sure she would love to give it to her for you. Does she know how you feel about Bella?" I smile. "She would love Bella to be with a good God-fearing man." I know I'm wrong but I can't help myself.

"Yeah, you're right." I watch Caleb walk away with a skip in his step, checking out booties as he passes them. I just shake my head and laugh at the fact that the poor idiot really thinks he has a chance with Bella. Even worse, his parents think he is going to be the next leader of this church. I have great respect and admiration for Pastor Lewis but I cannot believe that he is blind to his son's indiscretions. I can't see Caleb being pastor of any church; at least not right now. His only focus is something else I can't mention in church.

"So good to see you, Beaunifide," I hear Pastor Lewis' voice say from behind me as I'm making my way out of the sanctuary.

I turn around and reach my hand out to shake the pastor's. "I really enjoyed that sermon, Pastor."

He pulls me in for a hug. "Enjoyed or needed?" Pastor pulls

away and looks me deep in my eyes. Now I am convinced God has been whispering in Pastor Lewis's ear about me. I'm not ready to 'fess up yet, but I'm sure it's written all over my face. I feel tears welling up in my eyes. Yes, I did need that word.

"So I will see you next week." Pastor pats my shoulder.

"Yes, sir," I smile. Daddy always said GG and Pastor were hustling for the Lord and it looks like they may have just hustled me. Within a week, God has gone from nonexistent in my life to the only thing on my mind.

10
Holy Flying Biscuits

Bella

Sunday, Angel and I drive over to GG's house in the Hummer. Inside, the air is filled with the aroma of soul food: cornbread, collard greens, macaroni and cheese, twice baked potatoes, biscuits, gravy, fried pork chops, and Beau's favorite, apple pie. GG threw down in the kitchen. As soon as we walk through the door, GG runs from the kitchen to give us kisses and hugs like she hasn't seen us in ages.

"You do know we were just here last night and you didn't greet us like this," I joke. Last night after I counted my money, I took Angel over to GG's so we could tell her that Angel was moving out and to get the rest of Angel's stuff. GG took the news better than expected. She actually looked relieved. I guess she is getting too old to be running after a 16-year-old. It didn't hurt that I have a plan to get Angel back on track. She is going to summer school and I'm going to hire her a tutor and take her to look at some colleges to motivate her. College wasn't for me, but once Angel stops fucking around and focuses, I know she will do well.

GG seems overjoyed about something as she runs back into the kitchen to check on the gravy. I follow behind her to help in the kitchen and to see what all the excitement is about.

"What's up with GG?" Angel asks. She must have noticed GG's elation too. Turning to face Angel, I shrug and continue walking backwards towards the kitchen. As soon as I turn back around I accidently bump into a glaring Beau, who is coming out of the kitchen carrying plates to set up the table.

"Watch out!" Beau barks at me with a nasty eye roll. I just got here and she is trying me already. I don't know why she has such an attitude. If anyone should be angry at anyone in this house it should be me angry at Beau. Or Angel angry at Beau. Hell, even GG has reason to take up issues with Beau; I'm pretty sure she didn't tell GG she was taking Angel's car, either. I stand there, towering over her as I purposely remain in her way. I glare right back at her just to show her I'm no pushover. Then I roll my eyes and proceed into the kitchen.

I kiss GG on the cheek. "What's up, gorgeous? Why are you

acting so giddy?" Beau walks back into the kitchen and loudly gathers silverware and napkins. She makes sure to rattle every cabinet and slam every drawer.

"Beau got saved!" GG exclaims.

I sigh. "I didn't know Jesus was Captain Save A Ho." Beau shoots me an evil look. Her glare is burning through me like daggers, but I keep going anyway. "I'm just saying, Holy water doesn't instantly kill ho-ness."

Beau slams the silverware she has in her hands onto the counter. "Jodete, puta!" she screams, saying 'fuck you, bitch' in Spanish.

I smirk. "See ,GG? She's cussing in Spanish. Hos can't be saved."

GG turns around and mugs me. "It's a process, Bella. Being saved don't happen overnight. At least she's making an effort, which is more than I can say for you and Angel coming to church just for the show. You ain't taking the Lord seriously," GG fusses.

"She needs Jesus more than us. She's out there in these streets having one-night stands. The ultimate ho!" I exclaim, pointing my finger at Beau.

GG gasps and bellows in disbelief. "Oh my! I didn't expect that from you, Beau. Bella maybe, but not you." I know GG didn't just call me a ho on the low.

"GG! I'm a virgin," I defend myself. "I have never had sex. NEVER."

GG looks surprised. "Aw, baby I'm proud of you. Way to keep it on lock. It's a gift, you know. You can't be giving away your gifts all willy-nilly." Then GG turns to Beau. "Suga, do yo' pussy need a check-up? We need to take you to a doctor and make sure everything is okay down there. Maybe get a pussy tune-up and have Pastor pray over it afterwards. Pastor has done many pussy prayers. He done even had to pray over GG pussy a time or two. Ain't nothing to be ashamed of. You gon' be alright, baby. You gon' be alright."

Angel bursts out laughing. None of us even realized she came into the kitchen until then. "GG, stop saying pussy," Angel scolds in her sternest voice, while doing her best to keep a straight face. "You are saved."

GG wags her finger at Angel. "Pussy is not a cuss word. You know what pussy mean? Look it up in a dictionary. Pussy means female va-gi-na." She annunciates each syllable slowly as she says the word. "And Beau needs a pussy tune-up and some prayer."

As dark as Beau is, she turns red with anger. "Check this out, GG. She calling me a ho, but today in church Caleb tried to hand me an envelope full of cash to give to Bella." It was my turn to mean mug. Shit, she better run me my money. I need that cash. "Bella is taking the tithe money from Caleb, probably in exchange for sex," Beau lies. That was low. Beau knows I'm not having sex with Caleb or anybody else. She's slandering my name. At least what I said was true—well, most of it. She may not be a ho, but she did have a one-night stand.

GG looks exasperated as she throws her arms up. "Oh Lawd, not the tithe money!" Angel bursts out in a fit of giggles. GG paces back and forth. "They out here hoing, Lawd. Oh, Jesus! My babies are some hos. Angel, please tell me not you, too. Please, Lawd, please." Angel doubles over, laughing uncontrollably. GG pulls out an envelope from her purse and holds it up in the air. "Is that what this is? Tithe money? You hoing for the ten percent?" She drops the envelope on the floor like it's poison on her fingers.

"GG, I am not a ho," I defend myself. "I still have my V-card." GG begins to shake and grips onto the kitchen counter for stability.

"V-card? What's that? Venereal disease? Jesus, Jesus, oh Jesus, help me!" GG cries out. Angel almost falls over laughing.

"No, GG, it means virgin." I am trying not to raise my voice at GG as I set the record straight, but Angel is laughing so loudly I have to yell just to be heard. "She's the sneaky ho," I say, pointing to Beau. "How dare you take Angel's car without speaking to me first? Primero el chanchullo, ahora esto." First the hustle, now this, I say to Beau in Spanish. "We're supposed to be partners...sisters!" I scream at the top of my lungs.

"I'm not a ho!" Beau shrieks. She bangs on the counter again, this time with a closed fist. "You're such a hypocrite," she says, glaring angrily at me. "Did you consult with me about Angel moving in with you? You did what you thought was best and so did I."

Angel manages to stop laughing long enough to guilt trip Beau. "You thought it was best to humiliate me in front of my friends like that?"

Beau looks annoyed that Angel is speaking up for herself. "You'll get over it. Get yo' grades up. How you barely passing Spanish and you speak Spanish just as well as you speak English? You on some ol' dumb stuff. Now *that's* humiliating. You never knew Daddy, but if you did, you would know Daddy didn't believe in second chances. He was all about school and education. How many chances do you think you deserve to get your grades up?" Beau talks as if Daddy wasn't a drop out and a drug dealer. And it doesn't matter what Daddy believed in because Daddy isn't here.

"Puta, you ain't Daddy!" I yell at her.

"And you ain't my momma!" Angel chimes in, rolling her neck. Beau looks like she is trying to restrain herself from choking Angel.

"Nah, I'm not yo' momma. I'm not a slutty flight attendant throwing my pussy at every high roller that rides a plane. She chose her drug dealer husband over you. That's the only reason you here."

Oh snap, I can't believe she just went there. "Oh, no she didn't!" I shout.

"I did," Beau retorts, "And what?" Beau throws her arms up in the air like she is daring me to do something. I look to Angel and she has tears welling up in her eyes.

Angel's mother was married when she got pregnant with Angel. She pretended Angel was her husband's baby. He was a Colombian drug lord and she was afraid that he would murk them both if he found out the truth. She only came clean when she learned Daddy died. She wanted Angel to know where she truly came from. When her husband got word that Angel wasn't really his child, he gave her an ultimatum: either Angel goes or he goes.

"Don't talk to my sister like that, slut bucket. You got hustled out yo' panties in one night, you ol' stretched out, baggy pussy ho!" I scream at the top of my lungs. I'm so pissed that she came for Angel like that. Beau reaches over and grabs one of the biscuits in the serving bowl sitting on the counter. I think her fat ass is about to eat it, but instead she winds up her arm and throws it at me. I quickly jump to the left to dodge the biscuit, but it still hits me on my shoulder. I didn't know biscuits had bounce like that, but apparently they do. The biscuit bounces off my shoulder and hits GG in the eye.

"My eye, my eye!" GG yells, flailing her arms around. "I got biscuit in my eye!"

"Hold on, GG," Angel says, rushing to her aid. "I'll get it out. Tilt your head back," Angel picks up a pitcher of ice water and pours it on GG's face.

"Ahhhhh!" GG yells out, shocked by the freezing water.

"Wow, you really *are* stupid!" Beau yells at Angel. "You trying to drown my—"

I cut Beau off by smashing her favorite homemade apple pie right in

82

her face. "I hope it tastes good." I push her back into the counter, where she grabs a pork chop and flings it at me. I duck and it slaps Angel in the face. Angel tries to run up on Beau, but GG grabs her by both arms. While I'm distracted by that craziness, Beau smashes the mashed potatoes all on the side of my face.

"Enough!" GG yells. "That is enough, all of you! Beau, you ruining my nice Sunday dinner. All this food just went to waste!" GG is furious.

"Me? Me! How is it *all* my fault? Bella started it when she called me a ho." Beau looks hurt.

"Because you are the oldest and you threw the first biscuit. Words don't hurt but a biscuit in the eye does. You should know better."

Beau goes from looking hurt to baffled. "I'm only a few days older and—"

"Don't talk back to me, girl. I don't want to hear it. You just got saved and look how you acting. Look!" She pauses to gesture toward the mess in the kitchen before continuing to lay into Beau. "You are being way too harsh on Angel. She didn't begin her education here and she's in one of the toughest schools in the nation. You need to give Angel back her car. And you need to apologize to Bella."

"Angel will get the car I paid for back when she gets her grades up," Beau sneers. "And Bella can go walk into a brick wall for all I care." I want to slap her for the way she was talking to GG. It isn't so much what she's saying, but how she's saying it.

"Beau!" GG exclaims, surprised that Beau is still talking slick.

"Nah, I'm done with y'all," Beau says before she storms out the house.

11
And the Beat Goes On

Beau

I still can't fully digest what happened at Sunday dinner. Angel can flunk classes, skip school, and lie to us all about it. Bella can choose not to go to college, not work, and hustle the pastor's son. But the one granddaughter who is responsible, college educated, goal oriented, and career driven is the one to get blamed for everything. I'm the one that ruined Sunday dinner. Yeah freaking right. GG's words are haunting my thoughts. I'm so far done with it all—with all of them. I have law school to focus on, and even with that I still have to deal with my classmates' bullshit. Can a chick catch a break?

At the beginning of the summer session Professor Ingram explained, "Don't be alarmed to learn that although law school is an individual journey in which you will determine how well you do, it is also a competition." So, as you can imagine, shit got quite competitive and the true nature of some of these scandalous mothafuckas quickly came out. From the beginning, I dedicated myself to my studies. I worked hard as hell at whatever I did and attacked each reading assignment like I wanted to be number one. Everyone saw it. I was well prepared and contributed to every discussion. After the first week, Professor Ingram pulled me to the side and told me he could tell that I had it. I asked what exactly *it* was and he explained that my drive plus the passion I showed was multiplied by the fact that I always carried myself like I was already an attorney. This included the way I dressed. While most students were still showing up in shorts, sneakers, and flip-flops, I was rocking some stylish business casual attire and I stood out. "Most importantly," he continued, "you have a natural gift for speaking and a comprehension of the material that surpasses many of the second year students and even some recent law school graduates I have encountered." He patted me on the back and told me to keep up the good work. I am sure that the other students overheard our conversation, especially since I could feel their eyes burning a hole through the back of my head. That is how the drama began.

A week after Professor Ingram told me how well I was doing, I am in class and, as usual I'm on it. I am prepared and participate throughout the entire lecture. Professor Ingram wraps up class and as I am gathering my books and laptop, Alexandria McCord, one of my classmates, walks up to me with a devious ass smirk on her face. She looks like the typical spoiled rich girl; a tall, skinny bitch with long bleach blonde hair and a tan.

"I knew your name sounded familiar," she smiles. "I mean, how common is the name Beaunifide?" I know this chick is up to some sneaky shit that has to do with my father. "If I had such an infamous name I would probably change it," she continues. By now she has an audience, which includes several students and Professor Ingram, who is still at his desk. I can feel myself ready to snap on this girl. I grip my Louis Vuitton handbag and take a deep breath as I tell myself not to punch her in her smug face and break that obvious nose job.

"It all makes sense. Now I understand how you can afford all that Louie and Prada, and that Maserati you drive. Your daddy was a drug dealer, right? Well, at least that is what the news articles I Googled alluded to. How ironic is it that my daddy was the lead federal prosecutor on your dad's case?" She smiles proudly and I can tell she is feeling herself and enjoying putting my business out there for everyone to hear. She flips her long blonde hair and bucks her eyes, waiting for my response. "Well, look at you now. Despite growing up on the wrong side of the law, you made it to law school. Your family must be proud. Now you can help all your 'hood rat cousins get out of prison," she smirks.

I stand silent for a minute, as I often do while contemplating the exact words I will use to annihilate a foe.

"I am so flattered by your interest in me. It is interesting to see that you found time in your schedule to Google me and my family, but let me assist you in your research—that's probably why you're not doing so well in our Legal Research class and why you're not going to be in the Law Clinic." I put her on blast before getting back to my father. "Before you draw conclusions, you need to make sure you have all the information. My father has never been linked to any drugs, regardless of the slanderous articles you have chosen to reference. The federal warrant was for tax evasion and he was never formally charged for that, either. Your dad did manage to have all my father's property and assets seized, however, this was over five years ago, so how this has anything to do with what I own, wear, carry, or drive today is irrelevant." I smile and flip my hair. *Yeah, bitch, my hair is long, all mine, and it's flippable, too.* "And it is interesting that you would bring up my family's business, especially seeing how your father, although indirectly, was the cause of my father's death. Have formal charges of bribery been filed against your father yet? That's right, I keep up with your dad, too. I hear he is under investigation for accepting a bribe in exchange for reducing a convicted murderer's sentence. I am sure that has your family walking on eggshells around the state of Indiana. How courageous of you to show your face in public. I am surprised you even chose to go to school here—talk about a pink elephant in the room," I laugh. "Well, at least you will be done with law school in time to work on his appeal, right? How much time is he facing?" I pat her on her shoulder. She is fuming and I am enjoying every moment of it. She has absolutely nothing to say and stands, obviously embarrassed, face flushed and mouth wide open.

Professor Ingram walks over and dismisses the rest of the students who had stayed around for the show. He asks Alexandria and I to stay behind. I had put Alexandria in her place, but I wondered if Professor Ingram would have to inform the school of my father's background and if it would become an issue for me. I am sure those who heard Alexandria talk about my dad will be cutting their eyes at me from here on out. Although, I didn't freely discuss my father or my upbringing, I have never hidden who I am, and I am not about to start. I am very proud of my name and who I am. Regardless of the life my father chose to live, he did it well. He was successful, and he loved and took great care of my sister and me. I am sure Alexandria cannot say the same, which is probably why she chooses to be called by her middle name and never talks about her dad.

"I don't know what you were trying to accomplish by calling out Beau's personal life, Alexandria, but that conniving behavior will not be tolerated by me and I am sure the dean would also disapprove." He dismisses her then turns to me. "You could have walked away." His expression is a mixture of disappointment and intrigue. Yeah, I could have and probably should have walked away, but I didn't. There was no way I was going to let that ignorant, snobby bitch turn her nose up at my father or me. "Don't worry, we knew about your father and hers before you were accepted to the school. I know you know better than to allow bullshit and people like Alexandria to throw you off your game." He pats my back and dismisses me.

I take a deep breath and comb my fingers through my hair. I don't have time for this shit. I need to focus on school. But for some reason I feel a little bad about calling her out in front of all those people, even though I elected to not bring up the fact that her brother is currently facing a serious sexual harassment suit at the law firm he works at. When I say I did my research on her father and her family, I am serious. I know her father's dirt like the back of my hand, including the name of his coke dealer in the city and the fact that he keeps mistresses up in Fishers. I could have ruined him publicly a million times over and even considered killing him, but I ain't no killer and don't need karma coming back on me.

Alexandria's father is the prosecutor who initiated the tax evasion case against my father, including the warranted search in which my father was killed. In my eyes, that's just as bad as if he had pulled the trigger himself. And his arrogant ass boasted about the seizure of my father's assets and ridding the state of Indiana and the Midwest of a drug lord, despite the fact that they never had any evidence to prove he was a drug dealer. I knew who Alexandria was from the moment I saw her and automatically assumed she'd be as gutter as her dad. Just like hustling runs through my blood, back stabbing and scheming runs through hers.

I am glad to get to my car and away from the bullshit that ensued today, but in a true coincidence of karma, Alexandria is parked right next to me. She drives a two-door pearl white Mercedes-Benz, and through the window I can see her leaning on the steering wheel, sobbing with a fist full of tissue. People love calling folks out but can't handle the shit when it is thrown back at them.

That's when it hits me—I feel convicted. Yeah, you know, that remorse you feel when you know God is displeased with your actions. GG talks about it often, saying it is God's way of chastising his children. I suddenly feel the urge to apologize. Although I am still new to the whole relationship with God and religion thing, I know this desire to apologize has to be God, because the old Beau would accidently, but really purposely, tap her car to get her attention, laugh in her face, and enjoy her misery. After all, she started with me. But, instead, the new Beau taps on her driver's side window, ready to set things right. Alexandria looks up at me with her bloodshot eyes and mascara running down her face. She rolls her eyes and shakes her head at me. Exactly what I expected. I motion for her to roll down the window. She hesitates, then reluctantly cracks the window.

"I'm sorry for that, Alexandria. I shouldn't have called your dad out like that. It was a knee jerk reaction from what you said about mine. The problems of our fathers shouldn't be a reflection of who we are." I expect some smart-ass comment or the cold shoulder. I envision her rolling the window up and speeding off, trying to take me out in the process, but she replies with a teary-eyed smile and a nod. She forgives me and I know she is sorry, too.

I feel relieved once I get into my car with a new perception of Alexandria. Maybe she isn't as bad as I thought. She was only doing what she had been taught to do, which is try to take out the competition. God never ceases to amaze me.

12
Don't Let Paranoia Stop Your Hustle

Bella

It is July and it's been six weeks since Beau's blow up at Sunday dinner. None of us have seen or heard from her since that night. Speaking for Angel and myself, we couldn't care less. I have nothing to say to someone who has nothing to say to me. Especially since she full throttle threw food at my face. GG tries to reach out to her, but Beau ignores her calls. GG said Beau is stubborn and will come around in her own time. I did catch GG secretly talking to the dean of Beau's law school to make sure she is still alive. Hmph, GG is better than me. Beau will call me before I will call her.

Anyways, I'm packing up to do my next hustle in Atlanta. It's Friday and the start of Black Expo weekend. During the day the expo is very enlightening with exhibits about health, finances, and black unity. However, at night it's all about concerts, getting wasted, and having fun. There are people from all over the nation flying in just for the parties and celebrity sightings. Teenagers usually walk around downtown scoping the scene or trying to join the festivities by finding an under 21 party. I know Angel and her little friends are going to get turnt up this weekend, therefore I have to give her some rules and guidelines. I don't like rules, but Angel is straight wild, even when I'm home. Ain't no telling what she does when I'm not around, so I have to lay down the law before I leave. I leave her with just two rules: 1) Don't tear up my shit, and 2) Don't have people in my house I don't know. "Fail to follow my rules and I will beat you down along with anybody else who want it," I warn her. Angel just nods her head like what I said went in one ear and out the other.

I hold up two dresses: a white bandage dress and a red bodycon dress with four straps that crisscross in the back. They're both so banging I can't decide which one to take. Angel snatches the dresses out of my hands and throws them down on my bed. "Where are you going anyway that you need dresses like that? And why can't I go?" she whines. She is so nosey. I knew all the questioning and begging to come with me would happen, which is part of the reason I haven't been on a hustle since she moved in. The other part is because I don't feel safe or confident hustling alone.

"Do you really want to go on a boring business trip with me during Black Expo weekend?" I try to reason with her. I tell her I am taking care of business because there is no way I am going to tell her about the hustle.

"No," she sighs. It kind of hurts not to be able to tell Angel about the hustle, but I don't want to corrupt her. She has a chance to live a straight and narrow life, and I don't want to interfere with that. Since she's been living with me we have become increasingly close—almost as close as Beau and I had been before she decided to quit the hustle. I pick up the dresses Angel threw down and carefully place them in my suitcase.

Angel asks me if I am ready to head to the airport. She is going to drive me and she seems a little too anxious to get me out of my own damn house. I guess she is planning to make the most of having a downtown luxury condo during one of the most epic weekends of the summer. I finish packing and tell Angel to grab the keys to the Hummer.

"Let me whip the McLaren," she pouts. There is no way I am going to let her drive that car. I already don't feel 100 percent about leaving her alone for the first time since Reggie's wacko ass stalked me to Chicago. I don't want anything to happen to her if he should happen to see the car and think it's me instead of Angel.

"How many times do I have to tell you I will break my foot off in your ass if I ever catch you in my car?" I playfully chide.

"Whatever happened to su casa es mi casa?" Angel complains.

"No es su casa y no es su carro. Beau got your car. You better get it from her," I laugh. Angel storms off to get the keys to the Hummer. I guess she doesn't find my joke funny. She's still a little sore about how Beau played her and took her car. I note in my head that it is still a sensitive issue for her and kind of feel bad for joking about it. Beau was definitely wrong, but Angel does have to be accountable for her actions. Had her grades been where they needed to be, her car would not have been taken, and now that it's gone I can't get it back for her because I refuse to talk to Beau. I don't intend on talking to her anytime soon, unless she apologizes and gets back in the hustle, point blank.

The airport is about a 20-minute drive from my condo, and Angel is working my nerves the entire drive there. She is complaining that the Hummer is too big for her to drive and about how she needs

92

more money for the weekend because she doesn't want to be broke. She is rambling about not wanting to go to church on Sunday because she will be too tired from the weekend and blah, blah, blah. After a while her words start to run together. Man, was I like this at 16? I look in the review mirror and notice the same car has been following us since we left downtown. My heart begins to race. *Oh no, not again.* I keep turning around to see if I can get a glimpse of the driver.

"Slow down, Angel," I say, trying to remain calm. She must be able to detect the panic in my voice, because, for once, she shuts her mouth and listens to me.

The car behind us doesn't go around us; instead, it slows down with us. *Shit, shit, shit.* What if it's Reggie again? I tased him last time, so he could have a gun on him this time. I'm supposed to be protecting my baby sister and I'm about to get her killed by a stalker.

"Uh, is everything alright?" Angel asks, concerned. *No, everything is not alright*, I think to myself as I turn and face forward.

"Switch lanes," I direct her. I know I am scaring Angel, but I have to be sure we are safe. I haven't seen or heard from Reggie in six weeks, but after that stunt he pulled, I can't put anything past him. Angel switches lanes and I watch as the car passes us. An elderly woman is driving. I sigh in relief and relax back into my seat. Angel doesn't bother asking me about the incident. She just continues driving to the airport in much-needed silence. Still, I can't shake the feeling that someone is following us. Paranoid, I continue glancing in the mirrors and looking into every car that passes us—just in case.

We arrive at the airport and I gather my bags. I kiss Angel goodbye and she pulls off. As I walk inside to check in, I feel a strong hand grab my shoulder. I swear my life flashes before my eyes. Reggie caught me. He will declare his undying love for me before shooting me dead then killing himself in a crazy murder-suicide. It will be all over the news: 'Indianapolis Businesswoman Killed by Estranged Lover.' And I will yell from my grave that he was never my lover! Hey, it could happen.

I quickly spin around, ready for a fight. To my relief, it's just the airport baggage handler. "Miss, you dropped this," he says, handing me my cell phone. "Do you need help with your bags?" Even though I'm relieved that I am not going to die a painful death in the airport, I still have terror in my heart. I haven't robbed anyone since Chicago, and, quite frankly, it's because I've been scared. Everything seems to be going wrong for me lately and Reggie's stalking ass was the icing on the cake, making me rethink my safety and confidence in doing this alone. There is a very real possibility Reggie will show up again. Unfortunately, financially speaking I have no choice but to do another hustle.

It's a short flight to Atlanta, about an hour and a half, but I decided to fly first class anyway and I am so glad I did. I really need the free alcoholic drinks to get Reggie off my mind. I wave at the flight attendant. "Another, please." I'm sipping my third cocktail while I wait for the coach passengers to board the plane. The flight is full, but the seat next to me is unoccupied. Thank goodness. I don't want a stank breath chatter-box sitting next to me. I finish my fourth drink and ask the flight attendant to bring me a hot tea to sober me up. I'm beyond tipsy and my little frame can't handle another alcoholic drink. One of the flight attendants begins to close the airplane door when I overhear another flight attendant tell her there is one more passenger coming down the walkway. Damn.

A tall, brown-skinned man wearing glasses enters the plane. His back is turned as he thanks the flight attendant, allowing for a view of his low fade haircut. The sides of his head are shaved, old school style like in the Fresh Prince of Bel-Air haircut. I only know one man whack enough to still wear that played out haircut: Reggie. Damn. Please tell me this man just did not follow me to the airport and buy a last minute ticket to Atlanta. That's some super stalker shit right there. The flight attendant shuts and locks the door as my eyes scan the plane in a panic. I have to get off this freaking airplane. I grip the arms of the seat tightly and can feel my heartbeat speed up. This man looks just like Reggie. Could he be his brother? Did he send someone in his place to do his bidding?

The man sits next to me after putting his carry-on luggage in the overhead compartment. Since he has luggage, this can't be a last minute flight for him, unless he keeps a packed bag in his car for unexpected stalking missions. Or even worse, what if Reggie found another way to put a tracking device on something of mine without me knowing it. He is incredibly smart and fully capable of pulling something like that off.

"Ma'am, here's your tea." The flight attendant places the cup on the foldout table in front of me and I hand it right back to her.

"Another cocktail, please," I exasperatedly request. I turn my phone completely off. I refuse to even put it in airplane mode. This Reggie look-alike might have some type of device to hack into my phone. Who knows? I'm not taking any chances. I can't sleep or blink my eyes for too long. I can't even turn my head to look out the window. I need to be able see what he is doing at all times. So for an hour and a half I just sit there with my eyes wide open, counting the seconds until we land and I can get the hell off this plane.

As soon as we get the green light to unbuckle our seatbelts and exit the plane, I jump up. Climbing over the fake Reggie, I snatch my carry-on and run off the plane. I look left and right, in search of baggage claim. Then I spot another Reggie look-alike and duck behind a group of elderly woman to hide. Look-alike or not I am still trying to lay low. One of the ladies must have thought I was trying to pickpocket them, because she hit me over the head with her purse. "Ouch!" I squeal. Please help me. I'm hiding from my abusive ex-boyfriend." The women all gasp in sympathy for me and block me from view.

I don't know what is going on. The fact that I was on the plane with a Reggie look-alike and there's another at the airport is truly freaking me the hell out. I try to calm down and shake the feeling of paranoia as I leave my shield of old people.

Despite still being shaken up from seeing the two Reggie look-alikes, I decide not to leave the city or abandon my hustle. I can't let one whacko stop my hustle. Besides, I may not have Greta, but I do have my taser. Anyone crazy enough to run up on me will get jolted. I just want to get this hustle over with, make my money, and get back home. I decide to go a strip club. Strip clubs in Atlanta are notorious for their baller patrons and their generosity. I am not taking my clothes off, but I will make more money than any of the strippers in the club tonight.

At the club I quickly find my mark and begin working my magic. I spot a short, light-skinned dude with dreads and tattoos all over his face and neck. He is a local rap artist that is famous around the city.

"What's he drinking?" I ask the bartender as I point and take a seat at the bar.

"Hennessy and Coke," he tells me. How typical. The only thing that would have been more stereotypical is if he was popping a bottle of Moet. "Would you like to send him a drink?" The bartender asks.

"No, I'll take it to him myself." He hands me the drink and stands there staring at me as if I didn't pay him for the drink and tip him well. I start to ask him what the fuck he is looking at, but instead I bite my tongue and order a martini on the rocks. As soon as he turns his back

I slip the Special K into the Hennessey drink. The bartender turns around to give me my martini.

"I lost my nerve," I blush, putting on my best girly voice. "Can you take this drink over to him, please?"

"Only because you look amazing in that red dress. I've never seen someone so pretty," he replies. "Lil' Yappy is one lucky man."

Lil' Yappy. I hope he's as stupid as his name is. The bartender takes the drink over to him and after they exchange a few words, Lil' Yappy looks over to me and grins. Boy, he sho' is ugly. I wink at him and watch him gulp down the laced Hennessey and Coke. Hook, line, and sinker. Now all I have to do is get him to leave his boys behind and come back to the motel with me. That shouldn't be hard. I stroll up and shoo one of his boys away so I can sit next to Lil' Yappy. I sit down and slowly cross my legs, giving him a seductive look. Then I pull out a stack of ones wrapped in a rubber band.

"How many bands to make you dance?" I ask, trying to keep a straight face.

"Shiiiit, how many bands to make *you* dance?" Yappy retorts. "Shorty, you got an ass on you. Fuck these skrippers."

I laugh. "How many bands do you have?" I ask, twirling my hair.

He pulls out a stack of hundred-dollar bills and waves it in the air. "As many as you want," he slurs. I can tell the Special K is already starting to have an effect on him, probably because he was already gone off something else.

"That's what's up. Let me show you where you can get a private dance," I whisper in his ear. The rapper tucks his cash away and we begin to walk out of the club. I already have a cab waiting. The plan was to get in and out as soon as possible. Mission accomplished. This was way too easy.

As we're walking out the door, another Reggie look-alike is walking in the door. I don't know if you've ever tried to remain sexy while almost shitting your panties, but yeah, it's pretty difficult. It takes everything in me not to take off running, but somehow, I manage to hold it together.

"Aye, baby you a'ight?" Yappy asks me. I must have been gripping his arm tighter than I thought.

"I'm cool, baby. I'm just excited to show you what I'm working with," I lie to the rapper. I don't care what anyone says, bumping into these Reggie look-alikes is no coincidence. My instincts scream, '*Girl, get the fuck out of here. Run, bitch, run.*' And that's exactly what I do. I pick up my pace, practically dragging him to the cab.

In the cab, I keep looking out the back window to make sure we're not being followed. By the time we pull up at the motel, Yappy is almost knocked out. Good. The sooner he passes out the sooner I can get my money and go the hell home. I slide the cab driver a hundred-dollar bill and tell him, "There will be another hundred for you if you wait until I come out." The cabbie nods his head.

I look both ways before pulling Yappy out the cab and putting his arm around my neck to help him walk to the room. I plunk him down on the bed and pull out my essential items: my taser, in case the real Reggie rolls up on me, and my cell phone for the count down. It will take a few more minutes before he is completely knocked out and I want to keep track of time.

While keeping Yappy in my peripheral vision, I walk over to the window and peek out. My eyes dart in every direction looking for any signs of Reggie. All I see is my cab, so I walk back over to the rapper whispering to myself, "Come on, come on. Be asleep." I tap his forehead, and he doesn't move. I quickly collect all the money I can find on him. He has stacks everywhere, even in the waistline of his pants. I am startled by a loud knock on the door, causing me to fall off the bed. I hold my taser like a gun as I crawl to the window and peep out. "Don't be Reggie. Don't be Reggie," I whisper. It is a prostitute knocking at the room next door. The fact that it isn't Reggie doesn't put me at ease. I'm on edge and I need to hurry up and get out of here before he finds me.

I crawl back over to the bed and take Yappy's sneakers off. Sometimes dope boys keep a few bills in their shoes. I find two hits of cocaine and three $50 bills. I take the fifties and leave the dope. There is nothing I can do with that. I don't get high and I don't deal. I get up off the nasty ass floor and stuff all the money into my purse. Another loud bang from the room next door startles me and I jump. The rapper moves a little, too. I react without even thinking and tase him. Then I realize he only flinched in his sleep. I grab my stuff and make a beeline for the taxi so I can head to the airport.

I finally feel safe once I'm at the airport. Ever since 9/11, airport security has been top notch. If Reggie is up to something, there are plenty of cameras, witnesses, and airport police that can take care of him. I start to nod off a little bit waiting for my 6:45 AM flight. I read a book to try to stay awake, but my eyelids feel so heavy. My phone rings and I almost jump out my seat. Other than Beau, I don't know who would call me at this time, and I know it's not her. The caller ID reads 'Front Desk Security,' I nearly drop my phone. It's the security at my condo. I pray that Angel is okay. If Reggie got a hold of her, I am going to get a hold of him by his balls and twist those motherfuckas off. Mess with me all you want. I don't care if he has me running for my life; I'll straight hospitalize dude over Angel.

I fumble with the phone a bit before finally answering. "Hello, Ms. Jones," the security office says.

"Yes," I answer in a shaky voice, waiting to hear some devastating news.

"Since you are one of our best residents, I wanted to give you a courtesy call," he says.

"Okay," I say, unsure of what's going on.

"The other residents are complaining about a party being thrown in your condo. It's out of control, ma'am. Someone threw a porcelain monkey out the window. Mr. Briski was taking his toy poodle out and it almost hit his dog."

I got that monkey while vacationing in India last summer. I sink into my chair. I don't know what to say other than I'm sorry. "I apologize. This is so embarrassing."

In a kind voice he says, "Please get this party under control. Not only will the police be called but the Homeowners Association will have to reevaluate your residency here."

I am heated. I can potentially be kicked out of my own home that I pay a mortgage on. "I'll be home in a couple of hours. In the meantime, I'll call my sister to handle the situation." I hang up the phone and my blood is boiling.

I call Angel's cell phone. She doesn't pick up. I call the house phone. It rings for a while then finally someone picks up. "It's Willy, baby," a man's raspy voice answers.

"Whoa, hold up. Who the fuck are you?" I bark.

"It's Willy D. Baby. Please say the baby," the voice says.

It dawns on me that a celebrity rap star just answered my house phone. "Wha…Young Will? Where is Angel?"

"Who's Angel?" Young Will asks.

"The little Colombian girl that lives there," I retort.

"Oh, you mean Maserati. Lil' Billi. A billi, a billi, a billi," he raps. Oh, hell naw. I know she's not whipping my Maserati. Now I really gotta get in that ass. She thinks she's slick. I told her she couldn't drive the McLaren, so she jumped in my Maserati.

"Lil' Billi?" I ask. I wanted to be sure he was referring to Angel.

"Yeah, my billionaire boss bitch. That's my boo. I love me some Lil' Billi," he informs me before he breaks out into a full-blown rap. "She lookin' like a billionaire. Built like a brick house. Long hair don't care. If she was a lil' older I'd marry her right here. But tonight I'm content in her millionaire suite sipping something sweet; vodka wit a Lil' peach. Watch her sweet self serve me something to eat. Kick up my feet on this Italian leather seat. Yawn, stretch out, I might go to sleep just to dream 'bout the next time we meet. I'm a Young Dollar Billionaire!" In the background I hear a crowd of people going wild, clapping and cheering for his freestyle. If I wasn't so pissed it would've been dope.

"I'm gonna post this on YouTube!" someone yells. "Go Willy! Go Willy!" It's obvious that the party is out of hand. Ain't no telling how much they damaged my condo.

"A'ight, a'ight, enough with the raps," I interrupt his freestyle. "Put my sister on the damn phone."

"Yo, Lil' Billi," he calls.

"Yeah, Willy D. Baby?" Angel responds.

"Lil' Billi, yo' maid on the phone."

Angel takes the phone. "Angel! Yo' maid, huh? I'm on my way home right now," I say through clenched teeth. "And when I get home everybody better be out of my damn house and you better have my place sparkling!" Angel tries to say something, but I cut her off. "I swear Angel, I'm going to put my foot so far up your ass you're going to be able to tell me what my toenail polish tastes like. Playtime is over! And you buying me another monkey!" I hang up on Angel before she can say anything. I look around and notice the whole airport is staring at me. I guess I was loud. Oh fucking well. "Mind your business!" I shout. Everyone's eyes quickly dart away and I go back to reading my book as if nothing happened.

A half hour later I board my flight. When I touch down in Indy I call a cab instead of calling Angel to pick me up as originally planned. I really can't believe her. I specifically told her not to have people in my house. She could've done whatever she wanted, but bringing strangers into my house is a major infraction. It is a major security breach, especially for a hustla'. That's how Momma Tanya was killed. Somehow enemies got into the house and murdered her. It's also the very reason I have a stalker now—because I let him into my home.

Angel is spoiled and wild. She has it too easy. At her age I had to hustle to earn my keep. She has everything handed to her. All she has to do is keep her grades up and she can't even do that. I got something to solve that problem though. She gonna learn today. I walk into my condo and survey the place. I can tell she tried to clean up, but it still looks like hell. My five-foot imported Italian ceramic vase is missing, along with a couch cushion. There are wine stains on the carpet and some nasty-looking yellow gunk on the wall. I had 15 bottles of vintage wine and expensive champagne on my wine rack. Not that cheap sparkling wine that they make here in the States, but real champagne that I bought while I was in Champagne, France. Now there are only two bottles of wine left. My flat screen TV is cracked. I go upstairs to my rooftop pool and, lo and behold, I find my vase and my couch cushion floating in the pool, along with something brown. I step closer to the edge of the pool to get a closer look, and…aw, hell naw! Someone shitted in my pool!

I storm down the stairs and bust through the door of Angel's bedroom. She is laying in her bed pretending to be asleep. I snatch the covers off her and throw them on the floor. "Angel! Get yo' stankin' ass up! I know you ain't sleep. There is shit in my pool. There is literally shit in my pool. Who shitted in my pool, Angel?!" I scream. She doesn't move, so I yank her up by her arm. "Didn't I say I was done playing with you?"

Angel tries to break loose, but my grip is too strong. "Lo siento, mi hermana!" she desperately apologizes.

"You only had two rules. TWO," I hold up two fingers in her face then use them to push her forehead back. "And you managed to break them both."

Angel explains how she ended up throwing a wild, raging party in my condo. "We went to the Young Dollar Billionaires concert and I guess I caught Willy's attention because he asked me to come backstage after the concert. Somehow we got to talking and I invited him back to the condo to kick it. I mean, he's a celebrity. He wants me to be in one of his videos."

I roll my eyes. "Two!" I yell again. "You almost had the police in my home! You tore up my shit, so you are going to start paying for my shit. Starting next month you will pay half of the mortgage." The look on her face is priceless. She was expecting to get yelled at, she was expecting to be placed on punishment, and she was probably expecting to have her cell phone or something of value taken away from her. She wasn't expecting to have to step up and be more responsible.

"How am I going to come up with that kind of money?" she asks in a frantic voice.

"We'll discuss it in the morning."

"It is the morning," she snarls.

"It's not morning until I go to sleep and wake up again," I snap.

"I'm pretty sure that's not how it works, Bella."

"Shut up. I want you to get up and finish cleaning up this place. I want the gunk off my wall. I want the shit out of my pool. I want you to take inventory of all the things that need to be replaced. I want this place to look exactly how it did when I left. When I wake up we will discuss how you will start earning your keep."

After going off on Angel for the party she threw, I go to sleep and don't wake up until 5 PM. I swear my sleeping schedule is all off. I was hoping to only sleep until 11 AM. I guess I was more exhausted then I thought. I sit up in my bed and I hear my stomach grumble. No, not grumble—more like roar. I haven't eaten in over 24 hours, since before I left to go to the ATL. I want to run to the kitchen and gobble down a fruit salad and a croissant, but I have business to attend to first. I was in such a rush to get out of Atlanta that I didn't even get to finish counting the money I made.

I grab my purse from the floor and empty its contents onto my bed. I organize the money into separate stacks of hundreds, fifties, and twenties. Everything else I push to the side. My count is up to $10,000 with plenty more to go when Angel flings my door open.

"You up yet?" she intrudes. I look up at Angel with a look of annoyance, not bothering to hide the money from her. There's no point; she already saw it when she unceremoniously burst into my room without knocking.

I watch her eyes light up at the big piles of money spread across my king sized bed. I ignore her, hoping she goes away so I don't have to explain myself. I continue to count the money.

"Whoa. Is that from your business trip yesterday?" she asks with her eyes glued to my money. Angel has no clue about the hustle. Beau and I have kept her and GG in the dark to serve a dual purpose. The first reason is, the fewer people that know about it, the less chance we have of getting caught up. Beau calls it plausible deniability or some shit like that. The second reason is, we just didn't want to upset them.

GG would spaz out and Angel just wouldn't look at us the same. So as far as they know, we make our money from our farm. In reality, it only generates a quarter of our income. The real money comes from the hustle.

Without explaining how or why I have all this cash, I tell Angel to sit down on my bed and help me finish counting it. This is my third big hit in a row, first that Rick Ross-looking dude, then Mr. Movado, and now Lil' Yappy. I can tell just by looking at the big pile of money that it's a lot. Even though I want to stop robbing dudes, I keep getting lucky, and every gambler knows you don't quit during a winning streak. We count and double count the money. The total comes out to $28,346 and that's just the cash. That doesn't include the jewelry I will sell to my connect, which will probably get me another $10,000. Not a bad turnaround from the $570 investment I put out. I spent $300 for a first class plane ticket, $60 for the motel, $10 for the drinks at the club, and $200 went to the taxi cab driver. That's what? A 550 percent return on my investment. Wall Street can't see me. I'm proud of myself for another successful hustle on my own without Beau—fuck her.

"So, we going shopping?" Angel asks, thumbing through a stack of hundred-dollar bills. My euphoric moment is lost. That's the problem with Angel. Everything she owns has been given to her. Maybe that's the reason she's not taking school seriously and is wilding out so much. Don't get me wrong; I'm down for a good shopping spree, but she has no clue what I had to go through to get this money. She doesn't know I could've been beaten, raped, or jailed while her spoiled ass was partying and almost getting me kicked out of my condo. $28,000 may seem like a lot of money, but in the grand scheme of things it's only a drop in a bucket. And right now my bucket is empty so a shopping spree is out of the question.

"Is my house cleaned?" I ask, trying not to snap. I place all the cash back in my bag and leave the jewelry on the bed. "Get up," I command, hopping up. Angel stands up. I push the bed, moving it over about five inches. I feel around on the hardwood floor by the headboard until I feel a slight nick in the wood, and I pull up several of the slats, revealing a safe. Angel gasps. I unlock the safe and put the purse full of money inside until I can make it to the bank on Monday. I place the jewelry in my jewelry box so I can easily access it before I see my connect later on.

"That is so cool," Angel says, gesturing to my safe. "Why do you have secret safe under your bed?" she inquires.

"Why haven't you answered my question?" I retort, still angry with Angel. "Is my house clean?" My tone of voice doesn't even phase her, which pisses me off even more. Nothing gets to this girl.

"Take a look for yourself," she grins. I exit the bedroom, leaving Angel standing near my dresser. "Wait, madam, let me give you the grand tour," she says in a fake British accent. She walks me around the condo, pointing out all the things that were cleaned up. "If you look over here we have a gunk-free wall," she continues in her Brit accent. "And take a good look at the sofa. All of the cushions have been dirt repelled and put back into place."

I laugh. "You mean you cleaned the couch?"

Angel grins and nods her head. "And that's not all, madam. Let me show you the grand finale." She walks me to her room. "Tada! I even cleaned my room!" she exclaims. I am impressed. I'm not sure how she did it, but the place is actually sparkling. It looks even cleaner than it was when I left.

"Have I redeemed myself, madam?" she asks. I turn and look Angel in the eyes. When I got home and saw the condition my condo was in I was seriously considering bringing Angel into the hustle to make her earn her keep. Maybe that's not such a good idea after all. She's a good kid and she should be able to live the life that was taken from me and Beau. Instead of making her hustle, maybe I should just make her do some work on the farm to learn responsibility. I sigh and flop down on Angel's bed.

"I don't know, Angel. I just don't know," I ponder aloud, contemplating it all. Angel thinks I am just answering her question.

"I'm sorry, Bella. What else can I do to make it up to you? Please don't make me go back to GG's," she pleas.

"I'm not going to make you go live with GG, but you do have to learn responsibility. I trusted you with my home, Angel, and you let me down. You only had two rules and you couldn't even follow them. Those rules were for your protection. Do you know I have a stalker? What if he wormed his way into the condo as another partygoer and did something to you to get to me? Then what?" I lecture Angel. I feel like GG or, even worse, Beau. Angel is silent. She looks down at the floor as I continue to lecture her. "Not only was there a security breach, but you tore up a lot of things. And I'm strapped for cash right now. Do you know how much I pay for the mortgage? $7,000. Do you have $7,000?"

"Well, I have $25,000 in my savings that you and Beau started."

"Shut up. You know what I mean. You only have that money because we gave it to you."

"You just made over $28,000 in one night. I can help you. I can be your assistant or something."

"Do you know how I made that money? I hustled it."

"Yeah, I know. You're a go-getter. You have to be to make money like that."

"No, you don't understand. I hustle. Sit down."

I pat the space on the bed next to me and Angel sits down. I swear her to secrecy. "We've already told you everything about Dad. How he was a drug kingpin, how he was killed, and how we lived on our own because we didn't want to live with GG, right?" I try to ease her into to what I am about reveal. Angel seems confused as to what this has to do with the house party she threw. I hesitate, still unsure if I should reveal the truth. I decide I will tell her about the hustle, but I won't bring her in on it. Knowing how I make my money and that it's not all glitz and glam may calm her wild side down. "Well, what we didn't tell you is…"

I tell her everything. How Beau and I make money, and the reasons why we started hustling in the first place. I tell her how the farm is just a front to cover our tracks from the government. I tell her the rules of the hustle and the importance of keeping a low profile so we don't get caught up. Once I start talking I can't stop. I end up telling her more than I initially planned to, including the reason why Beau and I are beefing. I even tell her how I got played out of a lot of money and how I can't quit now, even though I want to, because I have to rebuild my cash flow. Not even Beau knows what Lorenzo did to me. That was something I intended to take to my grave, but I find myself pouring my heart out to my baby sister. It's therapeutic for me to finally have someone to talk to about it. When I finish talking to Angel I look up at her and all I see is her wide grin.

"I want in!" she exclaims.

13
Forgiveness Even If...

Beau

I gaze out the window at the bright July sun as I study. Over the last two months I've felt a transformation and I know it is God. I feel like that 8Ball and MJG song, *The Things We Used To Do.* I don't want do the things I used to do anymore. Although the hustle is in my past, I can't help but think about the things I have done and I feel bad about them. I feel even worse about the beef I have with my sisters and the fact that we still haven't spoken at all. Still, I can't bring myself to call either one of them.

I have, however, been talking to GG a little bit. Yeah, it took a while, but after she jacked me up after Bible study one Tuesday evening I knew I had to at least make peace with my GG. GG calls, interrupting my studying, and we end up having the same conversation we always seem to have about forgiveness.

"I'm always the bigger person, GG. Why must I continue to turn the other cheek?" I plead my case. But as usual, I feel bad. I know she is right and forgiveness is what God wants, but it isn't what I want. I feel a certain freeness not having to worry about what Bella and Angel are into. I know both of them are as stubborn as me. If I wave my white flag, Bella will try to talk about hustling again and I am done with that. Angel will start asking about her car and she doesn't deserve that back.

GG starts quoting the Bible on me. "Then Peter came to him and said, 'Lord how often shall my brother sin against me, and I forgive him? Up to seven times?' Jesus said to him, 'I do not say to you, up to seven times, but up to 70 times seven.' You give that some thought, Beau." GG sighs deeply. I can hear desperation in her voice. I know that she is more than ready for her girls to stop beefing. "I will see you at Bible study tonight." It is a statement; not a question.

"Of course," I giggle before I hang up the phone.

Busy is the one word that accurately sums up my life. School, internship, and shadowing Ms. Jacqueline keeps me going. I enjoy shadowing Ms. Jacqueline the most. I love watching her in action. Her legal practice is currently focusing on corporate law and business acquisitions. I enjoy watching her walk into meetings and own them, with all eyes and ears on her during presentations and negotiations. It's exciting to know that will soon be my life.

While I was on the phone with GG, Ms. Jacqueline had called and left a message. "Hey, stop at the office around 5 if you're available. Got something to share with you." I can hear excitement in her voice and I'm instantly intrigued to find out what it's about. Every Tuesday evening I have been attending Bible study at 6:30, so hopefully the meeting with Ms. Jacqueline won't take too long.

When I decide to get into something I go all in, and God is no exception. Not only am I attending Bible study on Tuesdays and church services on Sundays, I am also taking a new members course at church that helps build foundations in the word. The class is really enlightening and continues to pique my interest in God and His word. I have been reading the Bible, no longer as a book, but as a guide to life. I am noticing how God is helping me handle different situations. Like with Alexandria, the girl I embarrassed after class; we have actually become study partners and have hung out a couple times after class. I don't usually make friends easily, but I can honestly say that she and I are becoming friends. I have to attribute that change to God.

"I praise Him with my words. I praise Him with my heart," I sing quietly as I walk to Ms. Jacqueline's office. It is located downtown in a big, chic gold and glass building. I am rocking some cream dress slacks, five-inch gold heels, and a gold satin shirt. I feel like I will fit in perfectly in this sexy office. I continue to hum as I wait for the elevator and can't help but to start dancing to the music in my head. Thanking God has become second nature to me. I see myself praying and talking to God more and more. I have begun to discuss everything with God, sometimes even what I wear or how I do my hair. I can't help but to laugh at myself and sometimes I think God laughs with me, too. I hop on the elevator and press the button for the 21st floor.

"Hold that, please!" a deep voice yells as the door closes. I have started texting on my phone but manage to hit the open button right before it closes all the way.

"Thanks," the deep voice says. For some reason it sounds familiar.

"No worries," I reply, without looking up.

After sending my text I glance up at the elevator numbers and notice that Deep Voice is going to the same floor as me. Ms. Jacqueline and her business partner lease the whole floor, so I am now a little interested in seeing who the voice belongs to, but don't want to be obvious. I start at his feet. They are big—no, huge. He is wearing a pair of Air Jordan IV Promise Lands. I am very familiar with them because I own over 15 pairs myself, many of which I have had since I was a teenager. His hairy, chocolate legs are showing from the shin down and I can see a Nike sign on the side of his basketball shorts. My heart races as my eyes continue to scan his body. I can tell he is really tall.

The elevator door opens before I see his face and he waits for me to get off first. I know that this guy is not Real, but for some reason I can't help but wonder what would happen if by some freak chance I run into him. I wouldn't know how to react. Deep Voice follows behind me as I walk down the hall and I'm still unable to catch a glimpse of his face as he holds the office door open for me. Karen, the front desk receptionist, buzzes me straight back to Ms. Jacqueline's office as usual. And then I look. I finally peek at Deep Voice's face as he lets Karen know he is there for an appointment with Ms. Jacqueline, too. I bust a right and walk down to Ms. Jacqueline's corner office to question her about Deep Voice. He is definitely not Real but he does appear to be a basketball player.

"Hey, you did say 5 o'clock, right?" I ask her.

"You must have run into EJ as you were coming in." Ms. Jacqueline gives me a side eye and a smirk. "That is what I wanted to share with you," she says. I hope she is not trying to play matchmaker. EJ is cute, but I am not thinking about dating at all. "I have previously informed you, my partner Abraham Finstein has been considering moving to the West Coast to be closer to family. If he does, he and I will still be in practice together."

"Yes ma'am." I smile, feeling relieved that she isn't trying to play matchmaker and intrigued about why I am here.

"As you know, both Finstein and I handle corporate law and I've recently been taking over some of his accounts." I begin to wonder if Ms. Jacqueline is starting to second-guess bringing me into the practice after I finish law school. She has let me go over some of the contracts and draw up a few presentations, which, although weren't perfect, she was very pleased with. Maybe Finstein is having doubts about my ability to be a good corporate law attorney and has put a bug in her ear.

I listen as Ms. Jacqueline continues to discuss the firm's plans, patiently waiting for her to get to the point. "Look, Beau, I am sure you will be a great corporate law attorney, but…" She stands up and begins to pace while looking out of her office window. She has a beautiful view of the city skyline and the sun is shining down on the hustle and bustle of the city. I just sit there, waiting to hear my fate. If Ms. Jacqueline reneges on our deal, I will have to rethink my whole life plan. "Finstein has another venture he has embarked on; one that is totally separate from the corporate law practice. He has two professional athletes that he represents. EJ is one of them. Finstein thinks you can be a great sports attorney. He sees something in you. It takes a certain type of gusto and personality to do well in sports law and he thinks you have it." Ms. Jacqueline sits back at her desk and looks at me, awaiting a response.

I don't have a response, because the only thing I can think about is the fact that Real is a professional basketball player and throwing myself into this profession ups the odds that I may run into him. But I can't tell Ms. Jacqueline I'm going to pass up the opportunity to do sports law out of fear of running into some man I drugged, had sex with, and then robbed his brother. Since Ms. Jacqueline was my father's attorney, I am sure that she wouldn't be surprised that I had committed some illegal acts, Nonetheless, I have not and will never discuss the hustle with her.

Although she agreed to take me under her wing after I told her I wanted to be an attorney, she made me promise that if I was doing anything illegal, it would end before I became an attorney. I promised her this and stuck to my word. But now, I sit here speechless. If the Real thing had never happened I would have jumped at the opportunity to practice sports law. I am sure it would be a lot more interesting and profitable than corporate law. But I just sit here, looking through Ms. Jacqueline, my mind stuck on Israel James and what I did to him.

"Beau, what are you thinking?" The puzzled look on Ms. Jacqueline's face lets me know that my silence is not the response she was expecting.

"Okay," I finally say. But I can tell this is still not the answer she was expecting. She expected me to be more enthused about this wonderful opportunity, which most new attorneys would kill for. "You caught me off guard," I laugh and to try to change the focus of the conversation. "For a moment I thought you were trying to play matchmaker."

"I can." Ms. Jacqueline raises an eyebrow and leans back in her chair laughing. She thinks it is so funny. Her cocoa brown skin turns red from all the laughing she is doing, and she seems to have forgotten my initial response. "Great. Finstein wants you to start shadowing him as soon as possible, and when the time comes, I will work with you on setting your curriculum to prepare you." Ms. Jacqueline stands up and gives me a hug.

My head is still reeling from the meeting with Ms. Jacqueline as I head to Bible study. It has been two months since I slept with Real. I asked God to forgive me for what I had done but it seems like it keeps popping up. GG does all that talking about forgiveness, but even though I have asked for it I am still tortured by what I did. I don't get this forgiveness stuff.

Pastor walks into the pulpit and begins his Bible study lesson. "Forgiveness," he starts off. As soon as the word leaves his mouth I laugh. I don't mean to, but the laughter starts before I can stop it. I silently excuse myself for the outburst as everyone at Bible study, including Pastor, pauses to look at me. GG taps my hand. "What is wrong with you, girl?" she whispers in my ear as Pastor begins talking again. Once again, God has put my thoughts and feelings on blast.

"There are several things you need to understand about forgiveness," Pastor continues. I take notes as I always do. He states that forgiveness is not something that can be tackled in one or two nights and that he will be focusing on forgiveness for the next four weeks. I had always figured forgiveness was a simple thing: you ask for it, receive it, and give it. But Pastor sets me right within the first five minutes of Bible study. He starts with the part of forgiveness that weighs heaviest on me. "How many people have asked for forgiveness, but you haven't forgiven yourself?" Pastor's words circle around in my head for the rest of Bible study. I haven't forgiven myself. I had decided not to. I had decided I would carry my sin around my neck like a Flavor Flav chain clock, always weighing me down and reminding me what time it is. It serves as a reminder of what I have done in my past and the fact that I never again want to be that person.

Pastor's words stay with me during the car ride home. Suddenly it hits me like a brick to the head. How can I move on and do better if I am not able to forgive myself and let go of the past? Maybe it is because hustling had been my life, and because of that I saw nothing wrong with it up until recently. Hustling was necessary for survival—a means to an end. Am I to be blamed because of my ignorance? Maybe not, but either way, the only way I am going to change my life is to forgive myself for the past.

It's not dark yet when I pull up at home. The sun seems to be sitting right in my neighborhood with a serene orange glow. After parking in the driveway and leaving my heels on the walkway, I walk over to my tree swing. It is a perfect summer night, with the sun still warming my skin and a soft breeze twirling through my hair. The swing came with the house, but I can count on one hand how often I have taken the time to enjoy it. I start to relax and let go more and more with every movement of the swing. As the sun sets, I begin to forgive myself of all my wrongdoing. I can visualize all my sins clearly like photos in my mind, and one by one they drop, slowly falling down, down, down like the sun descending on the horizon. This must be what Pastor meant. I feel every wrong I have done leaving me. The sun feels like a warm smile from God accepting me and giving me peace. I continue to swing, reveling in the quietness, the freeness, the bliss that is God's forgiveness.

"Beau," a voice startles me. I am so within myself that the voice seems to jolt me back into the world from somewhere else. I almost think it is God who has called out to me until I see Jason walking up the driveway. "Can we talk?" He stops in the middle of the driveway, hesitant to walk up for fear of what my reaction might be. In the two years since I bought my house he has never been so bold as to just pop up, but he has picked the perfect time to come.

"Yes," I finally answer him after a moment of just staring at him.

"I won't take long." He sits next to me and starts swinging. He still wears Sean John. I had introduced him to the fragrance and it was perfect on him. He looks the same, too. I hadn't looked directly at him in almost two years. He looks good, though. "I am sorry, Beaunifide. No, I am more than sorry for what I did to you...to us. I know without a doubt it was the worst and best mistake of my life." Jason stops swinging and looks over at me with his hazel eyes glowing in the semi-darkness. "I've met someone." Not exactly the words I was expecting, although I knew that he had someone. I had noticed him with her at church. I couldn't really tell what she looked like, but I had noticed her baby bump. I don't say anything. I don't know if he is expecting me to say something or not, but I don't.

"I can't move on with her, because I haven't forgiven myself for what I have done to you. Maybe that is because I don't know if you have forgiven me." He is right. Just like I had held on to my own unforgiveness, I had held tightly onto his, too.

"I forgave you." I look over at Jason, whose look of disbelief mixed with shock and amusement makes me smile.

"When?" His puzzled face turns serious. Yeah, I certainly hadn't been giving off the *all is forgiven* vibe.

"Just now." I laugh because it funny but true. As soon as he walked up I forgave him. Jason burst out laughing, too, a familiar sound that reminds me how much fun we used to have together.

"Thank you," Jason says. I feel the sincerity in his thanks. "I really love her, Beau. She is nothing like Keyona. More like you: intelligent, sophisticated, and independent. You know I never wanted to be with Keyona. It really was just a one-night stand." Jason had always tried to convince me that was the truth, and I believed him. As much as Keyona thought having a baby with him would make him want her, I am sure it did the opposite. I could never see Jason with some 'hood rat chick content with mediocrity, so I never doubted it was anything more than just a one-night thing. It was his betrayal that ruined us.

"I know." I pause and stop myself short of crying. I am relieved to finally let it go. I feel that letting him go is setting me free to move on and maybe someday find love like he has. My thoughts instantly turn to Real. Will I ever be free of him? Even though from here on out when I think of relationships I will not think of Jason, I feel as if Real will always be sitting in the back of my mind. You see, Jason was a choice, but Real was a desire—one that still marinates in my mind.

"Can I show you something?" Jason snaps me out of my thoughts again. I have once again drifted somewhere else. Not that place where I feel close to God, but a space where my thoughts of Real live.

"Alright," I agree to his request. The small velvet box seems to appear out of nowhere, and although I know exactly what it is, I wonder why he wants to show it to me. He must think we have quickly come to a place where I am okay with seeing the ring that should have been mine, and knowing that some other woman will be living the life that should have been mine. He opens the box and, even in the dark of night, I can see the four-karat ring shining. It is beautiful; good quality and well crafted. I know he is seeking my approval.

"I know you've always had an eye for these things." He takes the ring out and hands it to me so I can get a closer look. I don't want to see it, yet alone touch it, but I will for his benefit. Maybe this is the final sign he needs from me that I have really forgiven and let go of him. When I lift my hand to take the ring, my stomach begins to turn. I feel like I have just eaten the most awful thing ever and I immediately run into the house. The contents of my stomach spew from my mouth as I cradle the toilet. Once I've released the last bit of bile, I brush my teeth and wash my face before finally going back outside.

I don't know how long I have been gone and I almost hope it was long enough for him to have decided to leave, but there he sits, swinging back and forth. He must have put the ring back in his pocket because I don't see it in his hand.

"Beau, I am so sorry. This was stupid of me. I don't know what I was thinking showing you that ring. God. I should go," Jason apologizes insistently for being so callous.

"It's okay. I'm good. That's not why I felt sick," I say, although in my mind I'm not sure. "Let me see the ring." I stick out my hand.

"No, Beau. It's okay," he refuses, looking up to see if I am making the face I usually make when I won't be taking *no* for an answer, which I am. He pulls the ring out and hands it to me.

"It is lovely." I look back at Jason as I stand by a security light twirling the ring in my hand. "You went to Yasef." I smile as I place the ring back into its box. "He did beautiful work. Congratulations." My congrats leave my mouth before I can change my mind about it. I am honestly happy for Jason, but for some reason this makes my hopes of love and family seem further out of my grasp. I will not allow the thought of always being alone haunt me. I have to believe when the time is right I will find the one.

"Thank you," Jason whispers in my ear as he gives me a hug. He walks off into the night, leaving me standing alone as I usually find myself these days.

In my empty home full of only my thoughts and feelings, I talk to God as I prepare for bed. I had given myself away to two men that I would never have as my own and that is a mistake I will never make again. I feel like my life requires some drastic changes. Celibacy is now at the top of that list. It is one of the many things I will commit to, along with leaving my past behind me. "Ojala," I whisper—'God willing,' because I know it will only be with God's will that I can.

14
Pierced Hearts and Deaf Ears

Bella

"Bella, we just got back in town last night. Why are we going to church instead of going to bed?" Angel complains. Since our long talk back in July we have been getting it in every weekend and splitting the money 50/50. I was hesitant to let her hustle at first, but she practically begged me and I figured it couldn't hurt. Two months later, we are making money and we are closer than we have ever been. I mean, I was her age when I started hustling. She wanted to do it because she knew I was broke and she wanted to help me get back on top financially while setting herself up for the future, as well.

I want to make sure Angel has some type of normalcy. So, we still attend church on Sunday with GG, and during the week, Angel attends school and studies with a tutor. I don't know if Angel was just gassing us about having a difficult time in school or if she was really struggling, but once I found her a tutor, her grades shot up. She went from being a C student to an A student. I guess it didn't hurt that I gave her extra motivation. I threatened that the hustle would be over for her if she got anything less than a B plus.

I step out of the passenger side of Angel's Maserati in the church's parking lot and blow a falling leaf out of my face. School started up last week and I guess Beau gave Angel her car back. I don't know how that came to be. I didn't ask Angel too many questions about it, and I still haven't spoken to Beau's petty ass. Excuse me, I mean petty self. I try not to curse at church. Anyway, I am just as happy as Angel that she got her car back. The nonstop complaining about not having her car has finally ceased.

I check my pink lipstick in the car's side mirror. It is the first Sunday of the month and that means Caleb will be passing out communion today. Even though I have no interest in him or his playa ways, I like to flirt with him to piss his mother off. I don't know what pisses her off more; the fact that she knows I don't want him and flirt with him anyway, or the fact that if I did want him, I could easily have him. It doesn't really matter. It's all kicks and giggles to me. Besides, the first lady is going to talk about me anyway, so I might as well give her something to talk about. As the wife of the pastor, I'm supposed to be able to look up to her, learn from her example, and feel loved by her. Instead of embracing and uplifting me, she constantly tries to embarrass and belittle me. I'm tired of being hurt by the people in my life that I'm supposed to trust the most. So if I can find a way to get a rile out of her, I'm going to take it just like I take everything else I want in life.

"Because it makes GG happy," I answer Angel's question about why we are going to church. I put my lipstick in my purse and sashay inside. Out of the corner of my eye I can see Angel trying to imitate my walk. How cute. GG is sitting in the second pew. There are three open spots that she saved for us. "GG you know Beau's not coming, right?" I inform her. Beau goes to the 8 o'clock service to avoid Angel and me. GG would love nothing more than for all of us to go to church like one big happy family, especially after Beau refused to come for so many years. But we are not one big happy family. We are a family divided. Team Hustle versus Team Skank. Besides, I don't know what I might do if I see her again after she attacked me at that epic Sunday dinner.

"Well, she said she might come. That's my baby, too," GG beams over how much she loves Beau.

"Yeah, a baby brown bear." I roll my eyes and Angel snickers.

"No! Not today, Bella." GG slaps my hand for talking about Beau, the golden child. I rub my stinging hand. I can't believe GG just hit the back of my hand like I am a 2-year-old. I don't want to say anything sideways to GG, so I get up and walk out the sanctuary into the hallway. There are a handful of people in the hallway talking amongst themselves. I notice a few of them glaring at me and my form-fitting dress.

Near the restrooms, I see Caleb playing the role of a good son, standing next to his mother who is speaking to one of the mothers of the church. I go over and greet them. "Good Morning, First Lady," I say, grabbing hold of her hand. "You are working that dress." The first lady has a look of disgust on her face. She quickly pulls her hand back like she could catch a STD just from touching me.

"Yes, I'm blessed and dressed appropriately," she counters. She blinks her eyes unnaturally. See, I try to be nice but, once again, the first lady snubs me.

I snap back, "I could never wear something like that and pull it off. I would just look frumpy and unattractive. But you look wonderful in it." I turn and smile at Caleb. "And you, have a blessed day," I say to him in my best sex kitten voice. I lean in, pressing my cheek against his puckering my lips, making a loud smooching sound just to get another dig at his mother. Satisfied, I walk away.

I can hear the first lady say, "Quick, somebody pour some holy water on my hand where that harlot touched me before I burn in hell."

"Hold on, I think I got some in my pocketbook," the mother giggles.

"Caleb, you come here, too," First Lady says. "Let me sprinkle your cheek."

I take my phone out to text Angel and see that Caleb has just texted me:

Have you ever had a quickie in a church bathroom?

I rub the tears out of my eyes and pull my hair back with my hand. I can't stand to be around these hypocrites another second. I know I do my dirt and I'm not right with God, but at least I don't pretend to be holier than thou. I don't belong here and I feel ostracized. Even GG is checking for Beau over me. For the past five years I've been the one coming to church all along when Beau wouldn't. But I get no credit for that. Even if I am only coming for GG's benefit, at least I'm here. I guess Beau is the prodigal child and I ain't shit. I text Angel from the bathroom: **Caleb is talking nasty to me and First Lady is talking shit. Let's go. I'm waiting in the bathroom.**

While waiting for Angel to come, Caleb messages me again: **Do you think I can make you scream in tongues? :p #Hallelujah.**

GG bursts into the bathroom, startling me so badly, I almost drop my phone. "You are not going anywhere, young lady. Get your behind in there and sit down," GG scolds. GG can't just be punking me like I'm some little kid or something.

"How do you know I want to leave?" I demand. She had to be going through Angel's phone.

"It popped up on Angel's phone. She left it on the pew," she admits. I knew it.

"GG, I'm ready to go. I'm tired and don't feel well. At least I showed up unlike some of your grandchildren," I complain.

GG looks me in the eyes. "You both need to end this feud you got going on. Both of y'all hard-headed and stubborn." It hurts her that Beau and I still haven't made up yet. I can hear the pain in her voice. To be honest, I don't know if I can forgive Beau. She left me for broke when

I needed her most. "And ain't nothing wrong with you, either," GG says. "You ain't sick. You just mad because I slapped you and First Lady said something slick to you. Baby, I'm sorry. I shouldn't of put them paws on you like that. Don't you worry about Lady Lewis, neither. Let your GG take care of it. Come on, baby. Let's go and get this word. Lawd knows you need it." GG gently grabs me by the hand and leads me back into the sanctuary.

I don't know what GG said to First Lady, but she avoids looking my way the entire church service. I know it has to be hard for her too, because from where she is sitting in the pulpit, I am in her direct line of sight.

The choir begins to sing and I find myself being moved by their voices. As long as I've been coming to this church I have never been moved like this. Typically I feel nothing when the choir sings. I usually just sit, thinking about the hustle I did the night before and how I'll spend the money I made. But this time, something comes over me. The choir does their thang and while listening to them sing, I temporally forget about how much I don't like First Lady and how upset I am with Beau. The songs they sing are up-tempo and uplifting. I'm so moved that I can't help but to stand and sway with the crowd. I still don't care for God, but I believe I can benefit from listening to something more uplifting.

The band starts playing the melody of the fourth song, and I raise my hands, ready to receive the message the choir is about to sing. Then Caleb walks out to the front of the choir with a mic in his hand, ready to sing the lead. He looks at me in a seductive way like he is about to sing me a love song instead of a song for Jesus. I drop my hands and try to keep from dropping my jaw. I lean over and whisper in Angel's ear. "Caleb has been texting me about poking me in the baptismal pool and trying to get me wetter than holy water and now they letting him lead praise and worship." Angel snickers and GG cuts her a sharp look that says *if I was closer to you I would backhand you.* To play it off, Angel cries "Hallelujah!" and does a little praise dance. She pumps her right arm back and forth like a chicken wing and moves her legs up and down like she is trying to step onto a roach. In all her foolishness, she bumps into the lady standing next to her, almost knocking her down.

GG reaches over me and clutches Angel's arm. "Stop playing with the Lawd, girl." Finally, Caleb stops squawking and the church choir retires. Pastor Lewis takes his place in the pulpit and begins this week's sermon, titled Victim Mentality.

I sit in the pew, feeling convicted as he preaches. "You are not a victim. How can you be a victim when you were made in the image of God? The hole you feel in your heart, that emptiness is an illusion by the enemy. As a child of God, it is impossible for you to have emptiness because God fills your heart with his love. But you don't recognize that love. Instead, you try to fill that emptiness that you think you have with materialistic things. But ah, things can't buy you love, and they sho' can't get you in good with Jesus. You have to learn to search for that love already inside of you by developing a relationship with God. I'm here to tell you the truth. And the truth is, God loves you and you lack nothing. So what momma wasn't there? So what you never knew your father? You can't use that as an excuse for bad decision-making. And you certainly can't use it as an excuse to push God away. God knows you. God is always there, whether you choose to acknowledge Him or not. At some point you have to stop playing the victim and start being victorious the way God created you!"

I hear Pastor loud and clear, but I'm not ready to give up the hustle. I still have to earn back what God let be taken from me. One day I may get right with God, just not today.

117

15
Rule Number Two

Beau

The summer session is over. It was easy for me and, of course, I ranked in the top ten percent of my class. The school gave us a break the last two weeks of August before starting classes again for the fall semester. But for some reason, by the beginning of the fall semester, I feel horrible. The fact that Bella and I haven't spoken in four months isn't sitting well with me.

Before our last fight at Sunday dinner, the longest I have gone without talking to my sister was the four days after our first fight when I threw her wine glass. Bella and I talked and were together so much that we were inseparable, but that had changed. I accidentally started to call her a couple of times when something funny or interesting happened. I even intentionally dialed her number once, but hung up before it rang.

Honestly, I think my issues with Bella are the source of my stress. My periods have become irregular. Starting in June I went from a normal five-day cycle to two days. I had some light spotting in July and my cycle never showed up in August. Even my appetite has changed. I love to eat and cook, but for some reason I don't have much of an appetite, not even for some of my favorite foods, like parmesan chicken. Just the smell of it makes me sick now. I wake up almost every day with a migraine and am so nauseated that I don't even want to drink water.

Enough is enough. After my period didn't show up for September, I made an appointment to see my doctor. I usually only go to the doctor once a year in November for my annual pap and physical, so Dr. Leon is surprised to see me. I have been going to Dr. Leon since I was a kid. He is a family practitioner, so he saw all of us; my dad, Bella, and me. We start with our usual conversation about what is going on in our lives. Dr. Leon asks me how law school is going, and then we get into why I am there. I tell him how I am feeling and his first thought is stress.

"Stress can cause irregular cycles and, depending on how you deal with stress, loss of appetite, migraines, and even weight loss can occur. You've lost eight pounds. Beau, with the demands of law school I am going with stress as the cause of your symptoms, but I am going to get a urine and blood sample just to make sure," Dr. Leon explains. After taking the blood sample, he hands me a cup and points to the bathroom.

Peeing is easy. I probably could have filled a couple of cups. Something else that has been odd about me in the past couple of months is constantly needing to pee. I leave the cup and go back into the room.

I start to feel cold waiting in the room for Dr. Leon. It seems like he is taking forever to get back. I've read every poster and pamphlet in the office while waiting, and am glad when he finally returns. "Hey, Doc," I smile as he enters. "So, I've been thinking, I know you probably want to prescribe some type of meds but I really don't like taking them." Dr. Leon isn't smiling. In fact he looks like he is sick. I begin to grow genuinely afraid as he stares down at some papers in his hands in silence. *Oh my God, what is wrong with me?* I think to myself. He looks like he is about to tell me I am dying.

"You're pregnant, Beau." Dr. Leon finally looks up at me. I instantly feel sick to my stomach and run to the bathroom. I know he didn't say what I think he said. I can't be pregnant. I don't even have sex. I haven't had sex since...Real. I scream and then begin to cry uncontrollably.

I can hear Dr. Leon and some other voices knocking at the door and asking if I am okay. "Hell nah, I am not okay!" I scream through the door. An hour ago I was stressed now I am pregnant. When I finally come out of the bathroom, Dr. Leon and three nurses are waiting in the room. "This has to be mistake!" I yell. "Dr. Leon, I need to take another test."

"Please calm down, Boofide," one of the nurses says, butchering my name.

"Who are you?" I ask, mean mugging the nurse. "Who is she?" I ask annoyed, turning to Dr. Leon.

"I tested your urine and then your blood. Beau, you are pregnant. From what you told me about your cycle the past few months, you could be as far along as three or four months. I would like to do an ultrasound just to make sure everything is okay with the baby. Everything will be alright, Beau." Dr. Leon places his hand on my shoulder.

I feel my hair sticking to the back of my neck and sweat dripping down my face. I place my face in my hands and close my eyes. I haven't cried in so long that I don't know if it is tears or sweat that I am feeling on my hands until I take a deep breath and release a sob. I am pregnant and it is Israel's. I am four months along. I don't need an ultrasound to tell me that the last time I had sex was in May. I rub my hand over my belly. It feels the same to me. I look at it and it looks the same, too. I don't know how I can be four months pregnant and my stomach is still so flat. With all the migraines and nausea, how could I not have noticed what is going on with me? Kids are nowhere in my plans right now. My plan is to finish law school, go into private practice, and make money. Then maybe find a man—the professional type, like a financial analyst— move to Brooklyn, New York, live in a brownstone, and travel the world.

Dr. Leon finally comes back with an ultrasound technician. Shit just got real, real quick. I've gone from having headaches and loss of appetite from stress to being four months pregnant and meeting my baby. *My baby*. The words just sound so surreal. I lift up my shirt and roll down my pants. The technician explains how the process will work and that if I want, we may be able to tell the sex of the baby. While the technician is preparing, Dr. Leon starts discussing my options.

"Based on what we know, abortion is not an option," Dr. Leon explains.

"It never was anyway." I shake my head then finally lower it. "Adoption isn't an option, either." I am going to be a mother.

The technician places some type of gel on my belly and begins rolling a small device around my stomach. "There," she finally says, and looks at me like I am supposed to know what she is talking about. And then I hear it; this rapid thumping sound, going what seems like a mile a minute. I look at the computer screen and see a tiny little body. I can definitely tell it is a baby. At this moment it all becomes so real to me. There is a real little person inside of me. I am seeing my baby and hearing its heartbeat for the first time. "Hold on," the technician says, moving the machine over my belly again. I hear more rapid thumping and look at the computer monitor with concern. "Is that normal?" I ask. The technician continues to move the device around my stomach as I stare at the screen confused.

The technician looks at me with a nervous smile. "I see what looks like another little hand reaching from behind." She points to the screen.

"Twins," everyone simultaneously says.

"Oh my God!" I scream out.

"Is there a history of twins in either yours or the father's family?" Dr. Leon asks.

"The father is a twin," I answer.

The tech snaps pictures and takes measurements. She presses down on my belly and we can see the babies squirm. "I am pretty small for four months and two babies." I start to panic. "Is that normal? Is everything okay?" Dr. Leon and the tech are quietly staring at the screen.

"They look perfect," the tech says, "They are both measuring at around 12 or 13 weeks, which is normal. Twins usually measure a little small."

"Right now your due date is March 12th," says Dr. Leon. "Twins usually come early, so we will just monitor you closely as time goes by." He gives me a fatherly smile and asks me if I am okay for like the millionth time in the past hour.

My answer is the same. "No, Doc." I smile nervously. I haven't had a moment to process anything.

"Would you like to know their sexes?" the technician asks with a smile. I can tell this is her favorite part of the job.

"Why not? What's one more surprise?"

"Okay, baby A is the one up front. Let's see." The technician pauses as she moves the little machine around my belly.

"Baby A is a girl." She then starts pushing on my stomach with her cold hands. "Trying to get the babies to switch positions," she informs me. Sure enough, baby A starts squirming again and switches positions with baby B. At first all we can see is baby B's butt mooning us, but the technician is persistent, and within a couple minutes baby B turns around. "It's a boy!" The technician excitedly says, pointing out my son's penis on the screen. A boy and a girl. Wow.

After asking me 30 more times if I am okay, Dr. Leon writes me a prescription for prenatal vitamins and an iron supplement. He tells me that my body will begin going through some changes very quickly, most notably weight gain. After setting my next appointment, I am free to leave. I am going to have to put all of the beef aside and call Bella. There is no way I can do this on my own, and she is the first person I want to tell.

I take the long way home to allow myself some time to think. I am still reluctant to call Bella, but by the time I turn into my community, I'm grabbing my phone out of my purse. It is a beautiful afternoon and my street is full of beautiful homes with beautiful yards and kids outside playing. This will be a great neighborhood to raise kids in and my house is more than big enough. I guess in some crazy way I somehow intuitively chose to live in the 'burbs, buy a big house, and have it paid off quickly because I knew one day I'd have a family.

I stop just short of my house when I notice the garage door is up. I know I didn't leave it open. I never do, and even if I had, it is set to close on a timer as long as no objects are in the way. My first thought is that someone has broken into my house. I couldn't care less about the material things in there, but I don't like feeling violated. Man, what else can go wrong today? I dial Bella's number and before I hit the call button, I see Angel's Maserati easing out of the garage with her ass in it. Angel looks me dead in my face and continues down the driveway.

I drop the phone. Bella has to be in on it. She is the only other person with a key to my house. This heifa' Angel has the nerve to ride up slowly on me and smile that devious Jones smile before she speeds off without saying a word. You know what? If Angel wants to ruin her life before it starts and Bella is down for it, forget them both. And if GG is so blinded by love that she can't see their faults, then so be it. I got much bigger things to prepare for and I know for sure I can't be stressing about anything now. I have to prepare for the biggest thing that will ever happen in my life, and, I guess, prepare for a lifetime of being hustled. I laugh to myself. Daddy always called Bella and I his only hustlers. He said we were the only people that could get absolutely anything out of him. Now it's my turn to get hustled.

16
Don't Let Your Past Ruin Your Future

Bella

I walk across the tarmac, rolling my small Louis Vuitton suitcase behind me. We are in the last couple of weeks of September, but it still feels like summer. It's a beautiful Saturday morning. I stop walking to let Angel catch up to me before I board the private jet. My legs are longer than hers, so I walk faster. I don't want to board the plane before Angel, because the owner of the jet is her connect. I want the first face they see to be of someone they know, so they won't go berserk when they see a random stranger walk onto their plane.

"Hermana, get on the plane," Angel urges.

"You first. I don't know these people," I tell her. I step to the side and let Angel take the lead. Angel and I hand our luggage to the flight crew. While Angel trudges up the stairs to the jet, I take a good look at it. It is one of the smaller ones, but I can tell from the outside that it is a top-of-the-line luxury jet. It looks like a Learjet and it's jet-black trimmed in rose gold. I wonder who the owner is and why I don't know them. I take it upon myself to know who all the power players in Indianapolis are, but apparently I missed one. I walk up the steps and, as I look inside, I think to myself that I need one of these in my life.

The jet is laid out nicely—even better than my penthouse condo. It is empty except for Angel and me. The owners aren't here yet. I walk to the handcrafted black leather sofa and make myself comfortable. I pull off my Jimmy Choos, kick my feet up, and adjust the little diamond shaped pillow so it lays with the curve of my back. The pillows are the same color as the trimming on the jet. The sofa is placed against the right wall of the cabin and across from it, against the other wall, are two oversized matching black leather recliners. Angel sits in the chair nearest to the door, swiveling back and forth. She pushes a button on the wall, which raises the black wooden venetian blinds hanging over the windows behind the sofa and chair. Between the recliners is a mahogany wooden table. In fact, the mahogany wood trims the entire cabin, adding an extra taste of elegance to the interior of the jet. Angel pushes another button on the table and a small double-sided TV monitor facing in her direction emerges from the edge of the table. I can see the slots where the other TV monitors will emerge so that each passenger can view their own personal screen.

"Girl, stop before you push a button that ejects us out the roof of the plane," I yell at Angel. She completely disregards me and pushes another button anyway. A retractable door slides back, revealing a player ass window in the roof of the jet. I didn't even know jets could have moon roofs. I sit straight up and we look through the moon roof in awe.

"See kid, stick with me and I'll have you going places," Angel says. She is feeling really proud that she arranged for a private jet to fly us to our next hustle in Los Angeles. It's not like I don't know anyone who owns or at least has a timeshare in a private jet. It's just that all those people are men who want to screw me and they would follow me like a puppy dog the entire weekend, blowing my hustle.

I absolutely hate flying to the West Coast because there are few flights that fly directly from Nap. There is almost always a long layover. Still, we need a change of scenery. We have been doing hustles nonstop every weekend along the East Coast. It's bad business to keep hitting up the same region back to back. It increases our likelihood of getting caught up.

Angel just happens to have a friend from school that owns a private jet, and she just happens to be going to Los Angeles the same weekend we are. I really don't think that it's a coincidence. I think Angel used her power of persuasion. However, I have a habit of not asking questions I don't really want to know the answerer to, so I can't say for sure. As long as she follows the rules and sticks to the plan, I don't care. This will be a 24-hour trip. When we arrive in L.A., Angel's friend will go handle her business, and we will go handle ours. Then we will meet up Sunday morning and fly back to Nap. We get in, we get money, we get out. And best part of it all is no TSA agents. Bada-bing. Bada-bam. Bada-boom.

I realize how much easier a private jet will make it to get in and out of cities discreetly and quickly. Beau and I should have put our money together and invested in a private jet a long time ago. I guess we had other financial priorities. Beau's priority was getting money for law school. Mine was purchasing my condo so I'd always have stability, and I even fucked that up because my condo is not fully paid for and I could lose it as soon as I fall behind on my payments. If I hadn't let my guard down and let myself get hustled out of one million cash, I wouldn't have cared so much that Beau quit and I would have no worries about making payments on my mortgage. However, I'm done beating myself up over it. I can't live in the past. I have to live in the moment and in this moment I have no worries. In this moment I'm moving forward to rebuild my financial security. In this moment I choose to be happy. I take a deep breath and exhale. I take in all the luxury that surrounds me. I relax and gaze at the sky through the moon roof.

"Kylie!" I hear Angel announce excitedly. I sit up and look over my shoulder. Angel jumps up and hugs a girl with long blonde curls. The blonde girl, Kylie, is about an inch taller than Angel. She is white but not pasty or pale. She has a little bit of color to her and striking blue eyes that I've seen somewhere before. I try to recall if I've ever seen her at the condo hanging out with Angel. A familiar-looking gorgeous man with short blonde curls enters the plane. He has the same striking blue eyes as Kylie.

"Oh, wow!" he exclaims, "The S. Pellegrino spokes model is on my jet." And then it hits me; it is the man I blew off at the restaurant in Chicago a few months ago. I feel butterflies in my stomach. Unlike when I first met him, I am no longer fixated with my money and men issues. I recognize him clearly. Oh, how stupid of me to let him slip away. I won't make the same mistake twice.

"Hi, Brian," Angel says with a hint of flirtation in her voice. I can't be mad at her for that. He is Brian Rose, heir to Ethan Rose and Company, a world-renowned, multi-billion-dollar pharmaceutical corporation founded and headquartered in Indianapolis. And he is some serious eye candy.

My eyes stay fixed on Brian as he politely smiles and gives Angel an innocent hug. He sits on the sofa next to me.

"Do you remember me?" he asks. Oh, I sure do. I feel embarrassed. I remember how mean I was to him and how I left him with the tab.

"Yeah, you're the obnoxious man that just wouldn't leave me alone," I say, trying to play it cool. After how I played him Chicago when I didn't know who he was, I can't now act thirsty just because I'm on his jet. He stares deeply into my eyes. I can feel Kylie and Angel looking at us.

"You want to know what I find remarkable?" he asks. He pauses as if he was waiting for my reply. I am lost in his eyes and don't attempt to reply. "I find it remarkable how amazingly rude you are. You are flying on a top-of-the-line jet for free and you can't find it in yourself to play nice."

Did he just throw me some shade? Yeah, he did. I can hear Angel laughing at me. Angel and Kylie take their seats in the reclining chairs and chit-chat about whatever the hell teenagers chit-chat about.

He is so fine. I wonder if there is such a thing as love at second sight. I want to kiss his luscious lips right then and there. Instead, I act like a lady, even though I want to let loose my inner slut.

"I apologize for being rude that day," I tell him. "I was having a bad day." It had to be a really bad day for me not to recognize a billionaire sitting right in my face. I can't say that I wouldn't have still been rude to him, but I wouldn't have tossed his business card out. Now I'm looking stupid, sitting on this man's plane and smiling in his face. I wish I could have a do-over of our first meeting, but what is done is done. I'm living in the moment. I can't change the past, so I might as well make light of it.

"You owe me an apology, too," I joke, "for me being rude to you." Brian appears confused as he looks at me awaiting an explanation. In a snarky tone I tease, "If you knew how to take a hint then I wouldn't have had to be so amazingly rude. Oh, and by the way, your plane is not top-of-the-line. It's one of the smallest that Learjet makes. If I was you I would've went for the 60 XR so we wouldn't have to be so cramped in this small space. But, hey, I guess I just have higher standards."

Brian chuckles. "Actually, I have a 60 XR, too. And I'm sorry I came on too strong when we first met. It's just that I didn't want to let you slip away. When you left the restaurant I was kicking myself because I thought I'd missed the chance to get to know you. I didn't think I would ever see you again."

"I accept your apology. I was feeling sad that day because I just got rejected from a modeling gig. I guess I took it kind of hard."

We talk about a little bit of everything. I've never encountered a man like him. He is clever and funny. He is a little corny, but I like it. From our conversation and the way he talks, he sounds like he is a Christian and has a deep love for God. Most of all, he seems to be sincerely interested in me for me and not for what's between my legs, but only time will tell his true intentions. As great as Brian may be, I don't know if I can actually get serious about him. Not after what my ex-boyfriend, Lorenzo, did to me. I lay my head on his shoulder. Although I am feeling Brian and enjoying his company, I can't stop thinking about the way my last relationship ended.

Lorenzo wasn't *drop my panties* fine like Brian, but he had a certain stature that demanded attention. Don't get me wrong; he didn't look like his parents had to tie a pork chop around his neck to get the family dog to play with him. I'm just saying he wouldn't win the award for most gorgeous man on the planet.

During some of our late night phone conversations at the beginning of the relationship, Lorenzo revealed that he was Italian and black like me. Just by looking at him you couldn't tell that he had any black in him. Unlike me, he was born in Italy and moved to the United States when he was a child. Standing two inches shorter than me, he was never self-conscious about me wearing heels when we were together. In fact, he loved the way my legs looked in heels.

Lorenzo had a lot of 'onlys' under his belt. He was the only person I could really connect with that understood what it's like to be bi-racial living in the Midwest. In this day and age you would think race was a non-issue, but apparently I'm not white enough to be white and not black enough to be black. On top of that, since I'm Italian I'm not really white, but I'm not really Italian either, because I'm black and wasn't born in Italy. Other people's perceptions of how I should "classify" myself are enough to make my head spin. Lorenzo understood the plight of being bi-racial and we would trade stories of our childhoods. My childhood was full of ignorant foolish people that would call me a mutt and try to fight me for no reason other than being bi-racial. Beau was always right by my side to help me fight, but there was no way she could understand what I was going through. She's not bi-racial and she had a choice to stand by my side and fight. I didn't have a choice. I was attacked and it was either fight or get beaten. We pretty much stayed to ourselves and were each others' only friends. Lorenzo had a similar childhood dealing with bullies.

He was the only man I have ever been in serious relationship with. I dated here and there, but I never saw the point of fully committing to someone that I had no plans on marrying. It's like playing pretend. I'm not about to play house with someone who can just leave me on a whim. I think people take commitment way too lightly, especially after seeing what happened with Beau and her ex and how my dad cheated on my mom. I was cool on commitment, until I met Lorenzo. We also bonded over the fact that we both lost our mothers at a young age. His mother

129

died giving birth to him. His Italian father raised him on his own just like my daddy did.

Lorenzo was also the only man that has come close to getting my panties. I've kept my virginity for a reason. It is one of the few things in this world that I have absolute control over. If so many guys want it, it must be special. No one is going to take my virginity until I'm good and ready. I'm not necessarily waiting for marriage, but you will have to be one extraordinary man to get it.

And lastly, Lorenzo is the only man to deceive me to the extent that he did and hustle me out of my own money. I can't believe I fell in love with a complete scumbag. I was with Lorenzo for almost a year, and while we were together, he was amazing. He never once pressured me into having sex and no two days with him were the same. One day we'd be wine tasting in Napa Valley and the next day we would be flying on his private jet to go horseback riding in Montana. He took me places where I never thought to go. Beau knew about him, but I never told her how serious we were. She just thought he was another one of my randoms that I kept in rotation. She didn't really care for him, even though she never had a real reason to dislike him. She would just always say there was something about him that was off. Well, she was right, but there is no way in hell I'm going to tell her that.

The entire time we were together he presented himself as a successful self-made businessman that owned multiple commercial real estate properties around the city. Turns out he is a made man, just not self-made. He was made by the Mafia. Shit got a little shaky for him in New York so he fled to Indiana until things quieted down. Law enforcement somehow caught wind of his whereabouts and arrested him. Well, that's a light way of explaining how our love story ended. The details of how it really went down are far more humiliating and damn near ruined me. I feel stupid that I missed all the major red flags. He would fly me around the country, probably to elude the police, but never once would take me to meet his family. For days I wouldn't hear from him. We never went out in public unless he arranged beforehand to have it private and secluded. Shit, I thought he was being romantic. And, to top it all off, he refused to be photographed.

A couple of weeks before I hustled Clifford's sleep apnea having ass, I entered into what I thought was a business partnership that would change my life for the better. Lorenzo and I partnered up in a residential real estate investment. We were going to buy up a bunch of old and condemned houses in the inner city, flip them, beautify and increase police presence in the neighborhood, and watch the money roll in. Since he was so successful in commercial real estate, it seemed like a no-brainer, and I handed him one million dollars as my part of the investment. I would be helping my city by creating new and safe housing, I would be establishing a future with the man I loved, and I would be making my own money legally. Despite not being married, it was the perfect exit strategy from the hustle.

A week and a half after I made my investment, I decided it was time that I gave him all of me. I was spending the night at his house like I often did. I loved going to his house. He had this huge multi-million-dollar estate hidden away in a gated community right off of 86th and Springmill Road. No one would ever find this neighborhood unless they already knew it was there. The neighboring communities were filled with regular houses and middle class families. It was exciting to be in a hidden gem. Lorenzo's master bedroom was on the first level. That bedroom is where the few pieces that were left of my heart were completely shattered.

We were lying on his king-sized bed butt naked in the heat of passion. The room was dimly lit by candles, giving off a sensual vibe. Our clothes were scattered around the room. Lorenzo's tongue swirled around the tip of my left nipple while he gently squeezed the right one. His hands and mouth felt like magic on my body. I could feel the wetness flowing from between my legs, dripping onto the comforter. This was it. I was finally ready to give up my virginity. My hand gripped his penis to guide him inside of me.

Boom! Police kicked open the door. I wanted to run and hide, but the police wouldn't even allow me to get under the comforter to cover myself up. They told me to keep my hands up where they could see them for 'officer safety.' Not a single officer in that room was looking at my damn hands. That's how I learned Lorenzo was involved in the Mafia.

Finally, after the police secured Lorenzo into handcuffs, they let me cover up, but I wasn't free to leave. They temporarily detained me at Lorenzo's house for questioning and bombarded me with non-stop questions. "Are you Marcello's wife? Oh, you don't know who Marcello is? You were just in the bed with him. How can you not know who he is? You thought his name was Lorenzo? No, his name is not Lorenzo; it's Marcello. Is Lorenzo the name he has been using to hide his identity for the last 11 months? I'm going to go out on a limb here and say you are not his wife? Ma'am, I need you to calm down; can you do that for me?"

Lorenzo...Marcello...whatever the hell his name is posted bond the next day and fled to his home country, Italy, with his wife, children, and my motherfuckin' one million dollars. Got damn it, that son-of-a-bologna-eatin'-bitch. I knew nothing about this man. He played me so far left it was right. I can overlook that fact that he lied to me about being in the Mafia. I can overlook the fact that he has children. What I cannot get past is the fact that he stole my money and is a married man. No wonder he wasn't tripping about me holding out on sex; he was getting it from his wife.

Oh yeah, and he wasn't even black! He lied about that, too. He knew all the right words to say to me to pull me in emotionally and financially. He sold me dreams then crushed them right before my eyes. I thought we had a future together. I wasn't his main chick. I was the mistress and I didn't even know it. That made me feel like I'm no better than my deadbeat egg donor, Sofia, for sleeping with a married man. Every day I strive to be a better human being than she could've ever been. That's why I don't do drugs and I'm still a virgin. But there I was, ready to give him my body, and risk disease and pregnancy for a man whose name I didn't even know. That's the type of shit Sophia would do. The only difference between me and her, is I didn't have an unwanted child and then dump her. Fuck Sophia and fuck Lorenzo. *Leave the past in the past*, I tell myself.

I feel a gentle nudge on my side as Brian pokes me with his finger.

"Bella are you asleep?"

"No."

"Yes, you were. I can't believe you fell asleep in the middle of our conversation," Brian laughs.

"I didn't fall asleep. I was just resting my eyes." Oh my gosh. I hope I don't have dried up drool on my face.

"You were talking in your sleep. Who's the bologna-eating son-of-a-bleep?" Brian raises his eyebrows.

My only response is to laugh. The flight attendant brings us some food: baked chicken, vegetables, and a croissant. I nibble on the croissant. I just woke up so I'm not all that hungry. Then something tells me to look out the window. I raise the blinds and look down. What I see is absolutely glorious.

"We're crossing the Rocky Mountains," Brian informs me. The mountains are almost completely white with snow, with little patches of grey underneath. I think to myself, *this is so amazing only God could have created this.* How can anyone look at something as magnificent as these mountains and not know there is a God? I'm so overwhelmed by the feeling of God's presence that I decide to do something I never do; I pray.

Um, God, it's me, Bella Jones. I'm not sure if you know who I am or even if you care. I'm not a prayer warrior like GG so I'm not even sure if I'm doing this right. We haven't been on the best of terms, but um, let's make deal. I know I do my dirt and all but maybe I can change. I just don't know how. So uh, please help me get over Lorenzo. Heal my heart so I can open it up to Brian if he's the man for me. If he's not the man for me, take Brian out of my life immediately and bring my husband to me. I really want Brian to be the one, though. If you can do this one thing for me I will know you really do care for me and I will change. I can't promise to be like GG, but I'll never hustle illegally again. Um, that's all. Amen.

17
Wifey, Baby Mama, Mistress by Any Other Name

Beau

No sooner than I found out I was pregnant with the twins, they wanted to make themselves known to the world. It feels like overnight my belly started poking out and my breasts got bigger, but thank goodness my ass hasn't gotten much bigger. I continue to rock dresses and pumps, but I am feeling more drained, tired, and hungry, as can be expected. So much has changed. I have become something of a recluse, only leaving to go to school or do some occasional shopping for stuff for the twins. I even stopped going to church. I already switched from the 11 o'clock service to the 8 o'clock one to avoid GG and my sisters, but once I started showing I stopped going all together. School is fine, though. I am doing well with my studying and class work. But I know it will only be a matter of time before gossip about my baby bump reaches the dean and academic advisors. Then I will be seen as the stereotypical black girl: young, pregnant, and unwed. I have chosen not to bring up my pregnancy to anyone at school, not even Ms. Jacqueline. Even if it is staring them in the face, I will just wait until someone says something.

I am due the first week of March, which is close enough to spring break that if all goes well, I can take off that whole month and technically only miss two weeks of class. I have thought about a nanny, too. I figure that within the next month or two I will start interviewing for the job. I think about GG. I know she would take great care of the twins and I would love for my babies to be taken care of by her. However, for the whole spring, summer, and now fall, I haven't really spoken to GG. I haven't spoken to Bella or Angel at all. I don't know if stubbornness is a symptom of pregnancy, but I was already stubborn before and now it seems like every little thing gets on my nerves. I don't want to deal with the smallest amount of foolishness, and that includes Bella, Angel, and their antics. I'm still annoyed that they stole Angel's car back. They were doing all that talking about me being a hypocrite and not consulting with them before I took Angel's car, but look who the hypocrites are now, because they sho' didn't consult with me.

About a week after my birthday, just before Thanksgiving, I finally receive an email from the law school dean to meet in his office. By now I am definitely showing. Ain't no hiding the fact that I'm pregnant. I wear a black dress, black tights, and some flat black knee boots. My hair is pulled back into a ponytail and I am carrying a small black briefcase. I have the law school rules and regulations where I highlighted the no discrimination clause and case law from a law student that sued a law school in conservative Texas when they tried to persuade and coerce her to drop out when she got pregnant. I have also written out a plan of action of how I can and will continue to keep up with my studies even though I will need to take between four to six weeks off after the twins are born.

"Have a seat, Ms. Jones," Dr. Spinx, the dean of the school, says as he closes the door behind me. I walk into the conference room where Dr. Spinx, Ms. Jacqueline, and Professor Jean Grand, my Criminal Law professor, are all sitting on one side of the conference table in front of me. I take a seat across from them and examine their faces. Ms. Jacqueline is smiling. Of course I know she's in my corner. Dr. Spinx is up in the air; he's looking over paperwork and I can't make heads or tails of whether he likes me or not. Professor Grand, on the other hand, I have been getting a bad vibe from all semester. I can feel her stare burning a hole through my forehead. She's not even trying to hide her discontent for me. She's upset that another student didn't get the judicial externship. There were only two spots and I got one of them. Of course she blames the black person. Isn't that how it usually goes? I am sure she felt there must have been some affirmative action need for minorities for me to be admitted into the school and get the externship. But I worked hard for it and I continue to stay on top of things.

"In light of your current situation, Ms. Jones, we called this meeting to discuss your future here," Dr. Spinx begins, peering down over his glasses at me. "Most of your professors speak very highly of you and we see that you did very well during the summer semester as well as the internship." Dr. Spinx looks at me and smiles.

"Thank you," I smile, confused about what is going on. I am expecting a lecture and some bull about taking a semester or two off. What I get is quite the opposite. Dr. Spinx and Ms. Jacqueline offer full support while Professor Grand is silent. Guess if ya' ain't got nothing nice to say...

"We know what you are capable of," Ms. Jacqueline smiles. "We can agree to allow you up to six weeks from physically being present in class after you give birth, as long as you keep up with all your required readings and any other assignments." I am sure Ms. Jacqueline advocated for me. Thank God for her.

"Thank you," I smile again. "I assure you I will continue to do well." I stand up and shake all of their hands.

"But you can be assured we will be keeping an eye on you," Professor Grand says. "We are committed to the success of the school as well as all present and future students. If you cannot be successful there are other students who will gladly take your spot."

Ms. Jacqueline asks me to stay a moment after the meeting. "You know you could have come to me, Beaunifide. I understand shit happens. Let me know if you need anything else." Ms. Jacqueline is the coolest woman I know.

"I will." I smile at her. God has placed her in the right position as my academic advisor to help me at law school and it is greatly appreciated. Having the babies is not going to interfere with law school or my career as an attorney. I am more determined than ever to succeed and become a great attorney. I leave the meeting feeling good about things.

As soon as I get home, I head to the twins' nursery to sit, as I often do. I find it peaceful. I had the nursery painted sky blue. It seems neutral enough for a boy and a girl, and it's my favorite color. I enjoy buying things for the twins. I even flew out to LA to shop at Bel Bambino, a trendy baby store where a lot of celebrities go for their little ones. I bought two cribs from the Pomelo Collection; dusty grey for my prince and light pink for my princess. I am set and ready for them to arrive. I have practically bought everything, and after each of my doctor appointments I hit up Baby Gap or Janie and Jack for clothes. Still, I know it will be hard doing it all alone and I pray to God so much about it. I know that if I tell my family they will totally be there for me. But I can't just call them and be like, *'Hey, how's it going? Miss you, and by the way, I am having twins in about three months.'* I feel some kind of way about my situation. I am pregnant by a guy I had a one-night stand with, who I was actually just supposed to rob. I am learning about giving things up to God. I had asked for forgiveness but I just can't let go.

I think about the situation all the time. I don't know how I am going to explain this to my children when they ask who their father is and why he doesn't want them. I will never tell Israel about the twins, even though it would be easy to find him. I have actually started watching basketball just to see him. I check for him in the Houston news and blogs. It all kind of makes me feel like a stalker, but I know it's the closest I'll get to him.

I wonder what the twins will look like. Hopefully my daughter will look like me; petite, chocolate, bow-legged, with my smile, of course. And my son, he can look just like his father. Hopefully they will both get my brains and his athleticism.

I love sitting in the babies' room. I sit in the rocking chair where I rock, rubbing my belly, and pray. I pray that my babies are healthy and strong. Mostly, though, I pray to God that I will be a good mother because I am scared. I can't even explain what exactly I am afraid of. I think I am scared of everything except loving them. I love them already. I am reminded of how much I love them every time I feel them move. When I rub, wash, or dress my belly I think of how much I love them. But I have absolutely no idea how to be a mother, and that terrifies me. It is not something I can plan or plot out. I will just have to go with it. The plush carpet tickles my feet. I can imagine them crawling on it and playing together. I am glad they will have each other like Bella and I had each other.

A knock on the door startles me. It is loud enough that I can hear it all the way upstairs. It is a quick, frantic-sounding knock. Whoever it is has come uninvited. I walk into my bedroom and grab my little .22 from between my pillows, making a mental note to find a new place to store it. I enter my walk-in closet and go into a small room where I have surveillance set up. At my door stands a very pregnant woman. I can't quite make out her face, but I can tell she has dark curly hair and is very fair-skinned. Her belly is poked out far, but her frame is still petite. I see and hear her bang on the door again and then she looks right up at the camera. I shake my head. It is Jason's girlfriend, wife, baby mama, or whoever she is to him. But why is she here?

I tuck my gun into my robe pocket and head downstairs. I open the door and stare at her. She is pretty and glowing. Her eyes immediately focus in on my baby bump.

"Oh my God!" she cries, with tears welling up in her eyes.

"See, I told you. That's her," a familiar ghetto voice calls out from the grey Tahoe parked in my driveway. It is darker than usual outside. Even the moon seems a darker shade of grey. I know it is Keyona in the car, and as I hear the door slam shut, I get into fight mode. I don't know about Little Ms. Perfect, but I can tell by Keyona's tone of voice that her ghetto self is ready to brawl.

"Bitch!" Ms. Perfect lunges at me with her hands stretched out towards my throat. I move to the left and watch as she trips on the threshold of the door, her curls bouncing wildly. I should let her fall. She is, after all, trying to hurt me even though she can obviously see that I am pregnant. But no, instead I stretch out my hands and grab Ms. Perfect's arms to try to catch her. Despite my good intentions, her downward trajectory pulls us both down. Ms. Perfect tries to break her fall with her hands. My knees hit the floor and pain quickly spreads up both my legs.

"Oh my God!" Keyona screams out, her eyes frantically darting between Ms. Perfect and me. I am sure this is not what she was expecting and I am definitely sure she wasn't expecting to see my belly full of life.

"I am fine. Don't touch me!" Ms. Perfect screams as she snatches away from me. I didn't notice I was still holding her arms. Her face is just as red as her hands, and she is shaking. Seriously, you show up on my doorstep in the middle of the night, you fall trying to choke me, and you are mad at me? Keyona just stands in the walkway, staring as Ms. Perfect leans on the door and catches her breath. Her red face is full of rage. She is looking at me like I am the devil, but for some reason I feel sorry for her. I don't know what lies Keyona has told her, but apparently it is enough for her to act crazy, disregarding any common sense she may have and, even worse, jeopardize the safety of her unborn child.

"Come in." I push the door all the way open. I need to make sure she is okay and call Jason. I will feel so bad if something happens to his baby. She hesitates for a moment and looks at me. Keyona stares from the walkway, still silent, eyes wide.

"I said I'm okay!" Ms. Perfect screams, rubbing her belly. She doesn't seem okay at all. I think she is further along than me, only because her belly seems to poke out a tad bit further than mine. I wonder what I would do if I were pregnant and thought my fiancé was cheating. Maybe I would lose all reason and snap, too.

"I am calling Jason." I start closing the door. I don't know what she or Keyona may try next, and I have no intentions on waiting at the door to find out. Ms. Perfect stares at me like she wants to kill me as I push the door closed.

"What would make you think I'd want to step foot in the home of my fiancé's whore?" Ms. Perfect begins at a whisper but is yelling by the time she gets to the word 'whore.' I'm tired of people disrespecting me. I haven't spoken to my own sister in months because she kept calling me ho, so I'm surely not about to take it from this chick. I slam the door in her face.

I stand staring at my door in disbelief as I listen to Ms. Perfect bang on the door screaming, "Whore, open the door and face me like a woman!" over and over again. She finally stops, and I debate whether or not I should open the door. Before I can decide what to do I hear a forceful knock and a deep voice announce he is the police. I don't know who called the police, but I'm relieved they are here to diffuse the situation. My pregnant body cannot handle any more drama, and I do not want to go into pre-term labor because of stress.

I immediately open the door and thank the officer for coming. "Officer, I'm so glad you are here."

The officer is consoling Ms. Perfect and has an angry expression on his face. "I don't know why you glad. I'm here to arrest your black ass." I am dumbfounded. He is a tall and dark, with an emphasis on dark, which makes his comment about my 'black ass' ironic. "Put your hands behind your back!" he barks at me. "You know the drill. I'm sure you've been through this before. How many times have you been arrested? Probably every month." He looks down at my belly. "Just a plain ol' pregnant thug. How many baby daddies you have. anyway? Now this white woman did things the right way. She got married before getting pregnant. You see that ring on her finger?" I look at the ring Jason had me examine before he proposed. "You thug-a-boos need to learn a thing or two on how to be a lady from a real woman. They know what they doing." I stand in shock as he rambles on about how great white women are. I thought ignorant people like Uncle Ruckus only existed in cartoons like *The Boondocks*. I can't believe people actually act like this for real. He grabs my arm.

"Wait! Why am I being arrested in my own home?"

He looks me dead in my eyes. "You don't live here. I'm arresting you for trespassing in this woman's home. The only way you could afford a nice house like this is if you were a drug dealer's main bitch or something. Why you here? What you trying to steal from these nice folks?"

I am so appalled by every word that comes out of his racist mouth. Here I am inside of my own home in a robe and nightgown, and he is seriously accusing me of breaking into someone else's house. I pull my arm away from him. "Hold up. I have proof I'm the owner. Let me go get you the deed." He grabs my arm again, squeezing it so tightly I'm sure it left a bruise.

"Now you going down for resisting arrest and criminal trespass. You don't pull away from me, girl." Furious, I shout in disbelief as he places the handcuffs around my wrists. He pats me down and finds my .22 in the pocket of my robe. "Bingo," he smiles, taunting me. "You are also going down for possession of a handgun without a permit. I hope you have a prior so I can charge you with a felony."

This man just assumes I'm a criminal and he's not even doing a proper investigation. My blood boils with rage. "This is racial profiling," I accuse him.

He and his back-up officer laugh. "You damn right. I don't like black people like you. I don't like you selling drugs and doing other illegal shit and bringing that drama to suburbs where me and my family lay our heads." He turns to Ms. Perfect. "Ms., I am sorry about this inconvenience. Please go on in the house and wait for your husband to get home." Ms. Perfect has a look of satisfaction on her face as the officer escorts me out my home in handcuffs. She stands in the doorway of my house, smiling as if she's just gotten the last laugh.

From the back of the police car, I watch them handcuff Keyona. I feel sorry for her being falsely arrested just like me, even though this is technically her fault for bringing that crazy white girl to my house. She is stupid for sticking around, especially after seeing how they treated me. If I would've known this black officer was going to be racist, I would have never answered my door in the first place. I know I don't have to talk to the police or answer my door. I may only be in my first year of law school, but I know my rights. I sit with my head hung low, embarrassed and pissed, contemplating how I'm going to get myself out of this situation as they cart me off to the county jail like a common criminal.

When I arrive at the county lockup, I'm thoroughly searched to the point I feel violated. About an hour later I have my Initial Hearing and finally get my one free phone call, which I use to call Ms. Jacqueline and ask her to bond me out. I pace back and forth in my cell, thinking about filing complaints and suing folks. My knees still hurt from falling on them, so after a while I finally sit down. God, who would have thought this is how my night would end? Just when I think things can't get any worse than being racially profiled and falsely arrested, Professor Grand strolls by my cell with several second-year law students. I know she does a criminal law clinic but what are the chances of her being here tonight? I bet she was there for my Initial Hearing and now she feels like she has ammunition to get me kicked out of the school. I can't hear anything she is saying to the other students, but the smug smile on her face as she points towards my holding cell explains it all. I feel like a caged wild animal on display being judged by each and every onlooker. I ignore the pain in my knees and again start pacing back and forth across the cell. Please let Ms. Jacqueline hurry up and get here. I begin to feel infuriated. All I know is when this is said and done I'm going to be paid, because I'm going to sue the mess out the Zionsville Police Department and the city of Zionsville.

18
How to Avoid Getting Caught Up

Bella

I sit on the couch in our Hyatt Hotel room in Toronto looking out the window. It's close to Thanksgiving and I watch as pedestrians hustle by bundled up in their coats and gloves. I have an awesome view that includes the CN tower. I wonder if we have time for dinner and drinks in the CN's rotating restaurant. I could really use a drink to get the sound of Angel's unending badgering out of my head. Angel has been werking— yes, werking with an E—every single one of my damn nerves ever since the Los Angeles trip.

"Hermana, what happened to putting la familia first?" she complains. "How many times will you ignore me for Brian? You'd rather be with Brian than make dinero?"

Gosh, all the questions. Yes, Brian and I have been spending a lot of time together since our Los Angeles trip back in September. Yes, I have haven't been hustling as much. Yes, Brian has become my priority. But that's what happens when you get involved with someone new. You have to spend time with your man to cultivate your relationship. How else can it grow from just dating to being married? Marriage is always the desired end game for me when it comes to dating.

As vain as it might sound, I always wanted to marry rich. I don't care about snubbing looks, snide remarks, or being called a gold digger. What girl dreams of marrying poor? Struggling to make ends meet? Surviving off of welfare to take care of her children? NONE. Call me a gold digger if you want, but I'm not marrying a broke dude. It's not all about the money, though. I don't want to be stuck in a loveless marriage, either. When I wake up in the morning and roll over to look at my husband, I want to be reminded how lucky I am to have married such an amazing man. I want love and money. That's where my true happiness lies and I refuse to settle; especially not after everything I've been through.

In Los Angeles, Brian did not want to part ways with me. Before the wheels of the jet hit the ground, he'd canceled his business meeting and asked me to spend the day with him. I couldn't turn him down. I

143

didn't want to. We could have done another hustle the next week, but how many times would I get the opportunity to have someone like Brian ask to spend the entire day with me? You just don't meet men like him every day, and I wanted to find out more about him. I was intrigued to see if he was a man of honor or just another dirt bag with a lot of money. So when he asked to spend the day with him, I didn't hesitate to say yes. I told him to give me a minute to cancel my "business meetings" as well. I pulled Angel to the side and told her what was up and she was livid that we weren't doing the hustle.

"If I'd known this was going to happen we could've flown coach," she said before taking her luggage and storming off with Kylie in tow.

If you are going to be in California you might as well do one of two things: go to the beach or go to Disneyland. Brian whisked me away on a helicopter to spend a day at Disneyland; just the two of us. Yeah, it might sound corny, but I found it sweet. Dinner and a movie would have been the typical thing to do, but I found it more romantic and magical walking hand in hand through the theme park.

I didn't see or hear from Angel until we boarded the jet to return to Nap. Brian was in communication with his sister, but Angel didn't want to talk to me. When we got home, she trudged straight to her room and slammed the door, giving me the silent treatment. I threatened to take the door off the hinges if she slammed it again, and do you know this heifa' had the audacity to open the door and slam it again? Yes, she tried me. I am a woman of my word, so I followed through on my threat by taking her bedroom door off the hinges. I broke my nail messing around with her and that damn door. The next morning I awoke to see she had put the door back up in defiance. I really wasn't trying to have an all-out war with another sister, so I ignored her defiance and made a peace offering to go get mani-pedis since both our nails were jacked up. We talked it out and everything was all good between us until I had to cancel another hustle…then another, and another. To say Angel wasn't happy would be a huge understatement. So when Angel suggested we do our next hustle in Toronto, I didn't hesitate. She has been wanting to go to Toronto for a while so, in an attempt to keep the peace between us, I agreed.

"Bella! Bel-la! I know you hear me."

"What, Angel?"

"What motel are we using tonight? Did you book it yet?"

"I'm about to in a minute. I'm thinking."

"Thinking about what? Brian? Seriously—"

"Girl, I don't want to hear it. I can't with you today so please don't start."

"You need to be thinking about my tuition. You know it's due. Beau paid her half. The school sent GG a final notice for the rest. If it's not paid by the end of the semester, I won't be able to enroll in classes for next semester. This is my senior year so that means—"

"I'm about to go and reserve the room."

It means that if I don't hurry up and come up with $15,000 in a matter of weeks to pay Angel's tuition she won't be able to graduate on time. It seems like every time I get ahead I get pulled right back. I grab my Birkin bag, a gift from Brian. I don't know how much he paid for it, but I'm pretty sure it cost over $12,000. I know for sure I can auction it off for at least $15,000 and then I will have enough to pay for Angel's private school tuition. But if I sell my purse, Brian will notice I'm not carrying it anymore. I have other purses I can sell, but I won't get as much as I could get for this Birkin. I walk towards the door, considering my options for making more money. "Shit!" I exclaim under my breath, realizing I forgot the Special K. I turn to Angel. "I forgot the—"

"Of course you did," she interrupts me, "but I remembered." Angel pulls out a small unmarked glass bottle and holds it up, smiling.

I smile in relief as I walk out the hotel room and head towards the lobby, digging in my bag for my MAC lip gloss. Once in the lobby, with my head still buried in the huge, never-ending purse, I collide into someone.

"Aw, damn," I say out loud. I look up to see two pairs of blue eyes staring back at me: Brian's and Kylie's. Feeling panicked, my knees buckle a little.

Brian kisses me on the forehead. "Babe, you really need to stop all that cursing. How can blessings and curses come out of the same mouth? Are you alright?" I nod, trying to figure out a way to bolt out of the hotel and away from Brian without it looking suspiciously weird.

"What are you doing here?"

"I came to see my baby at work."

"Huh?"

"I want to go on set with you and see what you do. Are you headed there now?"

145

DONISHA DERICE & JAI DARLENE

When I told Brian I would be in Toronto this weekend it was like I broke his heart. He was so disappointed. He said he had a big surprise for me this weekend, but I told him it would have to wait until I got back because I had business to attend to. He kept pressing me for more information about where I was going, and I hate to lie to the ones I care about, but I had no choice. There was no way that I was going to tell him that I was brushing him off to go rob some dudes in another country so that I can afford to pay my mortgage. The hustle is something he would never accept. So, I lied and told him that I had a modeling gig and that Angel was going to accompany me so I could show her the ropes of the business. I never imagined he'd pop up on me.

"Brian, this is unacceptable. You can't follow me around like this. You look like a stalker. And I'm not taking you to the set with me. You'll just be a distraction." I hope that I sound convincing as I chide him in my sternest voice, despite wanting to fall into his arms, kiss him, and, once again, drop everything to spend the day with him.

"Bella," Kylie chimes in, "when I found out Angel would be here, I begged Brian to bring me. He wasn't going to come at first. Don't blame him. Blame me." I cut my eyes at Kylie. Great, just great. I may end up getting dumped before all is said and done, because a little 16-year-old wants to play with her friend.

Brian reads my face and jumps back in the conversation. "I just wanted to spend some time with you. You fly with me sometimes when I'm on business trips, so I didn't think it would be a problem." I sigh in frustration. I have no clue what to do. There is no modeling gig for them to watch. I ask Brian and Kylie to wait while I make a phone call. I walk to the other side of the lobby and sit down on a sofa facing Brian to make sure he doesn't creep up on me while I am making my call. Angel picks up and before she can say *hello* I start talking.

"Angel, Brian's here."

"What the hell?!"

"I know, I know."

"This is some straight bull, Bella."

"Listen, I need you to do something for me."

"What you need to do is get Brian out of here."

"You need to go get me some outfits, hire a photographer, and reserve a location for a photo shoot."

"What?! I'm not doing that. What's wrong with you?"

146

"We need to fake a photo shoot. He thinks that's why we're here."

"Where am I supposed to get the money to do that?"

"You have money, Angel."

"I don't have rich boyfriends giving me Birkin bags and giving me money to renovate my condo. We're supposed to be out here making money, not spending it. You want me to spend twenty 'leven hundred dollars on some bullshit."

"I know, Angel. Damn. Just make it happen. We can't hustle tonight, but after the shoot you can hang out with Kylie."

"Kylie's here? Okay, I'll do it."

"Really?"

"I gotta go. Bye."

Angel hangs up the phone. Thank goodness Kylie came. Angel did a total one-eighty when she found out her friend is here.

I fake a smile and walk over to Brian. "I wanted to call the photographer to make sure it was okay to have you on set. He said it's cool."

"Great!" he replies with excitement.

I massage my forehead, wishing that I could rub away the stress that I'm feeling. Kylie asks to go up to the room with Angel. There's no way I can let that happen. Kylie can't know that the photo shoot is fake. I need to get Brian and Kylie out of the hotel and distract them while Angel sets up the fake photo shoot. I take them next door to a movie theater that shows independent films. This buys Angel almost two hours to get everything ready. I cross my fingers and hope she can pull it off.

The movie is just letting out when I receive a text from Angel: *It's done. A car is waiting for you outside the hotel.*

We walk outside and Angel is leaning coolly on a black Lincoln Navigator dressed in new everything from head to toe. I can see her ass went shopping while we were in the movies, because she didn't pack that shit. Angel is rocking the hell out of a shaggy fur vest with a leather back. Underneath her vest she wears a drapey shirt with a large gold studded cross on the front. She has on some red skinny jeans and Stella McCartney knee boots that cost more than a grand. I know because I've been eyeing them in the fashion magazines for over a month now. Angel knows she is throwing me a jab by buying herself a new outfit that she is ultimately going to charge to me. I want to be mad about how much money she spent on just those boots alone, but I have no right to be angry since she had to scramble to organize my cover up. And I have to admit, she does look fly.

"A car was arranged to take you and your party to the location," Angel announces. I don't say anything to Angel as I silently slide into the SUV.

Brian squeezes my hand, grinning from ear to ear. He looks so proud of me. He thinks he has an independent working woman. "You excited?"

I shake my head. "Nah, it's nothing new to me. Just work." I hear Angel snicker at the front I am putting on. The SUV treks up some hills in a residential area. I look out the window at the row houses. The neighborhood looks like a cross between yesteryear's New York City and London. It has an old-timey feel that makes me wish I could step back in time into an era that was much simpler than the 21st century; an era where I don't have to lie to the ones I care about or steal to make ends meet; an era where I can make and sell knit blankets or some shit like that.

We pull up in front of a castle. A freaking castle. Angel arranged for my photo shoot to take place at Casa Loma. I try my best to contain my excitement, but I know it is written all over my face. I hop out of the SUV and stroll over to the photographer. He has a large camera around his neck and is adjusting the lights he has set up outside the castle. I introduce myself and he directs me inside where I can change clothes and do my makeup.

"Honey, help me get dressed," I call for Angel. I can feel her eyes shooting darts in the back of my head as she follows me to the mock dressing room. Inside is a rack of high-end clothes, shoes, and a makeup table. "How did you do it?" I ask with excitement. This girl should be an event planner for pulling all this off in less than two hours. I was only expecting a small room, a change of clothes, and a guy with a camera.

Ignoring my question, Angel pulls an electric blue evening dress from the rack and hands it to me. The dress is glamorous. It's an off-the-shoulder sequined sheath dress with a small court train and a high split up the thigh.

"So we're not talking now?" I confront her as I put on the dress.

"Sit down so I can do your make up." Angel is being cold as ice.

I sit down and I try to get through to her again. "Angel." Silence. Angel gently strokes my face with a brush dipped in foundation. "Angel,

148

I know you're mad. I promise I will make it up to you." Silence. Now I am starting to get angry.

"Close your eyes," she orders.

"How much did all this cost anyway?" I ask as Angel works eye shadow onto my eyelids "You went all out."

Angel stops painting my face and sets the makeup brush down. "I only did what you asked me to do," she says through clenched teeth.

"Yes, but I didn't ask you to do all of this. How much did this cost?" I ask again, straining hard to keep from raising my voice.

Fuming, Angel rolls her eyes and exhales deeply. "If you must know," she begins, raising her voice just short of a yell, "those clothes were free. I told the stores I was an assistant for a celebrity. And this place cost—"

Kylie walks in, interrupting our conversation. "There you guys are. I've been wandering from room to room looking for you." Angel and I both stare at her in silence.

"I'll send you my itemized bill," Angel says, setting down the makeup brush. "Come on, Kylie. Let's go." Angel clutches Kylie's arm and storms out the room. I grab a pair of diamond-encrusted stilettos from the rack and follow behind them.

Angel marches out of Casa Loma dragging Kylie behind her. Brian is patiently waiting outside near the Navigator checking his email on his cell phone. Angel and Kylie fly past him and jump in the car.

"Where are you going?" Brian asks, before she can close the door. "I thought you were supposed to be learning." Brian looks puzzled.

"I've learned enough." Angel slams the door shut. Brian and I watch the Navigator drive down the hill and out of sight.

"Babe, don't worry about it," I tell Brian.

I walk over to the photographer and ask him where he wants me to pose. He points to the tower, so I walk over to it and lean against the blanched bricks. I arch my back and elongate my neck. The camera flashes. I angle my face towards the camera and smile with my eyes, or *smize*, as coined by Tyra Banks. The camera flashes. "Work it, babe," I hear Brian say. I smile at his encouraging cheers. I'm having so much fun and I have to admit I'm feeling myself.

I position my leg to emphasize the high split in the dress. I bend over and grab my ankle. "No, babe. No, don't do that," Brian waves his arms for me to stop. It's obvious he thinks my pose is too provocative and doesn't want me bending over showing my big ol' juicy donk to the world.

"I'm showing off the shoes, babe."

"Just stick your foot out like this." He hilariously sticks one leg out and pops his hip. I cannot stop laughing. This man is always making me smile and laugh. It's one of the many things I love about him.

I do a few more wardrobe changes and the photo shoot wraps up a couple of hours after we started. I have no idea what the hell I'm going to do with all these pictures I just paid for, but at least I enjoyed myself. Angel hired people to clean up the dressing room and collect the clothing, so all that's left for me to do is change and roll.

After the photo shoot, Brian and I go sightseeing. We visit the Distillery District and the Ontario Art Gallery. The distillery has a lot of small shops selling overpriced jewelry, knick-knacks, and clothing. At the art gallery, Brian is particularly interested in viewing the Inuit art of Canada's Aboriginal people. I didn't even know Canada had Aboriginal people. I thought they were only in Australia. That's what I love most about Brian; he expands my horizons and I always seem to learn new things with him.

Brian takes me to the CN Tower for dinner. We skip the long line to get in and enter inside a security scanner. It puffs a strong gust of wind on me to scan my body for explosive substances. The stupid scanner blows my natural curls out, making my hair look poofy. I'm pissed. I want to look perfect for Brian while observing the entire city in a 360-degree view over what I hope to be a romantic dinner. We enter a glass elevator and Brian embraces me as we sky rocket over 1,000 feet into the air. I don't know which view is more breathtaking; our panoramic view of the Toronto Islands or my view of this amazingly handsome man. The elevator lets us out in the middle of a rotating restaurant, which, surprisingly, is empty. The hostess greets us and sits us at our candle-lit table.

"I reserved the whole place just for us," Brian admits. I gasp as we are joined by a string quartet serenading us with beautiful, soft music. I am speechless.

"Bella, I did all of this because I want you to know just how much I love you."

I'm shocked by his words. "You love me?" I was not expecting for this to happen so soon.

"Yes, I love you."

"I love you, too, Brian." At least I think I do. If it's not love, it's pretty damn close.

"Good, because if you didn't love me I wouldn't be able to give you this." Brian hands me small velvet jewelry box. I open it and inside is a gorgeous necklace with platinum key pendant. The key has a row of diamonds streaming in single line from top to bottom and engraved on the back are the words "My Heart Is Yours." This is the first time Brian has ever told me he loves me. Tears of joy stream down my face. I never expected for him to fall in love with me this quickly. And as much as I want him, I know I just do not deserve this man.

19
The Beginning and the End
are All that Matter

Beau

My belly and I trudge through the snow, making our way to the Town Court for my pre-trial hearing. It's New Year's Eve and although it usually snows around this time, it is already turning out to be one of the coldest winters ever. I go through security hoping I don't run into anyone I know from the law school, especially Professor Grand's ol' hating self. I know the moment she saw me sitting in that jail cell she ran to go get the police report. I'm positive she is the one who told the dean about my arrest. Now I'm on academic probation pending the results of this case. It doesn't matter how well I perform academically; I can still get kicked out of the school if I'm convicted.

I feel the twins kicking and I rub my belly. I hope my stress is not affecting them. As soon as I make it through security I pull the hood of my coat over my face and go up the elevators to my courtroom. Even though I know I'm not in the wrong, I'm so embarrassed about being arrested and having to appear in court that I want to hide and shrink away. Ms. Jacqueline is already here waiting for me. As soon as she sees me she tells me to take off my coat, and I reluctantly comply. She wants the judge to see my professional attire and baby bump.

The judge takes the bench and, thankfully, Ms. Jacqueline has sway with the court bailiffs and gets my case called up first. We take our seats at the defense table. After the judge says good morning to the deputy prosecutor and Ms. Jacqueline, he gets straight to the case. "Ms. Price, I have reviewed your motion to dismiss for failure to state a cause as well as your request for expungement of your client's arrest on this case. However, the State never filed a written response to your motion. State, what is your position on the defense motion?" I feel butterflies in my stomach or maybe it's just the twins moving. All I know is I'm nervous as heck. If he doesn't grant my motion that means the case will be prolonged and I will have to actually litigate it in a jury trial.

The prosecutor remains seated as he speaks. "I've reviewed the motion and the supporting exhibits, including the surveillance video provided by defense counsel and I have no response. I leave it to the court's discretion." I am a little confused as to why they just didn't agree to dismiss, especially since they brought charges against Jason's fiancée.

"Why didn't they just say they have no objection?" I ask Ms. Jacqueline.

"They won't agree because of your pending civil lawsuit against the city," she whispers to me. "By agreeing they would be conceding on the record that they were in the wrong for your false arrest."

The judge looks at his file and then to Ms. Jacqueline. "Very well. In regards to the motion to dismiss count one, Criminal Trespass as an A misdemeanor, I reviewed the deed to the home in which the defendant is alleged to have trespassed and I find that she could not have trespassed on her own property. Motion granted as to count one. As to count two, Carrying a Handgun Without a License as an A misdemeanor, I have reviewed the handgun license submitted to the court and I find that, not only did the defendant indeed have a license, but she was in her own home, in which she did not need a license in the first place. Motion granted as to count two. And as to count three, Battery as a Level 6 Felony, based on what I reviewed on the video, the alleged victim banged on the defendant's door multiple times and when the defendant answered, the AV became belligerent towards the defendant. When the defendant tried to close her door to diffuse the situation, the alleged victim forcefully entered the home, attacking the defendant in her clearly pregnant state, and even after she was attacked she still tried to help the alleged victim. Motion granted as to count three. Motion granted to count four, Resisting Law Enforcement, as well. The defendant cannot resist an unlawful arrest."

The judge pauses and looks at my very pregnant belly before going on. "As to the motion to expunge the defendants arrest for these allegations, I find that the prosecutors did not do anything wrong on their part, however I find there was a lack of investigation on part of the arresting officer. The defendant attempted to show the officer documentation of her innocence. Not only did the officer refuse to look at it, but he barraged the defendant with disparaging and racist comments. Finally, he dragged her to jail in her obvious delicate state while the real intruder trashed her home, including her unborn children's nursery, causing thousands of dollars in damage. I find that there was no probable cause to arrest the defendant in the first place and order that her record be expunged. Next case."

"Thank God! And thank you, Ms. Jacqueline!" I exclaim, hugging her in relief.

"Thank yourself. You drafted the motion," she compliments. "I just signed my name to it."

We walk out the courtroom and I stop Ms. Jacqueline before reaching the elevators. "Can you get the transcript of what the judge said for my civil case?"

"No need. The city wants to settle. How does $200,000 sound to you?" she smiles.

Now I'm beaming. "Make it $500,000 and you have yourself a deal."

"Done." She presses the button for the elevator.

"One more thing. I don't want to press charges against Jason's fiancée." After how she trashed my house I shouldn't care. Shoot, all she had to do was speak up and I wouldn't have been arrested in the first place. Now the tables have turned. All the charges have been dropped against me and she is facing charges for residential entry, battery, criminal mischief, and burglary. I don't really understand the burglary charge, but Ms. Jacqueline explained that burglary is when someone breaks and enters into your home with the intent to commit a felony, and since the damage she caused when she wrecked my home is well over $2,500, she is charged with criminal mischief as a felony.

"Unfortunately, it's not up to you. You get to have your say in the matter, but ultimately the prosecutors make the final decision. And since you are about to take them for half a million, they are not just going to drop all charges against her. They are going to want her to pay in some way; they'll probably even want her to pay restitution."

I shake my head. I feel sorry for Jason. He finally found someone to be happy with and now his whole life is being turned upside down by this incident. I don't believe his fiancée is a bad person, and I don't think she deserves to be labeled as a criminal and felon any more than I do. She just made a bad choice. "Is there anything you can do?" I inquire.

"I'll talk to the prosecutor and inform her that you are not interested in pressing charges or being dragged into court to testify against her. I'll ask her to dismiss the burglary charge and offer a diversion to her remaining charges."

"What's a diversion?"

Ms. Jacqueline explains, "A diversion is an agreement to withhold prosecution where the State agrees to dismiss the charges against the defendant if she admits that she is guilty, does some community service work, and takes a class. It's usually only offered to those with no criminal history. Her arrest can't be expunged like yours was."

I think a diversion is a perfect solution. "Please, push for a diversion." We give each other hugs and goodbyes. Ms. Jacqueline goes across the street to her office and I go home to change before my doctor's appointment this afternoon.

When I get home I kick off my shoes and walk straight to the refrigerator. The babies are hungry and I am craving a prosciutto sandwich and red velvet cake. I look at the to-do list I keep on my refrigerator and I check off *Get case dismissed. Sue the shit out the city and get paid* is still left unchecked on my list because I am still in negotiations for my settlement. But the very first thing on my list, *Stay focused and make the grade*, is checked off. Grades came out a couple of weeks ago in mid-December. Tort Law, A plus. Criminal Law, A plus. Property Law, A minus. Contracts, A plus. Civil Procedure, A plus. Legal Writing, A. Yeah, I already knew I was acing everything. School is the least of my problems.

Now that my criminal case is behind me, my biggest problem is my pregnancy. I want nothing more than to have a natural and healthy birth, but because I'm having twins and I'm so petite, Dr. Adleberry, my obstetrician, feels that I'm high risk. My appointments are now weekly, which usually doesn't happen until the 36th week, and I'm 33 weeks.

After I finish eating my sandwich and cake, I leave for my weekly appointment. When I arrive the nurse greets me excitedly. "You know the routine. Hop onto the scale." I get on the scale and watch that little weight tip all the way to the left. It's almost insulting. "You gained four pounds from last week," the nurse enthusiastically announces. I have gone from 135 to 160 pounds over the past seven months. I have started to feel particularly huge over the past month, and my feet are a little swollen. I traded in heels and dresses for leggings and J's so my feet and big belly can breathe. All I want is to be comfortable. Today I have on some black leggings, a grey and red Law School hoodie, and black, grey, and red Jordans. I know it's New Year's Eve and all I want is to get in and out so I can go home to a half gallon of cookies and cream and watch the New York ball drop. But first I have to make sure my little loves are good.

Dr. Adleberry comes in a little while after I enter the room. "Beaunifide, your blood pressure is very elevated and you have gained four pounds within the last week. And looking at your feet I can tell they are swollen. I believe you have preeclampsia." Dr. Adleberry looks through my chart. "Preeclampsia can be life-threatening for you and the twins. Depending on the test results, you will either be giving birth today or be on bed rest until you go into labor."

My heart drops. Neither option sounds good to me. I want to follow the birth plan I made. I want to have my twins naturally without any drugs. I even picked out music to listen to while in labor.

My heart begins to race as I consider how this could affect the twins. I have done some reading on the condition but I'm not prepared to deal with having it. "Today?" I ask Dr. Adleberry. I'm not due for 6 ½ more weeks. It is too soon.

"Remember I told you twins often don't go full term, so we anticipated you going in between 34 and 36 weeks, especially with your small frame. I am going to transport you to the maternity ward and start running some tests. Everything will be okay, Beaunifide. Your little ones will be here and healthy when it is time," Dr. Adleberry says, attempting to comfort me.

"So, I won't be able to deliver vaginally? What about my birthing plan if I deliver today?" I ask.

"No, it will be a C-section. I know you had it all planned out but life doesn't always go as we plan." Dr. Adleberry leaves the room.

Left alone while waiting to be transported, my mind wanders to the first sermon I heard Pastor Lewis preach and my heart begins to hurt. King David had taken something he wanted and he paid for it with the life of his child. I know the wrong I have done in my young life. This year has changed me and I will never be that person again. I am still learning how God works and I know he isn't tit for tat, but I also know I must reap what I have sowed. *Please, God, protect my babies. Please give me a chance to raise them, love them, and hold them.* I wipe tears from my face as the hospital attendant comes with a wheelchair to transport me. I am hooked up to monitors to watch both babies' heartbeats, my heartbeat, and my blood pressure. If my blood pressure was already high I can only imagine where it is now that my mind has been going a mile a minute. All I can think about is how Izzy and BJ are doing.

Dr. Adleberry informs me that my fluid levels are also a concern. "Are you ready to meet your little ones?" she smiles. She informs me that the twins look great but that their heart rates are fluctuating. "Right now the twins are measuring at about four pounds each, but that is only an estimate. Also, because they are premature, their lungs may not be fully developed. They will have to remain in the NICU until they reach five pounds and we feel confident that their lungs are functioning at the level of a full term baby." Dr. Adleberry is trying her best to assure me that everything I am going through is common for women giving birth to multiple babies, but it doesn't help. I can't stop worrying and she can tell, especially since I am hooked up to these monitors. "You need to do your best to be calm because what happens with you is also affecting the babies."

The nurse dims the lights and I am left alone again with my thoughts. After a while Dr. Adleberry comes back and tells me that I will be prepared for the C-section within the next two hours. Lying in the hospital bed is uncomfortable and the twins are flipping and turning every which way. I don't think they like the monitors. I'm not allowed to get out of the bed without assistance from the nurse, so I feel trapped. I figure this is how the twins must feel, too.

I pull out my phone to call Bella and her picture pops up as I start to dial her number. I begin to sob and my hands are trembling as I continue dialing. I can't believe we haven't spoken in over seven months. It finally hits me how much I miss her. She is my best friend and was my only friend for most of my life, but she doesn't even know I'm pregnant. I rub my stomach as I wait for her to answer. After about three rings I am sent to voicemail. I never considered that she wouldn't answer my call. "Oh my God," I begin to cry even harder. I don't want to go through this without her. I call her phone a second time. Three rings and the voicemail again. I don't want to leave a message. I honestly don't think I can even talk I am crying so hard. I dial her number a third time, praying that she will finally answer.

"Really? You haven't called me in seven months. Let me guess; you don't want to start the new year with any bad blood between us," Bella sarcastically laughs. Hearing her voice, sarcasm and all, makes me smile but I don't speak. I'm scared to open my mouth. Scared of what will come out. All I've been doing for the past hour is crying, so I'm not sure what will happen when I try to talk. I also don't know how to tell my sister that I am pregnant and about to give birth in like an hour. Bella says hello a couple of more times. I can hear the irritation in her voice. And if she hangs up now I am sure she will not answer her phone again.

I finally open my mouth and all that comes out are sobs. I just weep into the phone. I can't manage to say anything other than "I" like twenty times in a row.

"Beau? Beau. Oh my God. What is wrong? Talk to me. Why are you crying? Where are you?" Bella frantically asks.

"IU hospital," I tell her, finally able to speak.

"I am on my way. It is going to be okay. I love you so much, sister. I am so sorry I haven't been there for you." I can hear Bella's voice quivering. She is now crying, too. I still haven't told her about the babies, but she can tell whatever is wrong I need her.

"I love you, too. And I am so sorry, too. Please hurry and get here," I sob even harder. For the first time today I feel okay, like everything will be alright. I close my eyes as I wait for Bella. My sister. My sister is coming.

Bella

"Okay, this is the last one," I call out to Brian who is patiently watching me try on dresses for the New Year's party that I am nervous as hell about. All of the who's who of Indiana will be there, including the mayor and governor. I'm not nervous about being around the elite or even Brian's parents. I have met Mr. and Mrs. Rose several times over the past three months and they are always pleasant and very inviting. I made sure they know I have my own money and that I'm not a gold digger. Now, I don't have anywhere near as much money as their family, but as far as they are concerned I am a multi–millionaire model and property investor.

I'm nervous because shit is getting real between Brian and me too quick. When we said we loved each other last month I couldn't help but to question it. I'm still not sure if people can really fall in love that quickly. It's been 15 weeks, 108 days, 2,592 hours and I feel like he is the one. But I made that same mistake with Lorenzo and it cost me one million dollars, my dignity, and almost my most precious asset, my treasure, my virginity. I don't want to slip up like that ever again. I did pray for Brian to be my husband, however, I can't put all my trust in God and believe that he is sincerely looking out for me. I need to be sure what

I have with Brian is that forever type of love before I give in 100 percent. And if this is really forever love, then I have an entirely different reason to be nervous. The lies. The lies I have told this man to his face. The lies I have told his family. The lies I have told to make them believe I am something I am not.

"Babe, you look gorgeous in every last one of those dresses. I don't care which one you wear." Brian smiles at me from the edge of his bed. I see sincerity in his eyes every time he looks at me. And when he smiles at me it feels like he is seeing my heart, not just my body and face. I decide that I am going to wear a floor-length silk dress by Oscar de la Renta. It is navy blue with a V neckline and a V-shaped back. I felt the most elegant and classy in that dress. It fits the occasion and my body perfectly. And Brian agrees like I knew he would. I take the dress off and throw on my silk Japanese kimono robe. I walk over to Brian, who is sitting at the edge of his massive bed, which looks like a pea in his enormous Geist mansion master suite. I think he had the bed custom made, because it is larger than a king-sized bed.

I have practically moved in with him. Forget the top drawer; I have my own walk-in closet. I lean down and give him a long, lingering kiss. He pulls me onto his lap and Brian wraps his arms around me tightly as we continue to kiss. Finally, he lets me go and looks at me, puzzled. "What was that for?"

"Why does there have to be a reason?" I pause and smile, staring into his deep blue eyes. I was about say I love you, something I hadn't said to him since Toronto. I didn't want to say it again until I knew for sure that our love is real. It was about to come out so effortlessly that I had to catch myself. I'm used to saying whatever is necessary to perpetuate the hustle and I know that is what Brian wants me to say. But I am not trying to hustle him. I have fallen for him. And for me to choose a man rather than his money, maybe it really is love for me.

"Is your family coming to the party? I hope they know they are more than welcome," Brian nervously asks. He has met GG before at Sunday dinner. He's even come to church a few times and liked it. He said it was a lot livelier and interesting than the Catholic mass he usually goes to. He knows about Beau, too. I told him how we had a major disagreement and aren't really talking, but he always asks about her.

"GG brings in every new year with the Lord and this one is no different. She said thank you for the invite, though," I laugh. "And Angel is going to a party in Chicago with Kylie and some of their other friends. Young Will is performing at midnight and they have backstage passes."

"I remember skipping out on this party when I was a teenager, too," Brian laughs. "What about Beau?" The way he says her name is as if he knows her. I haven't spoken to her in over half a year, but I find myself talking about her more and more to him.

I'm not mad at Beau anymore. Actually, I miss her like crazy. So many things have happened, good and bad, and I am used to sharing everything with her. But it's been months since shit went down at GG's house and we are both too damn stubborn to call first. I don't need or want an apology. I want my sister. "Yeah, about that...I still haven't really talked to Beau," I finally answer Brian. I'm happy. Really happy. Happier than I have been probably since before Daddy died. However, Beau isn't here to share it with me, and thinking about that takes away from my happiness. I wonder what she is up to, and how her first semester of law school went. I am sure she aced that shit.

I lay flat on the bed as Brian walks around. I hope he doesn't go asking a bunch of questions about Beau. I have told him as little as possible about why Beau and I are beefing. I most definitely didn't mention the hustle. I told him a half-truth that we disagreed about disciplining Angel when she performed poorly in school. The bed feels good and I just want to rest for a few minutes without thinking about shit, including Beau. While lying in his bed I don't want to think about how I just took some dude for his money last weekend in Philly when he thought I was making a property acquisition. I don't want to think about who I really am—a hustla' and a taker. I want to just be the girlfriend of Brian Rose, Bella the investor and model. I want to be normal, and right now, that is how I feel, so I just lay on the bed enjoying the feeling.

"Man, are all black women as stubborn as you, or do I just happen to be marrying the most stubborn black woman in the world?" Brian breaks the silence.

"What?" I ask, sitting up on the bed. I am sure I heard him correctly, but I can't believe he just said he was going to marry me. I look over to him. He is on one knee with a velvet box displaying a diamond ring. He is serious. I feel my whole body shaking.

"Look, I was going to wait and ask at the party tonight. I had it all planned out, real romantic. I was going to ask at the stroke of midnight right as all the confetti fell, but I know you. And even though I know that I know that I know...I mean, Bella Amore Jones, I knew from the first time I met you, not on the plane, but at that restaurant, that I wanted you and I would be with you for a lifetime. But if you don't feel the same way I don't want to find out in front of hundreds of people. Shoot, you are not about to embarrass me in public."

He continues to talk; his lips are moving, but I can no longer hear anything he is saying. My heartbeat is throbbing in my ears and I can hear every breath I'm taking. The wetness on my face must be tears and I feel them falling down to my chest, and flowing like a stream into my lap. He is serious. This is it. This really is a forever type love. I think back to when my daddy asked what my hustle was going to be and I burst out laughing.

My legal hustle was never really about money at all; it was about love. I had been proposed to over six times and each man was rich, but I always said no. I knew that each of those other men loved my beauty, loved the image of me, and I knew I didn't love none of their asses. I could have chosen any legal hustle: lawyer, doctor, scientist, but even as a teenager I wanted a hustle that would give me something much more than money—love.

"Yes!" I scream, and I continue to scream until Brian pulls me down to the floor and kisses me so deeply I can feel his energy all through my body.

Brian and I lay on the floor together, staring into one another's eyes. I love getting lost in his deep blues. Esmeralda, the housekeeper, bursts into the room like a tornado, hair blown every which way, and holding a broom, ready for attack. She heard me scream and is coming to the rescue. I have no doubt that any woman from Colombia can fight and she came prepared. Brian and I laugh. I could have laid on the floor with him forever and been happy. He slips the ring onto my finger and Esmeralda screams. She has been keeping the secret for over a week and is ecstatic that Brian finally asked. The ring is a three-carat diamond surrounded by a halo of white diamonds. The color of the center diamond matches my eyes and is cut in the shape of an emerald. It is perfect and beautiful. It is exactly me. Yeah, most people would think I would want some huge 20-carat rock, but nah, not really. I am glad my future husband chose a ring that shows that he knows me.

I can't stop staring at the ring as I get ready for the party. I keep looking at it and touching it. I am still in shock about what just happened. Remembering my prayer about making Brian my husband, I whisper, "Thank you, God" into the air as I slide into my dress.

By the time the car pulls around in front of the house, I look and feel like Cinderella. Now I have my Prince Charming and feel confident I will have him for the rest of my life. Right now I am in a dream and it is perfect—a modern day fairytale.

We arrive at the party. The packed ballroom is exquisite. Everyone screams congratulations as soon as Brian and I enter the ballroom. Literally all eyes are on us.

"You look breathtaking," Mrs. Rose says, hugging me tight. I instantly think about my mom, Tanya, and how I felt every time she hugged me. "Isn't my daughter stunning?" She asks no one in particular, whirling me around. "I'm elated to have another daughter." Mrs. Rose ushers me around the whole party introducing me to everyone. It is a little overwhelming.

After meeting just about everyone at the party, including the mayor and governor, I find my way back to Brian. "Are you sure you are ready to be my mother's daughter?" he whispers into my ear, laughing. Mrs. Rose or Mom, as she ordered me to call her, is aggressive, bold, fiery, and determined to get her way. She's a lot like me. She is gorgeous, and about 5'10" with natural blonde hair. She also has major sex appeal. I know because I've invited her up to my rooftop pool and she looked damn good in a two-piece bathing suit.

Mr. Rose is much more reserved than his wife, but he is fine as hell. If he is any indication of what my Brian is going to look like in 20 years, I have a lot to look forward to. Mr. Rose is about 6'2" and very well-built with sexy salt and pepper hair. He has the same heavenly smile and deep blue eyes as Brian.

"Welcome to the family," Mr. Rose says, hugging me. Brian's parents are definitely not what I was expecting. For billionaires, they are so down to earth and humble. Yeah, they like the finer things, but they aren't offensive with it. Being raised in Geist and going to a top-notch private school, I grew up around some of the most arrogant, rude, and snobby mothafuckas in Indianapolis. Brian's family is nothing like that. I feel loved and accepted by them.

Brian and I dance around the room, and even though the place is packed I feel like it is just us two. I want to dance my way into the new year and my new life. I feel my purse vibrate as we slow dance but accidently hit the reject button as I'm pulling it out. I am shocked to see Beau's name on the screen. She probably thinks I rejected her call on purpose. I shake my head and sigh.

"What?" Brian looks at me confused.

"Beau just called and I accidently rejected the call. I am going to the ladies room to call her back." As I make my way to the ladies room Mrs. Rose stops me for pictures. I can feel my phone vibrating again. Hell, I haven't spoken to Beau in seven months. What's five more minutes? I ignore the call and go to take photos with Brian and his family. There is a professional photographer and Mrs. Rose has us feeling like we are at a real photo shoot. We pose together, separate, as couples, sitting, standing, and dancing.

After the millionth picture I finally excuse myself and tiptoe to the restroom to call Beau back. I always knew she would break first and I am glad she did because I'm so excited to talk to my sister. I have so much to tell her, starting with my engagement. My phone rings again as I make my way into the bathroom. Even though I am so happy to talk to her I still have to give her a hard time. I answer the phone with slight sarcasm in my voice. Then Beau tells me she's in the hospital and I panic. I run out the bathroom, unable to stop crying. Brian immediately notices something is wrong.

"She is in the hospital. I gotta go," I cry to him. I don't know what is going on, but the way Beau is sobbing I know it must be serious. I gather the hem of my dress and run to the door with Brian and his parents following behind me.

"Hey, hey, what's wrong?" Mr. Rose asks, looking very concerned. Brian explains what is going on to his parents as I wait for the driver to pull around.

"Stay," I beg Brian. It is going on 11 o'clock and I don't want to take him away from the party.

"You're my wife. I'm not letting you go alone." Brian holds my hand as we rush to the car. As scared as I am, I'm so relieved to have him with me.

I don't call GG or Angel to let them know what's going on. GG is at church and she doesn't have a cell, so there is no way I can contact her. Angel is in Chicago and I don't want her rushing home stressing. So I just sit in the car silent. I have a death grip on my phone, staring at it in case Beau tries to call. Although IU Hospital is not very far from where we are, it seems like it's taking forever to get there. Everything seems to be moving in slow motion.

We finally arrive and the emergency room receptionist directs us to the maternity unit. I don't know what to think.

"You didn't tell me she was pregnant," Brian says. He looks confused, and hell, so do I.

"She's not," I say confidently like I know for sure, but honestly, what other reason would there be for her to be in the maternity unit? "I don't know," I say, choking on my words. "I don't know what has been going with my sister and I feel bad about it. Over some stupid ass foolishness." I start crying all over again as we finally make it to her room. "What the fuck?" the words leave my mouth before I can catch myself. Beau is lying in the hospital bed with a huge ass belly. Her eyes are closed like she is resting. How could I have not known my sister, my best friend, is pregnant?

"Hey," Beau groggily says. "I am so happy you are here," she smiles at me. "You look so beautiful." Whatever pain medication she is on has her feeling good. Beau's hazy gaze turns into a serious mean mug when she sees Brian standing behind me.

"Beau, this is my fiancé, Brian." I smile as Beau's mug turns confused. As many proposals as I have turned down, I bet she wasn't expecting me to get engaged to someone she's never met. I can't help but to laugh. I let Beau know I will be right back and walk Brian to the waiting area. "You can go home, babe. We will be fine." I rub his head as he sits in a chair. "I am sure you didn't imagine bringing in the new year in a hospital waiting room." I shake my head.

"Like I said, you are my wife and I am not going anywhere," he sternly responds. I can tell when he means business and this is definitely one of those times. I smile and hold his hand.

"Ms. Jones," a voice calls from the hallway. A short round nurse is waiting with some scrubs in her hands. "We are ready to take your sister into surgery. Just waiting on you. Please go change and meet us back at the room." She hands me the scrubs. I feel like I am having an out-of-body experience. I change and head back to the room where a doctor and team of nurses are waiting. Beau doesn't say anything; she just reaches her hand out to me. I hold her hand and brush the hair from in front of her face as the doctor and nurses go to work. The curtain blocking my view prevents me from seeing what they are doing, but I am looking at Beau anyway. I swear I am more nervous than she is and I have so many questions to ask her.

I consider it may be inappropriate to ask while she is lying there about to have a baby pulled out of her, but I can't hold it any longer.

"Why didn't you tell me you and Jason were still messing around? And why isn't his ass here?" I lean down and whisper.

Beau looks at me. "You really want to get into that now?" she laughs. My eyes grow large, expressing my interest in knowing what happened. "You know me well enough to know that when I'm done, I am done. Jason messed up and he is not the father. I got pregnant in May." Beau gives me the eye. She wants me to read between the lines. The only person I remember her having sex with in May was…

My mouth drops open. "Oh my God!" I yell, startling the people behind the curtain working on Beau.

"Is there something wrong?" a nurse peeks around the curtain and asks.

"I am fine," Beau laughs. I am not fine at all, though. I have a million more questions but I don't ask. I just look at my sister.

"It's a girl," I hear the doctor say over faint cries that come from this little life she has just pulled out of my sister. She comes around the curtain and shows us the baby. "Time," she asks a nurse.

"23:59," the nurse answers as she takes the baby out of the doctor's hands. I glance over at her. She is so little.

"Israel," Beau whispers the baby's name to me. The doctor goes back behind the curtain and what feels like only a second later I hear more cries.

"It's a boy," the doctor calls out again. My eyes dart over to another little crying life that the doctor holds up. "Beaunifide," Beau smiles at me. She named the boy after her and our father. The doctor asks the time again and another nurse tells her 00:00 and takes Beaunifide.

"They look great, Beaunifide," the doctor smiles and congratulates Beau. Beau smiles and I just sit bewildered. Beau has a look of peace and tranquility about her. The doctor stitches her up and the nurses bring the babies over. They are perfect. So beautiful. Beau and I both cry. I hold Israel and Beau holds Beaunifide, and we just sit and stare at them. "Happy New Year," the nurses and doctor say before they exit the room, leaving Beau and I alone with the twins.

"Yes, it is a happy New Year," I smile at Beau. My sister and I ended the old and brought in the new together and all is well.

20
Ghosts of Hustles Past

Bella

Five years later…

I gaze out over the garden as I wait for Esmeralda to bring my breakfast. Brian is out of town on business, so I'm enjoying the morning's beauty and silence alone. A sweet breeze sweeps over the table and I smile. I sometimes want to pinch myself to make sure this is really my life. I am still in my fairytale. Being the wife to an heir of a multi-billion-dollar empire is wonderful. A beautiful mansion, luxurious vacations, endless everything, and most importantly, a man who loves me more than anything money can buy. Brian treats me like I am his everything.

Now don't get it twisted. I haven't turned into some type of trophy that is all about appearances or some rich socialite that does nothing but shop and party. I've never liked to party, anyhow. I have actually become rather philanthropic. Or more philanthropic, shall I say. I think donating dresses to Proms for Girls counts as being philanthropic. Proms For Girls is a charity that gives prom dresses to low-income high school students. I've been donating my high fashion dresses since I was a teenager.

I may have been philanthropic, however, my mother-in-law, Momma Kimberly, schooled me on being a humanitarian, and I think I took to it rather well. I chose a cause that assists orphaned children. I am the founder of Sophia Tanya Love Thy Children, which not only raises money, but also places orphaned children with families. I definitely wouldn't consider myself the typical orphan, but I figure any kid I can save from the life I once lived or something even worse is certainly worth my efforts. I am proud of what I am doing and have found peace in it.

"Mrs. Rose," Esmeralda's thick accent breaks through the morning quiet as she hands me the phone.

167

"Hey, you weren't answering your phone," Angel says, sounding frustrated.

"I left my cell in the house."

"Anyway, I'm having a little get-together tonight and I want you to come through. You gotta meet my boo, so I really, really need you to make it a priority to come. I already know Beau isn't coming out on a week night so pleeeaaase come," Angel begs. Sometimes I can't stand her spoiled behind. I don't have anything planned tonight but I am not excited by the idea of hanging out with Angel and her boyfriend, either. She has a new one every month.

After I married Brian I asked Angel what her legal hustle would be and she told me she wanted to be a video vixen. I didn't think she was serious but she most definitely was, and who am I to judge? Angel has been in everyone's videos from Young Will to Chris Brown and she's dated a bunch of them, too. But I must say, she is getting paid. She had taken over the mortgage for the condo over two years ago and has completely paid it off.

"Your definition of little is very loose. How many people, Angel? I am not trying to come to some big party." She had got me like that a couple of times before. Once I showed up at the condo while they were filming a rap star's video and they had the audacity to ask if I wanted to throw on a bikini and get in it.

"Okay, so Jay plays pro basketball here in Nap. He's a guard. There are going to be a few players and a few girls. No video stuff or rappers; I promise." Angel sounds excited. "Plus, I told Jay about your foundation and he said he and a couple of the guys would like to make a donation when they meet you tonight." Angel's playing the charity card. She knows I am a sucker for my kids and I can't deny the fact that she has raised over $500,000 for the foundation.

"Okay, I will stop by for a little while. Hey, this is Brian calling. I'll see you later. Love ya, chica." I hit the button to switch over the call to Brian.

"Hey, babe." Brian's voice still gives me butterflies. I miss him like crazy even though it's only been two days.

"When will you be home?" I ask. If he is set to be gone for more than a week I usually go with him.

"Tomorrow. I can't wait to see your beautiful face," he sweet-talks me. "I had a dream about you last night. You were wearing that black teddy. You know, the sheer one with the lace lining. You were laying on the bed waiting for me to come." I smile at the hint he's dropping.

"No," I cut him off. "I think I was naked with a pair of silver Christian Louboutins." I'm dropping him a hint of my own because I want a pair. "I am standing in front of our stripper pole right now." I can hear Brian's breathing getting heavier.

"You got a stripper pole put in our bedroom?" Brian asks excitedly.

"It was going to be surprise for when you got home. I'm going to climb to the top of the pole just as you walk in and slide down into a full split." Shoot, I'm exciting myself, but now I have to find someone to install a stripper pole before tomorrow afternoon.

"Babe, I've got a meeting in about 15 minutes. I have to go. I love you," Brian says, rushing me off the phone.

I chill for the rest of the day and at about 8 o'clock I start getting ready for Angel's party. I'm definitely not about to get dolled up to go over there. I throw on some skinny jeans, a simple black blouse, and comfortable green pumps. I pull my hair into a ponytail, put on little lip gloss, and I am ready.

I hear the rhythmic sounds of R&B as I approach Angel's door, and I am getting a good vibe from the music alone. The last time I came to one of her get-togethers she was blasting rap music and there were half-naked chicks lurking in the hallway. I walk into the apartment and the lights are dim. I immediately grab a glass of red wine from a server wearing a little French maid outfit. Okay, the maid is looking a little slutty, but it's still an upgrade from what I am used to seeing at one of Angel's shindigs.

"Que Bella," Angel greets me and kisses me on both cheeks. She is wearing a cute little strapless black dress with blue and gold pumps that match her makeup. It is a very interesting combo but it looks good on her. "See, I told you it would be nice," Angel whispers in my ear, smiling. Okay, maybe my little sis is trying to grow up a bit. I smile as I peep out the scene.

There are a bunch of tall men and a gang of model-looking chicks. The blue and gold Angel is wearing starts to make sense as I realize they are the colors of her boyfriend's team. I don't really keep up with sports that much but I do know he helped take the team to the Eastern Conference finals last season, and I remember the news reporting he just signed a contract for $19 million. Jay's cute with light-skin, hazel

169

eyes, and dimples. Most importantly, he actually knows how to hold a conversation. One would be amazed, or maybe not, at the number of professional athletes I've encountered who can't hold a conversation beyond basketball to save their souls.

Jay and I chat a bit about my foundation and I'm surprised at how knowledgeable he is about it. He tells me he was orphaned as a baby and I can see in his eyes it still hurts him to talk about it. He wasn't as lucky as Beau and me. The State of Indiana raised him until he was 18 years old. Jay not only offers a generous donation, but to do a PSA for the foundation. Tonight is turning out to be nothing like I expected.

"Me gusta tu novio," I say to Angel, letting her know that I like Jay.

"Yo tambien," Angel gushes that she likes him too.

Angel and I mingle a bit and I meet quite a few of the players. I look across the room and see Kylie hugged up with some tall chocolate guy, who I assume is also on the team. Honestly, I worry more about her than I do Angel. I have taught Angel about hustling and being hustled. And the same blood that runs through me is in her, so I know she will always come out on top. Kylie, on the other hand, is a girl gone wild to the fifth power. There is nothing crazier and more reckless than a rich white girl who gets white girl wasted. Kylie embodies most daddy's nightmares—a girl who likes drugs, thugs, and partying.

"B," Angel calls out to me. "Come here. I want you to meet Real James. He just got traded to the team. He's one of the guys I was telling you that would like to make a donation to the foundation." Angel's words all but stop my heart. Real James. It can't be. My heart starts racing as I turn around, hoping that it is not really him. I mean, there has to be another Real James playing pro ball. But there he stands, and I feel like I am looking at my nephew 20 years from now. He looks exactly the same, except he is now rocking a full beard like the one Clifford had when we first met them. Oh my God. What if Cliff is here, too?

In a panic, my eyes dart around the room. I don't see him but I can't be sure he's not in here somewhere. He could be out on the patio or something.

"Hey, how are you doing?" Real stretches his arm out to shake my hand. I take a deep breath and play it cool.

"I'm great, and you?" I smile at him and quickly look away to Angel who can see the distress in my eyes.

"Umm, hey, I just remembered I need to check on which wine the servers are using," Angel smiles nervously. "Come help me, B."

I don't think Real recognizes me, but still, I've got to get out of here.

"Oh my God, Angel, you don't know who that is," I whisper after we excuse the servers from the kitchen. Angel just looks at me confused. "Real James. Israel James. Basketball player and the father of your niece and nephew," I explain. Angel now looks just as shocked as I do. "I got to get out of here ASAP. I don't think he recognized me but I don't want to give him the opportunity to. Did he come with anybody?"

"You know what, he did come with some big Rick Ross-looking dude." I watch her expression turn into one of worry as the light bulb goes off in her head. If she didn't instantly remember the story I told her about how we hustled them, she does now. It was the worst hustle of my life and it seems as if it has come back to haunt me.

"Look, I got to leave before they see me." I begin plotting my escape. "Walk towards the door," I instruct Angel and I follow behind her, looking around for Real. He isn't standing where we left him. As I near the door I exhale in relief. Real hadn't recognized me after all and I will be able to easily slip out the door. I pull my phone out and start to call Beau, but it goes to voicemail. Angel stops dead in her tracks, causing me to bump into her. When I look up, I see why. Real and Clifford are staring right at us, whispering to each other. The looks on their faces send chills down my spine. They look like they want to fuck me up, and after what Beau and I had done to them, I can't blame them. I am not trying to find out what they are thinking about doing. All I want to do is walk my ass out the door and hope they don't follow.

"Come on." I grab Angel's hand and pull her out the door as fast as my heels will allow. She's struggling to keep up, and I'm practically dragging her down the seemingly endless hallway. If we make it to elevator, we're good...I think.

Someone opens the condo's door and I hear a remix of Beyoncé's "Haunted" bellowing into the hallway: *What goes up, ghost around / Ghost around, around, around.*

The ghosts of my past have returned to haunt me. I don't look back to see who opened the door as I quickly debate whether to take the elevator or the stairs. I decide to dash down the stairs, but before I can reach the stairway door, I feel a hand grip my arm tightly.

171

"Man, I knew I recognized yo' ass," Real says, glaring at me with disgust.

"I been dreaming of the day I run into yo' scandalous ass," Clifford says, gripping my arm tighter. I don't bother trying to break free. I just stand there looking at him. I know an apology isn't what he wants, but I feel like I have to.

"I am sorry."

"Bitch, fuck yo' apology. I want my money." Clifford pushes me up against the wall and snatches my phone.

"What are you doing?" I ask, trying, unsuccessfully, to grab my phone from him.

Clifford dials a number on my phone and I hear another phone begin ringing. He pulls the ringing phone out of his pocket and then uses it to dial another number. "I know you didn't think I was gone let you leave here like that." He takes his hand off my arm and grabs me around my waist, pulling me in close to him.

"Get the hell off my sister," Angel warns, walking up on Cliff. I can see the fire in her eyes as she gets up in his face. He pushes her with his free hand and his grip gets tighter around my waist. I can tell Angel has had one too many glasses of wine because she stumbles back and falls into Real's arms. Clifford places his other hand around my neck. Man, I wish I'd never stopped carrying Greta. Five years out of the game and I thought I was safe without her.

"Man, fuck all y'all bitches. You better be glad yo' ho ass sister didn't give my brother nothing!" Clifford yells. If he only knew Beau did give Real something—something major.

"Enough!" I shout. My patience is running short. "You want your money? I got that. You can get it, but what you won't do is keep disrespecting me and my sisters. You and your brother are not innocent. Y'all thought y'all was taking some hos back to the 'tel and y'all got played. Chalk it up to the game. And as a matter of fact, your fat ass has sleep apnea and that's really why you were messed up that night. I probably saved yo' life, 'cause if it had been some random bitch she would have left you there. And you…" I turn to Real, looking him up and down. "You made a move on her; not the other way around. You wanted her." I shake my head and push Cliff's hand from around my neck. I can tell he let me push it away, but he keeps a hold on my waist and starts laughing. He thinks this is a game. This is crazy. Ultimately, I gotta hustle us out of this. He just wants his money, so I am going to make him an offer he can't refuse.

"Look, obviously you have my number. Give me a day or two to get the money together. I will pay you double what I took. So what's that? $140,000?"

"You must think I am dumb or somethin'. You walk away and I won't see yo' ass ever again. All you have to do is change your number," Clifford laughs sarcastically. "But maybe when your husband calls me back I can discuss things with him." He stares at me smiling. "Too bad you have him saved in your phone as 'Hubby.' I just called him. I'm sure he will be glad to find out who your scandalous ass really is. Shit, he will probably pay me way more than what you're offering." His smile turns to a look of disgust as he rubs his hands together. Unbelievable. He is trying to blackmail me.

"Are you serious?!" I yell. I feel like I am catching on fire I am so hot. There is no way Brian can find out about my past. He would not understand. I have spent the last five years changing my life. I have to think of a way to fix this. I cannot lose Brian. "How much?" I solemnly ask Clifford as Angel and Real stand there staring at us. I can see worry and sadness on Angel's face. Yes, I am willing to pay whatever to protect my marriage. But will it ever end? If I give him whatever ridiculous amount he comes up with, how do I know he won't come back for more? Pastor Lewis' voice pops into my head as I remember one of his sermons. I am reaping what I sowed. After years of hustling men out of their money, it is time for me to pay for it.

"$2 million," Clifford replies. I can tell he is dead serious.

"Okay," I quickly reply, although I have no idea how I am going to move that much money without Brian knowing. I have managed to put $1.1 million into a private account, but getting the rest is going to be hard.

"What? Yeah right! Bella, he is out his damn mind!" Angel yells. I shush her. I have to do what I have to do.

We all just stand there. I am waiting to see what Clifford wants to do next. I am at his mercy right now, powerless. His phone starts ringing and he answers, "Hello." Oh my God, it is probably Brian. I feel my heart about to pop out of my chest. "My bad. I must have dialed the wrong number." He looks over and smiles.

The blare of music loudens as someone opens the condo door.

"What the fuck, Clifford?!" I hear a woman's voice scream from down the hall. I look to see two angry-looking women heading towards us. One of the chicks is short and thick with an a'ight face. The other chick looks like the typical light-skinned pretty girl. She looks mixed, probably with black and white. She is about as tall as me and skinny as a twig. "You are so damn disrespectful!" the short and thick one yells, glaring at Clifford. Clifford hands me my phone and backs across the hallway. When the chicks get to the elevator, where we are all standing, they mean mug Angel and me, looking us up and down. "He's married," the thick chick steps in front of Angel and me. Lord, I know she is not about to try to fight over his whack ass.

"Does he know that?" I turn my nose up at her, take Angel's hand, and start walking towards the condo.

"We're not done!" Clifford yells up the hallway at me. I don't respond as I walk into the condo and slam the door behind us.

Before I can lock the door, Angel gets to talking a mile a minute. "What are you going to do, Bella? You can't give him that much money? Why would punk out like that and agree to give his ass $2 million?!"

"You know I can't let Brian find out about my past. Act normal; go over there with your man. I'm gonna wait a few minutes to make sure they are gone. Then I got to get out of here." I hug Angel tight. I don't know what my next move is going to be with Clifford, but I have to talk to Beau. I call Beau, and it goes straight to voicemail. I check the clock. No wonder; it is 10 PM, Beau turns her phone off every night at 9 o'clock. She gotta stop doing that shit for reasons like tonight. I find Angel and give her another hug and kiss. My heart is still racing even after I make it to the elevator and into my car. I am nervous that Clifford or Real will jump out at any moment. I can't wait to get home to Greta. She will never leave my side again.

21
Just When You Think...

Beau

"Thank you, God," I whisper into the air as I sit up in my bed and stretch. Thanking God is the first thing I've done every morning for over five years now, however, I don't thank God for any one thing in particular. I have so much to be thankful for: life, my beautiful children, my wonderful family, and a successful law practice. But lately the one thing I have been really thankful for is the peace God has given me. I'm not talking about the peace and quiet I enjoy every morning before the twins, Izzy and BJ, wake up, nor the peace that comes from not having to hustle or feel like I constantly have to look over my shoulder. No, the peace I am talking about is the peace I got when I went to the alter and asked God to forgive me of my sins. I had left every hurt I'd felt and pain I'd caused on the alter, and got up free and at peace. I had given my life to God and, in return, God had given me peace and so much more.

I hit play on the music app on my phone and *Already Here* by Brian Courtney Wilson starts playing. No matter how many times I hear that song the feelings it evokes never change. I sing along to the song, feeling every word of it. I put the song on repeat and begin getting ready for the day. Waking up every morning at 5 with God helps prepare me for the day ahead, no matter what is to come. Today I have a 9 AM flight to Chicago to go over a contract with one of my clients, Vick Daniels. He is an all-star player for the professional basketball league, and I have negotiated a deal for $95 million. Vick is 27 and, with this contract, I have secured his spot with the Chicago team for the rest of his career. For that I will be receiving a $1.5 million bonus for getting him exactly what he asked for and that is in addition to my base pay. After I meet with Vick, I have to fly back to Indianapolis to meet with Angel's boyfriend, Jay, to go over an endorsement deal with him. He has left me a message about introducing me to a teammate who is looking for an attorney. I love my job; I'm my own boss and, not only do I make my own hours, but I make well over seven figures and am good—nah, great—at what I do.

I think the biggest perk about working for myself is being able to cook breakfast every morning for my little ones and being at home in time to tuck them in every night.

"Bonjour Mademoiselle et Monsieur," I say, placing Izzy and BJ's plates in front of them at the kitchen island.

"Bonne maman du matin," the twins tell me good morning in French. Yeah, that's right, at five years old my babies are fluent in both French and Spanish, just like Bella and I were at their age. We wake up speaking a different language every morning. I am paying La Petite Elementary School over $15,000 a year in tuition per kid and my investment is paying off.

For breakfast we are having omelets, croissant, and hash browns. "God, thank you for this food for the nourishment of our bodies. Remove all contamination and bless the preparer," BJ blesses the food. We finish breakfast and it is off to school for the kids. Afterwards, I have a plane to catch.

I touch down in Chicago at 9:30 and go straight to my satellite office to meet Vick. I am about my business; no flirting, no personal talk, no lunch "meetings," and no media. I explain the documents to him and have them signed by 11 AM. I'm in, I'm out, I get paid, and I'm on to the next one. By 1 o'clock I am walking into my Indianapolis office and contemplating what I am going to have for lunch.

"Hey, Ms. Jones," Mindy, my receptionist, greets me as I speed by her without even looking her way. I understand why Ms. Jacqueline had hired her; she is young, slender, and tall with big boobs, which means she appeals to the type of clientele we work with. But she is a bit of an airhead. All she has to do is answer phones and escort clients to our offices. How hard can that be?

"Ms. Jones," I can hear her voice behind me. Dang, how can she walk so fast in that extra tight skirt? "Your 2 o'clock was early so I offered him and his guest a drink and seated them in your office," she smiles.

"In the future please just have them wait in the waiting room." I flash a smile back at her.

"Well, since he is your brother-in-law I thought it was okay," she explains. Gosh, she is working my nerves. Just because Jay is dating my sister does not make him my brother-in-law. I ignore her and walk into my office. Mindy follows me in with the documents that should have already been on my desk.

Jay stands up and gives me a hug. "This is my new teammate,

Israel James..." Jay continues to talk but his voice is drowned out by the throbbing of my heart in my ears. Oh my God. It can't be. But it is. I feel sick to my stomach and stand speechless as I look at him, trying my hardest to remain calm and act normal. I focus on my breathing and attempt to maintain my professional demeanor. He looks good—better than I remember—and he smells the same. I shake his hand and try to gauge whether or not he remembers me. I mean, he was drunk the night we met so maybe he doesn't. God, I hope he doesn't.

I take the documents from Mindy and hand them to Jay to read over. I glance over to Real, trying not to stare, but I need to know if he recognizes me.

"Israel James...isn't that your daughter's name? What a coincidence," Mindy giggles. Note to self: fire her. I mug her and she can tell I am not pleased. Mindy's annoying laugh causes Jay and Real to look at her puzzled. While their attention is diverted, I catch a glimpse of myself in the mirror and run my fingers through my hair. I just got off a plane and I want to make sure I don't look a mess seeing Real for the first time in five years.

"Yeah, that is a coincidence," Jay says as Real cuts his eyes over at me.

"Thank you, Mindy," I smile, giving her the cue to get the heck out of my office.

"No problem, Ms. Jones. And oh yeah, your sister has called a bunch of times. She said it was urgent."

"Thank you, Mindy," I repeat more aggressively this time. Finally she leaves, closing the door behind her.

"Yeah, that is quite a coincidence." Real grabs a picture of the twins off my desk and looks at me. He knows. God, what am I going to do? I thought that chapter of my life was over but my past is here staring me right in my face. "These are your children?" Real turns the picture around for me to look at.

"Yes." I grab the picture out of his hands and set it back on my desk. Real's stare pierces through me. I don't know what he is thinking but I am sure a million and one things are going through his mind just like they are running through mine. I stare back at him.

After I first had the twins, Bella and I discussed if I would contact Real to tell him. I'd obviously decided against that, but I had thought of plans for what I would do if I ever ran into him and he recognized me. But now, with him standing right in front of me,

177

everything I thought I would say has left me.

"Looks great. Where's a pen so I can sign?" Jay says, oblivious to what is going on. I am relieved that he broke up the awkward staring match between Real and I. "See, that's what I am talking about; Beau be getting that money." Jay looks back and smiles at Real.

"Yea, I bet she does." Real looks at me with a weird devious grin.

I grab my phone out of my bag. I hadn't turned it on since last night. I have 42 missed calls from Bella and 22 texts. I wonder if she knows about Real. That would explain why she's been blowing my phone up. She went over to Angel's place last night for a get-together. He must have been there. I only have to read the first three text messages to get the gist of what happened last night.

There is no way I will let Bella pay Clifford $2 million dollars. While I wait for Jay to sign the documents I send her a text: ***Call him back and tell him that you will pay him $200,000, which is more than twice the amount you took. Then turn your phone's voice record because he is going to threaten you. Cut him off before he gets into details of the hustle and hang up. When he calls you back, let him know that what he is doing is extortion, which is a major felony. Give him my number and I will handle the rest.***

I send Bella one more text to let her know Real is sitting in my office.

"Thanks for everything, Beau." Jay stands up after he signs all the documents. This has been the most uncomfortable 20 minutes of my life. Real is still sitting in his seat staring at me and I have no idea what is about to happen. God, please help me. "You ready?" Jay looks down at Real.

"I think I am going to stay back a minute to holler at the attorney." Real looks over at me and smiles.

"Sorry, I have another appointment. Maybe you can set something up with my receptionist on your way out." I start walking towards the door but he doesn't budge. Dang, I am going to have to deal with him right now.

"It won't take long. I'll catch up with you in a few, Jay." Real and Jay pound fists.

"Ah, man, you know we are supposed to be meeting our girls for lunch," Jay says, shaking his head. "I don't have time to get cussed out by somebody else's woman."

I walk Jay to the elevator, contemplating cutting out myself. I do not want to go back into that office.

After a few minutes I decide I have to go back. As I pass her desk, I glare at Mindy who is now chewing gum and talking on the phone. That better not be one of our clients' ears she's smacking gum in. I slowly walk back towards my office, looking at the art and plaques on the wall, which include my diplomas and portrait. Real probably had time to prepare for this meeting, at least more than me. I think he knew who I was as soon as he saw that picture and read the name under it. I dreadfully go back into my office.

"You are by far the most scandalous person I have ever encountered and I am professional athlete," Real starts in on me as soon as I enter. He has picked up the picture of Izzy and BJ again. I close the door and stand by it. I have nothing to say. He is absolutely right. What I did to him and what Bella did to his brother was dirty. "My brother is getting his money back. Maybe I should get what you took from me, or better yet, finish what we started." Real sits the picture down and is in my face before I can move. He is wearing Acqua Di Gio, the same as when we met. Real grabs my butt as I back into the desk. I feel his warm breath on my neck. He is pressed against me. My heart is pounding against his chest and I still say nothing. "We can do it right here." Real picks me up and sits me on the desk. I feel that tingle down there as Real's hands move up my skirt, squeezing my thighs.

"Stop," I finally say, pushing his hands off of me as I pull my skirt down.

"Nah, ain't that what you like? At least that's what you used to like. You fucked me good before." Real pushes up on me again.

"Stop," I repeat, raising my voice a little. He is relentless though. He pushes up on me until I am scooted back on the desk and my legs are not touching the floor. "Please," I plead with him.

"I don't really want yo' ho ass anyway. I just wanted to see if you were going to give it up as easily as you did when I met you. What I really want to know is why you'd name your little girl after me." Real finally backs away from me. Him feeling up on me I can deal with, but not this; not the questions. "Man, don't try to say these are my kids. You fucked me on sight so ain't no telling who these kids' daddy is. It sure as hell ain't me. You not gone get shit from me, trust that." Real looks so pissed. The way I see it, I have two options: lie and tell him the twins aren't his, or tell the truth.

He continues talking, hitting me with all sorts of money-hungry gold-digger jabs while I debate what I should say. Before he showed up in my office I had no problem raising my children with a horrible half-truth that I didn't know their father; that the worst mistake I had ever made brought me the greatest blessings I've ever received. But now, with him sitting right here, how can I deny them something I've held onto my whole life? Something that has gotten me through so much of life—a father's love.

"I know what I did to you was wrong," I calmly say, "but know it was never with the intention to become pregnant. I didn't come looking for you. I would have never come looking for you. You found me and that's the truth. What you do with it is now your choice. I named her Israel James because I felt like it was the only part of her father I could give her." I have a seat in one of the guest chairs and sigh deeply. I am finally free, regardless of what he says and what happens after today. I am free of my past once and for all.

Real sits down without saying a word and grabs the picture of the twins again. I know it is a lot to process and I will give him as much time as he needs. Next to me sits my past, present, and future in this man. Whatever he decides to do will change my life from here on out, and I honestly don't know what I want him to do. If he chooses to go away and have nothing to do with Izzy and BJ, I will continue with the plan I already have. However, if he does choose to go away, I know I will feel some kind of way about it, because I would be the cause of my children never knowing their father. On the other hand, if he wants to be in their lives, him meeting the kids will be the easy part. Having to deal with him, any questions he has, and his disgust of me will be hard to manage. What if he wants to try to take my kids from me because he thinks I am a terrible person? I choke on that thought and let out a gasp. "Excuse me for a moment." I grab my phone and walk into the hall. I feel like I'm on fire with emotion and just want to explode.

Contrary to what Real probably thinks, I do have another meeting. Yeah, it is over the phone and will take all of five to ten minutes, but it is still a meeting all the same. I have Mindy transfer the call to the conference room and I grab a fax I need. The call is from a sports agent who hired me to look over his client's contract. He is as busy as I am, therefore, I am relieved that he takes it well when I rush him off the phone. I'm just too emotional to talk business right now. After I finish my conference call I go back to my office. As much as I am dreading it, I have to handle this with Real before 4 o'clock so I'm not late to pick up the twins.

"They look like me," Real says, still staring at the picture. "I mean, he looks exactly like me and, God, she has my..." He shakes his head.

"Your smile," I complete his sentence. He smiles and places the photo back on my desk.

"I want to meet them," Real says, looking up at me. I haven't sat down since I came back in the office, so what Real just said nearly knocks me off my feet. I don't know if I am glad that he wants to be a part of his children's lives or terrified that his meeting them might be the first step he'll take before dragging me into court for a nasty custody battle.

"Of course. We can make arrangements." I smile and pull up the calendar on my phone. At least I will have a little time to figure out how I am going to explain Real to the twins and GG. I never told her who the twins' father was. For all I know she probably thinks Bella was telling the truth about me being a ho. This is going a lot better than I could have ever imagined, though. He has stopped snapping on me and actually seems sincere about wanting to meet the kids. Thank you, God.

"Nah, I want to meet them now. Unless you got another meeting or something," Real says sarcastically.

"Actually, I do have another phone call I need to make." I roll my eyes. I have four missed calls from a blocked number and I am sure they are all from Clifford about his money. "But regardless, I don't think we should just jump into you meeting the kids so quickly," I explain to Real, hoping he will think rationally.

"They are my kids, right?" Real looks me up and down. Maybe I spoke too soon about things going well.

"Yes," I answer, looking him straight in his eyes. I hope this doesn't turn into another awkward staring contest. Dang, he still looks very handsome with a well-shaven goatee and reminds me so much of BJ.

"So for five years you kept this from me and now you're telling me I should wait even longer to see my kids." I can tell Real is getting upset. I need him to understand that I am not trying to keep the kids from him. I just need some time to think. The way he is looking at me, I can tell that the time is going to be now or never. "The first time I saw my father is when I signed my first basketball deal. I hadn't seen that man in 21 years, but obviously he knew exactly who I was 'cause as soon as I signed that contract he was waiting with his hand out, talking about I got

181

my skills from him. I looked into his eyes and saw myself staring back at me because we looked just alike, but I felt nothing for him. So I know how it feels not to have a daddy, and now that I know I'm a father I refuse to be like that." Real stands up and looks down at me. I can't lie; I am a little intimidated. I mean, here I am, 5'2"—well, 5'7 in my heels— and here he is, 6'3", towering over me, with a scowl on his face that looks like he means business.

"Yeah, I know you probably want more time, but you had five years to figure out what you would do if this happened. You're a smart woman. I am sure you already have something planned. I know you are a good liar, too, so whatever story you got to tell ya' man, I'm cool wit'. I am going to meet my kids today or we are going to take this to court." Real rubs his head, sighs, and closes his eyes in frustration. I cringe over what he just said. The thought of going to court and possibly losing my babies is unbearable. I have done some messed up things and he knows it and could probably prove it in a custody battle.

"Okay, um, I need to step out to make a phone call, then I guess you can follow me to the school and, um, we can go somewhere." I am willing to agree to just about anything to make sure he doesn't get the law involved and try to take my babies from me.

"I didn't drive so I will just ride with you." Real looks at me like he knows he has me in a bind that I can't get out of. Man, I feel like I am getting punked and Ashton Kutcher is gonna jump out laughing at me any moment now. This is nothing like the way I thought things would go. I expected him to deny them and scream about paternity tests, but he didn't. He is doing the exact opposite.

"And by the way, I don't have a man that I have to answer to, and if I did I wouldn't lie about this. Believe me, I've learned my lesson." I walk out of the office and answer my cell. It's Clifford and, unsurprisingly, he's being belligerent and calling me all kinds of names, but I don't care. He's just mad because I chin checked him with Bella's voice recordings and got him to agree to the $200,000. Besides, I know I'm not that person he and his brother met five years ago, so his words don't phase me. I tell him he can pick up his money tomorrow at my office. I then call Samantha, who after all these years is still my personal banker, to make sure she can have the money ready as soon as the bank opens.

I turn around to go back in the office, but Real is standing in the hallway mugging me. Five years ago I couldn't stop thinking about him and what he thought of me, now I have the opportunity to make amends and convince him I am real. God, give me the words to say to him. "Look, I can only imagine what you think of me, but I've changed. I've changed my whole life. I mean, honestly, I think what happened with you saved my life and I am sincerely sorry you had to be involved with my hustle," I apologize as we walk to the car. "I understand you must be in shock and probably want to get a DNA test, and I'm perfectly fine with that. Just don't do things behind my back," I tell him. Real doesn't say much. Actually, he doesn't respond to anything I am saying.

We get in my car and I begin to contemplate what I will tell the twins. With traffic it usually takes between 30 and 40 minutes to get to the school, so that is how long I have to figure out what I am going to say.

"So you and your sister were prostitutes and stole money from y'all tricks?" Real finally breaks the silence.

"No, not at all. We stole from hundreds of men and you were the only one I ever slept with. Actually, you are only the second man I have ever slept with in my entire life. And as for my sister, please believe she did not have sex with your brother or any other mark," I reply matter-of-factly. "There was something about you. I did like you. I did want you. My attraction for you was much more than just physical and I let my guard down and messed up," I try to explain, but I feel like Real isn't paying me much attention and probably doesn't care what I have to say. It kind of hurts because I never did let go of my feelings for him. I never forgot about Real and how I felt when I met him. And the twins are a constant reminder of him. But I know what I did has ruined any chance for us. He won't even look at me. He can't see how much I've changed. I guess I will forever be that chick that drugged him, hustled him, and got pregnant by him.

"It's a nice day out. I was thinking maybe we can take them to the park," I suggest as the sun warms my face. I glance over at Real who is texting on his phone.

"Yeah, that's fine. I just want to meet them," Real answers without looking up from his phone. He doesn't say anything else and, honestly, I don't know what I'm expecting him to say but I want some type of reaction or response. I want him to care, but with his eyes glued to his phone he seems too busy to do so.

The silence is racking my brain as we arrive at La Petite. The parking lot is empty, as usual. The school closes at 5:30 and I am usually one of, if not the last parent to pick their kids. I nervously run my fingers through my hair. It's time. I have to face the twins and tell them the truth. Well, they don't need to know the whole truth. I will leave out the part that Mommy had a one-night stand. All they need to know is that Real is their father and he found Mommy at her office. Yeah, that's it. This situation will be easier for them to digest if I add the twist that he has been looking for them all this time and wanted nothing more than to meet them.

"You ready?" Real gets out of the car and closes the car door.

"What are you doing?" I jump out of the car. "No, stay here." I step in front of Real, placing my hand on his stomach. Real grabs my hand and pulls me closer to him. "Let my hand go," I say, trying to pull away from him.

"Hey, Beau," I hear a voice call out from behind me.

"Michelle, Mike, how are you all doing?" I smile. Michelle and Michael Stewart are parents of one of the twins' classmates. They look like the perfect little couple; well-off, educated, affluent black people.

"Great," they answer in unison.

"Have a great weekend," I smile and walk past them towards the door. Real and I are still holding hands and I can hear Michael and Michelle whispering. I have never brought any man up to the school and Real looks exactly like the type of man everyone would expect me to date, being a sports attorney. Wearing basketball shorts, Jordans, and a Nike T-shirt, everything about Israel screams basketball.

"You can let my hand go now," I say, snatching away from Real as we walk into the school.

"Buenas tardes Senora Jones," Martine, the front desk administrator, greets me as I approach the desk to check the twins out. "Quien es el hombre guapo?" She throws Real a confused smile and glances back at me.

"Me llamo Real. Yo soy papa de Israel y Beau. Mucho gusto." Real reaches out to shake Martine's hand. I don't know if I am more shocked that he speaks Spanish or that he just told her that he's the twins' father. "Senora, necesito ser poner en el lista de mi hijos," Real tells Martine he needs to be added to the twins' list at school.

"Que necesita firmar una papel." Martine looks over at me and I grin and nod my head. She smiles and walks away to get the papers.

"What are you doing?" I pull Israel to the side and whisper.

"Ensuring that you won't try to keep my kids from me," Real says with a straight face.

"Look, please go wait in the car. Let me explain to them what is about to happen. Imagine how you felt an hour and a half ago," I exasperatedly try to reason with him. I hate losing control over the situation and Real is forcing me to follow his every move. I'm too scared of what will happen if I do otherwise. I really do want to know what he is thinking and what his motive is. I mean, I am glad he is accepting the kids, but something is wrong with this picture; he is being overly accepting.

"Okay." Real grabs my keys and walks over to Martine to sign the papers before going to the car. I watch him walk out before I go to the twins' classroom.

I stand in the doorway of the twins' class as they sing and dance to La Cucaracha.

"Vamonos mis amores," I call out to them after the second go-around of La Cucaracha. Izzy's curly ponytails are bobbing around and BJ's long legs are skipping towards me. They have no idea their lives are about to change. "Hey, so I have a really big surprise," I tell them as we walk down the hall. My palms are sweating. I take a deep breath before continuing. "There is someone in the car who is very excited to meet you." I smile nervously. The twins smile and begin to walk faster.

"Who?! Who?!" they repeatedly ask, sounding like a couple of owls.

"Your dad," I spit out the words and they stop dead in their tracks in the middle of the parking lot. I look over at Israel whose eyes are big and bright. I try to continue to walk but BJ doesn't budge.

"Really?" His face lights up.

"Yes, and I was thinking we can skip basketball practice and go to the park." I know the twins will have millions of questions and I sure am not trying to get a million more from the parents at practice, most of which go to the same church as me. Not to mention, I have no idea what to expect of Israel. He might tell everyone that walks by that he is the twins' dad. Shoot, then there's Brandon...I forgot all about him. He is the kids' basketball coach who I have been talking to for a few months. Brandon is cool. We've even gone on a few dates. But I definitely don't want him asking questions that I don't have the answers to.

Real gets out the car as we are walking up.

"So you're my dad?" Izzy doesn't waste any time starting with questions.

"Yes," Real smiles.

"What's your name?" Izzy continues with the questions.

"Can you continue your interrogation in the car?" I ask as I open BJ's door while Real helps Izzy in.

"My name is Israel James. What's yours?" Real asks, snapping her seat belt.

"My name is Israel James, too. Where have you been? Didn't you want to see us?" Izzy asks the question I have been dreading.

"Well, it took me a really long time to find your mommy, but now that I am here I promise I won't ever leave you, okay?" Real looks over at me with a stare of blame. Eh I've gotten used to it by now.

We arrive at the park and I let Real spend time with the twins as I sit on a bench texting Bella and Angel. They are just as shocked as me when I tell them how Real had reacted. Real, Izzy, and BJ look like they have always known each other as they laugh, talk, run, and play. I sit back watching. I never ever thought a day like this would come and now that it is here it is so beautiful and perfect. I let Bella know that I am meeting up with Clifford tomorrow and am giving him the $200,000. I'm not tripping about the money. The $35,000 Bella had given me from that hustle has been collecting interest over the past five years. I have never touched it and now it is coming in handy. I can sense Bella's relief through the phone. We have dodged another bullet.

Angel sends me an interesting text message: *You know he has a GF n she will come for you. His bro will prolly help her.*

She is right, I have another dilemma on my hands. I am sure his family and girlfriend are going to feel some kind of way; especially Clifford, because of the circumstances in which the twins were conceived.

That's his problem, I reply. I can't worry about what anyone else thinks. Seeing my children with their father makes sense, regardless of how I feel or how Real feels about me.

"Izzy is getting cold," Real informs me. "The sun is going down. We should probably get a move on it." Real carries Izzy and holds BJ's hand. She is a daddy's girl already.

"Okay," I smile. "So do you want me to drop you off at home or...?" I look over at Real as we put the kids in the car.

"Nah, I'll call a taxi," Real replies.

"No, Mommy, can he come over for dinner?" BJ asks. I look over at Real, hoping he will decline.

"You know what guys? I think he probably has to get home. Maybe another night." I smile at the twins and hold my breath, hoping he will say no. I just want this day to be over. I need a glass of wine and my sisters.

"I'd love to," Real says, winking his eye at the twins.

"Of course you would," I sigh. I guess my glass of wine and sisters will have to wait.

"Thank you," Real looks over and whispers to me. I can only muster up a smile in response. Once again Real has taken control and all I can do is follow.

On the way home I stop to pick up a pizza. Israel and the kids wait in the car, and I call Bella while I run in to grab the pizza. "Don't come yet. He's coming for dinner," is all I can get out before I hang up the phone and get back into the car. As I head towards the house all I can think about is the fact that now he knows where I work, where the kids go to school, and he is about to be at my house. There's no going back. I don't think I would if I could, though. They look so happy together and the twins can't stop talking to him. We look like one big happy family. Real even looks over at me a couple of times and smiles.

"Mommy, is that Coach Brandon?" BJ points at a tall light-skinned man shooting baskets in our driveway as we pull up. I have never invited Brandon over. He must have gotten my address from the basketball registration form, but I don't know why he would pop up unannounced. We are definitely not on that level. I ask Real to take the pizzas and the kids into the house and hand him my keys. Just when I thought nothing else crazy could happen today this man decides to pop up at my house.

"Hey, Coach Brandon," the kids say before they go into the house with Real. Brandon smiles and waves then looks at me like I have done something wrong.

"What are you doing here?" I question Brandon. Man, dudes be catching feelings just as bad, if not worse, than women.

"You haven't been returning my calls and I didn't see you at basketball practice, so I felt like I needed to come check on you to make sure everything is okay. But now I know why...sheesh." Brandon continues to shoot the ball. I refuse to feel bad about this. He is wrong for stalking my address and coming over uninvited. "I mean, you tell me you like me and just want to take it slow then I see you here with some other cat eating pizza and hanging out at the crib with the kids—things you don't even do with me. You got me here waiting on you. You got me here believing you when you saying you want to take it slow, and

187

then…then...this. I'm cool, Beau," Brandon says, pausing and looking over at me.

Really? Is he really acting like this after three, maybe four dates? "For one, it's never cool to pop up at somebody's house like this. I told you I've been busy with work, and everything I told you, I meant. As far as the guy you just saw, I don't owe you an explanation, but you're reading into stuff that is not even there." I shake my head. I am totally turned off. "He is the twins' father." I roll my eyes at having to give him an explanation he doesn't deserve.

"Oh," is the next thing that comes out his mouth. The expression on his face says it all. He looks like he just lost a fight.

"We aren't together," I reassure him. His face immediately changes. He grabs my hand and pulls me towards him. I pull back before I hit his chest. "Don't show up to my house unannounced again." I leave it at that and walk away.

"I feel like everything happens for a reason. God is in everything; even in me popping up unexpectedly," Brandon tries to reason with me.

I cut my eyes at him. "Don't bring God into your foolishness."

I walk in the house Real and the twins are sitting in the family room with the pizza. "What are y'all doing over there?"

"Hey, you guys told me we could eat in here for family movie night. Aw, man, I done got played by some five-year-olds. My bad; we didn't get anything on your fancy couch," Real apologizes. I can see he is feeling like he has made his first parenting mistake.

"How y'all gonna start the movie without me?" I smack BJ in the head with a pillow and grab a slice of pizza. I sit in my favorite recliner and kick my legs up. The twins usually squeeze in with me but they decide to sit on the couch with Real. I am not jealous, though. Real is like a new Christmas present that they want to play with all the time when they first get it.

After pizza and ice cream the twins are good and full. It won't be long before they are asleep. This is usually how our Friday nights go. I am surprised the twins make it halfway through the movie before dozing off. Even Real has fallen asleep. He is sitting up with his head against the back of the couch, and the twins are under each of his arms. I grab my cell phone to take a picture of the three of them. Tomorrow I will print it and hang it up in the twins' rooms. I take a couple more pics and text them to Bella and Angel. This is definitely one of those *have to see it to believe it* moments. I caption the photo *God works in mysterious ways.*

"Hey." I look over at Real as I pick Izzy up from under his arm. "Y'all were sleeping good," I smile. Real picks up BJ and follows me upstairs to their rooms.

"This is a nice house," Real compliments. I wait for a jab, some type of mean-hearted joke about how I paid for it, but it doesn't come. We lay the twins in their beds and then walk back downstairs to the living room. "Thought you didn't have a man to answer to," Real says as he helps take the dishes into the kitchen.

"I don't," I reply and leave it at that. I quickly call a cab to get him out of here. I'm glad he connected with the twins, but I'm ready for him to go, especially if he is going to start interrogating me. How in the world did I go from being single to having two men questioning me all in the same day? I don't owe him any answers, either.

"I mean, you should have invited him in so we could meet. I want to know who my kids are around and I am sure he was worried about me," Real continues.

"Like I said, I don't have any man to answer to. So we are all good," I shrug my shoulders. Awkward much.

"Yeah, I bet," Real's sarcasm returns. I feel like he is putting his walls back up. It seems like I have taken one step forward and two steps back. I'm pretty sure he thinks I'm lying about Brandon and that I'm still the same chick that drugged and sexed him five years ago.

Real and I exchange phone numbers before his cab pulls up. Then he is gone and I am left to sort out what just happened today and how I am going to deal with him from here on out. God…

189

DONISHA DERICE & JAI DARLENE

22
When the Kettle Finally Meets the Pot

Bella

I roll my Bentley into the parking lot of GG's church. Well, I should say my church. It's just not GG's church anymore. Brian and I officially joined as members years ago soon after we got engaged. Becoming a member was intense. We had to take eight weeks of new member's classes and I had to have multiple one-on-one counseling sessions with Pastor Lewis. It was worth it, though. I made a promise to God that if he helped me I would turn my life around. God made good on his part, so I had to do mine. Pastor helped me work through my abandonment and trust issues, which ran deep. I swear, God relieved me of so many burdens and has forgiven me for so much wrong that my heart leaps with joy whenever I think about how good He has been to me. Especially since God helped me put the Clifford fiasco behind me. I faced my past and made things right by repaying what I stole from him and now I am back to normalcy.

It's Friday, so I am not here for a church sermon. I'm here to volunteer. I walk into the church's cafeteria and First Lady is walking in from the kitchen. She is rocking a cute bob cut and a black and white Ann Taylor pantsuit. "Bella, honey, there you go. I was just about to come looking for you," Lady Lewis playfully fusses with me. We greet each other with a hug.

"Let's get to work," I tell her. First Lady and I partnered up and formed NOC, which stands for Nourish Our Community. It's a charity organization we started together to feed a four-course meal to over 750 needy families in Indianapolis once a week. We also give away enough food supplies to last them the other six days of the week. Most people don't think about feeding the needy until November and December when the holidays hit. They forget about the other ten months of the year. There are some food drives that feed the poor daily, but their funding is lacking and the meals are usually meager and nasty tasting. NOC fills the void by feeding the needy all year around. The meals we provide are delicious gourmet dishes.

We go into the kitchen to help the other volunteers prepare the

191

food. "Mrs. Bewa, you late," I hear a small squeaky voice say, mispronouncing my name. I am late. I would love to say I'm late because I have my hands full juggling Sophia Tanya Love Thy Children, Proms for Girls, and running my household. But truth be told I was really busy giving my husband a private dance on our newly installed stripper pole before he flew out to a business meeting. I flipped and twirled on the pole, giving him a happy ending before he left. I knew I was running late, so I took a quick shower and slipped on a bright yellow maxi dress. I was in such a rush that I didn't put on any panties before leaving.

"Can I see ya' purse?" a different squeaky voice asks. The two squeaky voices belong to Caleb's children; Camesha, who is six years old, and Calvin, who just turned five. Caleb has three children, two on the way, and four baby mommas. Turns out Caleb had a secret baby, Camesha, who no one knew about until a year after her birth. While First Lady was busy shaming me, Caleb was getting busy making babies. Caleb's parents didn't find out about the baby until they received a subpoena served at the church to appear in court for child support. Camesha's mother will admit in a hot minute she only filed for child support because she was pregnant with his second child and she found out he had another baby, Calvin, on the way with another woman. These women were fighting in the church parking lot, pregnant bellies and all. It was so messy I thought they were filming for a reality show called Real Baby Mommas Of a Preacher's Son.

After First Lady found out about Camesha and Calvin we had a heart-to-heart. She told me she should have tried to embrace me instead of condemning me. In fact, she admitted she was ashamed of how she treated me and that her actions were not God-like. And I forgave her. It's like Pastor says, harboring unforgiveness is like drinking poison and hoping someone else dies. We've become very close since then and we talk frequently.

I feel a tug on my purse again. "Let me see ya' purse," Calvin says to me.

"Boy, get off her purse. What's wrong with you?" First Lady fusses at her grandson and I laugh. I know what little Calvin wants. I pull two small pouches of fruit snacks out of my purse and hold them out to Camesha and Calvin. Full of smiles, they greedily grab the pouches. "What do you say?" First Lady asks them.

"Thank you," they say in unison and run off giggling.

"And when do you and your husband plan on having some of

those running around?" First Lady probes, pointing at Camesha and Calvin. Brian and I have been trying to get pregnant for the last two years to no avail. Our doctor says nothing is wrong with either one of us fertility-wise. We were told these things just take some time. It's frustrating because I look at Caleb, who is having baby after baby without even trying, and I'm struggling to get pregnant. Adoption is always an option but the process can take years.

I shake my head. "Sometimes I think it just won't happen for us." First Lady places her hands on my stomach. My stomach grumbles a little bit because I'm hungry. I'm a little embarrassed, but I try to pretend like it didn't happen. I close my eyes and lift my hands.

"Lord, open her womb. OPEN," She shakes her hands on my stomach and it grumbles again. I don't know if her prayer will work, but it certainly can't hurt. Open, womb, open. Maybe I should place my hands on Brian's balls and say, "Open, testes, open." Or maybe not. I will jump at any reason to touch his balls.

After we finish serving dinner to the needy families I give my hugs and goodbyes to First Lady and the other volunteers. I grab my purse and check my cell phone for messages as I walk to my car. Beau texted me a picture of her, Real, and the kids. Angel texted me, too: ***Did Beau tell you about Brandon? He's calling me looking for her #Stalker.***

I don't know why, but I find Beau and her little love triangle hilarious. Beau spent so many years avoiding men and relationships and now she has two men bidding for her attention. I'm placing my money on Real, though. When he first started coming around Beau used to send pictures of him with the kids. Now she's sending family pictures with her and Real looking like a couple.

A day doesn't go past that I don't talk to my sisters, and every time I talk to Beau she is with Real. She's at the park with Real and the kids, cooking dinner for Real and the kids, taking the kids to a Disney movie with Real. Real, Real, Real, Real. Let her tell it, she's just letting Real come around for the sake of the kids. Yeah, she gets the side eye for that. The kids can have a relationship with their father without her spending so much quality time with him. But I think it's cute and I hope Beau and Real work it out. I think it was love at first sight for her and he was the one that got away. Now, she has a second chance at love.

Once I reach my car, I notice there is a piece of paper under my windshield wipers. Did Brian leave a sexy note on my car? I am all smiles in anticipation of what the note might say. I reach for the note and

193

read it: ***Bella, amore mio, my sweet zeppole. Do you think you can get away from me that easily? Just because we haven't spoken in a long time doesn't mean I'm not watching you. You may be married but you will always be mine. I'll see you soon.***

"Ugh!" I scream. Reggie's stalker self has some nerve leaving a note on my car like this. I ball up the note and stomp on it. But that doesn't seem like enough. I'm still angry, so I pick up the crumpled note and throw it across the parking lot like I am pitching a baseball. Forget Reggie. He's just trying to get under my skin. He's still been sending me Christmas and birthday e-cards over the years despite me never replying and blocking his emails. But this is going too far. At least I have Greta strapped to my leg. I always feel better with her nearby. Reggie picked the wrong time to mess with me. Last time I tased him; next time I'm taking out one of his knees. He can't stalk me with no knees.

Clutching my purse, I quickly get in my car and race to GG's house. I told her I would stop by. She is making me a good home-cooked meal. I make a mental note to call Beau to see what legal measures I should take just in case I have to kill Reggie.

When I arrive at GG's she is all hugs and kisses. "How's my baby girl doing? You okay?" I know she can tell I am shaken up about something, but I decide not to tell her about Reggie's note. No point of making her worry about something Beau and I can handle ourselves.

"I'll be alright, GG. I'm starving and I'm ready to eat." My appetite has picked up since I've been with Brian. It's true that when you are happy and in love you eat more.

"I cooked some meatloaf, corn, and macaroni and cheese," GG says, guiding me to the kitchen. I make a plate of corn and macaroni and cheese, and leave the meatloaf. Just because my appetite is bigger doesn't mean I have to eat meat on a daily basis. I still need to keep my body tight and right for my hubby.

I finish with my plate and curl up on the couch, laughing and joking with GG. I end up dozing off and am startled awake by a call from Angel. GG dozed off, too, and is asleep in the recliner.

"Hermana, I'm throwing a party tonight. You coming through?"

"Heck nah! You know what happened last time I went to one of your parties," I say, referring to when fat head Clifford hemmed me up and tried to extort $2 mil out of me.

"Well, it's not really a party; more like a get-together."

"That's what you said the last time. It's only a get-together," I say in a mocking voice.

"Whatever. What you scared for? I thought everything was all good now. Didn't Beau handle that?"

"She did handle it, but I'm still not messing with you—"

THUMP!

I jump at the sound. "What was that?" Angel asks, concerned. I don't know, but it has to be something big for it to be loud enough for Angel to hear over the phone. The noise wakes GG up. She goes into the kitchen and looks out the window into the backyard.

"It's the trash can. The squirrels must have knocked it over. Bella, go pick it up before I get garbage all over my yard. I got to use the ladies room." GG heads towards the bathroom and I look out the kitchen window and see the trash can tumbled over and rolling under a big bush. I tell Angel I will call her back and put my cell in my purse, leaving it on the counter while I go outside. I bend over to pick up the trash can and suddenly feel a pair of strong hands grab me and pull me down. I try to yell, but a big wad of cloth is stuffed in my mouth, muffling my voice. I fall to the ground hard and then, everything goes black.

23
Fights, Real Talk, and Make-Ups

Beau

"Mommy, look! Daddy scored again!" BJ points at the scoreboard, jumping up and down.

"I see. I see," I smile at him. Izzy chants the cheer I taught her and shakes her blue and gold pom-poms. She's been cheering the entire game. Real has invited the twins to every home game since he met them and I get to go by default. He always gets us nice seats in the family section, but we opted to watch from a suite. One of the perks of being a sports attorney is suite seats whenever I want, although up until now I had never taken advantage of it.

Real had bought BJ several of his jerseys and had some custom cheerleader outfits made with his name and number for Izzy. I usually just rock a team tee, although tonight I am wearing Real's number 21 jersey, because the twins have repeatedly asked me why I never wear one. It's nothing petty. I actually have a legit reason why—Real's girlfriend, Skylar. I am not trying to cause trouble in their relationship, even though he initially didn't tell me about her. Bella, Angel, and I figured she was the chick that was with Clifford's wife that night at Angel's condo. About a month and a half after Real had met the twins, we all went to dinner so the twins and I could meet her. Real had shown interest in keeping the twins while I went on a business trip and I made it clear it wasn't going to happen until I met the woman he lives with. I needed to see how she interacted with the twins. She was nice and talked with them at dinner. They seemed to like her well enough. And even though I know it was fake, she acted nice toward me and tried to keep up conversation. But I am not crazy; she is a woman who wants to keep her man and the twins and I are a threat to that.

"Don't leave my kids alone with that woman," I smiled as Real walked us to the car after dinner. Real assured me she is cool and, although she was initially upset about finding out he had children, she was accepting of it and wanted to have a relationship with them, too. "Don't leave my kids alone with her," I repeated. I was smiling but I was dead serious. I promise it was nothing personal and I am most definitely

197

not jealous of Skylar. But I have seen women and athletes in similar situations, and not all of them had happy endings. I know me, and if she so much as looks sideways at my babies I will have to see her.

Things with Real and I are actually going very well, though. He isn't taking any more jabs at my past indiscretions and he is committed to being a good—no, great—father, and that is all I can ask for. After meeting GG, Real has even come over for Sunday dinner and started attending our church. Of course GG persuaded him to attend with her "God is the key" speech. I mean, who can turn down a God-fearing woman after getting full off of fried chicken, mashed potatoes, macaroni and cheese, green beans, hot water cornbread, and apple pie?

"Mommy, don't forget Daddy said to meet him by the locker room after the game," Izzy whispers in my ear and then continues to cheer. Real had promised to show them where he hung the pictures they had drawn for him. To see them with Real you would not believe that they had only known each other for three months.

Indiana beat Miami 112 to 98 and I am glad they won, because I wasn't sure about taking the twins down there to see him if they had lost—a riot might've broken out. It was game six of the Eastern Conference Finals and the series is now tied 3 to 3. The Fieldhouse is on fire with the chants and cheers of fans. I figure we will wait a few minutes before leaving the suite.

"Hey, Beau. You all are still here?" Jack Bronson, the general manger of the team asks, walking over.

"Yeah, Israel promised to show the kids his locker after the game," I smile. I have gotten a few questions about Real being the twins' father from some of the team staff and players, but I have concocted a good cover story about Real and I wanting to keep the kids away from the business until they were a little older. It seems to have worked, and since Real didn't really start getting a bunch of media attention until the playoffs, there wasn't any suspicion about him trying to hide the kids. It seems like Indiana is the perfect spot for Real. He met his children and is doing big things on a good team. He has told me how reluctant and frustrated he was about being traded to Indiana, but that he now sees that it was the best move of his life. Everything happens for a reason.

We see Real waiting outside the locker room as we approach it. "Hey, I thought y'all had stood me up." He is already dressed in a blue and gold jogging suit and matching gold basketball sneakers. The twins run up to give Real a hug and I snap a few pictures. "Hey, Beau. What's up?" Real smiles at me before going into the locker room.

"Bitch, you think you slick!" I hear someone yelling from down the hall. Ah, man, who wife done got upset? I turn around to watch the drama unfold and I see Skylar marching towards me. What in the world? She can't possibly be talking to me. "You money-hungry, scandalous ass trick. You think you got him? You ain't got shit!" she continues to yell as she storms down the hall. I look around like everybody else is doing, acting like she is not talking to me but I know she is. Unfortunately, I have no idea what she is talking about. She is wearing skinny jeans, Real's jersey, and sneakers, no earrings or make up, and her hair is pulled up in a ponytail. She looks like she is ready to fight. God, I do not want to beat her down but, if she—.

Skylar swings her open right hand towards me before I can finish my thought. I step to the right and throw her a left to her face. She tumbles to the floor. "Oh my God, bitch, I am going to kill you!" she screams from the ground, holding her jaw, which is already turning bright purple and red. Out of pure natural instinct, I kick her before she can get up and put my shoe on her throat, applying pressure every time she tries to push my leg off.

"I could crush your larynx and you wouldn't have anything to say, you ignorant little girl." I remove my foot and she scampers to the wall, holding her throat. Everyone stares quietly, not moving. Skylar finally stands up and pulls a phone out of her pocket.

"I am calling the police," she whimpers.

I laugh at her stupidity. I don't know what's up with these chicks starting drama and getting mad when they get touched. "Go ahead because there are a number of witnesses that not only heard you yelling profanities at me, but also saw you swing on me first." I shake my head and wait to see what she is going to do next. Skylar stands motionless, holding her phone.

"What the hell?" Real finally exits the locker room with the twins and sees Skylar standing in a corner.

"Really? She's cool, right?" I look at Real and take the twins' hands and leave. I need to get out of here ASAP.

The twins are asleep by the time we get home. I put them to bed and grab a bottle of wine and a glass, and sit on the couch. After drinking half of the bottle I forget about the throbbing pain in my left hand. It actually isn't swollen, which is good. I don't remember the last time I got into a fight. I open and close my hand. I can't even consider what happened with Skylar a fight, but I know I was wrong and I could have handled it differently. I'm just glad the twins didn't witness their mommy cold clocking her. I want them to always see me in a professional light and handling difficult situations diplomatically. I'm going to have to have a conversation with Real about his girlfriend. She obviously has some type of jealousy issues going on about the twins being in Real's life. I can understand her feeling some kind of way about finding out only three months ago that Real has kids, but if she has issues she should have approached me and we could have discussed whatever was on her mind.

I hit the reject button for at least eight of Real's calls and don't read any of the texts that he sends. I know we have to talk, but I'm not in the mood right now. I have managed to remove every bit of drama from my life to make sure my twins would never have to deal with any foolishness. I know that Izzy and BJ definitely need their father in their lives. He really is amazing with them, but he's going to have to get Skylar in order.

I see headlights pulling into the driveway. That better not be Real. Obviously I don't want to get into this with him tonight. I peek through the curtain and see Israel's bright gold sneakers walking up. I grab my phone and text Real: *GO HOME*.

"No," Real says through the door. "I'm not leaving, Beau, so open the door." Real starts knocking on the door.

"They are asleep," I say, reluctantly opening the door.

"We got to talk." Real comes in and plops on the couch. He smells like liquor—Hennessey or something dark.

"Have you been drinking? How do you expect to have a rational conversation?" I grab my wine glass and take a seat on a chair.

"I have been drinking but I'm not drunk," he says. "I'm so sorry for what Skylar did." Real seems sincere and sorry as he stands in front of me apologizing.

"I...we cannot have that around our kids. I can't make you break up with her but I don't want Izzy or BJ anywhere near her."

"I know. Believe me, that was the last straw." Real rubs his head with both hands. What does he mean by last straw?

"So this isn't the first time she has acted up like that?" I question Real.

"Nah, it's not like that, Beau, and she hasn't in front of the kids. I don't even think she feels like the twins are the problem. It's you," Real explains.

200

"Me?" I sit my glass on the table. "Then you have done a horrible job of reassuring her that there is nothing going on between us." I roll my eyes. "Unbelievable. What did you do to make her feel that way?" I expect him to say nothing, which is probably the problem.

"Before the game tonight, I told her I still have feelings for you and that she needed to move out." Real looks into my eyes before leaning in to give me a kiss. It is long and deep. I should push him away but I don't. It feels *so* good. I place my hands around his head and I feel his hands wrap around my arched back as he leans onto me and the chair.

"What are you doing?" I ask, finally pulling away from his lips and scooting back on the chair. I can't lie, I liked it, but I'm not sure if this is what we should be doing. We should take things slow. Get to know each other more. Go on an actual date. Yeah, we have been spending a lot of time together, but only with the kids. I want to go on a date before we start making out in my living room. More importantly, I want to know if this is for real. I don't want to get Izzy and BJ's hopes up by making them think their mommy and daddy are going to be together and then things fall apart between us.

"I was so shitty with what you had done, but I looked for you. I still wanted to see you. I wanted to explain away what had happened that night, because I didn't want to believe you were that type of person. I was hoping that you didn't know what your sister did to my brother until after the fact, and that you disappeared because you were just too embarrassed to show your face. I wanted to believe that our connection was real. I have never in my life felt a connection to any woman like I did within the first five minutes of meeting you," Real confesses. I can feel my heart racing as Real sits in front of me expressing how he feels. "I think I have feelings for you, Beau, and I hope you do, too. And I know I said some mean shit to you when we first ran back into each other, but I didn't mean it. I wanted you then and I still want you." Real pulls me in towards him. I feel his hands gently rubbing my back as he presses his head against my stomach. I wrap my arms around his head, hugging him close to me, and in the moment, it is real. The connection I felt for him when I met him five years ago; the feelings I have always had for him. Damn, this is what I have dreamt about.

I decide I am not letting Real go and I am not letting this moment go. I bend down to my knees and look him in the eyes. I can feel his heart beating just as fast as mine. My kiss falls deeply on Real's lips and when I pull back, his lips and body follow me to the floor. Each kiss he places on my neck feels like ecstasy and my body quivers with every gentle touch. "You don't know how much I have dreamt of this…of you," Real whispers in my ear as he raises his jersey over my head. His tongue circles my neck before nestling between my breasts. I don't know how my boy shorts came off, but as he kisses his way down my stomach I know he is a pleaser. The first time we had sex he knew exactly what to do to please me. Now it's my turn. I pull Real's head up as I feel his warm breath on my vagina.

"What?" Real pauses like he has done something wrong. I just smile at him as I roll him over so that I am on top of him. I feel him hard through his basketball shorts. I part my lips so my breath tickles his ears as I kiss him. I know he is ready but I want to savor every moment. I move my hips slowly back and forth as his hands grip my back and then my ass. I can feel his heavy breaths and heartbeat as I kiss his chest, slowly making my way to his dick as my hands pull down his shorts. I begin to massage his head with my mouth and stroke his shaft. I can tell his toes are curling as he moans. He can't control himself.

I wait until he is just about there, more than ready, and get on top of him. He feels so good. I ride him slowly back and forth, up and down. I ignore the pain from not having had sex in so long, feeling every inch of him as I ride. I know I am tight. I lay on his chest, squeezing my thighs into his as I speed up. I feel myself climaxing as he grips the small of my back. "Oh my—" I kiss Real to stop him from screaming out and quickly roll off of him before he cums.

I sigh in satisfaction and can't take the big grin off of my face. It was all, and even more, than I imagined. It felt so right there's no way it could have been wrong. Everything within me is feeling like he is the one. I can only hope he feels the same way. But Real doesn't say anything. He doesn't even look at me. No regrets.

"So what now?" I look over at Real as we lay on the floor. We haven't said anything since we finished and I have laid there silently for as long as I could. I don't want to ruin the moment, but I need to know.

"I want us to try," Real looks into my eyes and says.

"I do, too, but there is something I need to tell you." I sit up and take a deep breath.

"What the fuck, Beau?!" Real jumps up. "I can't take anymore secrets or surprises from you."

"Calm down. It's nothing like that." I can only imagine what he is thinking. Real starts putting on his basketball shorts. He looks worried about what I have to say.

"I hadn't been with anyone since you. I know you may not believe me, but it is the truth. What happened that night I met you and what happened to your brother changed my life. I am so sorry it happened, but it was the best thing for me because it made me see God. I saw all that God had done for me. God gave me a second chance. God gave me life." I wrap the throw blanket lying on the couch around myself and go stand by Real, who is looking out the window. "I haven't slept with anyone because I made a vow to God and myself to change." I take Israel's hand and he looks into my eyes. "I would love for us to give it a try, especially since for the last five years every time I looked in the twins' faces I saw you and wondered what could have been if I hadn't been hustling." I choke on the last few words. All of this seemed impossible and now I am ready to let it all go. "I can be there for you emotionally, but not physically. I cannot serve God and be the woman God wants me to be and have sex outside of marriage. And no, I am not saying I want you to marry me like right now. What happened tonight was good, but I can't do it again." God, I hope he understands.

Real doesn't say anything for what seems like forever. I am starting to feel crushed, but no regrets. "Is that it?" Real looks down at me and I nod my head. "Well first off, I can tell it's been a long, long, long time," Real laughs. I couldn't have been that bad. It's like riding a bike, right? I punch Real in his arm. "A'ight Tyson, I think you have beat enough people down tonight. And that wasn't what I meant by saying it's been a long time, but I can tell." Real smiles and, yeah, I know what he is talking about. "I really don't know how I feel about that. I can only say I will try." I smile, letting him know I accept his answer. It is all I can ask for.

"So now that you done using me you putting me out?" Real asks.

"You can stay tonight, but we can't make a habit of it. Don't want either one of us getting tempted to do something." We go up to my bedroom and climb into bed. He wraps his arms around me and it feels so right. Within moments we are both sleeping peacefully.

"That's you," Real says, tapping my shoulder, waking me up. I don't want to roll over, open my eyes, or anything. "The phone...it's ringing." Real taps me again. It's the house phone. I finally sit up. Other than businesses, only one person ever calls that house phone.

"It's my grandmother. It must be something important for her to be calling so late." I grab the phone with panic and fear mounting in my heart. God, what is wrong?

24
A Ten-Second Keepsake

Bella

I hit the ground hard and my head lands on a stone about the size of a baseball, knocking me out for four seconds. Four seconds might not seem like long, but it is an eternity to me. Even though I am blacked out, I can hear his movements. I can hear him tear duct tape and stick it over my mouth to keep me from spitting the dirty cloth out. I can feel him reach down and I know his next move is to pull up my long maxi dress. I have no panties on. Damn, out of all the days that I actually do wear panties, today had to be the day I give easy access. I will myself awake and force my eyes to jerk open after the four seconds of eternity. I have to stop what is about to happen—my rape.

Reggie is overtaken by obsession. He reaches for the hem of my dress and pulls it up at the same time I reach for Greta. She is strapped to my inner thigh with a garter belt. I grip her slender handle, mentally preparing myself to kill Reggie. Just shooting to injure him won't be enough. I would get away tonight, but who knows when he'd be back to finish the job. This dude is absolutely insane. I have to shoot to kill, but something in me doesn't want to do it. Maybe I'll just shoot him in the dick; that will stop him from attacking me or anyone else ever again. Yes, I will shoot his dick off. I'm not a killer, but I am a fighter. I did the calculations in my head. Four seconds to duct tape my mouth. Five seconds to reach for Greta. Eight seconds to dismantle the safety and in ten seconds I will shoot him in the balls. Ten seconds from when this began this whole thing will be over. Reggie will be flapping on the ground and holding onto what's left of his balls. The police will be here and this will all be over. I'll be safe once again in ten seconds.

I feel the hardness of Reggie's penis on my leg and I throw up a little bit in my mouth. I swallow it back down so I won't choke on my regurgitation. The thought of Reggie touching me has always disgusted me. With Greta in my hand I take the safety off and I am ready to fight. He grabs the gun and says something in Italian. My adrenaline is pumping too hard to hear the actual words he says, but the voice I recognize. This is not Reggie. Terror rolls over my body, immobilizing

205

me. Reggie I can fight. Reggie I can beat. Reggie I have beaten before. But this is Lorenzo. I can't beat him. No one beats Marcello Ricci and lives to tell about it. He's above the law, and let him tell it, above God Himself.

I think back to how I was humiliated when I was willing to give him my virginity. How the FBI bust in through the door when I was butt naked on his bed with his penis in my hand. After Lorenzo was arrested and I was released from being questioned, I went home and cried for hours. And when I was finally done crying I hopped on my laptop and Googled Marcello Ricci to find out who he really is. He is rumored to be the mastermind behind many gruesome murders, but the ones that stuck in my mind the most were not the ones of fellow criminals or snitches, but of women. I scrolled through photo after photo of women who were rumored to have been murdered by Lorenzo at the orders of his psycho jealous wife. One slain woman was pictured missing her eyeballs, because his wife didn't like the way she looked at Lorenzo. Another woman was shown with her tongue ripped out and sticking out of her butt crack, because she flirted with him. And there were many pictures of women who were alleged to be Lorenzo's mistresses with mutilated vaginas.

My mind goes over all the scenarios that can happen to me. He can rape me and kill me. That is my best option and the best possible outcome. He can rape me, then circumcise me, and hand me my own clit right before killing me. Or maybe he won't just stop at my clit. Maybe he will carve off my nipples and save them as keepsakes. He might even rape me, drag me off, and torture me for days before killing me. All I know is three things for sure: One, I am going to be raped. Two, I am going to be killed. Three, this will not be over in a total of ten seconds.

He snatches Greta from my paralyzed hands. I hear a thump as she lands and feel my heart thump with it. All hope is gone. Barebacked he roughly penetrates me. I once yearned to have this moment. Five years ago I wanted him to enter me and I wanted to give him all of me. But that was five years ago. Today I hate him. I don't want him anywhere near me and I hope he does kill me, because there is no way I can face my husband after this. I whisper, "Jesus, help me." It is the only thing I can think to do, but Jesus isn't coming to my rescue.

As Lorenzo humps and thrusts in and out of me, I lay there silently crying but compliant. I do not try to fight him at all. I am dry as a piece of toast, but he's not. He put a lubricant on his dick so he could slide in and out of me easily. He is clever. The lubricant will reduce my injuries and if he manages not to cum inside me there will be no DNA. No injuries. No evidence of rape. And if he does leave traces of his DNA he can argue that I wanted it. He can say I wanted his cock forcefully shoved inside me, because I was wet for him, and he will walk away scot-free. So, maybe he's not going to kill me, after all. He can argue it wasn't rape but there is nothing he can argue for murder. There is still hope left.

Finally able to move, I squirm underneath him and try to scoot backwards. Lorenzo moans. "Yeah, yeah, rock your hips, baby. You fucking whore, you. You want this dick. You finally get poppa's good dick." I am enraged. I am fighting to get from under him and he thinks I am reciprocating his movements, like I want to be raped. He cups my left titty with his right hand and then pinches my nipple. I punch him in his hairy barrel chest over and over again. I hit him with a left, right, right, and left. He pins my arms down and leans close to my face, still humping me. His rhythmic thrusts are continuous like he is dancing to some music playing in his sick rapist head.

"How do my wife's panties taste?" he whispers in my ear. My eyes bulge at the disgust of what he is implying. "You know she wanted you dead, but for the first time ever, I refused. I didn't want to kill you, because I hadn't fucked you yet. She knew that, but she didn't care. She wanted you dead, because she knew I loved you more than my other whores. You were a threat. So the night I was finally going to take your virginity she called the police on me. My own wife tipped the feds off, because she was jealous of your long legs and green eyes." Lorenzo caresses my leg. "She said I was never going to kill you and demanded to know why." He moans in my ear and yanks my hair. "Your virginity was mine. I ordered you to wait for me." He thrusts hard as if he is trying to beat me with his erection. "But you gave your pussy away to some white boy. I am going to fuck you and kill you and then fuck you again. I dishonored my wife for you and kept you alive. And this is how you repay me."

I feel his slimy tongue slide down the side of my face. This motherfucka' just licked my face. I can feel the blood rush to my face. "You're mine, and you are going to die with me cumming inside you." My arms are still pinned. I kick my legs and try to scream, but the sound is muffled by his wife's panties. Lorenzo puts his hands around my throat, cutting off my circulation. My nostrils flare as wide as they can as my lungs desperately heave for air. He squeezes my neck harder, humping my pelvis to obliteration as he stares into my eyes, never breaking contact. He is still thrusting to the same music, but now he is dancing harder. "Oh, amore mio. I'm cumming. I'm cumming." His body convulses as he loses control.

I can feel him ejaculate in me and I want to die. I surrender to the unrelenting pressure around my neck. I stop trying to draw in air in his chokehold. With his wife's panties in my mouth, my eyes dim, and everything fades to black. This time I won't will myself awake. This time I won't force my eyes to open.

I hear an explosion and Lorenzo's grip loosens from my neck as the full weight of his body collapses on top of me. His penis is still inside me. I lay perfectly still, afraid, and unsure of what just happened. I am frightened that I am still alive. And I'm mad that I'm not dead yet.

25
Pigs' Feast

Beau

My mind is racing as I speed down I-65. All GG said was that she needed me to come right away. I asked Real to stay with the twins and reassured him I wouldn't be leaving unless it was an emergency. I have no idea what is going on, but I start freaking out even more when I see Bella's car in the driveway. What is so important that she had to call both of us? God, please don't let my GG be sick.

"Back here, Beaunifide," I hear GG's soft voice coming from the back yard. It is silent and dark outside. GG's outdoor lights are off.

"GG, what's going on? I hit the corner of the house and freeze. Bella is sitting on the back porch steps covered in dirt and blood. She is sobbing and rocking back and forth frantically. GG is pacing up and down the walkway. I see a body lying in the yard with blood leaking from the head. "Is that Lorenzo?" I look over at Bella. She doesn't say anything. She just continues crying and rocking.

"He raped her!" GG cries. "That nasty, filthy low-down pig hurt my baby so bad. I had to…I had to stop him."

I know what I have to do. I step in front of GG, halting her pacing. "GG, take her in the house and clean her up."

"We got to call the police. It was self-defense. Lawd Jesus, what have I done?" GG claps her hands together and starts whispering prayers.

"No," Bella and I both say at the same time.

I take GG by her shoulders and look her in the eyes. "GG, there is a dead white man in your yard. The reason he is there won't matter. Take her in the house." I guide GG toward Bella. "Take care of her." I stroke Bella's matted hair. "Je t'aime de tout mon coeur," I tell Bella I love her with all my heart and give her a hug and kiss on her forehead.

GG looks back as she walks Bella towards the door. "What are you going to do with the body?"

"I'm gonna take care of it," I answer GG.

I don't know what exactly went on here tonight, but I know I have to take care of it. I will not allow this sick monster to destroy my family.

I move GG's and Bella's cars out the driveway and back my Lexus in as far into the back yard as possible. I didn't exactly come over prepared to dispose of a dead body. I lie my head on the steering wheel. God, I don't know if what I am about to do is right. I don't know if I am wrong, if GG is wrong, or if Bella is wrong. God, let it all be on me. I snatch the tarp off my father's '82 Chevy Camaro, which has been parked in GG's backyard since my father died. My daddy promised the car to his first born grandson so there it sits waiting for my father's namesake to be able to drive it.

I find three guns in the yard Greta, GG's Smith & Wesson, and Lorenzo's pistol. I also find one shell casing near his head. No bullet, though; it must be still in his head. I empty all the guns and put everything down Marcello's shirt. I place the tarp on the ground. You know how they always say dead weight is heavy? Well, they ain't lying. I kick and roll him onto the tarp and wrap him up. I drag the body about four feet to the car and I pause to catch my breath. I struggle to get Marcello's body in the trunk but I'm not able to lift it off the ground. I pause again to catch my breath and think how I am going to lift this body. I feel around on the tarp, searching for his head. When I find it, I pull the body into a sitting position with the back leaning against the car. I get in the trunk and begin to tug and pull the tarp, slowly sliding his body up into the trunk. After what seems like forever, I finally get the entire body inside and wipe the sweat off my forehead.

Exhausted, I go inside the house to get a drink of water. GG is sitting at the table. "Where is she?" I ask.

"She just dozed off in my bed. Beau, what are we going to do? I just keep praying this is a nightmare and God is going to wake me any moment." GG puts her head in her hands and starts crying.

"I need her clothes, your clothes, everything; even y'all shoes. And get me some clothes and shoes to change into," I instruct GG before I grab a flashlight and trash bag from the kitchen drawer and go back outside. I am no expert but it looks like he died right where he was shot. I scan the yard for blood or anything that may have fallen off of him. I only see one spot with blood. I grab GG's garden hoe and start shoveling the blood-soaked dirt into the trash bag. I dig about three feet until I don't think there is any more blood mingled with the earth. I will have GG plant a small flower bed or something in that spot.

I walk back into the house and GG is sitting in the same spot I left her in, but she has changed. I see a pile of her and Bella's clothes on the floor next to her feet. I see semen and blood splattered on Bella's yellow dress and am enraged at what that sick bastard did to my sister— how he violated her, how he hurt her. Tears are running down my face in anguish for what my sister and grandmother went through tonight because of that monster. Suddenly, I begin to feel at peace. I remember that he is dead and I am glad. I find comfort in knowing he can never hurt Bella again. I kneel down and grab GG's hand. "GG, pray to God to forget about tonight. Ask God to take the pain of tonight away from you and Bella. Ask God to forgive me for what I am going to do, and ask God to give you peace for what had to be done. But, GG, never talk to anyone but God about what happened here. Look at me. You understand me, right?" GG nods that she understands. I quickly change into the clothes she sat out for me and find her still seated at the kitchen table when I get ready to leave. I put the soiled clothes in a bag and kiss GG goodbye. "Go be with Bella. I will call and check on y'all in a few." I wait to close the door until I see GG get up and head towards her bedroom.

I carry the bag to the trunk and am about to pop it open. Suddenly I freeze; I hear noises coming from inside the trunk. He can't be still alive. I saw blood pouring from his head where GG shot him, and he didn't move the whole time I was wrapping his body up. Oh no, if he is alive the guns are in there with him. I open the trunk and he moans in pain as he squirms in the tarp. I feel for his head, place the trash bag on top of it, and apply pressure. To avoid thinking about what I am doing, I focus on my knuckles. I watch the skin on my knuckles turn from brown to red. He continues moving for a couple minutes and then his body goes limp. I continue to apply pressure even though he is not moving anymore. I want no doubts that he is dead. It's always these horrible individuals that have nine lives. It seems like getting rid of the body is going to be easier than killing him.

Disposing of a dead body may seem unfathomable to the average person, but I am my father's daughter and I know a guy. As one can imagine, in my dad's line of business he had to get rid of enemies, and that is where the farm and Uncle Frank came into play. Growing up, Bella and I loved going to the farm to ride the horses, feed the chickens, and we even learned how to milk the cows. The farm was in my mother's name, so the feds never knew about it. Nowadays the farm basically pays for itself and for Uncle Frank's services. We sell organic milk and eggs. There is also a stable that is rented out. The crop land is rented by a farmer and used for corn. I enjoy taking the kids out there and watching them do the things Bella and I did as kids. Its only 20 minutes from my house and they love feeding all the animals, including the pigs.

I remember asking my dad if the farm was where he got our Christmas ham. He told me no and that the pigs were his pets and the most important animals on the farm. I never understood that until one day I overheard a conversation between Daddy and Uncle Frank. Daddy asked how the pigs' dinner turned out last night. His question seemed weird, but I guess it was a pretty normal inquiry until I heard Uncle Frank's response. "They ate everything, but Bingo choked on Chink's big balls that he always bragged about before you popped him." Uncle Frank and Daddy laughed until they noticed I was behind them. I was 15 and well aware of my dad's line of work and, honestly, I was more shocked at the fact that the pigs ate the guy than hearing my dad say he killed him.

Daddy and Uncle Frank explained everything to me. Chink was an up-and-coming drug dealer that had come to Nap from Kokomo. He set his sights on taking over Haughville and the whole Westside, but my dad was a threat to him since my dad was still running things despite transitioning out of the dope game. Chink and some of his goons had the balls to come to our neighborhood in Geist and threaten to kill Bella and me if my dad didn't fall in line. By the time everything was said and done, our pigs feasted on Chink and the three guys he brought with him.

"What about the skulls?" I asked curiously.

"They eat them, too, after I grind them up," Uncle Frank explained, which led to my next statement.

"I knew that accent came from somewhere. Uncle Frank, you're like a mafia hit man," I said, my eyes aglow.

"Retired hit man," he smiled.

"Promettimi non potrà mai parlare di questo con nessuno, Bella. Nemmeno tua sorella. Promessa," my dad looked at me sternly and made me promise not to ever tell anyone, not even my sister. I knew he meant business and he knew I would never tell a soul.

Daddy gave me a kiss, Uncle Frank gave me a hug, and they sent me on my way. As I strolled away I heard Uncle Frank say, "Tuo primogenita," your firstborn in Italian, and I turned back to see them looking on at me. I just smiled and kept walking.

Now I will need Uncle Frank to do for me what he used to do for my dad. I take I-65 North and get off at the Lafayette exit to get to our farm in Zionsville. It is a straight shot up Lafayette Road. I'm not nervous; just anxious to get there. I know what needs to be done and the sooner I get to Uncle Frank's, the sooner this will be over. While driving I listen to 2Pac's *Friend Like Me*. I want to call Real, but it is four in the morning and I hope he is asleep and not suspicious of me leaving out so late. I really haven't even had enough time to process what had happened between us.

The flashing lights behind me catch me off guard. I saw the Zionsville police officer about a quarter of a mile ago and knew he was behind me, so I made sure I was within the speed limit and I haven't changed lanes in miles. The only reason he is stopping me is because I am black. Every time they see me driving my Lexus in this predominantly white community they run my license plate number, see my unique name, and pull me over for no reason at all. I have gotten pulled over so many times since purchasing my house in Zionsville that I had to file a formal complaint with the ZPD. This is the last thing I need tonight.

I take out my license and registration, roll down the window, and assume the position with my hands on the steering wheel all before this old Barney Fife-looking officer makes it to my car. I read his badge as he shines his flashlight in my face.

"Do you know why I stopped you?" he asks. *Because I'm black, duh,* is what I want to say, but I don't. Even if there wasn't a body in my trunk, I know that keeping my mouth shut is all I need to do.

"No, sir, I don't," I answer him.

"You were speeding," he lies.

"No, sir, I was not," The words leave my mouth before I can stop myself.

"Are you calling me a liar, girl?" I can hear the indignation in his voice.

"No, sir, I am not trying to assess your character," another slick comment slips out.

"Your license and registration." He spits to the ground and then snatches my information out of my hand.

"What's a girl like you doing with this fancy car?" he asks as he looks over my registration. *I am a drug dealer,* I think to myself but keep my mouth shut.

"Keep your hands on the steering wheel," the officer orders before walking to his car. God, please just let him give me my ticket so I can go. I'm only ten minutes from the farm. "Here," he says, handing me a ticket for $190. "Next time watch your speed." Thank you, God. I've never in my life have been so happy to pay a ticket for something I didn't do. I roll up my window and keep up Lafayette towards the farm.

I can see Uncle Frank walking from the main house as I pull up. I didn't call before coming, so I make myself known before the pigs end up eating white and dark meat for dinner.

"Zio buongiorno," I say good morning to Uncle Frank. He knows. Uncle Frank knows why I am here without me saying a word. I back into the barn, pop the trunk, and Uncle Frank has the body out in no time.

"Guns?" He looks over at me.

"Three. The shell casing and clothes are wrapped up in there," I answer him.

"Good...good," Uncle Frank kisses me on the forehead. He doesn't ask any more questions about who or what is in the tarp. He only sends me home. "Tu sei la figlia di tuo padre," he says before I pull off. He's right, I am my father's daughter.

Once home, I take off all my clothes and toss them in the laundry room. I feel filthy and sweaty, so I decide to take a shower downstairs. I tiptoe into the bathroom. I really want to wash my hair along with every other inch of my body. I want to wash away what happened tonight. I hope Real doesn't hear me and is still asleep. It will be hard to explain why I came home and took a shower after going out so late at night.

Real's back is turned to the bedroom door as I go into the closet and grab a T-shirt. He doesn't move. I hope I can get at least a couple of hours of sleep as I slide into bed behind him.

"Is your grandmother alright?" Real asks. Dang, I wonder how long he has been awake.

"Yes, she will be fine," I answer Real. He wraps his arms around me and kisses the back of my neck. Lying with Real right now feels so amazing, especially after all the wrong done tonight. I close my eyes and drift off to sleep.

26
Silent Torments

Bella

Why, God? Why? I pace back and forth in my room with tears streaming down my face. I seem to be doing a lot of that lately. I keep replaying that night over and over in my mind. I have no clue what Beau did with the body; she won't tell me. I know I shouldn't care as long as I don't have to see him again. But I want to look at him one last time and make sure he is dead. I want to spit on his cold dead body. I want to kick him and trample his grave, but Beau won't tell me where he is so I can't do any of that.

I rub the back of my head. It still hurts from the fall. I haven't taken any pain medications. They never make me feel better. They make me feel nauseous, exhausted, and like I'm not in control of my own body. Right now what I need more than anything is to be in control. So if that means I have to feel the pain in the back of head then I will gladly endure it. My head pain is not the only pain that I've be enduring. I can still feel his hands strangling me. I can still feel him on top of me. I can still feel him inside me. I can still feel his wet, gross tongue slithering down my face. No amount of medication will take this pain away.

I slam the wall with an open hand as hard as I can to release some of my tension. Instead, I hurt myself. I shake and rub my hand. Another pain, but at least I created it. I scream out an awful cry of agony and Brian runs in the room from the en suite bathroom with nothing on except a look of concern. He stepped out of the shower when he heard me scream. He is getting ready to go to New York for another business trip. He is abandoning me again when I desperately need him here with me. Had he been home I would have never gone to GG's that night. I would have gone home to my husband and none of this would have happened.

"Babe, what's wrong?" he asks, stroking my hair. *What's wrong? What's wrong, you ask? Another man fucked me while you were away and now you're leaving me again. That's what's wrong.* That is how I want to reply. Instead I tell him I hit my hand on the wall. He assumes it was an accident and I don't correct him.

He grabs both of my hands and kisses them repeatedly. "You have to be more careful. There, is that better?" I nod and he leans in and gently kisses my neck. I back away from him shunning his kisses. "Jesus, Bella, what is wrong with you?" Brian asks, frustrated.

It's been six weeks since I was attacked by Lorenzo and six weeks since I've made love to my husband. There is something very wrong with me, but I can't tell him. I can't tell my husband that I let another man screw me behind a bush like a common whore. I could have stopped him. I could have shot him. I had enough time to shoot. I had ten seconds to fire Greta at him, but fear stopped me. Fear seized me and took control of my mind and I hesitated. I hesitated long enough for him to take Greta and toss her. It was like my subconscious wanted it and prevented me from protecting myself. Even if Brian understood my whorish ways I know he wouldn't understand murder.

The cover-up makes it look like we're guilty. Beau told me she was the one that actually killed him. She is the attorney, so I guess I'll have to trust her judgment. I know she did what she had to do. And, honestly, I'm glad he's dead because it would have either been me or him. But what she did could be considered murder. Now I've gone from a victim to an accessory of a crime, which is another aspect of my life that I have no control over, and another aspect of my life that I have to hide from Brian. My own husband doesn't even know who I truly am. A liar. A thief. An adulterer.

"Don't bring Jesus into this!" I yell. I grimace at the family Bible we keep on the nightstand. Jesus doesn't want to be involved in my shenanigans; that's why he allowed Lorenzo to do what he did. I thought God forgave me. I turned my life around and it still wasn't enough. I thought Clifford popping up and making me pay back the money I stole from him was my karma, but God still wanted vengeance. God doesn't love me. He set me up and hustled me. He made me believe he loved me and would help me change for the better. And just when I thought my life couldn't get any more perfect, he snatched it all away.

"We haven't made love in almost two months. You barely let me touch you. Overnight you changed and you won't tell me why!" he yells back at me. Tears well up in my eyes. I can't handle Brian being upset with me.

"Please don't go. You are always traveling. Stay," I plead with him.

"Stay for what? Blue balls?"

"Marriage is more than sex."

"I offered to go to marriage counseling, but you refuse to leave this house. Look at you. When was the last time you showered?"

I feel embarrassed. It's true; I don't know when I showered last and there is no way I am leaving our estate. Home is the only place I feel safe, especially since I don't have Greta anymore. No one can get past our security unless I want them to. And I'm definitely never going over GG's again. Beau and I have begged her to move. Before he died, Daddy even offered to buy her a nice house in a gated community, but she always refused. She gave us some bull about how no one was going to run her out of her own house she paid for and has lived in for over 40 years. Damn GG, if I'd just gone straight home that night.

I try to blink away the tears, but they rush down my face. I stand still, crying silently. Brian gently kisses my forehead and apologizes. He walks me into the bathroom and directs me to sit at the vanity table while he runs my bath water. When the Jacuzzi tub is full of warm water, he helps me get in. He shampoos my hair and bathes my body, not saying a word the entire time. When he is done cleansing me he dries me off and lays my naked body on the bed. He positions his body over me and his eyes change from blue to gray. His blonde curls darken, and his nose broadens. Brian's face is morphing into Lorenzo's. I yelp and try to crawl away backwards like a crab. Brian jumps up, confused. "What in the world, Bella? You act like making love to your husband is rape." He walks towards the walk-in closet and before he enters it he turns and says to me, "I just want my wife back." He goes inside the closet to get dressed.

His phone vibrates on the bed and I pick it up and look at it. Emily, his business partner, sent him a message. I put in his passcode to unlock the phone and read the messages. Brian texted her, *Happy Birthday, beautiful*. And Emily replied, *Thanks, hun. Maybe we can celebrate after we close this deal*. I can't believe my eyes. Beautiful? Hun? I wrap myself in a sheet and storm to the closet, throwing his phone down at his feet.

"Is this why you won't stay?" I accuse. He picks up the phone with worry lines on his face. He reads the messages I am referring to and his face lightens up like it was all just a misunderstanding. But there is no misunderstanding. I clearly saw those texts.

"This is nothing," he nonchalantly tells me. "You know that."

"Calling another woman beautiful is not nothing. Are you having an affair?"

"Babe, look, I didn't think something like that would bother you, because I've been friends and business colleagues with her for years. You know I didn't mean anything by it. I'm sorry. I won't do it again."

"You're only sorry you got caught. She's your ex. How could you possibly think it wouldn't bother me that you and your ex are calling each other pet names?"

"Um yeah, my ex when I was like 14 years old. I wasn't trying to hide anything from you. What is this really about? First you push me away and now you're accusing me of cheating."

"This is about you fucking around! I'm not giving it up, so you decide to get it from somewhere else. She's always wanted you. She wished she was me! I don't believe this is happening."

In a calm voice Brian says, "Don't turn this on me. You know I am not cheating. You are the one that won't talk to me. You are the one not taking care of yourself. These are your issues. Let me know when you work them out. Until then, I have money to make and an empire to maintain." He walks out, slamming the door and knocking the Bible to the floor. I pick it up and it's open to the book of Job. I start reading it and I feel what Job's wife tells him. After God took away everything from Job—his money, his children, and his health—she told him to let go of his integrity and to curse God and die. I should curse God and die. He's taken everything from me, too.

27
99.9 or 50/50

Beau

While every day Real and I are growing closer and closer, my sister is falling apart and destroying her marriage in the process. I cannot imagine what Bella went through that night and I know she isn't intentionally pushing Brian away, but she is. They haven't had sex in two months. She won't leave the house unless she is with Brian or me. She has abandoned all of her charity work. And she's sleeping all day in the dark without even getting up to bathe. Worst of all, my already picky eater of a sister isn't really eating anything, and what she is eating she can't keep down.

Brian calls me. He has been out of town on business for the last two weeks and is worried about Bella. "I would call her myself, but after that argument we had I don't think she will answer my call. I mean, the last time she got into an argument with you she didn't talk to you for almost a whole year," he confides in me. "I suggested counseling—I mean, for both of us. I don't know what happened. Everything changed overnight and she won't talk to me about it." I can hear the desperation in his voice. "Beau, I don't know what to do. I am scared to leave her alone. Maybe I should cancel the rest of my appointments and come home." Brian sounds stressed.

"No, don't cancel. I will take care of her," I reassure Brian.

"I love your sister, but if she doesn't tell me what's going on...I...I just don't know what to do. Should I come home? Would it even matter? I know she tells you everything, Beau. Does she still love me? I mean, what has she told you?" Brian is extremely worried and concerned about Bella. I'm not going to let her lose him. It's not my place to tell Brian about Bella's rape; it should come from her. Besides, if Brian knew what happened to her then he would want to go to the police. And the last thing I need is the police digging around for answers. Still, I do think Brian needs to know.

"Brian, I know for a fact she loves you. She hasn't told me anything, either, except that she keeps having nightmares." Technically it's true. She hasn't spoken one word to me about her rape except to tell me that what scared her the most was the look in Marcello's eyes; she said they looked soulless and that she sees them every time she closes her eyes. God, my sister needs help or she will go crazy. "But I can guarantee you whatever is bothering her is something major that has nothing do with you. Marriages go through high points and low points, and right now you all are just at a low point. I know you guys can work it out. I will go check on her today," I try to comfort Brian. I hope it's working.

"You promise?"

"I promise."

I hang up the phone. Luckily I had already decided that Bella is going back to the doctor and made her an appointment last week. She went to the doctor the day after the rape. She had all kinds of tests run on her and they all came back negative, however, something is definitely wrong, and if it isn't physical it must be mental. I am going to take care of my sister. I have to help her get back to herself. If Bella doesn't get better soon, it will mean Marcello has won. It will mean he has succeeded in tearing her apart and ruining her life.

I head straight to Bella's and when I arrive Esmeralda buzzes me through the gate. I walk through the door and I ask her if Bella is doing any better. Esmeralda shakes her head a solemn no. I press the button for the elevator, but decide the stairs would be quicker. I hurriedly walk up the stairs and go to the master bedroom.

"Come on, B," I say, pulling back the curtains in Bella's room. They have floor-to-ceiling windows and she has the curtains pulled so tight that you can't even tell it is daylight outside.

"Not today," Bella groans from somewhere under the bed sheets. She knows about the doctor's appointment and hasn't even gotten up to get ready.

"Nah man, you been *not today*-ing me for over two weeks. We are going today." I sit on the bed and start digging for my sister. "Look, let's go. You are going to see Dr. Anderson in like an hour. Personally, I don't care if it's with or without yo' butt washed, but the doc might be a little offended." I finally find Bella's head buried under a pillow.

"Okay, okay." Bella reluctantly agrees and sits up in bed.

"Eww, and wash your hair and shave that mustache." I laugh and get a smile out of Bella. "Shut up. I don't have a mustache." Bella heads to the bathroom.

"Whatever. All light-skinned girls have mustaches. I can't blame Brian. If that was what I had to wake up to I'd go on a business trip, too." I keep cracking jokes, doing my best to lighten the mood and lift my sister's spirits. I can hear her laughing from the bathroom so it seems to be working. I haven't heard that sound from her in long time and it is music to my ears.

I grab a black Bebe jogging suit from her closet and lay it on the bed. *I don't have anything to wear* is not going to be an excuse today. "Hey, hurry up. We need to be there in like a half an hour." I knock on the bathroom door. I know she is procrastinating. Bella finally drags herself out of the bathroom.

"This is what you pick out for me?" Bella holds up the jogging suit. "You are rocking a dress and stilettos, but you grab me a jogging suit and sneakers?" Bella rolls her eyes and heads towards the closet.

"For one," I begin, stepping in front of the closet door, "I have to go to work after the appointment, and where are you going?" I look over at the disheveled bed. Bella's eyes follow mine. "Exactly. Two, if you were worried about how you look, you would have washed your bum more than 40 minutes before it was time to go. Now get dressed."

"Whatever." Bella walks back to the bed. She takes her robe off and I can't believe my eyes. Brian had said she'd lost some weight, but seeing Bella in her bra and panties she looks so frail. The jogging suit, which normally would've hugged her small but shapely curves, just hangs off of her. I want to say something, but I don't want to offend her. I know how much Bella has always cared about her body image and I don't want her to overreact and refuse to go to the doctor.

Bella looks over at me. "I know he called you." Her usual bright green eyes look dull and tired.

"He's worried about you—really worried." I am sure she already knows, but him calling me means he is at his wit's end.

"I know, Beau. I wish I could tell him why. I really wish I could, but I don't know how to tell him without telling him that...you know." She is referring to the fact that I killed her rapist. After I told Bella what happened with Marcello we debated on whether we should tell GG that she didn't actually kill him. Ultimately, we decided that she would have been even more upset knowing that we could have saved his life but didn't. Regardless of who took that monster's life, my sister is still struggling with what he did to her. The fact that she can't talk to Brian makes it even worse.

"I got a story," I inform Bella as we pull up at the doctor's office.

"What?" Bella looks over at me, confused. We had sworn to never tell anyone what happened, but the way it is tearing her apart, I know the only way she can begin to heal is for her to at least tell Brian about the rape.

"He died in a car accident following a high-speed chase after he raped you."

"I don't know if that will work. Brian will still be upset I didn't tell him. And what about the police reports and news? You know the media would have eaten that up." I had thought about that, too.

"Because he died in the car accident you refused to make a formal report, knowing the media would have swarmed to the story. And just tell him the truth about why you didn't tell him about the rape. Bella, I know you are ashamed and hurt and pissed about what he did, and also afraid of how Brian will react, but this is not your fault and your husband loves you unconditionally." I hold Bella's hand as we walk into the doctor's office.

"Okay." Bella looks over at me and smiles. She looks like she is feeling relieved already.

It doesn't take long for Bella to be called back, and Dr. Anderson gets straight to the point. "Bella, you have lost 12 pounds in less than two months. I am going to do blood and urine samples." Dr. Anderson looks concerned. Bella describes how she hadn't really been able to eat for a while and that everything she did eat came right back up.

Dr. Anderson sends us to the lab so they can take her blood and urine for the tests. "I think I am going to call Brian when I get home and tell him I want to talk." Bella looks over at me and smiles. I can see life filling her eyes and body again. "What happened will not ruin my happy ending. Thank you, mi amor," She rubs the platinum key pendant that Brian gave her when they were dating. I think it's wonderful that she still wears it. I just smile. It is almost impossible to believe that Bella and I will both have our happy endings.

"So enough about me," Bella says. "What's up with you and Real?" Bella and I leave the lab and go back to Bella's room. I can't stop smiling. I tell her about how happy I am and how great everything is. Real and I haven't slept together since that night and it isn't affecting our relationship. Real goes to church with me on Sunday and to Bible study on Tuesday. We always have good conversation, but talking about God and his word is taking our relationship to another level.

"The other day he read Proverbs 31 to me." I close my eyes to hold back a tear.

"The virtuous woman," Bella says, grabbing my hand. "You are a virtuous woman, Beau, and Real better recognize how blessed he is to have you." She always knows the right thing to say, but I am the one who feels blessed to have him after everything that happened between us.

"Speaking of Real, we are supposed to be having lunch. I need to let him know I may be running late." I grab my phone and step outside of the room.

When I look at my phone and see I have eight missed calls from Real, I immediately call him back.

"You fucking lied to me!" Real yells in my ear before I even speak. "They aren't my kids, Beau. How could you do this to me? More importantly, why would you do this to the twins?" I can't speak. I don't know what to say. I don't understand where this is coming from.

"What are you talking about? They are yours," I choke out before he starts going in on me again.

"No the fuck they aren't. You can't help but to lie. I guess that is just who you are. I am holding Izzy's DNA results showing 99.9 percent I am not her father. Fuck, how could I fall for yo' scheming ass twice?" Real rants.

"You did a DNA test? The only thing I ever asked of you is to let me know if you wanted a paternity test. The twins are yours; that I am sure of." I feel myself getting upset and walk outside towards the car.

"You know what? I wondered why you were so adamant about me telling you if I wanted a paternity test. I guess this is why!" Real yells. I know the twins are his. There is no doubt about that, but he won't even listen to me. "I had every sign since the first moment I met you and you drugged me. And then when I see you again you got dudes popping up at yo' place. You leaving odd hours of the night. You on this *I have changed* Godly thing, but you ain't changed. Damn, to think I broke up with my girl for you. I'm glad she's taken me back. Skylar was right about you all along. You're still a scandalous plotting ass chick. Man, you had me. I fell for all your lies all over again. The way you mislead those kids into believing I'm their father, I should call CPS. I'm sure they will be able to dig up something on your conniving ass."

"Real, listen to me, please!" I plead with him. I know he can hear the panic in my voice. The last thing I need is CPS probing through my life.

"Don't ever contact me again. I love those kids. They deserve a better mother than you. God. I can't believe this shit." Real hangs up before I can say anything else.

I am at a loss for words and just want to go somewhere and cry. I try to hold back the tears and be strong while I wait for Bella, but I begin to sob. I pace back and forth, trying to get myself together. I don't know what just happened, but I am feeling a combination of confusion, frustration, sadness, and anger. Whatever test results Israel was talking about are wrong. I grab some tissues from the car and try to get myself together before going back to Bella's room, but I can't stop crying. I see Bella walking to the car. She isn't smiling. God, please, I don't know how much more I can take and Bella is at her breaking point.

"Hey B, you ready?" I look into Bella's bloodshot eyes. She has been crying.

"What's wrong?" we both ask one another. She can tell I've been crying, too.

"I'm pregnant," she whispers.

"Real doesn't believe the twins are his," I tell Bella as we pull off.

"What? What happened?" Bella looks over at me, confused. I ignore her question. I know her problem is so much bigger.

"What are you going to do? Who do you think is the father?" I ask Bella. Being pregnant explains the throwing up and weight loss, but I know it will only add to her stress.

"I don't know. I don't know," she sobs.

After a few minutes of silence I speak up. "I can take you to a place to get a DNA test done while you are pregnant to find out. Do you want me to make you an appointment? I can probably get you in by next week."

She tearfully nods her head. "Beau, I can't keep this baby if it's not my husband's," Bella chokes on her words.

"I know, mi amor, I know." I hug Bella as we go into the house. I'm not going into work today. My sister needs me and I need her.

28
Tumbling House of Cards

Bella

Lately I have been eating everything in sight and I have gained the 12 pounds I lost back. But I am still an emotional mess and the only thing that is keeping me from losing it all together is my Bible and my prayers. After I had that argument with Brian, I thought I was going to have a mental break down, but I kept reading the book of Job over and over again, reflecting on how God restored everything Job loss plus more. Every day I pray that my mind is restored and that the baby I'm carrying is my husband's. I also pray for forgiveness for what I will do if it's not his. Even though Brian and I haven't exactly made up, we have been communicating. However, I still haven't told Brian about the rape. And I don't want to tell him about the pregnancy until after the DNA results come back. Pregnancy is supposed to be beautiful and fun, but I am too afraid to be happy. I am scared that this baby might be the child of the monster that raped me.

I look in the bathroom mirror and rub my stomach. I'm not showing at all. Well, except for my breasts which seem enormous, but everything else looks the same. I always wondered how I would look pregnant and hoped to be sexy like Demi Moore when she posed pregnant on the cover of *Vanity Fair* wearing nothing but her diamond earrings. I want to work out as much as I can during the pregnancy so that the only thing that gets big on me is my belly and breasts. I'm going for a jog since my research shows that it is safe. I haven't been to the gym or on the trail since…since I was violated.

"Hey, babe," I answer Brian's call as I head down the street.

"I called the house phone and you didn't answer," Brian says. He's been in New York on business for almost six weeks and he hasn't come home since our fight. I usually fly out to be with Brian when he is away on long trips, but given my situation, I find it hard to face him.

"On my way to the trail, then I have a meeting with First Lady about NOC," I reply. I am really trying to get back to me and my normal routine. I miss my life. I miss my husband. I miss living. "I wish you were here, mi amor. It is such a beautiful day." I start a light jog down the

225

street. The sun is shining down on me and beautiful reds, oranges, and browns are filling the trees and lawns.

"I miss you too, Bella." The words sound so good leaving his mouth and entering my ears, but I can hear uncertainty in his tone and can tell there is a *but* coming. "But I can't live the way we've been living for the past few months," I feel Brian's anguish. I can't go on living like this either.

"I want you to come home," I begin to plead my case. I had it all thought out. I plan to tell him that I am ready to talk and that Pastor has agreed to do marriage counseling with us. I plan to tell Brian the story that Beau and I had come up with. I want him to know about the rape and that it is the reason why I have been acting the way that I have. I know the word *story* makes it sound like I am going to lie to him, but how Lorenzo died will be the story, and I've decided to stick with Lorenzo dying in a fiery car crash after a police chase.

I don't know what Beau did with the body, but I hope she cut him up into little pieces, starting with his legs and torso while he was still alive. I hope that he suffered terribly. I wanted him to hurt badly for what he did to me. Lorenzo stole something from me. He took away my choice to only be with the one man I chose to be with for the rest of my life. I feel tarnished, dirty, and unworthy after what he did to me. But I am determined to move on with my life.

"I will be home tonight," Brian answers after what seems like an eternity of silence. It feels so good to hear him say it.

"Are you sure? I don't want you to rush home if you have business." I cross my fingers. I made that comment as a gesture, but I really want him home as soon as possible.

"Yes, I'm sure."

"Okay." I am sure he can hear the elation in my voice.

"I got to go. I love you." He hasn't said those three words to me since he's been in New York. I never doubted that he loved me, though, and I will always love only him. We hang up and I continue my jog.

The first three miles are harder than usual, so I jog home. I am used to running ten miles in an hour, but today the three miles take almost 40 minutes. I blame it on being rusty and the pregnancy. I don't care. It feels so good to be outside. The cool breeze, the sun's rays, the waves and *heys* from other joggers that I have grown accustomed to seeing on the trail—it all feels good.

"Mrs. Bella, I see you've gotten back out on the trail again."

Esmeralda is beaming at me when I return home. I know she would never say anything but I think she knows I am pregnant. Aside from Beau, She has been the only one with me just about every day. When she hears me throwing up she always comes to my rescue. I usually lie and tell her it's some type of stomach virus and she brings me ginger root tea.

"Si, I am feeling so much better." I give her a hug. All I can think about is soaking in the tub and getting ready for Brian to come home. I let Esmeralda know she and the rest of the staff can take the remainder of the day and weekend off. "Hasta Lunes," I say, bidding her farewell until Monday before jogging upstairs.

I put on soft jazz and light candles before getting into a warm bubble bath. I enjoy a long relaxing soak, preparing for my husband's return. Lobster Alfredo, yeah, that's what I will cook tonight. He loves that with red wine. I don't know what time Brian will be home, so I need to make sure I am ready as soon as possible. I jump out the tub and browse through my clothes in my closet. I decide on an outfit that isn't too sexy, but still alluring. I rub some cocoa butter onto my skin and lightly spritz myself with a little bit of Brian's favorite perfume.

Still naked, I sit in a dream-like daze. I finally feel like my life can get back to being mine. The house phone begins to ring but I ignore it "Mrs. Bella, telephone," Esmeralda says, knocking on my door. I thought she was gone by now. I put on my robe and go to the door.

"Que esta haciendo?" I ask with a confused smile.

"I know, I know. It rang just as I was leaving." She hands me the phone and walks out of my room. I glance at the caller ID and don't recognize the number.

"Bella speaking." I wait for a response. I know someone is there. I can hear them breathing.

"Bella," a voice finally says in a faint whisper. It is Kylie.

"Hey, love. What's up?" I grab my cell phone while I wait for her response. She sounds like she has been partying all night, as usual. She probably has some wild story to share. I have seven missed calls on my cell. All the calls are from the number Kylie just called me from. My heart starts pounding. Something is wrong. Why wasn't she calling me from her cell or her condo? The number can't be the jail.

"I'm in the hospital," Kylie cries out just as I am thinking it. "I got beat up." I have so many questions, but she answers the most important one right before she hangs up. "I am going to be okay." I can hear the pain in her voice.

I throw on a jogging suit and my spiked Aldo sneakers. I want to look as laid back, casual, and unrecognizable as possible. The media loves eating up the stories of rich kids F'ing up and I don't want to draw any attention.

As I drive I come up with multiple scenarios that might explain why Kylie got beat up. She could've been talking crazy to someone. She has a very smart mouth. Or maybe she was messing with someone's man. She is good for that, and she doesn't care if he has a wedding ring on. If she wants him, she gets him. And then there are the drugs. Kylie has been in rehab once for cocaine and pills. But honestly, I don't really think she is addicted to drugs. She's just the typical rich party girl that does what she wants, and for Kylie, that includes getting high, partying, and not giving a shit.

The lights are low in the hospital room and Kylie's back is turned towards the door. Her gown is slightly open and I gasp at the bruises I see. Almost her entire back is purple and blue. My gasp must have been pretty loud because Kylie slowly lifts her head and struggles to turn towards me.

"Don't move." I swallow my cry and quickly walk to the other side of the bed.

"It's okay," Kylie tries to reassure me, straining to smile. I grimace at the sight of her. Her face is as black and blue as her back. One of her eyes is black and swollen shut, and her jaw is poked out like she took a right hook from Muhammad Ali.

"Who did this to you?" I clench my fists and feel my blood boiling. Kylie's pretty little face is almost unrecognizable and her hair is matted and all over her head.

She spreads her busted lips to smile at me again. "Still got all my pearly whites," Kylie says, winking her one open eye. I give a faint chuckle, but I am still horrified at seeing her like this.

"Have a seat." Kylie's bandaged hand appears from under a thin white cover. I take a glimpse outside as I grab a chair from under a dust-covered window. I am sure this is not the hospital of her choice. She is in the public hospital where all uninsured and low-income patients are brought. To put it lightly, the hospital is old and dusty. Not dirty by any means, but not well maintained. The hospital has been open since 1952 and doesn't seem like many changes has been made since.

"Who did this to you?" I ask again, looking her up and down in disbelief.

Kylie shrugs her shoulders. "I don't know. Last weekend I was out partying with Angel and we decided to hustle some dudes just for fun, you know?" My heart skips a beat.

"Hustle?" I'm sure my confusion and anger are apparent. Kylie has some questions to answer before we can even get into what happened to her last night. "What do you mean hustle?" I ask, raising my voice before I can catch myself. I grip the arms of the chair as I wait for her response.

Kylie begins telling me how she and Angel have been hustling off and on for the last five years. "Just for fun, you know?" Kylie casually explains. Angel and Kylie did their first hustle in LA the day I met her and Brian. She tells me about all the hustling she and Angel have done and how she finds it exhilarating. It is like a drug to her.

I am speechless. I open my mouth but am unable to form any words. I know this is all my fault. I brought Angel in and when I cooled down on hustling she recruited Kylie. This had all gone on behind my back, right under my nose. I just stare at Kylie as she finishes her story.

"Someone saw me. I was rolling on some X and must have been too careless. After Angel and I went to the bathroom to…you know," Kylie pauses to allow me to mentally fill in the blanks. Sounds like Angel imitated what she learned about the hustle from me step-by-step. "Two women approached me and told me they saw what I had done and unless I did something for them they would walk over to my mark and tell him. They snatched my purse and took my ID. I was so scared that I agreed. The good thing, though, is that they didn't see Angel. I was to meet them at the club Thursday night. They already had a mark picked out for me and told me to drug him, get him to a room they had already gotten, and leave him there. They said I could keep any money that was on him and then just leave him there passed out and they would handle the rest." Kylie slowly sits up in the bed. They, they, they. I want to know who these chicks are. It sounds like they set her up.

My mind weaves in out of Kylie's story, trying to grasp what they had been doing. I want to be mad at Angel for hustling behind my back and mad at Kylie for being so careless. But the tears running down my face aren't from anger. I'm crying because I know I am to blame. I created a monster in Angel. She had quickly become consumed by the hustle—more than I had ever been—and I'd ignored that. I couldn't bring myself to look at Kylie. I did this to her. I changed my life and tried to leave the hustle in my past, but it continues to haunt me. God, I have

DONISHA DERICE & JAI DARLENE

to make this right.

"Bella, are you okay?" Kylie grabs my hand and squeezes it as tight as her feeble frame can. I want to tell her the truth; no, I am not okay. I feel mentally and physically sick and angry. But, instead, I just ignore her question altogether.

"Who are these women that approached you? Where is the mark?" I question Kylie as I wipe the tears from my face with my jacket sleeve. I need answers, I need to know how to find these people and make them pay for what they have done.

"I was so high, Bella, I barely remember what the women look like. One was tall and light-skinned. The other was short and dark-skinned. But the mark, the police showed me a picture of him and they want to charge him with aggravated battery. But he didn't do it." I can hear the anxiety and worry in her voice and I can see it on her face. "I barely got him to the motel room. He was so gone on the drugs that he could hardly walk and he was big as hell. I mean really big." Kylie's one good eye grows big as a saucer to help illustrate her point. "He passed out about 15 minutes after I got there. I called a cab, took the money, and walked out, and that is all I remember until I woke up here. Shortly after I came to, some police came to interview me."

"And what did you tell them?" My mind is now focused on fixing this. I know I am going to need to get Beau involved for legal advice and story strategy.

Kylie shook her head. "Nothing. They had me on meds, so I acted incoherent and they left quickly." Smart girl. "I fucked up majorly, Bella. What am I going to do?" Kylie starts freaking out. I can see her brain spinning thinking about what will happen if they find drugs in her system or in the mark's system.

"I am going to call Beau," I say and step out of the room. I'm still not sure of everything that is going on, but I know Kylie needs legal advice.

"Beau, I need you to meet me at the public hospital, like right now." I know she can hear the panic in my voice. "No, I am fine. I can't talk over the phone, though. Just call me when you get down here and I will meet you outside." I rush Beau off the phone as a detective walks into Kylie's room.

"Ms. Mason, please give me a call if you remember anything," a tall, well-built, white guy in a blue shirt and tie says, handing Kylie his card. "Right now we are charging Mr. James, but we need your official statement."

"Ms. Mason?" I look over at Kylie perplexed after the detective walks out.

"I had a fake ID on me. I haven't told them my real name. Will I get arrested for that? I am so scared, Bella." Kylie starts breathing rapidly and the monitor shows her heart rate increasing. I tell her everything is going to be okay although I really don't know. "The guy, Clifford James, I know without a doubt he didn't do this to me." My jaw falls in my lap once the name leaves her mouth. There is no way she is talking about him. Or is there? It is all starting to making sense already.

"Calm down, love. It is going to be alright. Have you talked to your parents or Brian?" I hope not.

"No, and you can't either. Not yet. Not my parents, especially." Kylie starts to freak out again just as the doctor walks in.

"Well, Ms. Mason, there is no neurological damage, but you did suffer a concussion. We will keep you a few more days for observation." The young, petite doctor reassures Kylie that she is going to be fine.

I get Beau's text that she's outside and walk out behind the doctor. "What is going on?" Beau asks as she grabs me in her arms. She squeezes so tightly I can hardly breathe. "The baby?" Beau mouths silently while looking at my stomach. After convincing Beau that I am okay, I tell her that two women beat Kylie up in a motel last night, and set Cliff up to make it look like he did it. I also give her a description of the women that Kylie gave me. "It is his wife and Skylar," Beau says, which is exactly what I had been thinking. "Where's Clifford?"

"Not sure, but the detective said he is being charged with the attack. Kylie said he was passed out when she got beat up," I continue to explain.

"Is she sure?" Beau asks. I let her know Kylie seemed 100 percent positive he couldn't have done this. "I can have the criminal part taken care of. I will get Clifford released and get him information about them dumb chicks. What he chooses to do with it is on him. Ughhh," Beau groans, clenching her teeth and rolling her eyes. She can't stand Skylar. Although she cannot definitively prove that Skylar had something to do with Real and the twins' DNA results being messed up, she knows she did. And if we are right about what they did to Kylie and Clifford, it solidifies just how scandalous she is.

"Oh my God!" Beau shrieks when she sees Kylie. In all that conversation about what has happened I forgot to warn Beau about

231

Kylie's physical condition. "We are pretty sure we know who did this to you." Beau gives Kylie the whole run down about our unbelievable history with Clifford and describes his wife and Skylar.

"That sounds like them, but why would they do this to me?" Kylie starts to get angry.

"I don't think it was about you. It seems like they were trying to set him up and used you as bait and the victim," Beau explains to Kylie. "What I don't understand is how you met him in the first place and why in the world were you in a motel with him." I've been dreading this part of the conversation and I dread Kylie's impending answer to Beau's question.

"Hustlin' him," Kylie says. Beau's eyes quickly roll over, looking me straight in mine, but I can't look at her. I don't know why I thought I could somehow avoid this.

"I'm going to get the ball rolling on a statement for you and get Clifford out." Beau kisses Kylie's forehead and gestures for me to walk out with her. I feel like I am going to the principal's office. I know Beau is about to go in on me. "Make sure she doesn't talk to the police before I get back," Beau tells me as she texts on her phone. I am pretty sure she is texting one of her attorney friends that specializes in criminal defense. "Look, I know you know what I am thinking so I am gonna keep it short, B." Beau stops right outside of the hospital and speaks without looking at me. "This right here can ruin us and everything we have worked for." I know she is right and I just want to ball up in a knot and cry. Everything could lead back to us if it is not handled right. Beau and I stand outside of the hospital without speaking a word for what feels like forever. Beau's fingers are moving at warp speed, still texting. I glance over at her phone, not to be nosey, but to check the time. I had rushed out of the house without a watch. It is already 6 o'clock.

"Brian." I had forgotten all about him coming home. I snatch my phone from my jacket pocket and see six missed calls, four of which are from Brian.

"Y'all talk yet?" Beau finally looks over at me and I can see concern—not anger—in her eyes.

"We're supposed to do that tonight." My eyes roll into the back of my head. I feel like I still have to talk to him, but about what exactly? I'm not sure I should still tell him about the rape, if I should tell him about the hustle, or even about Kylie getting beat up. I had no intention of telling him about the hustle. I didn't think I would ever need to until now.

"Tell him everything." It's like Beau is reading my mind. There is no way he won't eventually find out about Kylie, and the only way to heal myself is to tell him about the rape, too.

"Hey, babe," I say, giving my best *everything is okay* impression when Brian answers the phone.

"What is going on, Bella?" He sounds irritated. "I couldn't reach you. I had to call a driver to pick me up at the airport because you didn't answer the phone."

"I am so sorry, babe. I forgot my phone over Beau's house and we have been out together." The lie effortlessly leaves my mouth. "I am on my way," I tell him and get off the phone as quickly as possible. "He's going to leave me." I start sobbing uncontrollably.

"No, don't say that. Everything will be okay." My sister holds me in her arms and tries unsuccessfully to console me.

"I-I-I have to make sure Kylie is okay," I try to talk through my sobs.

"Go home. I will stay with Kylie until she goes to sleep." Beau continues to hold me. To look at us you would think someone had just died and, honestly, I feel like this may be the death of my marriage. Beau holds me for a while longer before popping me on my butt. "Go get 'em," she smiles at me. I can no longer avoid the inevitable.

233

29
I Am Not Rachael McAdams

Beau

"How is Real doing?" Pastor Lewis asks as I walk into the sanctuary for morning prayer. I am so tired of people asking me about Real. GG asks, Ms. Jacqueline asks, every male member of the congregation who likes basketball asks, but most importantly, the twins ask.

"Can we call him? Why hasn't he called us?"

I don't know how to answer them, so I have been lying. "He's busy with work," is the lie I normally tell the twins, but they are by no means stupid. About a week ago, Izzy came to me with her big brown eyes watery.

"He doesn't love us anymore," she whimpered. It took everything within me not to break down and cry with her. It was breaking my heart. I keep trying to call him and he never answers. All I want is for him to talk to me. I know he is the twins' father and I know a DNA test will prove it. I have to prove it, not for myself, but for him and, more importantly, for the twins. I spent the whole five years of their lives accepting the fact that they would never know who their father is, but when that changed, when he walked into their lives, it felt right. The closer we got, the more it felt...well, it felt like there could be something between us...like we could be a family.

"Of course he does," I smiled at her. All I can do is smile and pray, and that's what I am doing at morning prayer today. I have been coming faithfully every Wednesday morning since I last spoke to Real.

"Let's pray." My silence must have said everything. Pastor Lewis grabs both my hands and squeezes them tightly. I have been praying endlessly about this and I let Pastor know that. "Put it in God's hands," Pastor smiles sincerely. "Father God, your will be done." Pastor releases my hands, smiles again, and walks away. I feel something from his words. *God's will be done.* Whatever is meant to be will be and I will just have to accept it. But my situation is nothing compared to what Bella is going through. As much as I pray for my situation I have been praying even harder for my sister. I don't know what exactly was said when Bella confessed to Brian, but I imagine all the lies she ever told Brian caught up with her. I've been trying to talk to her about it, but every time I see her or call her she begins to cry uncontrollably. Although it's not official, they are separated and Brian has gone back to New York indefinitely.

As soon as I turn on my phone it starts chiming, indicating that I have several missed calls. I unlock my phone, hoping one of them is from Bella. She hasn't returned my calls in two days and if I don't hear from her by this morning I am driving over there. Before I can even check my missed calls and pull out the church parking lot I hear the Roots' *You Got Me* sounding from my phone. *If you are worried 'bout where I been or who I saw or what club I went to with my homies baby don't worry, you know that you got me.*

It's Real. He is finally calling me. I sit in the parking lot staring at the phone as the call goes to voicemail. I have been praying for this but now that it's happening all I can do is stare at the phone. No voicemail. I want to call back. I want to explain things to him, and make them right, but I am not going to look desperate. I have to laugh at myself. I wonder if God is laughing, too. All that praying about it and now I want to act hard like I'm not stressing it. Wow, that is the fourth call from Real. The first was at 12:46 AM. I scroll through my call log. I'm kinda feeling like he is probably just calling about that drama with his brother, his girl, and his sister-in-law. Yeah, that's it. I had given Clifford the information about those scandalous chicks, told him to do with it what he pleased, and haven't heard from him since.

I sit my phone in the cup holder and start driving to work. It's been so long with no word from him, but now that I got his brother out of some major stuff and implicated his treacherous girlfriend in the mess, he all of a sudden has something to say to me.

Travis McCoy's *Billionaire,* Bella's ringtone, is singing from my phone. Just what I need; to hash things out with my sissy. She hasn't really been in the mood to talk about her problems, but she is always available to hear mine.

"B, you will never guess who's been blowing my phone up today," I start in before she can get a word out. Yeah, I am sure she already knows who.

"What did he say?" For the first time in weeks I hear a hint of excitement in her voice. She can't wait for me to spill the tea.

"I don't know," I laugh. I take her deep sigh as a sign of disappointment. I give her the whole scenario about how I think he's just calling about Clifford.

"Right, so you have been praying to God for him to call so you can talk to him. Does it even matter why he is calling? Who cares if he's calling about Clifford? Just make sure you say everything you need to," Bella advises me. She is absolutely right. I have been asking God for him to contact me and I need to accept the opportunity. Regardless of the reason Real called, God has answered my prayers.

"Listen to you with the sound advice. Sounding all Joyce Meyer mixed with a lil' Dr. Phil on me. So, let's get on you. Have you talked to Brian?" Bella has left the conversation wide open to discuss her situation and I am determined to give her the best advice possible just like she has given me.

She hesitates for a few seconds. "No, don't start, Beau." Bella's demeanor instantly changes. "Our situations are totally different."

"Look, we are both in the predicaments we are in because of the hustle, point blank. And because of what we did in our past, the men in our lives don't trust us. Right?" I sum up the gist of our problems. Bella never told me exactly what went on the night she came clean to Brian, but I do know it went bad. Bella called that night sobbing and screaming that it was all over and that he had left her. In that moment I knew that was exactly how she felt, and the fact that Brian hasn't made contact with her since he left has her going crazy.

"You know what you need to do." This is not a question for Bella to ignore but a command for her to call Brian and talk their problems out. I see my sister falling apart, even worse than she had right after the rape. I am concerned about her well-being as well as that of her unborn child.

"I love you, babe." That is Bella's not-so-subtle way of telling me she is about to hang up on me.

"Go, damn it!" An angry voice and blaring horn draws my attention to the fact that I have been sitting at a green light for I don't know how long.

If you are worried 'bout where I been or who I saw or what club I went to with my homies baby don't worry, you know that you got me. I take a deep breath.

"Hello," I answer. An eternity passes with just silence on the other end of the phone while I await his response.

"Beau, I am sorry," Real's shaky voice finally speaks up just as I am parting my mouth to say hello again. His words bounce around in my head as I wait for him to say something else. Maybe he is waiting for me to say sorry, too, but I have nothing to be sorry for. I just listen. I can hear his quick breathing as I imagine him carefully picking his next words. "I didn't do those tests; she did, but..." Real pauses again. I know the *she* he is referring to is Skylar. I knew she was behind it from the beginning, and obviously now he does, too. "She did the test behind my back. I was so pissed when she told me she did it, but then she showed me the results." Another pause. I don't know if Real is trying to give me time to digest what he is saying or if he is struggling with what he has to say. I pull into my office parking garage and remain in the car. I have been praying for this conversation. I have planned out every word I would say if given the opportunity, but now I just wait for Real to finish his story.

"My neighbors have been on vacation in the Caribbean and just got home yesterday."

"What?" I am confused and wait for clarification.

"The Simons, you met them before. Izzy and their daughter had that play date at Build-A-Bear." Yes, I know who he is talking about, but I still don't understand their relevance to our situation. "She swabbed both of the twins and sent off separate tests," Real explains. "Janet brought me some mail they had accidently received." Suddenly it clicks. Skylar changed the results on one of the tests but not the other. "I called you as soon as I found out." I hear apologies in between his words. I understand exactly why he acted the way he did. I'm not mad at him, but I am on fire with anger for Skylar. That stupid conniving bitch hurt my babies.

"Where is she?" I calmly ask Real, talking over him as he continues to explain. I don't need to hear any more.

"What?" Real asks, confused.

"Skylar. Where is she right now?" I talk through my clenched teeth, trying to mask how enraged I am.

"She better be getting the rest of her stuff out of my house. I'm so pissed. I can't anymore. I should've never gotten back with her." Real sounds about as angry as I am at just the thought of Skylar.

"So she is at your house right now?" I pull out of my parking spot. It'll take me 20 minutes to reach her if traffic is light. I don't know what I am going to say or do when I see her, but she will know what she has done.

"Hey, don't go over there," Real says, finally catching on. I am already on I-65 heading north. "Beau. Beau!" I hear Real yelling as I sit the phone down. I will have my piece with her, and if she tries me I will enjoy every punch I lay into her. I turn the radio on. I don't have time to fumble through my music player on my phone. I push 80 MPH on the highway. I'd preferably listen to *Hit 'Em Up* while preparing for war. Pac always gets me hype. But this morning I am going to have to settle for Hot 96.3 and whatever popular song they decide to play after the commercial break.

If you are worried 'bout where... The ringtone keeps playing as he keeps calling me. I'm not trying to hear no voice of reason. I turn the radio up just as the DJ starts playing *Bandz A Make Her Dance*. I burst out laughing because bands are going to get her ass whooped today, with her thirsty self. I am sure she enjoyed the lifestyle that came along with being the girlfriend of a professional athlete. She saw all of it slipping away and did what she thought necessary to keep Israel. And it had almost worked. She had gotten him back, but at what cost? Neither one of them know what I have been through because of her lies. I have been hearing echoes of Izzy's little cries for weeks. I've been forced to look into the faces of my two hurting children and lie to them. My eyes water just thinking about it.

God, what am I doing? You have answered my prayers, Lord, and just that quick I allowed the devil to distract me. I turn the radio down and grab the phone. I don't need to confront Skylar; I need to pray for her. She is a sad, desperate woman—desperate enough to ruin the lives of two innocent kids. With that in mind, there is no telling what she may try to do if I confront her. Lord, you say love your enemies. Bless those who curse you, do good to those who hate you, and pray for those who spitefully use you and persecute you. Obviously Skylar is trying to hang on to Real, maybe for some of the same reasons I like him. I get off the exit for Real's place and turn right instead of left. Thank you, God, for stopping me from getting into unnecessary drama.

I wait for Real to call me back as I decide to take the street route back to my office. I need a little more time to clear my head and figure out what I am going to say to Real. I have been so mad about Skylar I ignored Real's obvious plea to be a part of the twins' lives again. I am sure they will be so happy to see him. Maybe he can come by today. As I continue to drive I check my phone. Real hasn't called me back yet. He is probably thinking I am on one for how I was acting. I had lost focus of what was important so quickly. I am almost scared to call him.

I turn the radio back up. "Hey, breaking news, y'all!" the radio

DJ interrupts Cee-Lo's *Fool For You*. I laugh at the irony of the song. I think Real and I have been some fools for each other ever since we first met. "Accident on West 38th Street and Michigan Road. Sources say NBA champ Israel James was involved. We're praying the basketball star is alright. Stay tuned for updates."

Pain shoots through my heart as soon as I hear Real's name. Oh my God. He was probably trying to get to the house and stop me from doing something reckless. "Please God, let him be okay!" I cry out. My heart is racing as I head down Michigan Road. "Please, God." I continue to repeat my prayer as I drive. I am shaking and crying. I see the flashing lights of police vehicles and fire trucks as I reach 42nd and Michigan. The south lane traffic is blocked all the way down to 38th Street. I park in a church parking lot on the corner and start running towards the accident. I see an ambulance and tow truck parked right off of the east side of 38th street. For some reason all I can hear in my mind is the hook to the Cee-Lo's song as I run down the street in my heels. *I'm a fool, such a fool for you.* I freeze as I see the rear end of Real's Range Rover smashed into the brick wall and fence of Crown Hill Cemetery. But no Real. I don't see him in the sea of people at the accident scene. Parked sideways near Real's car is a blue Chevy Impala with its front end smashed in. I slow my pace to a walk as I get closer to the scene and stop in the middle of the street looking for Real.

"Ma'am, ma'am, you can't stand here," an officer trying to direct traffic says to me. I stop right in the middle of the one clear lane that remains open on the east side of West 38th street. I walk towards the ambulance, squeezing my fists so tight I am cutting off circulation to my fingers.

"Ma'am, you shouldn't be over here," another officer says, walking over to me. I feel like I am in a daze. It's like I am in a movie or something and everything I hear and see is a blur. "Ma'am," the officer tries to get my attention again.

"Where is he? Where is Israel?" I finally cry out, still trying to look through the crowd of police, firefighters, paramedics, media, and bystanders. I still don't see Real. I ignore the officers and walk towards an ambulance parked sideways near both of the totaled vehicles.

An officer touches my shoulder. "Ma'am, I can't just let you walk through here." I shrug off his hand and keep walking. I can't stop. I have to find Real.

God, please. Where is he? I grow more and more worried with

every step I take. My body is shaking uncontrollably. "Ma'am!" a loud voice yells at me.

"Where is he?" I cry out again. I am not trying to hear what anyone has to say. I have to find Israel. Every worst-case scenario runs through my head as my eyes dart through the crowd for Real.

"It's okay. She is with me," I hear Real's voice call out, although I can't see him. I look back to see an officer about two seconds from snatching me up. Hearing Real's voice eases the tension, but I am still so scared. I have to lay eyes on him.

"Beau." I try to find Real as he calls out my name. I shudder and finally exhale when I see him standing near the ambulance. Relieved beyond belief, I start running through the crowd towards him. "Thank you, God!" I yell out as I run to him. I can see cuts and scratches on his face as I get closer, but he is okay. A smile crosses his face. I finally stop running and walk up to him. What was I thinking? That this was gonna be some Rachael McAdams, *Notebook*, *Time Traveler's Wife* love scene? Like I was gonna run up to Real and he was gonna lift me up into his arms and kiss me passionately? Yeah right. I stop a few feet away from him and finally take a moment to catch my breath and let my heart stop racing. I look him up and down as I collect myself and try to find words to say.

"Come here, man." Real reaches his long arms out and pulls me into him. I can't help but to start crying uncontrollably. Real wraps his arms around me, rocking me. "I am okay. Shhh, shhh, don't cry," he consoles me, but I can't stop crying. Less than five minutes ago I thought he could be dead or badly injured and now I have him in my arms. I squeeze him as tightly as I can. "Ahhh, I do have a bruised rib, though," Real loosens his arms from around me and grabs my face into his hands, pulling it up towards his. I give a chuckled cry. His face is a blur through my tears and I don't know he is coming in for a kiss until his soft lips are pressed up against mine. My hands go from around his back to around his head as our kiss lingers. "Whew," he sighs. For just those few minutes I forget about everyone around us. It felt like it is just him and me. That is until the sound of clapping and cheering startles me. I am blinded by cameras flashing from the crowd as news reporters shove microphones in our faces. Wow, this *is* just like a movie love scene. Nah. This is better. This is real.

241

30
The Beginning of the End

Beau

I twirl my engagement ring off of my finger and place it my purse. I want to tell Bella, but I know it is not a good time. I turn down Bella's road and there are reporters and photographers surrounding the house's gate. I honk the horn to get them to move out of my way.

"Hey, Beau, any comments about your sister's husband filing for divorce?" a reporter wearing a TMZ shirt shouts through my closed window. He is so close to my car I could roll down the window and punch him in his throat. This is why I don't like the media. Bella hasn't told me about any divorce so I don't believe it. I pull up TMZ's website as I wait for the gate to Bella's estate to open. I don't know why I am entertaining this foolishness but I guess I should know what it says just in case Bella has seen it, too. **ROSE MONEY FLOURISHES AS THE FAMILY WITHERS.** Accompanying the article is a copy of Brian's divorce filing, posted big as day. Oh my God. Bella.

I use my key to let myself in. Even the house seems sad and gloomy. With the curtains pulled shut and very few lights on, the cold house doesn't just feel empty; it *is* empty. Bella has laid off all of her staff with pay. She said all she wants is to be alone. All the staff has left except Esmeralda, who refuses to leave. I thank God for Esmeralda because Bella does not need to be alone.

"Hi, Ms. Beau. Mrs. Bella is in the living room." Esmeralda tries to greet me with a smile, but even her disposition is sad.

"What's up, B?" I throw on my best happy face. Bella is curled up on the couch. She just looks at me—no, she looks through me. I sit next to Bella and say nothing. Nowadays I really don't know what to say to her. Nothing seems to be any consolation. Sometimes we just sit in silence for hours at a time. Bella is gripping a manila envelope with both hands. I wonder if it is the baby's DNA results or the divorce papers. God, give my sister strength. Give her peace. Give her a chance. Bella cannot give up on Brian, the baby, or life. God, please help my sister. I stare at Bella who still hasn't said a word to me. I can only imagine what is

243

going through her mind. Why do we always have to be so strong? Why does it feel like our family just can't catch a break? As soon as there is a glimmer of light, darkness tries to snuff it out.

"Where is it?" Bella finally speaks, leaning over and placing the manila envelope on the table.

"Where's what?" I have no idea what she is talking about.

"Your ring, Beau. Where is your engagement ring?" Bella grabs my hand and starts turning it every which way like my ring is going to magically appear on my finger.

"Huh?" I pull away. How does she know? I dig in my purse for the ring and slide it onto my finger.

"It's even prettier in person." Bella pulls a tablet from under her blanket. Big as day, Media Takeout has a picture of Real and me hugged up, walking down the street with the twins, the ring shining on my finger. On the same page there is a picture of Bella and Brian that looks like it's been torn in half. The story title reads, **A TALE OF TWO SISTERS.** I don't need to read the story to get the gist of it. They are playing on the fact that I have just gotten engaged the same day Brian filed for divorce. "Brian and I aren't the only ones making rounds on social media this morning," Bella shakes her head. I hate how the media always tries to twist things and put dumb spins on people's lives. "You know I am happy for you, Beau. Don't let my disastrous ending mar your happily ever after," Bella says sincerely, grabbing my hand again.

"What? No, it's not over. Brian is going to come back. You have to believe that, Bella. I don't understand why he would leave you after you told him about the rape. You did tell him, right?" I look over at Bella whose eyes are watering like a flood of tears are about to pour from them. She won't look at me, though. "Tell me everything, B. What happened that night?" I pull Bella's face up, forcing her to look me in my eyes. "What are you keeping from me?"

Bella

"Girl, it was horrible," I sob "I don't know what to do. Ever since that night I can't eat—"

"That ain't nothing new. When do you ever eat?" Beau jokes, trying to get my tears to stop flowing. "Hold up. I think I got some nuts and berries in my purse."

"Shut up. I'm serious." I am not laughing. Beau stops giggling and allows me to continue to tell her what happened.

After I left Beau with Kylie, I was flying up I-465 North to get home to Brian. I was excited to see him after he'd been gone for so long. In our five-year marriage we have never been apart for more than a few days. However, I was more nervous than anything. He was already a little irritated with me for not picking him up from the airport, and all my plans to butter him up with a romantic dinner of his favorite dish went out the window when I had to rush to Kylie's side. Not only did I have to tell him that I was raped and may be pregnant with my rapist's child, but the fact that I was placed in a position where I had no choice but to tell him about the hustle had me on edge. I already knew he wasn't going to take any of the news well, but I thought with the help of marriage counseling with Pastor Lewis we could work it out.

I arrived home and parked my Aston Martin in the garage next to the Bentley, but I hesitated before going inside. I had rushed home but now that I had arrived, what should I say? What exactly should I tell him? When I met you I was drugging and robbing dudes and now your little sister was almost beaten to death because of the hustling I used to do? No. I told myself I should first give him a passionate kiss and then ease him into it by leading with the less negative parts. I would tell him about the rape and the baby first. And after he digested that, I would tell him about Kylie and the hustle. We could even go back to the hospital together and check on her.

I slowly walked inside the house and Brian was waiting for me in the kitchen with a glass of whiskey. A feeling of dread came over me; Brian only drinks whiskey when something is really bothering him.

"Hi, babe." I walked over to him and leaned in to kiss him on the lips. He pulled away and I looked at him like was he was crazy, because I had no clue as to why he would pull away from a kiss hello. I know we have our issues but that's no reason for him not to kiss his wife. It was already going bad and I hadn't even told him anything yet.

"Where were you and why weren't you answering your phone?" Brian asked with a snarky attitude. "Before I left you accused me of cheating. Are you?"

Oh no. The way I've been acting, closed off and rejecting his sexual advances, it did look like I was having an affair. I have done a lot of things wrong in this relationship but infidelity is not one of them. I needed to set the record straight.

"No, Brian, I would never. I was at the hospital. It was Kylie.

245

She got beat up really bad."

Now Brian was looking at me like I was crazy. "No, she's not. On the phone you said you were with Beau. Don't lie on my sister. That's so not cool."

"I'm not lying. She's at the community hospital."

"Community hospital? Oh, hell no. There's no way my sister would be at that rinky-dink hospital, and if she were, I would have known already. My parents would've called me immediately when they found out."

"She's there under an alias. She didn't want the media to get ahold of the story and she certainly doesn't want your parents to find out. I was the first person she called. She was beaten up by Real's girlfriend and his brother's wife."

"What?! Media or no media, I'm calling the police. No one puts their hands on my sister and doesn't see the inside of a jail cell." Brian pulled out his phone.

"No! No, don't." I grabbed his phone from his hand in a panic. "You can't call the police. I mean the police are already involved, but they don't know the full details. If you call the police and reveal her real identity they will...I don't know. You just can't call the police, okay?"

"Why? You sound like a lunatic. What the hell is going on, Bella Amore Rose? Tell me everything."

"Well..." With fear in my heart, I took a deep breath and let it all out. I told Brian everything. I told him about the hustle, how Kylie got beat up, and how she got involved in it because of me.

"Whoa, so you pretended to be a prostitute and then robbed people? Were you ever actually a model or real estate investor?"

"No."

"So what the fuck am I? Your ultimate hustle or something?" I remained silent as he continued to go in on me. "You think I'm supposed to feel better because you quit after we got engaged? All that means is that the gold digger hit it big when she landed a billionaire and didn't have to prostitute anymore."

"I was never a prostitute. You know you were my first."

"Call it what you want, but I call it prostitution. You probably never loved me."

"I do love you! It's not about the money."

"I don't believe that. That's just one more lie to manipulate me so that you can continue to live this lavish lifestyle."

I reached for his arm, but he pulled away, "I'm done with you. I'm done with this. Don't call me, text me, email me…hell, don't even fax me. I want nothing to do with you. As far as I'm concerned this marriage is over. It was based on nothing but lies, anyway."

I screamed for Brian not to go as he stormed out of the house. The door closing behind him echoed with finality. I fell down to the floor, hysterical. Esmeralda rushed over to me. She had been listening from the dining the room. "Mrs. Bella, you should have told him you're pregnant first," she said as she helped me up.

"Wait," Beau interrupts my story. "What did Brian say about the baby? And the rape? He still left after you told him that?"

"I never got the chance to tell him. He left. Everything happened so quickly."

Beau shoves her phone in my face. "Call him now."

"Don't you think I've tried that? He was serious when he said don't call him. He changed his number and blocked my emails."

"Dang, girl. So what are you going to do?" Beau asks. I solemnly shake my head. I don't know. I really don't know. "Well, what about the DNA results? You can't wait much longer if you're going to…you know." Yes, I know that I need to hurry up and make a decision about whether or not I am going to get an abortion. I love my sister for not judging me for considering it.

"You want to know?" I pick up an open envelope containing the DNA results from the coffee table and hand it to Beau. "Here."

Beau begins to take out the results. "Did you read it yet?" I stare at her, not saying anything with tears in my eyes. "You know our hustling caught up with me too and everything eventually worked out for me, so I know it will for you," my sister says, trying to comfort me before she reads the results. "No matter what…" says Beau, gently rubbing my hand as she stares into my eyes, "All's well that ends well."

I look back into Beau's eyes. "Except for when it don't."

ANOTHER HUSTLE COMING SOON…

Donisha Derice's Acknowledgements

James 1:17 says, "Every good gift and every perfect gift is from above." Thank you God for my gifts. Thank you God for placing me where you did; my family, my city, my education, and my job all led me to this point, living a dream doing something I love.

I would like to thank all of my family and friends for their love and support. Most importantly, I want to thank my parents, Mark and Mary Council. But there are no words to express how thankful I am. Who I am is because of y'all always loving me, encouraging me, supporting me and believing in me. I appreciate all your help in making this book happen. Without you there may have never been *The Hustle: A Means to an End*. You watching my babies gave me the opportunity to write and pursue my dreams. I love you, Mommy and Daddy.

To Donnell and Rihyan, my beautiful gifts from God, you two are my life, my motivation and my everything. I hope and pray that by seeing Mommy follow her dreams you will be encouraged to follow yours and never give up on them.

For my first critics, Mena, Sugano, and Jay, thank you, thank you, thank you for taking the time to read the book. Thank you for your encouragement. It was motivating. Thank you for your suggestions/opinions. They made me a better writer. And thank you for taking this ride with me.

To my publisher, Vanna B. and Hope Street Publishing, thank you for liking what I wrote and believing in it enough to take a chance on some first time authors.

To my friend and co-author, Jai Darlene, I had the book idea for years but was never able to put it down on paper. In less than a year we brought Beau, Bella, and *The Hustle* to life. *The Hustle* is the first, but definitely not the last.

Finally, to every book lover that enjoys a good story, I hope you love this and know this is only the beginning.

Jai Darlene's Acknowledgements

Having gifts differing according to the grace that is given to us, *let us use them* (Romans 12:6.) I thank God for the gift of writing and for the wisdom to know that it is my gift. I pray that God continues to use me for His will and strengthen my gift every day.

I want to thank...hold on, let me go into the other room. It's hard for me to concentrate over Bella's crying. And Beau is distracting me, as well. She's pacing back and forth, trying to think up a hustle to get Brian back with Bella. Okay, I'm in another room. As we were....

To all the readers who downloaded this book to their e-readers, Kindles, iPads, and Nooks, stopped by a library, or purchased a copy from a book store, **THANK YOU!!!!** I hope you enjoyed it, and that it was as thrilling and entertaining to you as it was to me.

I want to thank my brother, Number Two. You are one of the first to read the original manuscript and I was afraid to let you read at first. If it was bad you would have clowned me to no end. I'm an artist and I'm sensitive about my work. Don't get me wrong; you fully support me in everything I do, but the jokes would have never stopped. To my pleasant surprise, you absolutely loved it and couldn't put it down. In your words, "I wouldn't have kept reading that book just because you're my sister. As I was reading it I was in awe and I kept saying, *I can't believe my sister wrote this. This is INCREDIBLE!*"

To my sister and dad, y'all really didn't do anything to help me write this book, but thank you, anyway. Just joking...kind of. No, seriously, Dad you gave me life and took care of me when I couldn't take care of myself, for which I will always be thankful. And as for my sister, you are the best big sister a little sister can have. I love you both.

To all my aunts, cousins, long lost uncles, and friends who reached out and called or blew up my texts the moment you heard about my book, I love y'all. That support touched my soul. I was not expecting that type of reaction from you and I thank you for it.

To the Glasser Family, thank you for your support during my transition period. It goes to show that you are not people who extend a helping hand just for pleasantries and really don't mean it. You all are amazing!

Oh, I can't forget Mena. You read the original manuscript, as well. Thanks for telling us when Bella was rambling, when something didn't make sense factually, when you preferred the surfboard, and for the many, many, many other insights and suggestions you made. We still owe you that Orange Leaf, girl. That froyo will give you life.

Chana, I mean Vanna, I often get you ladies mixed up. Thank you for everything you have done and are probably still doing to get this book out to the public. You've done an incredible job and I appreciate your cleverness, wit, experience, and knowhow. I look forward to working with you on future projects.

Most importantly, I want to thank my love, who read three versions of this book. Who quotes lines from this book. Who fully supported me writing this book, even though that meant less quality time for us. I would litigate cases all day and write all night, which didn't leave much time for us. Thank you for being so understanding and supportive.

Lastly, but certainly not least, because this book would not have happened without you, thank you K. Derice for opening up to me about your dream of becoming an author. Little did you know I had the same dream. Great minds think alike and once we put our heads together, everything just flowed miraculously. Philippians 2:2 says, "Fulfill my joy by being like-minded, having the same love, being of one accord of one mind." As we developed our writing relationship and friendship I learned one thing for sure: we are definitely like-minded, and working with you has given me joy.

If I forgot to thank anyone charge it to my head and not my heart. Just insert your name right here: _____, thank you! You are the best and I couldn't have done it without you!!!

To all the Bellas and Beaus in the world, remember you are made in the image of God. There is nothing he can't get you through. Life may not be what we want it to be, but life is what we make it to be.

Donisha Derice

Donisha Derice is an up-and-coming author bringing her creativity to life by penning tales of fiction. Born and raised in Indianapolis, IN, Donisha had only dreamed of being two things: a lawyer and a writer. Receiving degrees in Paralegal Studies, Criminal Justice, and Public Management, she worked as criminal defense paralegal for over four years. After realizing she no longer desired to become an attorney, Donisha decided to follow her other dream. Her first novel, *The Hustle*, was completed while Donisha's plate was full with motherhood, college, and her full-time job. Writing a book and receiving a publishing deal all within a year, Donisha knows she has found her true passion and calling—and it is in writing.

Connect with Donisha:
www.facebook.com/donishaderice
www.twitter.com/donishaderice
www.instagram.com/donishaderice